PRAISE FOR NAIMA SIMONE

"Passion, heat, and deep emotion—Naima Simone is a gem!"

—Maisey Yates, *New York Times* bestselling author

"Simone balances crackling, electric love scenes with exquisitely rendered characters."

—*Entertainment Weekly*

"Every romance reader should be reading Naima Simone's books."

—Hypable

"Simone never falters in mining the complexity of two driven, wounded, wonderfully decent people who grow and heal and eventually love together."

—Sarah MacLean, *New York Times* bestselling author

PLAYED

OTHER TITLES BY NAIMA SIMONE

Secrets and Sins

Gabriel

Malachim

Raphael

Chayot

Guarding Her Body

Witness to Passion

Killer Curves

Bachelor Auction

Beauty and the Bachelor

The Millionaire Makeover

The Bachelor's Promise

A Millionaire at Midnight

Lick

Only for a Night

Only for Your Touch

Only for You

WAGS

Scoring with the Wrong Twin

Scoring off the Field

Scoring the Player's Baby

The Sweetest Taboo

Sin and Ink

Passion and Ink

Blackout Billionaires

The Billionaire's Bargain

Black Tie Billionaire

Blame It on the Billionaire

Billionaires of Boston

Vows in Name Only

Secrets of a One Night Stand

The Perfect Fake Date

The Black Sheep Bargain

Rose Bend

Slow Dance at Rose Bend

The Road to Rose Bend

A Kiss to Remember

Christmas in Rose Bend

The Love List

With Love from Rose Bend

Trouble for Hire

Mr. Right Next Door

The Husband Situation

The Single Dad Project

Fairy Tales Unleashed

Bargain with the Beast

A Perfect Fit

BURNED Inc.

Heated

Ravaged

Love on the Radio

Jesse's Girl

Don't You Forget About Me

Please Don't Go, Girl

Other Titles

Grading Curves

Sweet Surrender

Flirting with Sin

Ruthless Pride

Trust Fund Fiancé

Back in the Texan's Bed

Her Best Kept Secret

An Off-Limits Merger

To Conquer a Bride

PLAYED

NAIMA SIMONE

Montlake

Published by Montlake, Seattle

www.apub.com

ISBN-13: 9781662519628 (paperback)
ISBN-13: 9781662519611 (digital)

Cover design by Hang Le
Cover image: © Inked Pixels, © Woskresenskiy, © mariakray, © Igor Link / Shutterstock

Printed in the United States of America

To Gary. 143.
To Connie Marie Butts. I will miss you forever and love you even longer.

Chapter One

ADINA

I hate stereotypes.

Not only do they help disseminate and ingrain misinformation, but they're extremely harmful.

Yet . . .

Yet this Black woman from Rhode Island doesn't know a damn thing about hockey. And doesn't really care to. Not just because I consider it a white-people sport, but listen . . . I'm a Patriots girl through and through. Blue and silver run amok in these veins.

And well . . . I'm a Black woman.

Sorry, not sorry.

All that said, I still never expected my first time in a hockey arena—if there ever was going to be a first time; please consult aforementioned stereotype—to be because of a fire.

Well, technically, not the actual hockey arena. The Pirates—the professional team from Providence, Rhode Island—plays downtown at the Dunkin' Donuts Center, along with the AHL's Bruins and Providence College's Friars. And yes, the Dunkin' Donuts Center, not the Amica Mutual Pavilion. The name may have changed on the stadium a few years back, but it will always be the DD Center to me.

Still, walking through the lower level of the Pirates' training facility, I never imagined this would be my introduction to the sport. Thanks to the sprinkler system and our hoses, my rubber boots slap through the half inch of water covering the floor. Ahead of me, Jared Silva, my partner and mentor on Engine 5, scans the locker room and adjacent therapy room. We arrived in time to contain the fire and prevent it from spreading to the rest of the facility, but smoke filled the area in a thick noxious cloud. Thank God for my face mask and tank.

"We're all clear." Jared's voice crackles over the in-mask radio, and I nod. "Hell of a way to start the season."

I laugh at his annoyed grumble. My mentor is a longtime Pirates fan, and knowing his superstitious self, he probably considers the fire a bad omen for the team. I don't necessarily believe in things like omens, premonitions, and shit, but even I have to admit, this isn't a *good* thing. I mean, if a fire broke out at Gillette Stadium, I'd start going to altar call *every* Sunday. Maybe even coming up off 10 percent more in tithes and offerings.

"Let's head out," Jared says. "This just makes me depressed."

I laugh. "Right behind you."

Even with all his turnout gear on, I can still peep the dejected slump of his shoulders. Shaking my head, I follow Jared toward the door leading to the complex's main hall. Luckily the flames had been contained to just these two rooms. That's all the owners of this place could be thankful for. The damage had been done, the sprinklers helping but not completely snuffing out the fire by the time we arrived. I'm no arson investigator, but I'd bet Dad's prized autographed Brady jersey that the cause was electrical. Maybe faulty wiring. Or too many plugs in an outlet. This facility isn't decades old, but it's not new either. People update cosmetically through the years but don't bother with the wiring. Y'know, the important things—rather than enlarging a locker size.

I give the locker room one last scan. Nothing to see but scarred wood, walls, smoke, and water as far as the eye can . . .

"What's this?"

My feet slow, and I squint behind my mask. With the smoke hindering visibility, I should've missed it. Hell, I nearly did. But before I can ask myself *What the fuck?* I veer off, away from the exit, and head toward the bank of lockers near the closest wall. It's not the soot-covered athletic gear that's grabbed my attention, though. Tucked against the bottom board is a . . . I squat down and pick up the object.

A book.

No. I flip it over a couple of times, feeling like Bilbo finding the One Ring. However, it's not an evil piece of jewelry or a book. A journal. Leather, with a thin strap circling the spine and edges, it's a little bigger than my hand. Water already stains the back and front covers, and droplets drip from it.

Surprise wings through me at finding a journal in a hockey locker room. Yeah, here I go, stereotyping again. But I don't know. When I think of the big toothless players, introspection isn't what comes to mind.

I see sensitivity training in my future.

Turning over the volume in my hands again, I study it. Really, I should mind my business and return it to the floor or tuck it into one of the lockers. But seeing as how I have no idea who it belongs to, I also don't know which locker to hide it in. Again, I don't know the culture of hockey or hockey players, but I can imagine my own embarrassment and anger if a book with my private thoughts ended up in the wrong hands. But if I just put it back where I found it, the water will ruin it more than it most likely already has.

And there's something in me . . .

That *something* has my chest pinching at the thought of just leaving it to be damaged. As if the words themselves or the thoughts captured in this bound notebook will also be damaged. It's fanciful, silly, I know. But I can't deny it either.

Sighing, I slip the journal in the pocket of my turnout coat before my brain even acknowledges what I'm doing. As if I've crowned myself its protector. *Shit.* I shake my head, scoffing, and the sound rebounds back to me inside my mask.

Like the owner, who could probably bench-press two of me, needs *my* protection.

Still, I don't remove the journal. The safest and most private option is turning it in to the facility's front office. They'll know who to return it to. I walk toward the door, not stopping until the October sunshine greets me as I push through the exit. A cacophony of sound—of calls from the other firefighters and the gathered crowd, camera flashes from phones, shouted questions from reporters—ripples on the air. They only become louder when I remove my helmet, mask, and hood. The cool afternoon breeze feels good on my sweaty face and neck. Shrugging off my air tank, more formally known as the self-contained breathing apparatus, I head toward my engine just in time to hear Jared griping to Cam Riley, one of our lieutenants.

". . . already had my doubts about the team's chances of going all the way this year. Yeah, we made it to the playoffs last year, but with Morgan gone and this new goalie they got . . ." He grunts.

"Morgan was great, but this new guy, Mont Hannah, he's good. You're just biased. The Pirates did well in preseason," Cam says.

But Jared snorts, jerking his gloves off and tucking them in his pocket. "So what if I am biased? Harry Morgan is one of the greatest goalies in the game. Or was. I still can't believe he retired. And I don't care what you say, the team's play shows it. The cohesiveness is off. You can always tell when the locker room isn't great by how they are on the ice."

"Look at it this way, Lieutenant," I say, setting my helmet on my head again and removing my own gloves. "Maybe this will light a fire under them for the season." When he turns and mugs me, I wrinkle my nose. "Too soon, isn't it?"

"Get in the fucking truck, Wright."

"Yep, definitely too soon." I snicker and climb into the engine.

Behind me, Cam coughs, but yeah, he's not fooling anyone. Including Jared. He opens the door and climbs into the front passenger seat. Jared follows behind me, and Michael, the last member of our crew, takes his place behind the wheel.

My eyes close, and a sigh eases out of me. A deep sense of satisfaction over another successful call settles in my chest, my gut. Yes, there was property damage, but no one died. Not in the fire and not one of us. I call that a win. Things can be replaced, buildings renovated. But neither can be done to people.

Opening my eyes, I take in Providence as it whizzes past outside the window.

I was born and bred in this city, and it has my heart. It's where my family lives, where I found my place and purpose. Yes, we have our issues, as any city does. As this country does. But I wouldn't want to live anywhere else.

Except maybe Middle Earth. Or Westeros.

But since I only have a 3 percent chance of ever living there, Rhode Island will do.

Minutes later, we pull up to our firehouse, a somewhat unassuming medium-size brick building that looks more like a church without the stained glass than a station. Built in the mid-nineteenth century, it's been my home away from home, and I wouldn't want to be assigned anywhere else.

Especially since, for the last thirty years, at least one member of my family has been a firefighter here. At the moment, there are three of us: me, my dad—the shift captain—and my oldest brother, Malcolm. Thankfully, my second-oldest brother, Malik, is assigned to another station across town. Believe me, it's both a blessing and a curse, working with family.

A blessing because I recognize the privilege it brings me, as far as being cushioned from the unease and harassment women can face when first being assigned to a house. Men being afraid they'll have to curb their language or that we won't pull our weight. Or men seeing us as targets for sexual advances. With my father and brother here, I've been insulated, protected from that behavior.

Well . . . for the most part.

Not going there today.

But it's still a curse because that protection can go overboard when they slip and see me more as their daughter and sister rather than a fully trained and competent firefighter.

Our engine rolls into the bay, and as soon as it's parked, we jump out. Peeling off the turnout gear is like shedding a heavy skin. Then we go through our normal routine. Check equipment, do inventory, replace and reload supplies for the next call. Afterward, I shower and dress in my station wear—black uniform pants and a long-sleeved black shirt with the Providence Fire Department emblem—and head toward the kitchen for some dinner. Terry, our rookie, is cooking, and he can burn his ass off. So yay!

Hours later, after Cam has us outside doing hose carries and rolls and after another shower, I finally sink to my bunk, the leather-bound book in my hands. Like back in the training facility, I stare down at it, flipping it from front to back. Why am I so drawn to it? Hell, right now, I really am feeling like fucking Gollum with the One Ring.

As I shake my head, a puff of laughter escapes me. This holds someone's personal, most private thoughts. Yet I trace the Celtic tree of life emblem on the front, then toy with the leather string wrapped around it. The longer I hold it, touch it, the stronger the curiosity stirs inside me.

It's wrong to pry. Wrong to even consider opening the cover and . . .

Dammit.

Even as the . . . *ickiness* writhes inside me like a pissed-off nest of snakes, I loosen the strap and slowly open the journal. There's no name on the inside flap or on the first page where it's typed *This journal belongs to* . . . with a line for the identification of the owner. Conversely, that makes me feel an iota better about violating this faceless and nameless person's privacy.

Or I'm just trying to justify what I'm about to do.

What I can't seem to stop myself from doing.

Slowly, as if I'm opening a box of precious treasure, I flip to the first page.

August 2

Dear Kendra,

Goddamn, I feel so stupid even writing that. You know I don't do this shit. The most I've ever written was a grocery list the one and only time you let me go shopping by myself. And we both remember how that turned out. A $500 bill and a shit ton of beer and beef jerky. But here I am, writing in a journal of all things. The therapist your father insisted I go see gave me this as homework. And if I want to keep seeing the ice, I have to cooperate. Apparently, I have an anger problem that's not getting any better. Your father better be glad he's not just my in-law but the owner of my team or else I'd tell him and the therapists to go fuck themselves. Yeah, sorry. I know that's your dad.

Well, since I have to do this and you're the only person I want to talk to, I'm writing this shit to you. Besides, as crazy as it sounds, I swear I can hear you in my head. And I feel closer to you. Like you're here right next to me. I said it sounded crazy, right?

I don't have anything to say.

Except.

Except I miss you. I miss you like fucking crazy, sweetheart.

And I need you.

August 8

Dear Kendra,

Last night I dreamed about you.

It was so real. You still wore that peaches and cream body lotion. Your voice, smile, touch—they all were the same. And even though I was holding you again, talking to you again, a part of me knew that it was a dream. That I had to take advantage of this time with you while I had it. But even knowing that, I woke up reaching for you. And the pain of patting those cold, empty sheets sent pain through me all over again. As sharp as if you've been gone two days instead of two years. I lay there in bed, staring at the ceiling, unable to move. Like the pain, the grief were physical weights pressing me into the mattress, smothering me.

For a moment, Kendra, I thought the unthinkable.

I wanted to follow you.

Shit, I can only admit this here, to you.

I haven't had those thoughts since the days right after you left. Why is it so hard for me to say "died"? I can't. Even years later, I can't say it out loud. Because it makes you being gone so fucking final. As if death isn't. And yet, I haven't said it in two whole goddamn years.

Which makes no fucking sense, right? If I want to follow you there, I should have the balls to say the words. I can hear you cursing me out for even thinking about it. You were always the bravest out of the two of us. I might fuck people up on the ice for a living but you? You were the one who was fearless, rushing into life, enjoying the hell out of it. Forcing me to go along for the ride.

I can't fucking do this without you, Kendra. I don't want to.

But we have Khalil.

He's my lifeline, my saving grace. I hate to put that kind of pressure on a five-year-old kid, but I swear, if it wasn't for him, I don't know . . .

Sometimes I believe . . . Shit, I feel ridiculous for even saying this. But sometimes I believe you somehow knew you wouldn't be here, so you gifted me with him. I will always have a piece of you here as long as I have him.

Yeah, I'm done after that.

I'm out.

August 21

It's been a minute, Kendra.

Not because I forgot about you. But because I can't stop thinking about you. And this—writing to you like you're sitting in the other room—started to become too hard. But maybe that's the therapist's point? Forcing me to talk? To purge myself? Shit. It feels more like bloodletting.

Khalil talked about you today, which prompted me to pick up this journal again. When I was fixing breakfast, he told me that I don't fix his pancakes like you do. Whipped cream smiley face with chocolate chip eyes. He didn't tell me before because he didn't want to hurt my feelings. Isn't that funny? And sad.

I'm the parent but he's worried about hurting me?

I'm fucking up, Kendra. In that moment, it hit me harder than it ever has before that you pulled the weight in this family. You were the heart of it. You were the light in it. And sweetheart, it's been so damn dark without you. I'm trying to keep it together for Khalil, give us a new normal. I even have him seeing a child therapist now so he's not as fucked up as I am. Forget what Jesus would do. I ask myself what would Kendra do, and I try and get it done.

Speaking of Jesus, your mom is on me about that. About going to church with them, saying you loved it and would be disappointed knowing me and Khalil weren't going. I told her she could take Khalil because a part of me knows she's right about that. Hell, I remember you promising me Sunday morning pussy if I'd go with you. And when I wasn't on the road, I did. More because you had fire pussy than a sermon, though. Don't suck your teeth at me. And Solomon, my ass. We both know it's true.

Now, though? I would be a hypocrite if I stepped inside a church. Shit, I'm likely to flip a pew than pray. Pray to who? A God who would take away my peace, my joy? A God who would take away the love of my life? A God who obviously enjoys suffering over love? Nah. I ain't got nothing for Him. But if I tell your mother that, she'd fall the fuck out.

So I'ma keep my mouth shut.

I got to go, sweetheart. If I don't get in there and read your son his story, he's going to raise hell. At least that hasn't changed.

Love you, Kendra. Always and forever.

September 2

I miss you like fuck.

I don't stop reading until the last entry, dated two days ago. I close the leather cover and lift my hand to my neck, and seemingly without my permission, my fingers close over the pendant under my shirt. My Saint Florian necklace. Or rather, my inherited necklace. My lashes flutter down, but I don't need to put my eyes on the pendant to see the engraved images of Saint Florian holding a flag and pouring water on an emblazed house or the ladder, hydrant, and letters *FD*. Or see the *Saint Florian Protect Us* above the engravings. They're branded into my memory from staring at the silver many times as it rested on a hard, bare chest. Keshaun's hard, bare chest.

Shaking my head, I refocus on the journal and not my heart slamming against my rib cage, pumping hurt, anger, and sadness through my veins. All moisture fled my mouth at about the fourth entry, and as I swallow, it hurts, like sandpaper dragging over new, sensitive flesh.

At some point, I realized the identity of the book's owner.

Solomon Young.

No, I don't follow hockey, but even most non-hockey-fans have heard of the Pirates' forward, especially if you're from Providence. Not just because he's one of the few Black players in a sport dominated by white men. And not only because he's apparently one of the best in the game, according to Jared.

No, even if you don't follow hockey, like me, most everyone in Providence still knows about him losing his wife in an automobile accident two years ago, leaving him a widower and his little boy motherless. It dominated the news, and not just the sports channels, for weeks. Even now, images of him—huge, his impossibly wide shoulders straining the seams of a black suit jacket, head down and dark shades covering his eyes as he walked out of a church, his hand wrapped around that of a small boy beside him—pop into my mind. Other men his size and width, all wearing dark suits and shades, surrounded him, a wall of muscle between him and the ravenous press. Again, I didn't have to watch hockey to guess those were his teammates. Giants, all of them, and wearing identical don't-get-fucked-up expressions aimed at reporters who got too close to Solomon and the boy I assumed was his son.

I lower the journal and smooth my hand over the cover, as if I can soothe the writer. But he and I both know a simple touch isn't enough to erase the pain of loss, of a grief that's entrenched so deep in the soul it's grown teeth and roots.

My eyes burn behind my lids, and I sink my teeth into the tender flesh behind my lip to fight the sting.

No one . . . I suck in a shuddering breath. No one has ever captured the ache, the emptiness, the powerless *longing* as this man did in words that are raw, sometimes brutal, at times ugly, but always gut-wrenchingly honest. My fingers, which haven't stopped clutching Keshaun's necklace, tighten, and the beveled edges of the pendant press into my skin.

A part of me feels like a disgusting Peeping Tom for intruding on his grief, his utmost private thoughts. So private he addressed them to his wife. The love they shared, the need drenching those words . . . they reflect what's in my heart, my soul. Though it's ridiculous, it's almost as if he's the only person who understands me. Dad, Mom, Malcolm, Malik . . . they empathize, but none of them have lost the person they considered their other half. The person who completed them.

Keshaun was that person.

No.

He was *my* person.

And losing him a little over a year ago—fourteen months, to be exact—had almost taken me out of here. Three and a half years with him, gone on a routine call to a house fire that ended up being anything but routine.

A shiver runs through me, and just like on my necklace, the other hand holding the journal tightens.

"Dina? You good?"

I open my still-stinging eyes and meet my brother's dark-brown gaze. A frown draws down his thick eyebrows as he leans over me.

My lips part to give my usual reply—*Of course. I'm okay*. But maybe because I've just finished reading Solomon Young's bitterly honest words, my throat closes around the lie, and I'm unable to shove it out.

Instead, I slowly shake my head, and Malcolm's face clears, sadness and understanding crowding into his handsome features. He and Malik take after Dad, with their tall, big frames, and right now, as he sinks down to the bed beside me, he uses that frame to gather me close and give me a safe place to lean against and on.

"No one expects you to be strong all the time, Dina," he murmurs, his arm wrapped around me. Pressing a kiss to my forehead, he gently rocks me. And I let the tears that I've been managing to hold back fall. "Let it go, baby girl."

I do.

Dimly, I hear footsteps in the room, several pairs. No one in this house would shame me for crying. No one here would judge me for mourning not just my fiancé but the firefighter brother they all lost too. But I still don't glance in their direction. I can't look at them . . . let them see me. So I bury my face deeper in my brother's chest, and I let the broken, jagged pieces of me out.

And underneath the heartache, the clawing sorrow, there's a bit of relief. This man, who has no idea I exist, gave me the gift of understanding, and like a valve that's been twisted, I release some of the pressure that has been building for over a year.

How do you thank someone for putting your feet firmly on the path of healing?

I don't know.

But I'll find a way.

Chapter Two

SOLOMON

I fly down the left side of the rink, narrowing my gaze on Ciaran and Erik, who skate down the middle and right side of the ice. Out of the corner of my eye, I keep an eye on Banks, who's trying to defend me. But that shit ain't gonna happen. He's good—wouldn't be on second line if he wasn't—but there's no way he's keeping me from receiving the pass from Erik.

Just as Erik slaps the puck, sending it sailing toward me, I drag my skates, and Banks sails by me while I slide my hockey stick forward, halting the progress of the puck. Grim satisfaction curls inside my chest, and I—

A whistle pierces the air.

"Young! Goddammit, offsides!" Coach yells, the call rebounding off the boards.

Fuck.

Grinding my teeth together, I halt the play, slicing to a stop on the ice.

Rookie fucking mistake. Especially for me.

I avoid the stares of Erik, Ciaran, and Mont, our new goalie. I don't need to look at them, and I don't need to glance down to see that both my skates crossed the blue line before the puck did. Yeah, offside is common as hell in hockey, but it's not a mistake I make. This is just a scrimmage before the first game of the season. But call me a perfectionist, arrogant, or whatever the fuck, I don't do it.

Except, of course, if it's today.

"Where the hell is your head, Young?" Coach Searles growls, and my automatic reaction is to snap a response, but I'm not crazy. Not only do I respect him too much for that kind of behavior, but he'll bench a player in a minute and doesn't give a fuck if he's first or fourth line or how many jerseys his name sells. He doesn't play that disrespect shit. "What're the rest of you standing around for? Face off!"

I skate to my position on the ice. Erik moves to the face-off spot in the neutral zone and gets in position, stick down, the center from the opposing team across from him. I don't pay attention to shit else but the puck. I don't glance around me to make sure the rest of my team are in their positions; I don't need to. We—Erik, Ciaran, and Ken and Ares, our two first-line defensemen—have played together long enough that we're more than a well-oiled machine. We're one body, one mind.

When I'm not fucking up, that is.

The whistle blows, and Erik slaps the puck before the other center even swings. Ciaran stops the pass and soars down the ice toward the other team's goal. At the last second, he shoots the puck toward me so fast it's a blur. But there's a reason I'm a left-winger: I'm fast as fuck. And accurate too. As soon as it unerringly connects with my stick, I slam it toward the net. The black disc bowls past the narrow space between the goalie's stick and his skate.

"Fuck yes!" Ciaran yells, pumping his gloved fist in the air.

Coach's whistle blows, calling an official end to the play. When I pivot around on the blades of my skates, he gives me a sharp nod. But just by the narrowing of his eyes, I know scoring doesn't get me off scot-free. He'll see me later.

Forcing myself to focus, I head back to the center of the rink and continue the scrimmage. This time with my head on straight.

An hour and a half later, I knock on Coach's office door, and after he yells "Come in," I twist the knob and enter. Gary Searle has been my coach for the last seven years, since I left the Edmonton Oilers for the Pirates. He's a legend, and not just because he's the only Black coach in the NHL. When he played with the Calgary Flames, he was a beast, right up there with Grant Fuhr and Jarome Iginla. And as a coach? He exceeds his athleticism and skill on the ice. And as a man? He's even better. When I lost Kendra, he grieved along with me. It's an honor to play for him, and I want to retire a Pirate.

But if I don't get my head out of my ass, that could be a pipe dream.

Sighing, I sink into the armchair across from Coach's desk and meet his steady dark gaze. In his midfifties, he still possesses the build that made him one of the most formidable centers in the league. I've seen him on the ice; don't let the salt and pepper in his hair and beard fool you. He'll still outskate and outscore a lot of these players out here.

"What's going on, Young?" he asks, getting right to the point. "You played like shit out there today. And it's not the first time this week."

Another quality I love about him. He doesn't sugarcoat shit.

As I scrub a hand over my short curls, then down my face, my scruffy beard abrades my palm, the slight scratchy sound echoing in the office in lieu of my reply.

"You're going to have to talk to me, Solomon. I need to know if you're in a good headspace. The first game of the season is in four days, and right now, you're not playing like you're ready for it. Give me something."

"I'm sorry, Coach. I know I haven't been my best out there lately."

"Yeah, I just said that. I'm asking why."

He might be digging in my ass, but concern laces through the stern tone. And it's that note that makes me spill the truth. At least part of it.

"I've been sleeping like shit the past few nights." Understatement. The truth's closer to me barely sleeping at all.

Dreams.

Part of me longs to go to lose myself in them, since it's where I find Kendra. But a bigger part of me doesn't want to encounter them. The pain of waking up and finding her side of our bed—the bed I shared with her for seven beautiful years—empty is like carving my chest out with a rusty-ass spoon. It's a fucked-up *Groundhog Day* that I would do anything to avoid. Even suffer insomnia.

"Are you still seeing the therapist?" Coach asks.

"Yes." When he gives me a hard, measured stare, I hold up my hands. "I promise I am, Coach. I wouldn't lie to you."

That's the other part of what's been fucking with me. Since the fire at our training facility last week, I haven't been able to find the journal my therapist insisted I keep. I hated it at first, but the activity soon became a lifeline for me. Became . . . cathartic. Things I could never speak aloud, I wrote. Things people would look at me crazy for ever admitting, I could include in that book because no one would ever see it but me. That shit changed with the fire.

The last place I remember having it was in the bag I carried to the locker room. My duffel bag went home with me. But the journal? Nowhere to be found. And the only place it could be is the training center. Which means it was destroyed by either smoke or water . . . or someone found it. All those private thoughts gone forever? Or all those private thoughts exposed to another person's eyes.

Both possibilities make my stomach clench around the acid rolling around in there.

"Good. I get it's not something you originally wanted to do, but I hope it's been beneficial. Men—especially Black men—tend to believe therapy is a stigma in our communities. It's a show of weakness or that it's a white-people thing. Those beliefs are pure bullshit. There's nothing broken or weak about you, Solomon. Most people would cave, crawl in a hole in their minds and not come out. But you're still here. You're still fighting. And counseling is part of that battle. Believe me, son, I've been there."

I clench my jaw, teeth grinding against each other. How could I forget that Coach was a widower too? Maybe because he's happily married again? The love between him and his wife is beautiful to see, and it tends to make me forget he's experienced the exact thing I'm suffering.

"Look, Solomon." He sighs, lacing his fingers over his solid stomach and peering at me from underneath heavy eyebrows. "Do whatever you need to heal. I remember the sleepless nights, the anxiety. The fear." He pauses, and when I don't contradict him, he nods. "But if you're exhausted and running on fumes, you're not going to be any good for Khalil, much less this team."

"I hear you."

"Good. Now get out of here. Go home and rest." Slapping the desktop, he stands. "See you tomorrow at practice."

Rising to my feet, I stretch my arm across the desk, and he grips my palm, squeezing it. "Thanks, Coach. I appreciate you."

"Same, Solomon."

Turning, I make my way out of the office and into the hallway leading to the rear of the arena. Erik shoves out of the locker-room door, and the center—and one of my best friends—falls into step beside me.

"Did he rip your ass a new one?" Erik arches a dark-blond eyebrow.

I half grunt, half laugh, throwing my duffel bag holding my change of clothes over my shoulder.

"No. Although he could've. But if I have a repeat of today, that might change."

Erik doesn't give me any kind of platitudes like *Nah, you weren't that bad* or *You're good.* Almost from the moment I joined the Pirates, Erik has been my boy. And he doesn't and wouldn't lie to me. Especially about hockey. He's one of those friends that'll give you shit raw and worry about how you took it later. Yeah, that's not true. He doesn't worry.

"Hey." He comes to a halt in the middle of the corridor. "Anything you need to get off your chest?" he asks instead.

I huff a laugh, because if I'm emotionally stunted when it comes to expressing my feelings, then Erik is pretty much in an emotional coma. This muthafucka can't even spell *feelings*, much less experience them. So, for him inviting me to unload on him?

I must've been more fucked up on the ice than I thought.

"I'm good," I say, expecting relief at me letting him off the hook to wash over his face. But it doesn't.

He frowns, his dark-blue gaze roaming over my face as if searching for a truth I don't have to give him.

"You played like shit, and you look it. You sure there's nothing you want to talk about? We can go get a couple of beers and—"

"And what? Get fucked up and then fucked? Nah, I'm good on that." I shake my head. "Look, man, I appreciate it, but I'm fine. Just tired."

Erik quietly studies me for a long moment, then nods. "All right. I'm going to believe you. But if you need me, need anything . . ."

"I know where to find you. And like I said"—I clap a hand on his shoulder and lightly squeeze—"I appreciate it. And you."

Even though sour swill sloshes in my gut as if I got drunk on my ass in the last hour, I mean it. I am grateful for Erik—for all my boys. I love them. And no matter how hard I want to snap for their fucking . . . gentleness with me, I don't. Because their concern and mother-henning comes from a good place. A protective place. As much as I want to lash out and yell to leave me alone and stop fucking pitying me, I keep that irrational anger locked down. It's not their fault that two years after my world imploded, I'm still trying to pick up the pieces.

"I'm good," I reiterate, probably more for my benefit than his.

Erik doesn't respond but his gaze calls bullshit, and I decide to ignore that too. Turning, I start down the hall toward the exit when I'm stopped again.

"Mr. Young. A moment, please."

Swallowing the heavy and irritated sigh climbing its way up my throat, I briefly close my eyes, then pivot back around. Can I just get the fuck up out of here and go home? I have a couple of hours before I have to pick Khalil up from kindergarten. After getting him straight and fed, I just want to end my day with me on my couch, feet kicked up on the table, watching *Inside Out*—again—with my son beside me.

"Yeah?" I ask, frowning as my gaze lights on a familiar-looking petite, slim brunette. Recognition flares a second later. Right. One of the front-office people. Can't remember the exact department, though. "I'm sorry, I don't . . ." I trail off, silently inviting her to supply her name. Especially if she wants me to call her by it.

"Natasha Mowry." She inclines her head. "Sorry to hold you up, Mr. Young, but if I could have a moment?"

Her attention doesn't shift to Erik, but the message is clear. At least to me. She wants to speak without an audience. My brows hike, curiosity roused, despite me hating that shit. I glance at Erik, who shrugs and bumps his shoulder against mine.

"I'll hit you up later to see if you change your mind about tonight." Giving Natasha Mowry a chin jerk, he continues down the hall.

"What can I do for you?" I ask her, attempting to conceal the impatience running rampant through me. Curiosity didn't trump the desperate need to end this day.

"There's a young woman in the conference room who'd like to speak—"

I shake my head, cutting her off.

"Sorry, but my PA handles all the fan shit. I'm not doing any meet and greets right now, but shoot an email to Alyssa, and she'll send her a signed jersey or something."

I'm already turning around when Natasha stops me again.

"Mr. Young, please, wait. This isn't a meet and greet. The woman is a firefighter from the city—"

"No more community service events either. I'm good with the Boys and Girls Club."

Her mouth firms at my second interruption, and I'm no mind reader, so I can't say for certain that she's calling me an asshole. But those narrowed eyes and flattened lips telegraph the message pretty loud and clear.

She's not wrong. My mother would pop the shit out of me if she overheard me being rude. Especially to a woman.

Still doesn't change my answer, though.

"I understand," she says, voice measured like she's doing deep-breathing exercises having to fuck with me. "This isn't about community service either. It has to do with the fire at our facility last week."

I blink. *That* grabs my attention.

"Yeah? What about it?"

"One of the firefighters found something of yours and would like to return it. She insists on giving the item only to you." Her mouth tightens at the corners, and once more I catch a hint of irritation. As if the stubbornness and audacity of the firefighter waiting in the conference room annoys her. "Ordinarily, we wouldn't allow a meetup between strangers and our players, but Mr. Talley okayed it. He spoke with the young woman and told me to tell you that you'll want to see her."

I stiffen at the cryptic message from my father-in-law, who's also the Pirates' owner. The fire. Something belonging to me. The firefighter wanting to return it only to me.

This could mean only one thing. My pulse thickens, slows. What were the odds?

Blinking again, I refocus on Natasha.

"Where's she at again?"

"The conference room next to the media room."

"Thanks," I murmur, then take off for the opposite direction of where I'd been headed.

A thousand thoughts whirl through my mind as my legs eat up the distance between the locker room to the front of the building. My heart hasn't stopped hammering against my rib cage, and I can't cleanly parse the emotions dogpiling one another. Anxiety, relief, anger—they're so tangled I can't pinpoint which one claims more real estate.

Minutes later, I approach the closed conference-room door. My hand hovers over the knob, and I give a harsh yet low chuckle. The fuck am I hesitating for? It's not like I'm waiting on an ass-beating on the other side of this door. Logically, I acknowledge that. But the fist of emotion lodged in the base of my throat?

That ain't listening.

"Stop being a pussy," I mutter to myself, forcing my fingers to close around the knob and twist. Pushing the door open, I move into the room.

At first, I don't see anyone. Just the long conference table with the built-in monitors and black leather chairs, along with the large screen mounted on the far wall. A softly clearing throat draws my attention to the corner directly across from me. The corner and the woman standing in it, like a child placed in fucking time-out.

Except there isn't a damn thing childish about her.

Curves that can't be street legal shove against a black long-sleeved shirt with a fire department insignia and dark pants. The uniform shouldn't really be flattering, at the very least, or sexy on anyone. But the firm breasts, full hips, and thick thighs possess magic or something, because she turns these boring clothes into something worthy of Pornhub. Not overweight by any stretch of the imagination. Still, no one could call her slender or thin. Thank fuck. Nah, that body belongs on a video set or hip-hop reality TV show.

But as bad as those curves are, it's her face that's a punch to the gut. My fingers fist at my sides, and I battle the twin urges to stare and look away. To gaze into that stunning beauty and to avoid it at all costs. Big, heavy-lidded, and densely lashed brown eyes. Delicately arched eyebrows with a small birthmark punctuating the corner of the right one. A proud nose with wide nostrils. Plump lips with a faint little dent in the middle of the bottom one, which is slightly bigger. A dip that invites someone to suck on it, familiarize themselves with it.

A dip that's the perfect resting spot for a hard dick about to slide up in that wide mouth.

I shake my head, my brows dipping into a frown that probably reflects the confusion and anger I can't suppress. The feelings I want no part of. Because I shouldn't be feeling *anything* toward this woman. No confusion. No anger. Definitely not lust.

It's not like I haven't fucked in the two years since Kendra's passing. That would be a lie, and one I wish I could claim is true. But ask me if I remember the names of those women. If I remember the faces. Shit, if I remember the nut. The answer is no to all of them. As much of an asshole as it makes me, I just needed to get off when my fist wasn't doing the job any longer. They were forgotten as soon as I came.

None of them, not one of those women, snatched me by the throat like this one does.

I don't know her. Not her name, not who she is.

But that doesn't stop me from detesting her in this moment.

Detesting her for making me feel something that had no business curling and knotting inside of me. Something that belonged solely to another woman. A woman who is no longer here.

"Solomon Young?" she asks, stepping forward, and damn if I don't catch myself from shifting backward.

The fuck?

I almost shake my head, not in denial of my name but at the silken stroke of that husky, low voice. Did she eat too much smoke on her job? That has to be the only explanation why she owns a sultry tone like that.

"Yeah," I bite out, and her pretty eyes flare wide a little at my terse response. *Shit.* Scrubbing a hand back and forth over my hair, I try again. "Yeah, that's me. Who're you?"

A small smile flirts with her lips, and once more, my gaze drops to that lush mouth. I hate that mouth. Hate that my dick tightens as if she's dragging that same mouth down the throbbing length of it.

"Sorry." She crosses the space separating us, arm outstretched. For a long moment, I peer down at it, but when that smile trembles just a little bit, threatening to fall away, I quickly grasp her hand, barely touching my palm to hers before I drop my arm back to my side.

Surprise flickers in her eyes, briefly scrunches her brow, but her expression clears, and the smile is back in place. "My name is Adina Wright, a firefighter here in Providence."

"Yeah, they already told me that. What's so important you had to come down here and see me?"

If my harsh tone takes her aback, this time she does a better job of concealing it. Instead, she nods and turns to a messenger bag sitting on one of the leather chairs. She opens it and retrieves something from inside.

My journal.

My breath snags in my throat, and my heart drums a discordant rhythm in my ears. How . . . ? I jerk my gaze up to her before returning it to the book I'd believed lost. The book that holds my very personal and raw thoughts.

"How did you get this?" I rasp, numbly accepting the journal and cradling it in my hands as if it's a newborn infant.

"I was one of the firefighters that responded to a call at your training center last week. Before we left the locker room, I noticed that"—she nodded toward the journal—"on the floor in water. The front and back cover are water stained, as are some of the pages. I didn't want to leave it lying there—I figured someone would be missing it. So I picked it up, intending to turn it in to your front office. But I forgot it was in the pocket of my coat, and I accidentally brought it back to the firehouse. I'm sorry it took me so long to return it to you. With you being a professional athlete, getting past the red tape and convincing the staff here that I wasn't a crazed fan took a little doing."

"How do you know some of the pages are water stained?"

"I'm sorry?"

I stroke a hand over one of the dark-brown spots on the cover, then lift my gaze to her.

"I said, how do you know some of the pages are water stained?" I repeat my question, eyes narrowed on her. "You made sure you personally hand delivered this to me."

"Yes." She nods, and her tongue peeks out from between her lips, moistening them. The clenching of my stomach only throws gas on the anger licking higher and burning brighter inside me. "It's personal, and I didn't want to risk anyone reading it."

"But you did." The flicker of guilt, faint but there in those brown eyes, betrays her and confirms my accusation.

"I didn't—"

"So you're going to lie to my face now?" I snap, my grip tightening on the journal until I swear I can feel the print of my words beneath my fingertips. "There's only one way you could know how damaged the pages are, and that's by looking inside the journal. Reading it."

"I'm not a liar," she says, and the thread of steel in that voice has my chin jerking toward my neck.

She's damn near a foot shorter than me, but that trace of hardness just granted her a few more inches. Hope she doesn't think that's going to back me down. I don't care if the bitch blew fire like one of those ugly-ass dragons on that crazy-as-hell show Ciaran obsesses over. She's wrong; she violated. So she can just take that fucking bass out her voice.

"You can say that shit with your whole chest if it'll make you feel better. I don't really give a fuck. But if you're going to stand here and try and convince me that you didn't violate my privacy, then yeah, li'l mama, you're not just a liar, but a goddamn liar."

Her eyes narrow, and she shoves her hands in the back pockets of her pants, and the stance thrusts her breasts forward against the shirt. Unbidden, my gaze dips to those full curves, and just as quick, I snatch my attention away from them. That flare of anger bursts hotter in my chest, like that brief slip tossed an armload of kindling on the flames. Anger at myself. At her. At the primal hammering in my veins, my dick.

"I'm not going to be too many more liars," she growls, and damn if that rumble, like a pissed-off kitten, doesn't skim down my chest, my spine, caress the small of my back. Before I can reply, she releases a weighted sigh and pinches the bridge of her nose. "Listen," she finally says, lowering her arm and meeting my gaze again. "Let me start over.

Because you're right, I did read your journal. And I had, and have, every intention of telling you the truth about that. I apologize for invading your privacy; it was wrong. I opened the journal to see if there was a name in the front so I could identify its owner. When I didn't see one, I—"

"Decided to keep reading when it was obviously none of your business," I finish between gritted teeth. "I call bullshit on that excuse."

My chest is cracked open, my skin peeled back. Exposed. I feel exposed. For the second time since I entered this office, the urge to demand she look away from me rises hard inside me, and only by sheer will do I force it and my vitriolic response down. Yeah, that's panic whispering to me, pressing me to lash out. Swiping at her is better than the alternative.

Hiding.

Retreating in shame at everything she read.

All the admissions, the pleas, the secret pain I unleashed on the pages of that journal trample through my head like the haunting and terrifying march of a hundred thousand ghosts. Ghosts of my past. My mind. My soul.

And she read every one of them.

Oh yeah, I embrace the rage. Wrap myself in it like old, comfortable clothes.

"I'm sorry, Mr. Young," she murmurs, and I ignore the softness of those four words.

"Fuck your sorry." I toss the leather-bound book on the conference table. "This wasn't yours; they were mine." *And Kendra's.* But I swerve around that thought like fucking roadkill in the middle of a rain-slick road. "Without an invitation or my permission, you invaded my thoughts, what was supposed to be a safe space. You infiltrated my—" My lips roll inward, trapping *pain*. My pain. "Your *I'm sorry* means dick." Jabbing a finger at the stained cover, I sneer, "So what're you really doing here? Did you want to personally return it to me so you could give me that sad-ass apology or to set a price? I can't imagine firefighters make that much in salary. But a personal journal from one of the city's professional hockey players? That's a come-up probably too good to resist. Tabloid sites would pay good money for that shit. So what is the going rate for a hockey player's letters to his wife?"

Her deep-brown skin blanches, and though it's nearly imperceptible, she flinches. Regret curls inside my gut but I extinguish the emotion before it can solidify. I don't know her from a glory hole in the wall. A pretty face and a badass body don't mean shit to me. Both can conceal the greediest soul. And since my years in the league, I've encountered more than my fair share. She's no different. Hell, she might be worse. At least none of those other people who tried to use me had access to my darkest secrets and pain.

"I wouldn't know the going rate, since I would never sink that low. And it saddens me that you apparently know people who would." When I part my lips to tell her exactly what she can do with her sadness, she holds up a hand, shutting down the response. "Mr. Young, I deserve your anger at my disrespect for and invasion of your privacy. And I've apologized for it. Several times. Yes, I know that can't undo what I did, and I regret it. But what I'm not going to do is stand here any longer and take your abuse."

Those words slam into me like a brutal check to the chest. I go still, the air freezing in my lungs before expelling on a low, long breath.

Abuse?

Shame, corrosive and searing hot, damn near raze me to the ground. Dark, turbulent memories bombard me, like that one word squeezed a trigger. Like a round of rapid gunfire, I'm blasted with the sounds of flesh slapping flesh, of pained whimpers, of a masculine voice raised in fury, his hateful tirade peppered with curses and insults. The sound of weeping and desperate pleas.

I blink, wiping a slightly trembling palm down my face.

Shit.

No. *No.*

Have I become that? Have I become . . . *him*?

But even as I repeat those anxious questions in my head, pose them to myself, my tone, my words flood back to me, sweeping over me, drowning me. And in this moment, I'm just a little terrified of who I've become in the last two years.

Fuck.

"Look—"

"No." She shakes her head. "I've accomplished what I came here to do, and I need to get to work. There's nothing I can say to make you believe that, as inappropriate as my actions were, I meant you no harm. And part of me wants to leave this . . . interaction right here. But I can't. Mr. Young, while I do wish I hadn't opened that journal, another part of me is glad I did."

My head jerks back as if her words clipped me in the chin.

"That same part is grateful that you decided to follow your therapist's advice and write down your thoughts, your heart. Because for a couple of hours, I felt understood. Seen. You did what I haven't had the courage to say or even acknowledge. And *that* I can't regret. Even if the man behind the words turned out to be a royal asshole." As shock and—fuck it, yeah—arousal reverberate through me, she rounds the end of the conference table, and when she halts several inches in front of me, she reaches into her pocket, then pulls her hand free seconds later. "Here. This is the other reason I wanted to personally meet you. Not to extort you but to give you the journal and this."

This is a small, rectangular card that she places on top of the journal.

"Thank you for giving me a few moments of your time, Mr. Young."

Without another look or word, she slips past me and leaves the conference room. Not that I have anything to say in response.

Because for a couple of hours, I felt understood. Seen. You did what I haven't had the courage to say or even acknowledge.

That soft confession ripples through my mind as I reach for the paper, pick it up.

A website address.

I flip the slip of card over, but nothing is on the back. Not what the site is, what it pertains to. Just the address.

My fingers start to curl around it, crumpling it. But at the last second, I stop and slide it in the pocket of my track pants. It seems to burn a whole through the knit-mesh lining, but I still don't toss it in the trash can by the door.

As I grab my journal, the peace I should've experienced at finally having it in my hands again deserts me.

Instead, a chaotic, messy storm of emotions gathers right behind my ribs. The all-too-familiar tenant that's anger mixed with the ever-present grief, powerlessness, and guilt. But there's a new member of that godforsaken circle.

Lust.

Lust has joined the party, and I don't know who I resent more for it, Adina Wright or myself.

Myself.

Definitely myself.

Chapter Three

ADINA

"Biiiitch. He said what now? Hol' up a sec." The voice of my bestie, Noni Crawford, blasts in my car's interior. "Damn, girl, are you trying to snatch my soul through these braids? I'm not gonna have one baby hair left on my head, fucking around with you."

I chuckle, shaking my head.

Monica, or Noni, as most people call her, has zero filter, and it's just one of the many reasons we've been best friends since the second grade. It's also why all her tenth-grade students adore her. You never have to think about what's on her mind; that mouth is going to tell you. Along with her unflinching honesty, though, she's fiercely loyal, unfailingly kind, and as protective as a mama bear over her cubs. As a kid who was a quiet-bookworm introvert, I was an easy target for bullies in middle school. But with Noni as my best friend, that bullying was shut down real quick. Usually by a quick two-piece to the face. Not that I couldn't defend myself. But with her, I didn't need to.

A lot of people use *BFF* as a catchphrase. For me and Noni, it's a promise.

Through the car speakers, a voice snaps back at Noni, and I wince, thankful neither woman can glimpse my face.

"Is that Minnie?" I ask Noni, referring to her fraternal twin sister, Minerva, also known as Minnie. "Tell her I said hi."

"Mmkay." Noni snorts, then says, "Dina says hi, Minnie."

Silence echoes in my car, and it doesn't take much to imagine the balled-up face Minnie's probably throwing Noni's way.

"Girl, you petty as hell," Noni mutters, and I snicker.

Minnie has had an issue with me since five minutes after I befriended her twin. Seriously. She's done things as small as not pass along a message from me to Noni and as big and hurtful as spreading rumors about me and one of Noni's boyfriends to drive a wedge between us. Noni stopped talking to Minnie for a hot minute over that one.

It used to bother me that my best friend's sister—her twin sister, at that—seems to hate me for no apparent or good reason. But in the last few years, I've just accepted that not everyone is going to love or like you. And that's more of a reflection on them than me. Still . . . I might've been a shy bookworm at one time and am a civil servant now. But I grew up with two older brothers, and we are adults now, not middle and high school kids. Minnie gets too slick at the mouth and she can catch these hands—who her sister is be damned. I'll just hope Noni can forgive me for that ass whooping.

Fortunately, it hasn't come down to that yet. Hopefully, it won't. But if there's one thing I remember from Pastor Todd's Sunday sermons, it's *Be ye ready*.

"Anyway, like I was saying," Noni says, aggravation rippling through her voice. "Biiiiitch! This fine-ass man said what now?"

I cackle even though the residual irritation and, yes, hurt from my interaction with Solomon Young brushes up against my sternum.

"Girl, who said anything about him being fine?"

"Miss me with that, Dina." Noni sucks her teeth, and though I can't see my bestie, I *can* see her roll her eyes. "Just because you don't give a damn about hockey doesn't mean the rest of the free world doesn't."

I bark out a loud crack of laughter. "You a whole-ass lie, Monica Beatrice Crawford! You don't know one damn thing about hockey."

"Damn, girl. The government name, though?" she mutters. "And 'scuse you. I *do* know a li'l something about hockey. But anyway, what does that have to do with *hockey players*? Have you seen him? Well, shit, yeah, you have. That muthafucka is make-my-pussy-a-ho-out-in-these-streets fine!" I crack up harder, and Noni's laughter joins mine. "Seriously, babe. He's like the only Black player on the team. You know we don't fuck with hockey, for real. But for him? Well, shit, I'd just fuck him."

"That's 'cause you haven't met his mean ass," I grumble, eyes narrowing on the road in front of me. "He's an asshole."

"Um, babe, I hate to point this out, but you did—hold on a sec." Low voices whisper argue in the background, and some shuffling fills the car. "All right," Noni says, several moments later. "Sorry. I didn't want to put your business out there in front of Minnie. I love her, but if she didn't braid the hell out of my hair . . ."

"And not charge you for it," I add.

"That too." She snickers. "But back to you. I hate to point this out, but if there's one thing I'm going to do with you, it's keep it real. You did read the man's private journal. You didn't really expect him to be happy and welcome you with open arms, did you? Hell naw. You're lucky he didn't have you thrown out of there. I mean, I don't know what was in there, but I can just imagine, given everything he's been through. And just from looking at him—which I have done, often, especially with one hand—he doesn't strike me as the kind of man who easily shares his feelings."

"First, ew." I scrunch my face. "Second, what would Shawn say if he heard you talking about this man like that?"

"Girl, please. Am I dead? No, really. Did my grandfather, the honorable Reverend Terrance Crawford, preach my eulogy and lead the congregation in 'Going Up Yonder' over my open casket? No? Well, then I can still look and appreciate."

Oh, did I mention Noni is a preacher's grandkid? Yep. And she lives up to the name.

Laughing, I shake my head. "And three," I continue, "I agree with you. He had every right to be angry. And I *told* his big head that. But I apologized over and over, and he was still rude as hell. And that made his ass ugly."

"Now, bitch."

I pull to a stop at a red light and lean my forehead against the steering wheel.

"All right, fine. Damn. He's sexy as fuck."

Her high-pitched laughter bounces off the roof and doors of the car, and despite the anger and embarrassment still taking up residence in my chest, I smile.

"I really can't stand your ass," I mutter, but Noni continues to crack up.

I lift my head, heaving a sigh.

There really isn't any point in lying to Noni . . . or myself any longer. Solomon Young might be an asshole, but he's a gorgeous, insanely hot one.

Of course, I'd seen him on the news before, and then, for good measure, googled him before I finagled my way into the Pirates' inner sanctum. So yes, I knew the left-winger—I have no idea what that really means—was easy on the eyes.

But nothing, and I mean *nothing* could've prepared me for the impact and power when he walked into that conference room. It's been some years since I was that painfully shy, insecure girl. But in that moment, when his huge muscled frame pushed into that room with a mug on his face that would have a Ringwraith having second thoughts about leaving Mordor, I became that awkward preteen again.

Oh, did I mention I revert to *Lord of the Rings* metaphors when I'm nervous?

And trust and believe, when that man looked at me with those stunning and gorgeous green eyes, I was *beyond* nervous. And tongue tied.

The pictures on the internet didn't compare to reality. Eyes the color of spring set in a face of sharp angles, blunt edges, and lush curves. Against his warm light-brown skin, the green seems even brighter, more intense, magnetic. I found myself falling into that bright gaze.

Then he opened his mouth.

While those lips, surrounded by a short, thick, soft-looking beard, were a work of erotic art that had my thighs trembling and aching to be wrapped around his head, once he started speaking, I only wanted to choke him out with said thighs.

God, what a dick.

And not the beautiful, mouthwatering dick print pressed against his black track pants either. Take me to the cross, that man is big *everywhere*. And I swear—though it seems impossible with the anger toward me practically radiating off his huge frame—he was *hard*.

I don't know why I just whispered that inside my head. Like I was trying to hide the thought of his hard cock from my own self.

Probably because I have no business sitting here in my car, squirming in the driver's seat, getting good and wet over that asshole . . . and his dick.

Shit.

"Is he as big in person as he is in pictures?" Noni asks, breaking into my thoughts and plucking them right from my head.

"Bigger," I grudgingly admit.

"What about his hair? It looks so soft."

Picturing the short, loose sandy-brown curls that proclaim a probable biracial heritage, I grind out, "Softer."

"Damn. Is he as pretty?"

"Prettier." I release another sigh. A much-aggrieved sigh, not an oh-my-God-let-me-worship-that-mouth-with-this-pussy sigh.

It's nuanced, but a big difference. "But then he ruined it." I suck my teeth. "I just wanted to punch him in the mouth. Wouldn't be the first time for him, I'm sure. Probably got fake teeth anyway," I mutter.

"I can't with you." Noni continues to get her amusement on at my expense. "I'm sorry, babe, but from what I've seen, that man could vote for Trump and I still might gift wrap this kitty cat for him."

"You're terrible. And a sellout." Shaking my head, I ease forward, pressing on the accelerator as the light changes.

"And is." The sound of a door opening and closing hits my ears, and a soft grunt.

"What're you doing?"

"Getting a glass of grape-cranberry juice. This whole thing has made me thirsty as hell. Anyway, he accused you of possible extortion, and then what? How did you leave it?"

"With me apologizing again and calling him a royal asshole."

An abusive one. My imagination wants to convince me that he flinched just a little bit when I lobbed that word at him. But she isn't a reliable source. She and my vagina are in cahoots about assigning Solomon Young softer, more human attributes than he deserves.

"Well damn." She chuckles. "Did he yank you up, spread you on that table, and tear that pussy up for getting loose at the mouth?"

God*damn*.

Now that's all I can picture.

And with all that anger writhing under that pretty almond skin, he'd probably tear my pants down my legs, literally rip my panties from my hips, and leave bruises on the inside of my thighs when he pushed them so far apart my hips would twinge . . .

"You're seeing it right now, aren't you?" Noni's cackle is positively deviant.

"I *really* can't stand you," I hiss. "And no, he didn't do that. The man looked at me like I was shit on the bottom of his shoe, not like he wanted to fuck. I didn't give him a chance to say anything since he could provoke Jesus into throwing a punch. I got my ass up out of there."

But not before giving him the link to my private online journal.

I don't tell Noni that; I don't know why.

Maybe because I can't even adequately explain to myself why I gave him access to that part of me. The painfully private side. The vulnerable side. The walking-wounded side. Saying it's because I violated his privacy so it's only fair that I return the favor is too . . . simplified. Too easy. It's more than that, because I didn't even know I was going to go through with it until I did. Giving him that card, even after he'd talked to me as he did . . . yeah, I can't make sense of it. And just thinking about him reading my journal entries has nerves marching down my spine like a battalion of ants.

My only saving grace? I'm never likely to see him again. It's not like firefighters and professional hockey players inhabit the same circles.

"Look, all kidding aside, Dina," Noni says. "I'm sure, given everything he's gone through, his demeanor is a little . . . rough. Not an excuse to be a bitch to people, but still, understandable. Plus, throw in him being an athlete, and somewhat of a celebrity one at that, the chances are high that people have come at him sideways on some foul shit. So he could be forgiven for thinking the worst."

I mug her even though she can't see me.

"Are you really defending him?"

"Buuut." She raises her voice over my objection. "He doesn't know you or your heart. I know both. And that's his bad and loss, not yours. So don't be over there, internalizing what he said. You know who you are, and one hockey player doesn't change that. You better walk like the bad bitch you are!"

I laugh, a little bit of the weight from my meeting with Solomon Young shifting and evaporating from my chest.

"Thank you for that. I knew there was a reason I kept you around." I hit the turn signal and turn on the street nearest the firehouse. "I need to go. I'm almost at the station. Send me a pic of your hair when ol' girl is done with it."

"Ol' girl?" Noni cracks up at how I referenced her sister. "Watch. One day you and Minnie are going to figure out y'all's shit and we're going to be a hot-ass threesome."

It's on the tip of my tongue to say I didn't have shit to work out with her sister since I didn't have the problem, but I'ma let her have it.

"Okay." At my dry response, Noni laughs again, then lets me go.

Minutes later, I park and climb out of my car, and my hand brushes against the hard piece of plastic still clipped to my shirt. The way I rolled up out of that arena, I completely forgot to return the visitor's pass to security. With more force than necessary, I tug the pass off and toss it onto the passenger seat. If I had a trash can nearby, I'd dump it in there. And maybe toss a match in for good measure. I don't need any more reminders of my ill-advised visit to the Pirates' headquarters or the hockey player with the pretty eyes and chain saw for a mouth.

Being in his presence had stirred something I wasn't prepared to encounter. Wasn't prepared to feel again. Guilt and shock twisted in that *something* like threads in a tightly woven rope. I draw to a halt in front of my car's hood, briefly closing my eyes.

For a second, I'd been Icarus, flying too close to the beauty and sensuality of that stern face, the power practically humming from that huge strong body. But then, the glint in those eyes, the anger and, yes, pain that he wore like that long-sleeved black shirt and those joggers he never should be allowed to wear in public sent me plummeting toward an emotional sea of my own.

Like Maya Angelou said, people might forget what you said, but they'll never forget how you made them feel. I'm paraphrasing, but still . . . it's true.

The exact words Solomon and I exchanged might eventually fade from my memory. But I'll never forget the hurt, shame, anger, and, God help me, lust that bubbled and seethed inside me.

I'll never forget that, for just a few moments, he made me feel alive. So painfully alive.

That, more than anything, makes me thankful I won't see him again.

Chapter Four

ADINA

"No, Ma. I didn't forget the wine." I push my car door open, stepping out with my cell phone pressed to my ear. With my free hand, I stretch across the driver's seat and grab the grocery store bag with the aforementioned wine.

"It's not that boxed wine you drink, is it?" Her disdain couldn't be clearer if she waved a hand in front of her nose and told me my alcohol choices were shit.

"No, Ma," I repeated, rolling my eyes. "Although I don't know why you're acting all bougie. I've seen you knock back some twelve-dollar wine before."

"All right, Adina. Don't get your li'l feelings hurt right before dinner. I've heard it's bad for the digestion," she says sweetly.

I snort. All my teasing aside, Dr. Viviane Wright might be a professor of history and African studies at Brown University, but it would be a mistake for someone to think the title and prestigious college meant she wouldn't verbally flay anyone who dared to play in her face. And she'd do it with a smile.

I love her to death.

"Fine." I huff out a laugh. "Can I get off the phone now since I'm right outside your door? This fifteen-dollar wine needs to breathe at least two minutes before we eat."

"Adina Joy Wright—"

"Joking. Just joking." I laugh, holding up a hand in surrender, even though she can't see the gesture. "I'm on my way in the house."

"Bye, girl."

She hangs up on me, and a grin spreads across my face as I shake my head. Bumping my hip against the car door, I shut it and glance around the neighborhood I grew up in. It's one of many in Providence yet unique unto itself. Just one of the many reasons I love my city.

What started as a port city that saw a healthy importation of sugar, molasses, and firearms as well as a brisk slave trade evolved and matured into a liberal, incredibly diverse place filled with universities, art, music, great food, and culture. A person can walk down a street and glimpse gorgeous murals, take a ghost tour through the city's east side, or catch a play at Rites and Reason Theatre at Brown University, one of the longest-running Black theaters in the country. The people themselves are an integral part of Providence's fabric. Loud, sometimes a little rough around the edges, colorful and self-deprecating, we are a community that thrives on our pride and ingenuity.

It's as much home as the colonial I grew up in.

I start up the walkway, and glancing down at my phone, I check my messages. Today and tomorrow are my days off, and Noni and I were supposed to get together for a girls' night. Since Noni suggested it, that could mean anything from binging Hulu and Chinese food to drinks at a strip club.

Nope. No message yet. Maybe I should—

"Adina."

I freeze. Every muscle locks up. I know that voice.

I know that *fucking* voice.

I slowly turn around, hand clutching the phone so tight my fingers throb in protest.

"What are you doing here?" I ask Solomon Young.

It's been two weeks since that day I went to return his journal. Two weeks since I calmed down and stopped flipping off every sign or ad about the Pirates. Two weeks since I put him and his journal in my rearview window.

Two weeks since I started believing he wasn't that fine or sexy.

Two weeks since I convinced myself that my reaction to him hadn't been that visceral.

How dare he make a liar out of me.

"Yeah." He glances down, and for the first time, I notice the brown paper bag he holds by the handles. "I'm sorry for popping up on you."

It's okay sits on my tongue, because isn't that the polite and automatic response? But I bite it back at the last second. Oh, hell nah. Rude is apparently our love language.

Wait. *Love language?*

I want to scrub my brain out with soap for even thinking that shit.

"And yet here you are." I spread my arms wide, my own grocery bag swinging, the two wine bottles clinking against each other. "And don't tell me you're just in the neighborhood. I'm sure Mount Hope is far from . . . wherever you live."

Wherever being a wealthier and more exclusive area than here. Not that working- and middle-class Mount Hope is a hole. Well, the area around Camp Street is a bit sketchy, but even that area is gentrifying. Like I said, I loved growing up here. It's friendly, quiet, a good place for families. A historically Black neighborhood, it remains diverse, vibrant, and thriving. So no, I love my childhood community. But I'd bet a year on kitchen duty that Solomon Young is not from around here.

"No. I had to do some finessing of my own to find out your address. Or rather, your father's. Someone at your fire station named Jared said you would be here. And he only told me that after my PA promised him tickets to the next four home games."

"Seriously? Ain't that some shit," I mutter, copping an immediate attitude. My godfather really sold me out for hockey tickets. Narrowing my eyes, I say, "So why did you go through all the trouble of hunting me down? After our last encounter, I have very little ass left, and I'm partial to it, soo . . ."

Maybe it's my imagination, but I swear his gaze dips below my waist, in the vicinity of my ass.

Yep, I definitely imagined that. Because when I look into those green eyes again, they're shuttered, as unreadable as the stoic mask he wears on his face.

"Sir?" I prop a fist on my hip, pouring so much attitude into that one word, surely he tastes it.

This time I don't imagine anything. Something flickers in his eyes, momentarily tightens his face at that *sir*.

Damn.

Let me find out Solomon Young gets off on freaky domination shit.

"I came to apologize. And bring you this"—he holds up the bag—"as a peace offering."

"A peace offering." I arch an eyebrow. "What? Does something explode in my face when I open it? Will something crawl out?"

"Are you for real?" A frown darkens his face, but just as quickly, it disappears. As if he just reminded himself that he came here to play nice. I silently snort. Yeah, right. I doubt he could find *nice* with both hands and a flashlight. "Here, man."

Reluctantly, I move forward and gingerly take the gift from his outstretched hand. Switching it to the hand still holding the wine, I peer down into the bag and pull out a green jersey. A green Pirates jersey, to be exact. With a Captain Jack Sparrow–looking guy on the front and number 19 on the arm.

"Is this"—I give the jersey a slight shake—"your jersey?"

"Yeah." He jerks up his chin. "I got it signed by the first line."

He says that like it's supposed to mean something to me.

I shrug, dropping the top back into the bag.

"We're football fans around here. But thanks." It should bring in a good amount on eBay.

He stares at me, squinting. "Ay. Don't let me find out you put my shit up on eBay."

I blink, my lips falling apart. How did he know . . . ?

"It's all over your face, ma."

"No, it's—*oh fuck*." I groan, squeezing my eyelids together. But when I open them, the person climbing out of a Mercedes parked behind my car is still there. Still approaching the house with two bouquets of roses in his arms. *Ma, what the hell?*

He isn't familiar to me, but then again, he is. I don't need to have met this man before to understand who he is and why he's here. I've met about eleven of them before in the last year. He makes a clean dozen.

"Oh, good, Kyle. You made it," my mother announces from the porch behind me, as if we all can't see *Kyle* standing there. "I'm so glad you're here."

I half turn as Ma descends the front steps, a wide smile stretched across her pretty face. At forty-eight, she could easily pass for a woman in her mid- to late thirties, even with the strands of silver glinting in her tight shoulder-length natural curls. Laugh lines crease the corners of her brown eyes, but otherwise, her walnut brown skin is smooth, gorgeous.

She might be able to pass for my older sister or younger aunt, but I can never forget this is the woman who birthed and raised me. And right now, it's only my respect and love for her that's keeping me from turning and demanding *What the fuuuuck?*

'Cause a bitch is tired of Viviane Wright playing the Millionaire Matchmaker. Sans the millionaire.

"Oh, we have another guest." Ma glances at me, curiosity gleaming in her eyes. "Baby, why didn't you tell me you'd invited someone else to dinner? Hi." She stretches out a hand toward Solomon. "I'm Viviane Wright, Adina's mother. And you are?"

I snort, and Solomon cuts a look at me even as he accepts Ma's hand, shaking it.

"I'm Solomon Young. A . . . friend of your daughter's."

"*The* Solomon Young?" Kyle grows animated like a live-action cartoon. "Oh my God, I knew you looked familiar. *Wow.* I can't believe this." If he held up a sign with **I ♥ #19** painted on it, I wouldn't have been more stunned.

This guy. I glare at Solomon. Somehow this is all his fault.

Ma shifts her attention back to me, a little furrow wrinkling her forehead. I shrug.

"I'm sorry, I hate to sound rude," she says. "But should I know you?"

"Only if you're an NHL fan, ma'am." Solomon dips his chin. "I play for the Pirates, Providence's team. But I understand if I'm not familiar to you. Adina informed me you're more football fans than hockey."

I almost snort again, but as if he's read my mind once more, he slides a don't-get-fucked-up glance my way, and I huff out a breath.

And squeeze my thighs. Because goddamn. That was hot as hell.

"Ah, okay. Well, that's ni—"

"Can I get a selfie?" Kyle cuts Ma off, already dipping inside of his dark-blue sports coat and emerging with his cell in hand. "Do you mind? Your arms are longer." He passes the phone to Solomon with a wide grin. He's not lying; Kyle isn't a short man, but Solomon is a damn giant. I might've looked up his stats: six feet, four inches and two hundred and thirty-five pounds. "That's awesome. Thank you, Solomon." Kyle cheeses as if they're pals.

Though that stoic, slightly menacing mug remains on his face, Solomon does take the phone, holds it at an angle, and snaps a couple of shots.

"Oh man." Kyle shakes his head, fingers flying over his phone after he accepts it back from Solomon. "I have to post these now. No one would ever believe me."

This whole thing has taken a sharp turn into the surreal. And by *surreal*, I mean the what-the-fuck-is-happening-here zone.

Ma clears her throat. "Uh, Kyle. Kyle?" She calls his name again, and this time, his head pops up, a grin still lighting up his face.

"Oh, I'm sorry, Dr. Wright." Chagrin seeps into his expression, and he tucks his phone away again. "I just got a little"—he waves a hand toward Solomon—"excited."

"Yes, I see," she murmurs. "Can I introduce you to my daughter?"

"Of course. My apologies." Shifting closer to me, he holds his hand out, and a whole lot of *Hell no* surges inside me. A handshake now, and I find myself on a painfully awkward and tedious dinner a couple of days from now that my mother's coordinated. "It's a pleasure to meet you. Your mother speaks very highly of you."

"Thanks," I say, quickly shaking his hand and dropping it. "You too."

"If I may?" He lifts the forgotten-for-a-selfie bouquets in his hand. "These are for you." He passes one to Ma and then extends the other to me. "And these are for you. Your mother didn't lie. You're as beautiful as she said."

Nope.

Uh-uh.

Not today, Satan.

Don't get me wrong. I'm sure Kyle is a nice guy. I mean, my mother loves me, so she wouldn't try to fix me up with a douche. But every man she has invited to a family dinner just isn't my type. I can't even identify what my type is, but it's not the parade of guys she's wined, dined, and off-loaded on me.

You don't know your type, huh?

The bitchy voice in my head pipes up.

And *without* my permission, my gaze slides over to Solomon. Today, he's traded a T-shirt for a black sweater and those joggers for black jeans and a pair of black-and-red retro Jordans. Swirls of black, gray, and blue ink peek above his collar, and I find myself staring hard, tracing each line, trying to decipher what the tattoos are.

Arousal throbs low in my belly, thumps in my sex.

"Dina." Ma elbows me in the side, and I mouth *ouch* to her.

Damn. I swear she has knives tucked under that shirt. She squints at me, nodding toward Kyle. Right. The flowers.

As I take them, Kyle smiles bright, and his regard dips down, lingering on my breasts, hips, and thighs.

Okay, no.

I can't. I just *can't*.

"Thank you, Kyle." I beam at him, and though Kyle's smile brightens, Solomon stares hard at me, green eyes narrowed. Taking the flowers, I sidle over to Solomon until I'm standing next to him. He stiffens, but I don't let that stop me from switching the bags over to the same one grasping the flowers and sliding my now free arm through Solomon's. "But I think my boyfriend might have an issue with another man giving me flowers."

"*The fuck?*" he hisses, but at the same time I laugh loud and brightly to drown him out. Unfortunately, it emerges sounding like I'm either drunk or *really*, really happy.

When Ma glances at the plastic bag with the necks of the wine bottles poking out, I can guess which option she's going with.

"Boyfriend?" Ma slowly repeats, her skeptical gaze roaming Solomon from the loose wavy curls on his head all the way to his large sneakered feet. "And why is this the first time I've heard about him?"

Because it's been a whole two minutes.

"Because it's new."

The suspicion doesn't fade from her eyes. "Is that right? How new?"

"Almost a month." Not a lie. Two weeks is almost a month. "But I thought it was time for Solomon to meet all of you guys. And what better time than our family dinner. Isn't that right, baby?" I tilt my head back, staring up at Solomon. Silently pleading with him to go along with this charade. At least for tonight.

And that beautiful face reveals nothing.

My stomach bottoms out, and nerves flood in. I widen my eyes, and honestly, I don't know if I'm begging or threatening him at this point.

His green eyes sharpen, narrowing.

Shit.

"That's right," he murmurs, and relief washes through me so strong I get a little lightheaded. "I'm happy to meet Adina's family."

"Hmm." The suspicion doesn't clear up from Ma's eyes, but I'm too relieved that I can deflect her matchmaking for the evening. As far as how I'm going to explain where my "boyfriend" went after this dinner? I'll cross that bridge when I come to it. "Well, not only is it nice to meet you, Solomon, but welcome to our home. Everyone, come on in. The food is ready."

She turns and heads back up the walk and climbs the front steps. Clearing his throat and with discomfort obvious on his face, Kyle follows, momentarily leaving me and Solomon by ourselves.

"Don't even say it," I mutter.

"That's ungrateful as hell. And here I could've blown up your spot. Shit, I still can . . ." He starts to turn, but I squeeze his arm into my side boob, stopping him from moving.

His gaze drops down to where his forearm is pressed to my flesh, and my nipples draw to almost painful points under my shirt and bra. God, they're doing the most. Thank goodness this bra is padded.

"Sorry, sorry. You're right. And I am grateful. I just . . . I wish I didn't have to need you," I admit, looking away from that bright, too-seeing gaze. "I came here this evening hoping for an easy, laid-back dinner with the family, and here my mom is, on her matchmaking bullshit again."

"Again?"

I wince. "This would be Prospect Number Twelve. And I've been on four terrible first dates. And Kyle . . ." I ball up my face. "Well, first of all, his arms were too short to take a selfie with you. Turnoff."

He snorts.

"Yeah, yeah, I know how shallow that sounds," I say. "But still. And second of all, he allowed my mother to coerce him into coming here. Nope. He's either trying to curry favor, or he's soft as fuck for letting my mother pressure him into coming here to meet me. Both of those are turnoffs too. Third, I love my mother dearly, but she can't pick men out for me for shit. She's oh and twelve."

"Eleven, actually. You didn't even give twelve a chance."

"You got that. But this is why I need you. At least for tonight, I cannot have her shoving mashed potatoes *and* desperate man at me. My appetite only has room for one of those."

The corner of his mouth quirks in an almost smile.

"Yeah, well, you owe me, li'l mama. And since I'm going to be lying on your behalf for the next couple of hours, not to mention probably looking at a grilling for not just being your new man but a hockey player, too, you owe me big."

"Fine," I mutter, tugging on his arm and guiding him forward.

"You might wanna get that attitude out your voice. I don't put up with that shit."

"You know what?" I snap. Then, at his arched eyebrow, I swallow my *Kiss my ass* down. Because I need him, and he knows it. Solomon Young has me by the proverbial short hairs, and he knows it.

Bastard.

Swallowing a sigh, I plaster a fake smile on my face. I need to start practicing now.

"You're right, *babe*. And thank you, *sweetheart*, for bailing me out. If you're ever on fire and you need me to put you out, I'm your woman. Bet."

"Okay, I see what type of time you on," he murmurs, climbing the front steps. "Don't worry. I can play games too."

With that ominous warning bouncing off my skull, I reach the front door, pull it open, and lead him into the house.

◆ ◆ ◆

"So, Solomon," Dad says, cutting into his thick slice of roast with his steady gaze fixed on my "boyfriend." I silently groan. Other than greeting Solomon and giving me a squinty side-eye, Dad hasn't said anything to him. My reprieve is over. "It's not often *my daughter* brings a *friend* home." He forks the meat into his mouth and eyes Solomon, who, to his credit, doesn't stiffen or shrink under my father's stare. I've witnessed that narrowed gaze make two-hundred-plus-pound firemen shiver in their turnout gear. "That must make you special."

"Dad, really?" I shake my head. He's acting like I'm twelve instead of twenty-six. And he wouldn't pull this with Malcolm or Malik if they brought home significant others—not that they have. I love my brothers, but they put the *whore* in *manwhore*. "A day may come when your daughter's pride fails, but it is not this day."

"Aw, shit. She's hauling out the *Lord of the Rings* lines." Malik snickers, stuffing a piece of corn bread in his mouth. "She must be nervous as hell."

I shoot him a mind-the-business-that-pays-you glare, then glance at Solomon, who peers down at me, an expression I can't read on his face. He studies me for another long moment before shifting his regard to my father.

"I don't know about *special*, sir," Solomon says, and his dark, rich rumble of a voice does *not* roll over my skin like a silken caress. "If anything, I'd give that compliment to your daughter. It's one of the first things I thought about her when we first met. She was real . . . special."

Son of a . . . I kick his foot underneath the table and try to hide my wince. God*damn*! Screw him and his Barney Rubble feet.

"Oh, that's sweet." Ma smiles at Solomon as she raises her glass of wine. Despite her initial skepticism and hesitation, she has fallen under his dark, broody spell. She's damn near forgotten about Kyle, and I've been trying not to stare too deeply into her eyes. The vision of bouquets and cream-cheese-icing red-velvet wedding cake dancing there is unnerving. "Speaking of, how did you two meet?"

"At the arena."

"After a call."

A heavy silence falls over the table.

"Well, which is it?" Dad asks, propping his elbows on the table and staring at me, then Solomon.

"Both," I answer quickly. "We met after that call at the hockey training facility. Solomon invited me down to the arena the next day for our first date."

"*You* went to the hockey arena? Who *are* you?" Malik asks, mock disgust dripping from his voice.

Okay, maybe not so *mock*.

"Oh, I've been down there. It's great," Kyle chimes in from across the table. "And the games are amazing. I have season tickets, and I'm all ready for Thursday's home game. The Pirates are going to kill the Ravens. Especially since we now have Mont Hannah as goalie. Sure, we're going to miss Morgan at that position, but Mont is showing real promise with a save percentage of .915. And he's only been in the league for two years. Imagine how much greater he's going to get."

Another silence descends over the table. Kyle scans each face, and the enthusiasm slowly disappears his smile until he just looks . . . confused.

"Okay, no, for real." Malcolm sets his fork and knife down on his plate and leans back in his chair. "What's going on? It's October, so no

April Fools' joke. But, Ma, you brought a hockey groupie here, and Dina brings a *player*. Somebody better tell me something."

"I'm sorry?" Kyle glances at my mom, then at Malcolm. "Did I say something wrong?"

"This is a Patriots household," Malik says. "No other sport or team exists except football and the Patriots. If you're not talking about Belichick or Brady, we don't give a damn. No offense," he tosses at Solomon.

He dips his head, lifting a forkful of roast and mashed potatoes to his mouth.

"None taken."

"Brady?" Kyle frowns. "He's not a Patriot any longer. He retired from Tampa Bay."

Malik's fork clatters to his plate, and I shake my head at Kyle.

Oh sweet, sweet summer child.

"Say that again. I dare you," Malik threatens.

"Once a Patriot, always a Patriot. Especially if you're Brady," Dad sermonizes, glaring at Kyle.

"Seriously, Ma?" Malcolm scowls. "Where'd you find this guy? And you actually brought him here to hook him up with Dina? What tomfoolery is this?"

I would feel bad for Kyle and his ass that's about to be handed to him, but his untimely and unwise homage to hockey saved my ass from my family's interrogation about my "relationship" with Solomon.

In desperate times like these, it's each person for themselves. Nah. He's on his own.

"Brady should've retired a Patriot." Solomon forks more roast into his mouth, chewing and swallowing before continuing with his blasphemy. "He's one of those athletes that just don't know when to step away from the sport. Even after winning a ring with Tampa Bay, that still wasn't enough for him. It's sad when you allow a sport to define who you are."

Malik gasps. Ma groans. Dad goes stony silent. Malcolm glares. Kyle gives him a look of such adoration I'm embarrassed for him.

And me?

I gape at Solomon in abject horror.

But he doesn't give a damn that he just committed blasphemy at my mother's dinner table. He keeps eating as if he isn't seconds away from a dogpile.

Why would he deliberately court death? We were in the clear. We . . . I glance across the table at Kyle again, then return my attention to Solomon.

Holy shit. Did he just throw himself on the grenade for Kyle?

Noooo.

This man verbally eviscerated me within seconds of us meeting, so why would he . . . ?

I frown.

"You gotta go." Malik jerks a thumb over his shoulder, his eyebrows a dark V over his nose. "We don't play that in this house. What would a guy who figure skates for a living know about football, anyway?"

Solomon breaks off a piece of corn bread and slides it in his mouth. And I really shouldn't be distracted by those full lips in the face of his imminent destruction.

Sure, he has my brothers and father by a few inches and pounds, but there are three of them. Am I expected to throw myself in front of my fake boyfriend? Like, what are the rules for that?

"Football players run on a field, catching balls. In hockey, we skate on razor-sharp blades, requiring balance and speed, which means when we hit the boards or each other, you can hear it in the nosebleed section. And all this carrying sticks while passing and shooting a frozen rubber disc that flies at speeds exceeding ninety miles per hour." He picks up his glass of wine, arching his eyebrow at Malik. "And figure skating is hard as fuck. Sorry, ma'am," he says to my mother.

She waves his profanity off, staring at him in the same way she did when I was fourteen and we visited Robben Island Prison and the cell where Nelson Mandela was imprisoned—fascination and awe.

"Hold up," Malcolm butts in. "You have skates, but football players wear spiked cleats. Take a cleat in the foot or leg and see how tough you are. And turf—especially in the winter—isn't a field of grass. It's like hitting rock. And every play in football means hitting against six-foot-plus, sometimes-three-hundred-pound fully padded men. Yeah, you get shoved in a hockey game, but we tackle over and over again. Football requires a mental and physical toughness that's superior to other sports."

Solomon shrugs, picking up his fork and finishing off his roast.

"Yeah, and when you do get hit, the ref blows the whistle, calling an end to the play. For us, you get hit, you don't get time to regroup and recuperate. You get up and play without stopping. That's stamina *and* toughness. Besides"—he arches an eyebrow and smirks at my brother—"we fight."

"You know what—" Malik leans forward, jabbing a finger.

"Hey, Ma, what about dessert?" I blurt out, leaning against Solomon, half blocking him from my brother's view. "Ma!" I grind out when she doesn't reply.

She blinks, straightening in her chair.

"What? Oh yes, dessert. I got it. Who's in the mood for pound cake and coffee?"

Dad glowers in her direction as she smiles at Solomon again. If I wasn't busy being a human shield for "my man," I'd find the shit funny. Dad knows as well as I do how exciting Mom finds a debate.

"Viviane, don't get snatched up in here," Dad growls.

"Please, Nolan." She flicks a hand toward him, then rises and picks up her plate. She rounds the table and lifts his as well. Bending down, she kisses his bearded cheek and whispers loud enough for everyone at the damn table to hear, "Hem me up, daddy."

"Oh God."

"You so nasty."

"I just ate!"

My and my brothers' shouts fill the room. Beside me, Solomon snickers. I shoot him a hot glare, and he looks at me, shrugging a shoulder.

Mom rolls her eyes and heads toward the kitchen.

But not before Dad smacks her on the ass.

I can't. I'm out. Don't get me wrong. I love that, after thirty-one years, my parents are still as affectionate and in love as ever. But they on one today. And between them and the death stare Malik is still shooting Solomon, I'm calling it quits.

"Okay, well, sorry, Mom, Dad. But I'm going to have to take a rain check on dessert. I promised Solomon I'd show him around Mount Hope. Ready, babe?"

He picks up his napkin and wipes his mouth.

"Sure." And if everyone else hears the dry note in the word, well, thank God for small favors that they don't comment on it. He's probably mad he can't eat more. "Thank you for a wonderful dinner, Dr. Wright. Nice meeting you, too, Mr. Wright." My father nods but with a flinty stare. Solomon turns to my brothers. And smiles. It figures the first time I see this man smile it's a wicked taunt. "You too. I'll be in prayer for the Patriots' season."

They both growl, and goddammit, I shove Solomon in the back with both hands.

"All right, see you guys later," I say loudly, injecting false cheer in my voice.

I'll be lucky if Dad allows me to cross the threshold ever again.

"You just couldn't resist, could you?" I mutter at him, my fingers locked around his wrist.

I drag him out of the dining room and into the hall.

"Your brothers started it," he calmly says, as if that isn't the most five-year-old shit ever.

Grumbling under my breath about knuckleheaded athletes with the emotional maturity of a spoon, I stop by the living room and snatch up the bag with the jersey. I can't leave that behind, because I'm 88.5 percent sure my father and brothers will have a barbecue in the backyard using the jersey as kindling.

And fuck that.

I'm *definitely* selling this bitch on eBay.

Chapter Five

SOLOMON

"What are you doing?" I frown, shoving the bills Adina set on the scarred mahogany bar back toward her. "Get that outta here."

"I brought you here, so that means I treat you to drinks." *Here* being a small one-step-above-dive bar in Mount Hope.

Ignoring her dumb-as-fuck argument, I hold up a hand, signaling the bartender. The pretty young woman with long black hair and tattoos running down her arms approaches me with a smile.

"Can I start a tab?"

She nods. "Of course."

"Put these two"—I circle a finger over our bottles of Sam Adams—"on there."

"No problem." She smiles again, and though I glimpse the recognition in her eyes, she doesn't say anything. Usually, I have no problem with fans approaching me, but right now I appreciate her restraint.

I turn back to Adina, and she mugs me. But I shrug and lift my bottle for a deep sip. The wine at her parents' had been fine, but it's not my preference. Give me a cold beer anytime.

"I can handle a few beers," she pushes with a bite in her tone.

"Fuck I look like letting you pay for me, ma. When I'm with a woman, I'm getting it." Her frown deepens and her lips part, but I beat her to it. "Yeah, call it sexist, whatever. Not gonna happen."

Her lips snap shut. And she lifts her beer for a long sip. After she lowers the bottle, she continues to stare at me, all her feelings and thoughts on her face.

So I'm low-key surprised when she says, "Thank you for not busting me out tonight and playing along as my man."

I dip my chin. "I take it 'Kyle' happens often."

She shudders, thrusting a hand in her thick brown-and-auburn curls. Last time I'd seen her, the shoulder-length tight coils had been tamed in a bun at the nape of her neck. And I do mean *tamed.* Tonight, that hair is free, an explosion of natural beauty. All through that shit-show of a dinner, the peach scent emanating from it had teased me. Tortured me. I'd wavered between scooting my chair over as far as possible without sitting on her father's lap and leaning over so I could fill my lungs with that scent.

It'd been so long since I'd buried my face in a woman's hair, the brush of the strands an intimate, sensory caress. I'd loved lying behind Kendra, inhaling the vanilla-and-cinnamon scent from her shampoo and conditioner . . .

The fuck.

Adina is not my wife. Could never be Kendra. So why the hell am I even *thinking* about this?

The beer ain't cutting it. I might need something more brown, stronger and guaranteed to drown my brain so it doesn't have ridiculous, traitorous thoughts.

"Too often. My mother is of the opinion that I've given up ever dating or trying to find love again. It's not her believing I need a man; she's too progressive for that kind of bullshit. I don't even think she cares if it doesn't end in a long relationship or marriage. She just doesn't want me to . . ."

"Give up," I finish for her when her voice trails off.

She gives me a tight nod, then takes another drink, her gaze skipping away from mine.

If I thought her body did magical things for her firefighter's uniform, then it's doing the Lord's work with these dark-denim skinny jeans, knee-high camel-colored riding boots, and green V-necked sweater.

Adina Wright has been heavy on my mind since she left that conference room. I've tried to evict her. Many times. But she's as stubborn in my head as she is in person. It's bugged me how our conversation ended. No, correction. How she saw me has bugged me.

I'll freely admit, I haven't given a fuck about much in these last couple of years. But that? I'm giving a fuck about it. So much that I made the effort of asking Natasha to get me Adina's information. So much that I had the guys sign a jersey so I could give that to her in apology.

So much that I pretended to be her boyfriend.

If I dwell on it long enough, I might realize it unnerves me that I've gone to all this trouble for a woman I barely know *and* who violated my privacy.

So I don't dwell on it.

"I read your journal," I say.

Again, Adina nods. "That's why I gave you the link," she replies and drinks more beer.

We're going to need more alcohol if we're having this conversation. I turn on my stool and, catching the bartender's notice, hold up two fingers. She smiles, and I return my attention to Adina.

"I almost didn't. Doesn't matter that you allowed me to read it. Still felt intrusive and none of my business. Add in the fact you only gave me access because you'd read my journal. It almost felt like you were coerced into it. Like I was on some get-back shit."

"But you still read it."

"Yeah, I did." Sighing, I pick up my bottle, but instead of lifting it to my mouth, I twist it back and forth between my fingers. "I'm sorry about the loss of your fiancé." I loose a rusty chuckle. "Shit, I feel like an asshole even saying those words, since I hated when people offered them to me. But I *am* sorry, Adina. No one should know that kind of pain. Especially when they're so young, when they have so much life to live. When they have a life to live with you."

She clears her throat, and I stare at the elegant column, inordinately fascinated by the motion behind that pretty brown skin. The V of her sweater exposes her collarbone, and her pulse ticks away. For a moment, I'm damn near hypnotized by the fast pulse. I want to feel it under my tongue.

Guilt and shame creep through my body, infiltrate my veins, and take a ride straight to my chest. My heart.

This is why it took me a couple of weeks to get off my ass and come find Adina. Not because I'm scared of her or her reaction to my offer of an apology.

I'm scared of me, of this unwanted and hated fascination with this woman who I have no business being within five feet of.

"You remember when I said I didn't have the courage to acknowledge or admit what you did?" she asks. I jerk my chin up in response. "I didn't mean being able to write down how you were feeling about losing your wife. Well, not all of it. You emptied yourself into that book. Gave voice to things that . . . scared me. Things I never confessed out loud, much less to my parents or brothers. Things that made me feel ungrateful and ashamed just for thinking about them."

"Suicide."

The ugly word echoes between us. Even with the loud chatter and laughter as well as a replay of a football game on the mounted television, it seems as if the word echoes, getting louder and louder.

Adina's gaze drops to the bar, and the bartender arrives with our fresh beers, removes the tops, and sets the cold, damp bottles on the bar top.

"Thank you," Adina murmurs to her. Switching out her empty, she tips the new one up to her mouth. And I pretend the act of her pursing those lips over the bottle opening isn't downright fucking lewd. After a moment, she says, "Yes." Another heartbeat of silence passes, and then she shakes her head. "All firefighters go to a call praying to make it back safe, without injury. Keshaun included. It's a slap in their face—it's like spitting on Keshaun's memory—to even consider ending my life. Not when our job is saving the lives of others and our own. I think a part of me felt like if I didn't write that down, I could deny the thought ever crossed my mind. But reading your journal made a liar out of me. It also, as terrible as it sounds, gave me relief. Because I wasn't alone."

I wasn't alone.

Yeah, I'm intimately familiar with the hollow emptiness that some underwhelming soul coined as *alone*.

"One thing I didn't read in your entries . . . after your fiancé passed, did you ever consider going into a different field? Losing someone in a fire and then having to turn around and face that same thing every day? I don't know if I could do it."

She finally looks at me and cocks her head.

"The thought of doing anything—hell, breathing—was painful at first. But I can honestly say not once did the thought of quitting my job come to my mind. Hockey isn't just something you get paid to do. I'm going to assume that it's your passion, sometimes your saving grace and your peace in the middle of a storm. It's the place you go to empty your mind when it's so busy, filled with too much noise and chaos that thinking is a lost cause."

I don't reply, even though she's absolutely correct.

In the days after Kendra's death, when I couldn't drag myself out of the bed to do anything, not even to care for Khalil—thank fuck for my in-laws—I would leave the house at one, two in the morning and go to the rink. It was the one place where everything made sense. It still is. Skating. The swish of blades over ice. The clack of the puck against my stick. The speed of flying down to one end of the rink and back to the other. They're all the equivalent of a slowly rocking cradle, lulling me into a peace, a calm that has become a rare commodity.

"That's how firefighting is for me," she continues. "How hockey is a passion for you, fighting fire is a calling for me. There's nothing else I'd rather do. Maybe it's my way of living for both of us. For continuing to do what he wanted above all else but now can't." She pauses, drags her short nail down the label on the bottle. "I don't know. And maybe I'm making it much deeper than it is."

I don't contradict her.

Who am I to say it's wrong to use his memory to get through the day? To grant more meaning to her decisions? She's talking to a man who used his son as the sole reason not to say *Fuck it* and walk away from it all.

"Also, it's in my blood. My brothers, my father, my grandfather—all firefighters. Sure, I had a choice, and I'm sure there are days when they wished I'd gone a different path. But in a way, I was born to do this."

My eyebrows shoot up, shock vibrating through me. Of all the things that had come up during dinner, the family occupation hadn't been one of them.

"You work with all of them?"

She laughs softly and sips from her beer. "I can hear the horror in your voice at the thought of that. And some days, the struggle is real. My dad, Malcolm, and I are in the same house; Malik is stationed in another one. And let's just say they can get a little . . . overbearing at times."

"Wouldn't have believed that shit."

Her grin is quick and dry. "Sarcasm duly noted. My dad's been a firefighter for almost thirty years. And being Black in the department brings its own set of problems, as you can imagine. The racism, bigotry, favoritism is as deeply entrenched in our culture as it is with the police. As a matter of fact, not too long ago, a Black firefighter was racially profiled and harassed by the police while he sat in his car right in front of his fire station in full uniform. No, we're not too far removed from that bullshit. Experiencing all of that, you can understand why he didn't want his daughter to not have to face dangerous situations on the daily but also have to deal with that shit on top of it."

I get it. As one of fewer than forty Black players in the entire NHL and the only one on my team, I for damn sure get it. Being called racial slurs or having animal noises aimed my way by players and fans ain't anything new to me. With the players, I can take it out on their asses on the ice. But with the fans? Nothing I can do but take that shit because my love for the game and my job is more important than some inbred muthafuckas who probably can't even spell the shit they yell at me. At least that's what I tell myself to keep from climbing in those stands and showing them these hands are good for other things besides holding a stick.

"So yeah, he can be overprotective. And my dad. I keep telling him he needs to lay off calling me *baby girl* and hugging and kissing me while on shift. Besides a couple of the EMTs, I'm the only woman there, *and* I'm the shift captain's daughter. It's giving nepotism." She shakes her head with a rueful smile. "But I've been saying it since I entered the fire academy three years ago. But Fire Captain Nolan Wright isn't listening. And it's only gotten worse in the last year."

I don't need her to explain that last sentence. From her journal entries, I know that her fiancé died within that time frame. And if I didn't get that, the subtle flexing of her jaw and the rapid blinking of her eyes give all the context needed.

"Are you . . . better?" she suddenly asks, and I arch an eyebrow. Clearing her throat, she lifts her hand to the chain around her neck. She toys with the pendant tucked inside her sweater for several seconds before dropping her arm. "It's been two years, and you're in therapy. Do you feel any better? Not as"—she shrugs a shoulder and twirls her fingers, as if that gesture can conjure the words she's searching for—"heavy?"

I inhale a sharp breath, straightening. After a second, I release it on a long, low exhale.

"I won't lie to you. Some days I wake up and want to knock all this shit over because I'm mad as fuck. Other days I wish God would come down and fight me face to face."

"You betta ask Jacob how that worked out for him. You and that hip gon' fuck around and find out."

I snort. "You got that. But those are the days I blame God and don't wanna have shit to do with him. Then there are days I have to force myself out of the bed." Damn near crawl out, when all I want to do is lie there and not move because even that's too painful.

"Solomon," she whispers and, reaching out, sets her small, long-fingered, elegant hand over the one resting on my thigh.

I stare down, taking in the size difference, her skin a few shades darker than mine. A circle of heat simmers, then flares to life where she touches me. It doesn't stay on the back of my hand, though. It radiates up my arm, across my chest, and shit, straight to my dick. Lust, guilt, and disgust at myself are a twisted mess in my blood, my gut. My cock doesn't give a fuck about the guilt or disgust, though.

"Then"—I swallow past a suddenly tight throat—"there are days when the weight on my chest lifts and I can . . . breathe. When I can go hours without thinking of her. Or I can laugh and not feel guilty. Or my heart doesn't seize up when my son talks about his mother." I loose another breath, pick up my Sam Adams, and, tipping my head back, down a healthy gulp. "What I'm trying to say, ma, is the answer to your question is yes and no. Grief isn't stationary; it's continuous and fluid until it's not. Day by day we find a way not to be dragged under. And each day you don't is a win." I stare into her brown eyes, glimpsing the sadness, the ache there. "Are you winning, Adina?"

"I . . ."

She bows her head and removes her hand from mine, circling the slender fingers around the base of her throat. I'm a piece of shit for wondering how those small hands would fit around me. How the softness of her palm would feel sliding up and down my hard dick.

Fuck.

I need to get the hell up outta here. Away from her before I do something I regret. Something I'll hate myself for.

"I'm winning more than I'm losing," she softly admits, dragging me kicking and screaming from the spiral I'm point-eight seconds away from tumbling into.

"Take the win." I drink down the last of my beer and set it firmly on the bar top.

"You want another one?" she asks, her gaze flicking from the emptied bottle back to me.

"No, I'm good. You?"

"Nope." She shakes her head. "We can head out."

"Let me go take care of the tab, and I'll be right back. Aht. Not interested in hearing whatever bullshit you about to let come out your mouth."

I rise off the stool and head toward the other end of the bar. But not before I hear a muttered "Mean ass."

Smirking, I take care of the tab and ignore the phone number scrawled on the back of the receipt. Even if I were in the headspace to date again—which I'm not and don't know when or if I will be—with this move, she wouldn't be an option. Hell, she couldn't even get the dick. For all she knew, Adina and I could've been together. It was grimy and rude as fuck for her to slip me her number.

Not caring if she's watching, I toss the receipt in the trash can near the exit. Adina arches an eyebrow in question, but she turns and opens the door, stepping through to outside, me right behind her.

We silently walk down the sidewalk, which is teeming with people either going into or leaving the restaurants lining the street. It's habit, but I stay to the right of her, providing a barrier between her and the street. When I took that position, she again arched an eyebrow but still refrained from saying anything.

It isn't until we're almost to our cars, parked one behind the other, that she says, "She gave you her number, didn't she?"

I briefly look at her before returning my attention to our surroundings. "Yeah."

"Damn," she scoffs. "How that heffa know we weren't on a date? I could've been your woman, and she up there being shady. I knew she was too nice," she mutters. Then, a short pause later, "Why didn't you keep it, though?"

"I don't do friendly pussy."

"Oh. Okay. Wow." Her steps stutter, almost stopping. But then, with a shake of her head, she resumes walking. Another brief pause. "Do you do pussy at all?" she asks.

My head jerks toward her, but she's staring straight ahead, not looking at me.

"Are you asking if I'm fucking?"

"Since your wife passed, yes."

"Yeah, I have."

She glances sharply at me before just as quickly shifting her gaze away. By this time, we've reached our cars, and she slides her hand into her jean pocket and removes her keys.

Against my better judgment, I reach out toward her and cuff her wrist. *Shit.* I grind my teeth against the electric charge that seems to transfer from her skin to mine. It crackles up my arm, over my shoulders, and down my spine. I should let go of that slim wrist with the deceptively delicate bones, but I don't. I almost . . . can't.

That's fucking ridiculous.

And to prove that I can, that there's nothing special about touching her, about *her*, I force my fingers to straighten and drop her like her skin brands me.

Here's where I should get my ass in my car and get the fuck up outta here. I apologized, did her a favor, and even had somewhat friendly drinks. Now we don't ever have to see each other again. Definitely no need for more conversation—

"Why does it feel like that bothers you?" I press.

Shit. Shitshitshit.

The corners of her mouth pull down. "It doesn't."

"That ain't what your face saying." I continue to poke.

"Don't flatter yourself." She gives me side-eye that I bet has been perfected on those brothers of hers. A sliver of amusement slides through me. Fucking with them might've been the most fun I've had in . . . well, a while. "I was just curious in general. How did you . . . ? I mean, it wasn't . . . ? Shit, I don't know what I mean."

"Yes, you do." Any traces of humor fade as I stare down into her troubled expression. Those full lips flatten—well, they try to. Disappearing that lush dick-tease of a mouth would take an act of God. Her lashes lower over her pretty eyes, and my fingers itch with the need to touch her chin, tilt her head back, and order her to look at me. I slide both hands in the front pockets of my jeans just in case they get any fucking ideas. "Ma, you might as well just say it and stop censoring the shit in your head. You can be honest with me. One, we'll never see each other after tonight. Two, we've already established that we're members of a club no sane person wants membership to. But there's no one else who would understand you more. Perks of this shitty club. And three, we've already judged the hell outta each other. You've read my private shit without my permission, and I was an asshole to you. Unless we pull out a shovel and start digging, our opinions of each other ain't getting much lower. So that pretty much makes me the perfect person to talk to. Ain't shit you say gonna shock or disgust me."

She tips her head back, her pretty face balled up.

"I really hate that you make sense," she growls, and if she guessed how cute as opposed to threatening she sounds, she'd stop that.

Sighing, she thrusts a hand in that thick-as-fuck hair, and an image of my fingers fisting those reddish-brown curls flickers in my head before I can block it out. I clench my teeth, battling back the acidic burn of guilt. And lust.

"I always do." The words come out sounding like they ran barefoot over a gravel road.

She squints up at me, then shrugs a shoulder. But that troubled expression creeps back over her face.

"How did you know it was time to"—she pauses, licks her lips, and I'm inordinately fascinated by the sneak peek of that pink tongue—"be with someone? That you could be with them . . . like that?"

She's having a hard time saying *sex*, and I'd find it amusing if worry and guilt didn't reflect so clearly in her eyes.

"The first time I fucked after she . . ." My jaw clenches again, and just seconds ago I found her inability to utter *sex* funny. But here I am, still unable to say *died*. Goddamn hypocrite. "It was a year and some months later. And afterward? I threw up like the fucking *Exorcist*. Couldn't even wait until I got home. I did it right there in the hotel parking lot. Being physically ready is different from being mentally, emotionally ready. I got off, but the guilt? It ate me alive, and it was like I cheated on her."

"Is it still like that?" she whispers.

"Adina." I sigh and rub a hand over the nape of my neck, staring over her head for several seconds before lowering my gaze to hers again. "For me, sex is just that—sex. Fucking. No emotions, no promises, sometimes no names. It's a need that I take care of when my fist is no longer doing the job. And even then, because I know what it's like to have just the opposite of that—making love with a person who means more to you than yourself—it's empty." I shake my head and a reluctant half smile curls a corner of my mouth. "I guess what I'm trying to say is there's no timeline. There's no 'right time.' There's no shame in needing to satisfy a biological, physical need. Or even an emotional one. I'm not one of those people who believe women have to be emotionally connected to a man to have sex. That's bullshit. But if you just want to lie next to someone again, feel them move inside you again, make you come again . . . then that's your right. That's your privilege."

Despite the evening shadows, I glimpse her eyes darkening. Catch her throat moving up and down on a swallow. Her arms wrap around her chest, and her lips part as if she's about to say something to me but then, at the last moment, changes her mind.

I shift closer—I don't know why, but I want to know what thought she shut down.

"Why, Adina? Have you been thinking about going there? Letting someone touch you?" Sinking my teeth into my bottom lip, I drag my gaze over her, lingering on the swell of her hips, the sexy thickness of her thighs.

Goddamn, baby girl is bad as fuck.

Inhaling, I trample down the heat sliding through my veins like the fires she's paid to put out. I've felt lust, need, in the last two years. But this . . . yeah, it's stronger, hotter. Different.

And I want no part of it.

And yet I don't tell her to forget about my questions. Don't tell her to forget about answering. Because no matter how much my mind scurries away from the truth, I want to hear it.

"Adina," I press, voice low.

She sucks in a deep breath, her eyes briefly closing. I brace myself for her response. But nothing, absolutely nothing, could've prepared me for her soft "Kiss me."

My head jerks back as if those two words are physical blows to the jaw.

"What?" I rasp.

Her eyes widen as if she can't believe she uttered the request. That makes two of us. Because . . . what?

She licks her full lips again and drops her head. But a second later, she lifts it again and looks at me unflinchingly.

"Kiss me. Please."

Her voice is soft, but it doesn't waver. There's no uncertainty, no doubt. Only the determination that's reflected in her dark eyes.

"Adina . . ." I shake my head, my fingers curling and straightening by my sides.

My palms itch, as if her soft-looking skin is already under them. And I swear my mouth is watering, anticipating the taste of her.

But there's no way in hell I'm kissing her. I didn't even kiss the women I've been with since Kendra. That's . . . no. I shake my head again.

Adina shifts closer to me, her hands raised as if she's about to set them on my chest. She glances down at them and crosses her arms.

"I haven't been intimate with anyone since my fiancé died. Not just sex. But nothing. No touching. No kissing. Not even held the hand of a man outside my family." Her arms fall to her sides, then almost immediately lift to resume her previous position. Then she shifts her weight from one hip to the other. "How will I know if I don't try? Can I be honest?"

I jerk my chin down in an abrupt nod.

Thrusting her hand in her curls, she sighs. "I love sex. Of course the physical act itself, but also the closeness. From the pleasure and the connection to the weight of a man on top of me. I loved the quiet moments afterward, where the sweat is drying and our hearts are calming as we're tangled up in each other. For three and a half years, I had that with Keshaun. I miss it. All of it. I know I won't have the emotional connection we shared, with another person. But everything else? I at least want to try and see if I'm ready for it or if I need to give myself more time."

"And you think I'm the person you need to experiment with?" I ask, arching an eyebrow, not attempting to hide my skepticism.

She shrugs, loosening her arms to hold her palms up. "More honesty? I don't have anyone else. Unless it's family or the people I work with, I don't have anyone else. Aside from the men my mom tried to set me up with—and God knows they don't count—you're the first man I've spent this much time with outside that circle. And you . . . *know*. So who better? There's no expectation. No feelings. No confusion. And what did you tell me earlier? I won't see you again after tonight. That kind of makes you perfect. It makes you . . . safe."

It makes you safe.

The pounding in my dick feels anything but *safe*. But it's that argument more than anything else she said that has me moving closer to her. That argument and the quiet desperation in her eyes that the light from the streetlamp clearly reveals.

And my own curiosity. My own need that already had me hating myself. But not enough to stop my hand from lifting and cupping the back of her neck. Her brown-and-auburn curls brush my skin, and those strands might as well have grazed my dick. That's how painfully good it felt.

Drawing her closer, I give her time to change her mind. When she doesn't, I slowly lower my head and press my lips to hers. Goddamn, they're so fucking soft. Closing my eyes, I brush my mouth over the corner of hers. Then move to the other side and repeat the caress. Her soft gasp bathes my lips, and I press another kiss to the center of her mouth, taking that sound for my own.

Her hands grip my sweater, balling the sides up in her fists. The hem of my sweater must've lifted because her fingertips glance against my bare waist. And that smallest of touches of skin against skin has me bricking up harder than ever.

I part my lips, introduce my tongue to her. And, tilting her head, she greets me. Hesitant, careful at first, I learn her mouth. And she educates herself on mine. With each lick, suck, and twist of our tongues, the kiss becomes hotter, wilder . . . nastier. Soon, I'm swallowing her moans, and she's drinking down my grunts like the beer she just took to the head. My other hand raises to the front of her throat, circling it as I dive deeper, demanding she give me more. I'm fucking that wide dick-tease of a mouth and demanding she take all of it.

A whistle and catcall of "Fuck her!" infiltrates the red haze of lust enshrouding my mind. Reality crashes over me in an icy deluge, and I snatch my hands down and off her, ignoring the tingling in my palms. The feel of her soft skin is branded into them, and though I scrub them down the sides of my thighs, I can't rid myself of it. Guilt streams in as if it were just waiting in the wings to remind me that I ain't shit.

I scrub my hand down my face, swiping the back of my hand over my mouth as if that could remove her taste from my tongue. But it's a fucking waste of time. Her rich, smoky flavor, like the rarest bourbon and the richest cream, will follow me into my dreams tonight. I just know it.

And that knowledge has guilt digging its claws deeper, towing shame along for shits and giggles.

"Really?" she whispers.

My gaze snaps back to hers, noticing her staring at the hand I have yet to drop—the hand I just swept across my mouth.

Fuck.

"Adina." I reach for her wrist, but she yanks it behind her, shifting backward several steps. "I didn't—"

"You didn't what?" Her kiss-swollen lips curl up in a hard yet brittle-looking smile. "Let me fill in the rest. You didn't mean for it to go that far. Didn't mean for your dick to get hard?" She deliberately drops her regard, and I don't need to glance down to verify that my cock is doing the fucking most under my jeans. "Didn't mean to like it?"

That smirk evaporates from her mouth as she lifts her eyes back to mine.

"And here I was, starting to believe that maybe you weren't the asshole I met in the conference room. That you weren't mean. But I was wrong. You're not mean—you're cruel." She closes her eyes, but a second later her thick lashes rise. And the hurt there . . . my chest hollows out. "And to think I felt safe with you. Looks like I was wrong twice in one night."

She spins on her boot heel and stalks the short distance to her car. I don't say shit as she unlocks it, climbs inside, and drives off. Even when the sound of her engine has long faded, I continue to stand there on the sidewalk.

And to think I felt safe with you.

Her words ricocheted inside my head, echoing in my chest.

Adina was right; I didn't mean for it to go that far. The kiss was her experiment, not mine. Yet I'd been caught up, tangled in her flavor; the slide of her soft, lush lips against mine; the sounds that rumbled from her throat. I wasn't supposed to *enjoy* that kiss. But the fact I had seemed just as much a violation as giving in and tasting her. My hubris had been in thinking I could have that mouth and control it. Control *me*.

"Shit." Tunneling my fingers through my hair, I clench my jaw.

After another long moment, I lower my arm and force my feet forward, stepping off the curb and rounding the rear of my car.

I'm the last person Adina should feel safe with.

Not when I'm a danger to myself.

Chapter Six

ADINA

I pull around to the back of the firehouse and park. After grabbing my bag out of the back seat, I climb out of the car, ready for my twenty-four-hour shift. As much as I appreciate the one-day-on, two-days-off schedule, I always look forward to coming in to work. But today, I'm *really* eager to get in here. It's been a couple of days since that kiss fiasco with Solomon, and I've spent all that time thinking and rethinking. About Solomon. About our conversation at the bar. About the kiss.

About the kiss.

Yes, it warrants repeating. Because I've done nothing but hit replay on how he dominated my mouth. For those few moments, it wasn't even mine anymore—it had his name stamped on it, and he claimed my mouth like he had the pawnshop ticket entitling him to it. What had started out as something I needed to test out, to prove, ended up being the biggest—and hottest—mistake I made in a long-ass time.

I don't even need to close my eyes or think hard to feel those soft, almost too-full lips pressed against mine, molding to mine. Or feel the tangle and slick glide of his tongue over and around mine. Feel that big calloused hand wrapped around my neck in a firm, slightly intimidating, and completely pussy-wetting grip.

But more, I don't need to try too hard to feel the burn of humiliation and shame that razed a path through me, leaving me in a pile of ashes in front of him. For real, I don't even know why I thought kissing Solomon Young was a good idea. Nothing about the man screamed *good idea*.

That's what I get for being impulsive.

For giving even the slightest amount of trust to the wrong person.

Never again.

Huffing out a breath, I enter the firehouse and head straight for the locker room to change. It's empty, and though that's a little unusual, especially at shift change, I'm grateful. For the last two days, I've felt like rejection and embarrassment are tattooed on my skin for all to see. And no amount of scrubbing can wash them away.

I'm so entrenched in my thoughts I don't notice the pictures and green and blue streamers until I'm damn near upon them. Jerking to a halt in front of my locker, I'm staring at the shit covering the front of it, seeing it, but . . . not. Because I don't understand what it all is . . . at first. Then . . .

Holy shit.

My eyes widen, pinching at the corners.

Are those . . . ? Is that . . . ?

Yes, and *yes*.

My groan echoes in the room, bouncing off the walls and the lockers. Printed-out pictures of me and Solomon standing close together on the sidewalk outside the bar. Pictures of us kissing.

Oh my God.

I squeeze my eyes shut, but nope. When I open them, the pictures are still there. *We're* still there. And from the amount of pictures taped to my locker, it's safe to assume others have seen it. And by others, I mean everyone in this firehouse. I pinch the bridge of my nose. Son of a bitch.

"Well, there she is," Mark, an EMT on my shift, crows, appearing at the end of the bank of lockers. He leans a shoulder against it, a shit-eating grin stretched across his handsome face. "Our very own celebrity. And apparently, a big fan of hockey."

Scowling, I yank open my locker and—*fuck me*—glare at the big green, blue, and white jersey with Solomon's number on it. I only know this because it bears the same number on the signed jersey he gifted to me.

"Haha." I jerk the jersey down and toss it behind me to the bench. "How old are all of you?"

It seems like the rest of the house crowds in behind and beside Mark, all grinning like twelve-year-old assholes. Well, everyone except for Malcolm, whose frown is damn near as dark as mine.

"Since when did you become a puck bunny, Wright?" Matt Husband asks. Unlike the others, his voice holds a hint of an edge. No one else seems to notice, but I can't miss it.

Without turning around, I give him my middle finger, then pull off my jacket. He chuckles, and again, it's not nice.

"Okay, enough. Lay off her." Jared shoves through the group, pushing his way to the front of them. "You all have work to do, and if not, come see me. I can find some for you." Good-natured grumbles meet his order. "But Wright." He pauses, and in the next second, a big smile blooms over his face. "You think you can get me Solomon Young's autograph? Y'know, since you're so . . . close to him an' all."

"Et tu, Lieutenant?"

Jared smiles wider.

"Ay, unless all of you want more of a show than you bargained for, then I suggest you clear out so I can change," I warn.

That does the trick of getting them to leave, but not without some more teasing and laughter. When they're gone, I plop down on the bench instead of stripping and grab my uniform. Propping my elbows on my thighs, I drop my head into my hands. I suck in a deep breath, count to ten, then slowly exhale.

Nope.

That did nothing to calm my racing pulse or silence the chaotic whirl of thoughts in my head.

This isn't good. Not good at all.

Not only did I make a huge mistake two nights ago, but now the whole world gets to witness it. God, I hadn't seen anyone taking notice of us, much less taking pictures. But somehow I forgot Solomon Young is a big deal, especially in Providence. Why didn't I foresee the possibility of this happening?

Oh damn.

Has Dad seen this? Malik? Malcolm definitely has. I mentally wince. After that disastrous dinner, Solomon is now their archnemesis. And I'd been caught literally kissing the enemy.

Sighing, I grip the bottom of my shirt, then pause.

I don't need to turn around to know that I'm not alone. The hairs standing on the back of my neck clue me in that Matt is back in the locker room.

"You had me fooled, Adina." He laughs again, leaning a shoulder against the locker next to mine. I glance over at him, arching an eyebrow. He's not a bad-looking guy. It's his pushiness and inability to take no for an answer that makes him so not my type. "And here I thought you just weren't ready to start dating again after Keshaun. I guess I was wrong."

He's not. Or not really.

Hell, after that kiss, I don't know anymore.

I *do* know him bringing up Keshaun has my temperature rising.

Forcing a smile, I toss my bag in my locker, shut it, and face him.

"Like I told you before, Matt. I'm not really in the headspace to start seeing anyone. And getting involved with a firefighter in the same house is messy as hell."

I've said this before. Four times before, to be exact. But here I go again. Being a parrot.

"That picture says different."

"That picture was nothing."

"Didn't look like nothing."

I grit my teeth. Why the fuck am I up here explaining this to him like he's my father when Dad didn't grill me like this? Hell, Dad's probably more upset over Solomon insulting Brady than the kiss.

"Look, Matt. I don't want to start any problems or cause any issues between us or at work. So like I said before, I'd rather just keep it at friends or colleagues. No offense or hard feelings, okay?"

He runs his gaze up and down my body, and I force myself not to shudder at the disgusting and fucking inappropriate gesture. If he were anyone else, I'd tell him to fuck right on off. But he isn't just anyone. Not only is he a coworker, but he's a driver engineer, which means his rank is higher than mine.

And he's an entitled man.

Rejecting a man isn't simple anymore; it's a double-edged sword for a woman. You never know if they're going to just accept it and walk away or call you all kinds of *bitch*es and *ho*s for daring to turn them down. Shit, it's not even unheard of for a man to put his hands on a woman, or worse.

Fucking shame I have to deal with that in my own house.

I have to be nice in the face of his bad behavior so the workplace isn't toxic, when he's the goddamn toxicity.

Being a woman isn't for the weak of heart.

I inhale a breath and force a smile.

"See you out there."

I give him as wide a berth as the rows of lockers allow and move around him, striding for the door, feeling his eyes on me.

I just had a shower, but now I need another one.

Not for the first time, I consider walking down the hall to Cam's or Jared's office and reporting Matt. Or hunting down Dad and Malcolm and confiding in them. It would be so easy . . . and it wouldn't. Not because they wouldn't believe me. They would. Especially Dad, Jared, and Malcolm.

But just two days ago I'd been complaining to Solomon about their overprotectiveness and them injecting themselves into my private life. Losing Keshaun—and how I loss Keshaun—broke me, and my family were witnesses to it. And no matter that I'm a capable, skilled firefighter: they can't seem to erase the broken me from their minds, their memories. Dad constantly checking on me, Mom trying to fix me up, Malcolm's and Malik's damn-near-feral need to shield and defend me. Sometimes it's suffocating. And it fucks with my head. If they believe I'm emotionally fragile or don't believe I'm strong, then are they right? They know me best, so . . .

The thought of being seen as weak turns my stomach.

The possibility of *being* weak terrifies me.

And it's that, right there—the chance that they're correct to worry about my strength, and the possibility of *proving* them right—that has kept my mouth shut about the shit going on with Matt.

This is my problem, and I can handle it. I *need* to. For my own fucking sanity.

I lost the person who'd been my partner, my confidant, my rock, but I'm fully competent and powerful enough to deal with my own shit. I'm not the young, inexperienced firefighter fresh out of the academy with milk on her breath. And I'm not the daughter and sister whom they had to literally peel off the floor of her bedroom after Keshaun's death. They don't need another reason to worry about me, and I refuse to hand it to them. Maybe later I'll tell them, after this bump in the road passes. But until then . . .

I got this.

I have to.

My cell rings just as I pull the door open and step out into the hall. It's way too early in the morning for all this heavy shit. Cursing under my breath, I retrieve the phone from my front pocket. A glance down at the screen reveals Noni calling. Sighing, I hit the green answer button and lift it to my ear.

"Hey, Noni."

"*Hey, Noni,*" she mimics. "That's all you have to say to me?"

I sigh, tilting my head back and blinking up at the ceiling.

"I take it you've seen the picture of me and Solomon."

"Bitch, yes! It's all over Beyoncé's internet. What the hell, Adina? And I'm mad as hell that I had to find out you kissed *the* Solomon Young from TMZ rather than from you, my best friend. That breaks so many friend codes that I'm embarrassed for you."

"I didn't say anything because I was trying to forget about it," I mutter.

"Forget about it? Why?" She gasps, and if I wasn't so upset at well, *everything*, I would've rolled my eyes at her dramatics. "Don't tell me he drooled in your mouth? Did he almost choke you with his tongue? Please don't break my heart by telling me a man that fine can't kiss."

She sounds so distraught I huff out a chuckle. "No, Noni, your heart is safe. He can kiss."

"Oh thank God." She releases a loud sigh. "So why did you want to forget about it?"

I throw a glance toward the far end of the hall. Even though I'm alone, I still stand and walk toward the sleeping quarters, which are most likely empty this time of day.

"Because yes, the kiss was great, but not seconds after it ended, he regretted it." Hurrying, I give her the abridged version of what happened on that sidewalk.

The silence is deafening when I finish my wrap-up. I pull the phone away from my ear to make sure the call didn't drop, but no. The line is still open.

"Noni?"

"I don't care how beautiful that muthafucka is, he's gonna have to see me for hurting you," she snaps.

Despite the situation and my run-in with Matt, I laugh, the love for my friend and her unmitigated loyalty pumping warmth through me and temporarily nudging aside the mortification and anger.

That loyalty almost has me spilling the truth about Matt. But one, she's crazy. And she don't play about me. I'd arrive at work to find Matt hemmed up against the nearest engine. First, I don't need those kinds of problems, and neither does she, being a teacher an' all. Second, Noni has never held her tongue about her concern over my returning to work so soon. As much as I love my bestie, she can't fully grasp my love of firefighting. Keshaun did. Always. That's why, beyond being my lover, he'd been my other best friend. The one whom I rarely had to complete a full sentence with. Because he knew. He *knew*. Trying to replace that connection, even with Noni, feels . . . disloyal, somehow.

It doesn't make sense. Not even to me. But I also can't deny how I feel.

Without conscious thought, I brush my fingers over Keshaun's Saint Florian medal, wishing, not for the first time, I had him here to touch instead of his cold silver necklace.

"I'm serious," Noni insists, thankfully dragging me back from thoughts of Matt and Keshaun. But unfortunately, continuing on about *him*. "He, of all people, should understand the courage it took for you to do that, and he shits on it? Nope. Me and him? We got a problem. Has he even called or reached out about these pictures?"

I shake my head, even though she can't possibly see the gesture. "No. Shit, I just found out this morning because of the crap they put on my locker. And from the short amount of time I spent with him, Solomon doesn't strike me as the kind of person who trolls sites or googles his name. He probably doesn't know."

"Oh he knows," Noni dryly says. "I agree he doesn't seem like he gives a damn, but he most likely has PR people whose job is to be aware of everything that's being said about him so they can either capitalize on it or go into damage-control mode. Nah, he knows," she reiterates, then sucks her teeth. "Which makes it really fucked up that he hasn't even called to check on you and see if you're good."

I step into the dorm-style room and close my eyes, telling myself I'm not bothered by Solomon's silence. As a matter of fact, it falls in with the behavior he's shown me. Still . . . I'm having a hard time convincing myself that I don't care. Hell, if I'd been kissing Kyle on that sidewalk, no one would've given a damn, much less snuck pictures of us. It's because of who and what he is that this is news and worthy of being plastered across tabloid sites. So, really, this is his fault.

Hell, right now with how I'm feeling, *everything* is his fault. From Eve biting that apple to global warming.

Asshole.

"Well, it is what it is." I shrug. "I'm sure this will blow over pretty quickly. I mean, it was a kiss, not full-on public fucking. Besides, yeah, he's an athlete, but it's not like he's Gronk." Damn, how I miss Gronkowski. The Patriots could really use him now. But anyhoo . . . "I give this a day before people are on to the next story."

"Okay, babe," Noni says, but I can't miss the skepticism practically dripping from her voice. "If you say so."

"I do. Watch. You'll see. Everyone will forget about this."

◆ ◆ ◆

Oh my God. Why haven't people forgotten about this?

I frown at the man hovering across the street from the firehouse. The camera hanging around his neck announces his identity. I clench my jaw until my temple throbs. I'm so sick of this shit. It was bad enough that two or three of them showed up on calls all yesterday, shouting questions at me and snapping pictures while I worked. They were a distraction and pains in the ass, not just to me but to my team. And though it isn't my fault, I still feel responsible. If not for those pictures . . .

"Shit," I growl, pushing out the door and stepping onto the back lot.

It's the end of my shift, and all I want is to get home, eat breakfast, shower, and get into bed. In that order. But I have to deal with a nosy-ass cameraman first. And after their rude and relentless intrusion over the past twenty-four hours, I'm so not in the fucking mood.

"Hold up, Dina." Malcolm appears at my side, cupping my elbow. I glance at my brother, and his gaze is narrowed on the reporter. "Fucking vultures," he mutters, guiding me forward even as he shifts his big body so he's partially shielding me from the camera that is already raised and fixed on us. "I can't believe that's a job that someone actually wants."

"I'm sorry, Malcolm." I sigh. One of my biggest pet peeves is when women apologize for others' shitty behavior, carrying and accepting blame that's not theirs. And here I am, doing just that. Another reason to hope Solomon gets a puck to the face. "I really thought this would be old news by now."

"What're you apologizing for? Are you the one over there violating someone's privacy and being a whole-ass nuisance? No. So cut that out."

"I know, but—"

"No *buts*." He marches forward but tosses a look at me over his shoulder. "This isn't on you. But we are gonna have a talk about you kissing that muthafucka. Bet on that. The fuck, Dina. After everything he said at dinner? You should be beating his ass, not tonguing it down."

"Malcolm, really?" Yeah, I'm not having that conversation. Ever.

"Yes, *really*. That's the—ay, get the fuck away from her car and outta my way." Malcolm abruptly stops in his tracks, and I almost bump into him.

Peeking around Malcolm's wide shoulders, I spy a huge white guy dressed in a black shirt and jeans. His dark hair is cut close to his head, and the short style emphasizes the strong, almost brutal lines of his face. Sunglasses shield his eyes, but I'd bet the stack of pancakes I'm about to destroy when I get home that his gaze is as sharp as the angle of his jaw.

"Ms. Wright," the wall says, tone low, even. And intimidating.

"Who wants to know?" Malcolm barks, his body damn near bristling with anger.

This guy outweighs him by at least fifty pounds and has no less than four inches over him, but my big brother doesn't dial back the attitude. The human wall doesn't react to Malcolm's hostility, though. His expression remains the same, and he remains standing by my trunk.

"I'm Graham. Mr. Young sent me to follow you home and make sure no one bothers you once you're there."

"A bodyguard?" Malcolm says before I can reply. He scoffs. "Yeah, okay. One, how do we even know you're who you say you are? And two, if anyone's going to protect my sister, it's going to be family. We don't need *Mr. Young* to do shit." He might as well have said we don't need Stalin to do shit. That's how much disgust he wrapped around Solomon's name.

Again, Graham doesn't directly respond to Malcolm but, instead, reaches into his back pocket and removes a phone. He taps the screen, then holds the cell up to his ear.

"Yeah, I'm here with her." Pause. "Uh-huh, yeah, got it." Graham's attention shifts back to me, and he moves forward, arm and cell outstretched. But Malcolm cuts him off from approaching me.

"Nah, bruh. Back up."

Graham doesn't lower his arm or the phone, but his hard jaw flexes, and though his poker face would fleece a lot of people out of their money, Malcolm's obviously working his nerves.

"It's okay, Malcolm." I fully step around my brother. He shifts again, trying to stay in front of me, and I pat his arm. "It's good. I'm good."

He mutters something under his breath, but I still move forward and accept the phone. God, I'm about to choke on all this testosterone.

"Hello?" I say.

"Adina." Solomon's deep, midnight voice rumbles in my ear. And I hate myself for the shiver that trips down my spine and echoes in my sex. Why can't he have a voice like Michael Jackson's? If all were fair, he'd sound like his balls were permanently stuck in his stomach. "Graham's legit. He's a part of my security. You can trust him."

"I don't trust *you*, so I don't know how you figure I can trust him." I flick a glance at Graham. "No offense."

He shrugs a massive shoulder.

"I get that, and I own it. But now isn't the time to be stubborn, ma."

I grind my teeth at the endearment. The *Don't call me that* dances on my tongue like an entire step team. But I swallow it down. Snapping that might reveal too much. If he doesn't affect me, then nothing he does should bother me.

Should.

"I found out about those fucking pictures yesterday. I'm used to this kind of thing, but you're not, and I'm sorry that you got caught up. I also know how aggressive and intrusive these trash-ass reporters can be. So please, let Graham do his job. I'm out of town on a stretch of away games and won't be back until next week or else I would be there myself."

"And make all of this bullshit worse?" I scoff. "No thank you."

"Adina."

He doesn't say anything else, and after several seconds, I blow out a hard, much-aggrieved breath.

"Fine." And there's nothing gracious about my tone. "But if you're waiting on a thank-you, I hope you're holding your breath."

Do I sound like an ungrateful brat? Possibly. Do I care? Not. At. All.

I jerk the phone away and hand it back to Graham, but Solomon's low chuckle still tickles my ear. Fuck him for even *that* being sexy as hell.

"Here." Graham silently takes his phone back, and I sweep a hand over my hair, my fingers bumping up against the bun at the back of my head. "I'm not leaving my car or riding in that . . . tank." I jerk my chin toward the humongous gleaming black Range Rover. "You'll have to follow me."

"That's good. Ready when you are."

"Dina, you don't need this guy. I'll follow you home and stay there just in case any more like him"—his lips curl into a sneer as he shoots the jerk still snapping shots an evil glare—"are hanging around."

"Thanks, Malcolm, but you don't have to do that."

"You're my sister. I don't—"

"No, you're as tired as I am." I squeeze his arm. "Besides, if you're there with me, you're going to dirty my kitchen up, not clean the bathroom after you shower, and take over my living room." He just snorts, but his mouth twitches in a reluctant smile. 'Cause he knows I'm not wrong. "I'm not going to take a check out of Graham's mouth either. It's not his fault his boss is an ass-a-hole." Graham arches an eyebrow, and I answer his unspoken question. "He's so much of an asshole he deserves an extra syllable."

This time it's Graham's mouth that quirks the barest amount.

"All right, sis." Malcolm pulls me into his side and slides an arm around my shoulders, squeezing me close. "Call me when you get home. Let me know you got there safe. I'll come by if you need me."

"I will, and I know." Wrapping my arm around his waist, I return his hug.

He remains in the same spot as I walk to my car, unlocking it with the key fob. I don't wait to see if Graham is behind me or not. If he's in Solomon's employ, I'm sure he's resourceful. Resourceful and possessing the patience and long-suffering of Job.

I start my car and pull away from the curb, beeping my horn at Malcolm. He holds up a hand, and I pull off. The entire way home, I keep peeping in my rearview mirror to see if Graham's still tailing me. And when I arrive home, I'm suddenly thankful for Graham's presence. As soon as I park, about four people rush to the sidewalk, blocking the path that leads to my house.

I don't scare or panic easily, but my heart soars to the back of my throat, lodging itself there. I can barely breathe, my pulse racing in time with the rapid camera clicks and flashes. My fingers tighten on the wheel, and for a moment, I can't move, the walls of my car steadily crowding closer and closer to me. I want to push out of the car and run. But I also want to huddle there on the seat, try to curl into a ball and disappear . . .

A firm, quick rap on my driver's-side window has my head jerking to the side. A wave of relief surges through me so powerful that if I wasn't already sitting, I'd sink to the floorboard. Graham stares down at me and points a finger down. Fumbling, I jam the unlock button a couple of times, and Graham opens the door, granting me just enough space to slide out so his big body remains between me and the press on the other side of the car. He settles a hand on the middle of my back, gently but firmly guiding me forward. A guy rushes around the hood of my car, and Graham outstretches a hand. The cameraman wisely pulls up short, or else he would've had a palm to the face. And that's a big-ass palm.

"Keep your head down and keep moving," Graham murmurs. "Have your house key ready. I'll come back for your bag later."

I follow his directions, bowing my head and striding forward, ignoring the questions thrown at me as well as the demands to look up for a picture. White noise buzzes in my ears like a live wire, and it's pure muscle memory that has my feet moving forward. In seconds that feel like hours, we climb the front steps, and with trembling fingers, I shove the key into the lock. Or try to. I manage it on the second try, and another surge of relief crashes through me when the door opens and I step inside my house.

"Wait right here," Graham orders, and I pause inside my postage-stamp-size foyer as he roams through my living and dining room, the kitchen, and the small office. He then ventures upstairs and, minutes later, descends the stairs, giving me a nod.

"It's all clear."

"Is all that necessary?" I ask, a little unnerved by his reconnaissance.

"Yes." He pulls his phone from his back pocket and tips his head toward the living room. "You're free to move around. I pulled the curtains in all the rooms, but just to be on the safe side, try and stay away from them, if you can. The lenses cameramen have today are ridiculous."

Pulled curtains? Stay away from the windows? Holy shit. What has my life turned into?

Graham doesn't wait for my answer but turns around, heading back toward my front door and peeking out the small window cresting the top.

Palming my forehead, I walk into the living room, glancing at the long light-blue curtains. I make my way to the couch and sink down on it, still staring as if I can see through the glass panes.

"Ms. Wright?"

I lift my head at the sound of Graham's voice to find him standing in front of me, his phone outstretched toward me.

"Yes?"

"Mr. Young would like to speak to you."

My eyes narrow on that cell as if it's hairy and has eight legs. I want no part of it. But Graham's arm isn't lowering, and that steady gaze silently informs me he's not moving until I accept the phone. Sighing, I take it.

"What?" I say, none too friendly.

"Graham's going to stay with you until the reporters go away. He'll sit outside your house and make sure they don't try to get any closer than across the street. I know you don't like it," he adds before I can voice my objection. Because I was about to voice it. "But just let him do it." A pause. "Please."

For the second time this morning, I mutter, "Fine."

"Good." Then, "Adina, I'm sorry."

I blink. Pull the cell away from my ear. Stare at it. Then put it back again. "Say what now?"

He snorts. "You going to make me repeat it, huh?" His low chuckle is a sensory caress that has heat curling low in my belly. "I'm sorry, Adina," he repeats, tone stripped of humor. "This is on me. I should've been more careful. I know better, and I wasn't thinking. I'm . . ." I can just picture that hard jaw flexing. "This is my bad, and I didn't mean to put you in this predicament."

Just earlier I was heaping all the blame on his massive shoulders and big-ass head. But now . . . it must be the shock from hearing him apologize, because I'm thrown. Thrown enough to grant him mercy.

"Yeah, well . . ." I clear my throat. "At least my Gram numbers have skyrocketed."

True. In the last few hours, I've gained tens of thousands of followers on IG. It's crazy how disappointed they're about to be with my content.

He gives another of those dry laughs.

"Well, at least there's a bright side. Are you good, ma? I can imagine how fucked up this can be for someone who's not used to it."

"The fucked-up part is that you *are* used to it," I blurt out. I'm tired. That's the only explanation for why I'm continuing this conversation with him when I can jump off right now. "How are you doing? I'm sure it's not exactly fun being caught kissing another woman when . . ." *When you're still obviously in love with your wife and the world knows it.* "When it's not as deep as they're making it seem," I quietly say aloud.

"People are going to believe what they want, no matter what I say or don't say."

"Right." I should leave it. Again, end this call, let this go. But instead, I ask, "Is your son okay? Khalil, isn't it? Seeing you with another woman that isn't his . . . mother," I finish on a murmur.

A long, heavy beat of silence throbs over our connection. And for a moment, I don't think he's going to reply. And heat scorches up from my chest, passes my throat, and pours into my face. Even though he can't see me, I duck my head, the embarrassment damn near a physical weight.

"Never m—"

"Yeah, Khalil. And he hasn't seen anything, that I know of. My in-laws have kept him away from social media."

My in-laws. Not *my son's grandparents.* Not *Kendra's parents.* But *my in-laws.* I don't know if it's a conscious choice of words, but I catch what isn't said. He very much considers himself still married and a taken man. And they aren't just his son's grandparents but his *wife's* parents.

The message is received loud and clear.

Suddenly, the urgent need to get off this phone is like a fire alarm clanging in my head, reverberating in my pulse, my veins. It's damn near a primal warning.

"That's good." I stand, restless. "Listen, I'm about to give Graham back this phone. I just got off work, and I'm tired. Thanks for looking out for me when you didn't need to."

Not granting him a chance to respond, I thrust the phone back at Graham and stride past him, out of the living room, toward the stairs. Am I running away? Quite possibly. But not from Solomon—from myself and my obvious penchant for rejection. Solomon Young is no good for me. And more importantly, he doesn't want to be. He might call himself riding to my rescue by sending Graham, but there's a big difference between caring and responsibility, duty.

I'm clearly the latter.

The sooner I accept that there's nothing between us but regret and bad choices, the better off I'll be.

Chapter Seven

SOLOMON

"I got it." I tap the back of the front seat, forestalling Graham from climbing out of the Range Rover to open my door.

I've been a professional athlete for twelve years—starting with the Edmonton Oilers at eighteen—but in a lot of ways, I'm still that boy growing up in North Preston, Nova Scotia, with a loving but hardworking single mother. She provided everything I needed—a safe home in a protective and close-knit community, clothes on my back, food in my belly, and an education. And though her paycheck didn't stretch for the extras, she found a way to make sure I stayed in the sport I loved.

Still, we didn't know anything about luxury cars, drivers, or security. And though I've been able to afford all three—and more—for the last several years now, a part of me will never be used to all this extra shit.

And having another person open a door for me when I have working hands and limbs seems pretentious as fuck.

If not for being so damn tired after a run of away games lasting more than a week, I would've driven myself. But Graham met me at the airport, and I was grateful as hell. Both me and my tired, bruised body. Now, though, pushing open the rear door and stepping out of the vehicle, that weariness and pain ebbs, swamped by the excitement and love rising inside me and swirling between my ribs.

A smile lifts the corners of my mouth as I climb the front steps to the white palatial home that belongs to my in-laws. The quiet of the Blackstone neighborhood is broken only by the soft chirp of nocturnal insects and the resounding chime of the doorbell I push. Kendra had a key to her parents' home—her childhood home—that she'd use when we visited. Despite my in-laws' encouragement, I've never taken that liberty. This is their home, not mine. And though I'm close with them, I haven't been able to bring myself to use the key that remains in Kendra's jewelry box that I packed up and put into storage for Khalil one day.

Moments later, the wide front door with its pristine arched windows opens, and Nate Talley, Kendra's father and the owner of the Pirates, stands in the doorway. Tall and on the lean side, he exudes authority from his unwavering gray eyes to the straight, powerful set of his shoulders. In his early fifties, he's a handsome man. But it's his wife, Caroline, who blessed their only child and daughter, Kendra, with her lovely features.

I smile at Kendra's petite mother as she walks up behind Nate, and like always, an invisible hand fists my heart and squeezes, twists. From the smooth light-brown skin to the loose shoulder-length dark-brown curls framing delicate facial features and brown eyes a couple of shades lighter than her skin to the slender build, Caroline is like a future vision of Kendra. So much, at times, it's difficult to look at her for too long.

"Hey, Nate, Caroline." I move forward, stepping into a foyer that I can't call anything but *grand*.

A black-and-white marble floor stretches beneath my feet, and a gilded ceiling soars high above us. The elaborate crown molding lends the spacious area an air that dates back to another era. Which tracks, since Kendra once told me this house was built at the turn of the twentieth century. Before Nate owned a hockey team, his family had their hands in everything from textiles manufacturing to banking to real estate. Given their generational wealth, I hadn't been surprised when he'd insisted I sign a prenuptial agreement before I married Kendra. A twenty-three-year-old hockey player fresh to the States wanting to wed his daughter after only knowing her for four months? Shit, in my head it sounds sketchy as fuck. But it was love at first sight for us, and if I had to sign away any claims to her inheritance, I didn't give a damn. I only wanted her, not her shit.

Moving into the living room, I scan the massive stone fireplace, floor-to-ceiling windows, and richly upholstered furniture. The room seamlessly pours into a just-as-elegantly-appointed living room that I've spent many dinners and holidays seated at with my adopted family.

"Where's Khalil? Sleep?" I ask Nate and Caroline, who follow me into the room.

"Yeah, we put him to bed about an hour ago," Caroline says. With a shake of her head and soft smile, she adds, "That was after two and a half bedtime stories that he managed to con out of me."

"You say that every night, and yet you always give in," Nate chides, but his gentle tone and own smile rob the sting out of his words.

Their love for their only grandchild is as obvious as the sadness that lingers in both of their gazes. At least, obvious to me. Due to complications with Kendra's birth, Nate and Caroline couldn't have any more children, and they spoiled her. It's a wonder she didn't end up a rotten bitch. Kendra would laugh when I said that to her. It says a lot about the kind of people the Talleys are that they raised a wonderful, grounded daughter. And now, with her gone, they've transferred even more of that love and protective nature to her son.

Not that I can complain. There are eighty-two games in a hockey season, and half of those are away. Without them caring for Khalil when I'm on the road, I don't know what I would do. Mom still lives in North Preston, and though I could hire a nanny, knowing he's with family when I'm not here comforts me. Eases the guilt of somehow failing him as his only living parent. Fuck, sometimes I feel like such a poor substitute.

"It's"—I glance down at the royal blue face of my Rolex Datejust—"ten after nine. I hate to wake him up, but it's been nine days since I've seen him."

"Why don't you go up, peek in on him, and then take the guest room across from his? He's asleep, and it'd be a shame to wake him up, get him dressed, and make him leave. This way, we can all have breakfast in the morning before you go."

Even though there's nothing more I want than to sleep in my own house, in my own bed, with my boy in his bedroom, there's a faint plea in Caroline's voice that I can't ignore. And they watch him like he's their own; I can give her—them—this.

"Yeah, that's fine. Let me text Graham and let him know we're staying."

As I pull my phone from the inside pocket of my suit jacket, Nate claps me on the shoulder.

"Good. And after you're settled in, come on down to the kitchen. We had Lenny prepare a plate for you since we figured you might be hungry when you arrived. We can talk while you eat."

Irritation pricks at my skin. If they had their chef already fix a plate, then they'd already planned on me and Khalil staying the night without asking me. That's the shit that is getting on my nerves more and more. I'm Khalil's father, his parent. But at times, they overstep, make decisions for him, for us, without consulting me. It's ungrateful as shit to be annoyed, considering all they do for the both of us, but . . . I swallow down the aggravation. But nothing. They're right about taking Khalil out after he was already down for the night, and I can't be mad at their thoughtfulness in feeding me.

I sound like a real bitch right now.

"Sounds good. Be right back."

As I stride out of the room, I head toward the stairs, then climb them two at a time. After turning right, I approach the closed door of the second bedroom on the right. I carefully ease open the door and quietly move inside, my breath catching in my chest at the sight of my son sprawled like a starfish on his custom-made *Black Panther* bed. His *Avengers* blanket covers one side of his small sturdy body while a thin arm and leg stick out from under it. Tight curls that are a blend of his mother's dark brown and my lighter shade crown his head, and his walnut-colored skin gleams in the muted glow of his night-light. Thick lashes hide eyes that he inherited from me and my father.

God, I love this little boy.

I clench my jaw, battling back the sting of tears. It's moments like these when I feel Kendra's absence the sharpest. When Khalil was first born until he was several months old, Kendra would sneak into his room at night and put a finger under his nose, checking to make sure he still breathed. I used to tease her about that until . . . until after she was gone, and I found myself doing the same thing.

Sighing, I near his bed, kneel down, and pull the cover completely over him, tucking all his limbs back in. He stirs but doesn't fully wake; once Khalil is out, he's out, and only a natural disaster could wake him. Maybe.

Placing a kiss on his forehead, I breathe in his scent of the lavender soap Caroline uses on him as well as the shea butter she rubs into his skin every night. A few moments later, I rise, sliding his Black Panther doll next to him. When I return downstairs, my duffel bag is waiting in the foyer, where Graham must've deposited it. My stomach grumbles at that moment, making the decision for me about whether to take the luggage up to the guest room now or head to the kitchen.

Head to the kitchen it is.

Like the rest of the house, the Talleys' kitchen is a work of art. Beautiful granite counters, top-of-the-line appliances, mahogany floors, big bay windows, a marble island, and a breakfast nook with a table large enough to seat a family of eight. Out the windows stretches a huge yard, complete with a stone patio, built-in firepit, a grill, and furniture. A pool, covered for the season, sits behind the entertainment area. Professionally landscaped trees and shrubbery provide privacy.

"Here you go, Solomon." Caroline sets a plate piled with baked chicken, green beans, and cabbage on the table. The delicious aroma has my stomach growling louder, and I beat it to take a seat. "Let me get you something to drink. Water? Wine? A beer?"

"Water is fine, thank you." I smile at her, picking up my fork. Not wasting time, I dig in. And moan around the first mouthful of food. Lenny can cook his ass off, even with something as simple as baked chicken and vegetables. I ate before we left Vegas to come home, but that was hours ago. "Please thank Lenny for me. He put his foot in this." I point my fork toward my plate before shoveling more cabbage in my mouth.

"I will, honey," she says, setting a glass of cold water in front of my plate, then rounding the table and sinking into a chair across from me.

Nate takes the seat next to her, and they sip coffee as I eat.

"Solomon, I wanted to wait until you got home to speak with you about that article and picture going around on the gossip sites and social media," Nate says, his gaze trained on me over the rim of his cup.

He sips from it and lowers the mug to the table, I guess waiting on me to say something, but I ain't got shit for him. That flare of irritation flickers again, hotter this time. I'm not this kid that he can call on the carpet. Team owner or not. Son-in-law or not.

"We just don't want people to get the wrong impression, honey," Caroline chimes in, leaning across the table and laying a hand over mine. "It's not just you we're worried about; it's Khalil, the team. Rumors have a nasty way of turning and becoming true in people's eyes. And we don't want to see anyone get hurt by something that's a nonissue."

"I don't see how anyone could get hurt by a picture." I continue eating, that irritation growing wings, blowing into embers of anger.

Doesn't matter that I'd already decided that kiss was a mistake and wouldn't be repeated. Doesn't matter that there isn't anything between me and Adina. They don't know any of that. But still, it has me hot that they'd relegate her to something as demeaning, as inconsequential as a "nonissue."

"We kept Khalil from seeing anything online, but he has friends in kindergarten who mentioned his daddy having a girlfriend. Probably something they heard from their parents. We can't protect him from everything, as hard as we try," Caroline says. "He asked us about it, and we explained as best as we could about how people can make up things, but I don't know if he fully grasps what we meant. So he may come to you as well, and you'll need to make it clear that there's nothing there and he doesn't need to be worried."

"He's worried?" I frown.

"He wondered if he was going to have a new mommy," Nate says, voice flat.

I stare at the half-eaten food on my plate, not really seeing it.

If he was going to have a new mommy.

My appetite fucked, I lift my head and meet Nate's. There's censure there, a hint of condemnation among the grief that has never fully dissipated.

And it burns like hell. Right down to the center of me that still churns with guilt because I not only kissed a woman who isn't Kendra but that I remember her taste, the texture of her lips and tongue, the sound of her soft moan.

"That's ridiculous, but I'll talk to him and make it clear." As clear as I can to a five-year-old without involving him in adult situations.

"Make exactly what clear, Solomon?" Nate asks, leaning his folded arms on the table. "We'd like to understand as well. I'm assuming, if the reports are correct, that she is the firefighter that came to see you at the arena. I thought her speaking to you was a onetime thing. When did it turn into something more? *Is it* something more?"

The *Ay, mind the business that pays you* sits on my tongue, but I bite it back, locking it behind clenched teeth. Nate's coming at me not as my employer but Kendra's father. And both are rubbing me the wrong way. Respect keeps those words tethered. Respect and who he's been to me and my son.

Because if it were anyone else, they would get the other side of me.

"It won't be repeated." I don't elaborate, and after a moment, Nate dips his chin.

"Good. Aside from Khalil's well-being, the season's just started and we can't afford any distractions. Not for you or the team."

We both know this is less about the Pirates or their season and more about me possibly bringing another woman in to my and Khalil's lives. That they want to preserve Kendra's place in Khalil's life. In mine. As if I don't. As if anyone could ever come in and replace her.

Yet none of that keeps me from getting hot. And not just on my behalf but Adina's. Yeah, I need to get to bed, because I'm not making any damn sense. I must be more tired than I thought because there's no other explanation that has me wanting to jump bad on my father-in-law over a woman I have zero plans on seeing again.

Even when Adina Wright isn't in front of me—or has her tongue in my mouth—she's a shitload of trouble.

Trouble I didn't ask for or want.

◆ ◆ ◆

"Daddy!"

The guest bedroom door flies open, and Khalil races in, his little face lit with a huge grin. I sit up in time to catch him as he launches himself onto the bed and into my open arms. It's been over a week since I've held my son, looked into his face without the use of FaceTime. At times, I worry that being away from him so much during the season will affect our relationship, have him feeling abandoned by me.

But then, I'm on the receiving end of this smile and the obvious love shining from his green eyes, and that gnawing concern lets up on me. For now. Unfortunately, worry and I are partners shackled at the ankles with only brief reprieves. Shit, since Kendra, it's like we have a muthafucking life sentence together.

"Hey, li'l man." I close my arms around Khalil, hugging him close. He obviously came to find me immediately after he woke up, because drool still crusts the corner of his mouth and smears halfway across the cheek I smack a kiss on.

"Daddy," he whines, swiping his palm across his skin. "I'm a big boy. I don't need kisses."

"Oh really?" I arch an eyebrow.

"Yeah." He balls up his face.

"Okay, then."

Without warning, I sweep his little body up and drop him on the bed, my fingers digging into his ribs. His wild, raucous laughter fills the room, and he curls his knees toward his chest, twisting and turning, trying to avoid my tickling. Grinning, I bend over him, peppering his face with more loud, smacking kisses.

Joy fills me, pressing against my rib cage, and the piercing intensity of it is almost painful. The sound of my son's happiness is a gift that carries no price tag, holds no sorrow. Every time I hear it, I'm so grateful. If I still prayed and didn't have problems with God, I'd thank Him for it.

"Stop, Daddy, stop!" he yells, giggling like mad.

I finally let up, and once I lean back against the headboard, he pounces on me. For the next several moments, we wrestle, him loosing growls like a baby cub. Rising from the bed with him scooped under my arm like a flailing sack of potatoes, I make my way to the en suite bathroom and deposit him on the counter.

"Get yo' funky mouth brushed. You almost killed me with that breath, man."

"Uh-uh!"

"Bet." Smirking, I grab two newly packaged toothbrushes Caroline faithfully keeps stocked in her guest rooms. After ripping them open, I squeeze a generous amount of toothpaste on Khalil's brush, run it under the water, then hand it to him. "Take care of that, bruh."

Mugging me, he takes it and goes to work. Snorting out a laugh, I follow behind him, and he mimics my actions. We spit, brush, spit, and rinse together. When I grab his toothbrush from him and slide it along with mine in the holder, he holds his arms out to me, curling his fingers.

"Daddy, c'mere," he orders. I bend down toward him, thinking he wants me to pick him up, and he huffs out a breath directly in my face. "See? I don't stink!"

"Okay, you got me." Chuckling and curling my hands under his arms, I lift him up, but he curls his legs around my waist and his arms around my neck, clinging to me and prohibiting me from lowering him to the floor. "Hey, how about you come to practice with me this morning, and then we can head over to the children's museum?"

The Providence Children's Museum is one of his favorite places to go, and we haven't been there in a while.

"Yes, yes!" he cheers, his arms tightening around me.

"All right, let's get a move on, then."

Moments like these remind me that he is still my baby boy, regardless of how much he protests my kisses. Smiling, I carry him back into the bedroom, and just as we clear the bathroom, the door opens, and Caroline pokes her upper body through the cracked space.

"Hey, I thought I heard voices in here." She grins and widens the opening, stepping inside the room. "Morning, Grammy's baby." She holds out her arms, and Khalil wiggles against me, and I lower him to the floor so he can run into his grandmother's embrace. She holds him close, her eyes closing as she buries her nose in his neck. I don't miss the whisper of pain that passes over her face, and it doesn't take a mentalist to figure out that she's thinking of Kendra. "How'd you sleep, baby?"

"Good, Grammy." He pulls away from her, smiling wide. "Guess what?" He doesn't allow her time to answer but announces, "Me and Daddy're going to the museum!"

"Is that right?" She glances up at me. "I thought you had practice this morning."

"I do. I'ma take Khalil with me. It's been a while since the guys have seen him. And he loves going to the arena." God, why does it feel like I'm explaining myself? Or asking for permission to spend time with my own son?

"But you're going to be busy, and he shouldn't be there alone. He could get into—"

"He's going with me, Caroline." I gently cut her off. "No need to worry. He'll be fine."

She looks like she still wants to argue with me, but then Khalil fists the bottom of Caroline's sweater and tugs.

"I'm hungry."

Snorting, I walk over to my duffel bag, drag back the zipper, and pull a T-shirt out. As I slip it on, I pad barefoot toward Caroline and Khalil.

She rises, switching her gaze from her grandson to me.

"Breakfast should be on the table in ten minutes."

I nod. "Sounds good. We'll be down as soon as I get dressed and Khalil into some clothes too."

"Oh, you go ahead and get ready. I can take care of him," she offers, already reaching for his hand.

"That's okay, I got him." I softly but firmly turn her down. Her smile falters, then fades. My heart constricts at her disappointed and hurt expression, but I don't take my objection back. It's been over a week since I've seen Khalil, and I've missed the little things—like getting him dressed in the morning. "We'll be down shortly."

She dips her chin in acknowledgment and leaves the room.

"Daddy, why is Grammy sad?"

I lock down the sigh sliding up my throat. God, if only that question had a simple answer. But grief . . . I shake my head. It's never simple. Not when it's mixed up with anger, regret, and guilt.

"Not sad, li'l man. She's just probably going to miss you spending the night with her and Grandad."

His face scrunches up. "But I'll be back. I won't leave like Mama."

Oh shit.

Pain howls through me like a starved, snappy wolf. It leaves behind claw marks, ripping my heart to bloody shreds. I swallow past a suddenly tight throat and blink back the burn in my eyes. And in the darkest, dingiest, most secret part of my soul, I yell and curse Kendra for leaving me to have this conversation with our son.

For leaving me.

Slowly, I hunker down in front of Khalil, meeting his green gaze on his level and cupping his shoulders.

"Son, of course you won't. Why would you say that?" I gently ask.

For a moment, fear whispers through his eyes, and God, if that doesn't tear me apart. No child should experience fear or uncertainty. Damn sure no child of mine. But he has. He's known loss, sadness, and fear. And it crushes me as his father.

Khalil shrugs. "I'on know."

"Khalil." I lightly squeeze his shoulders. "Yes, you do. Now, c'mon. Remember, we don't keep secrets. You can tell me anything. Why would you say you don't want to leave Grammy like your mama?"

He shrugs again, but then he whispers, "Mama left our house and went to heaven. I don't wanna go to heaven. I don't wanna leave Grammy and Grandad. They'll be sad if I go. You and me all they got."

Anger hums beneath my skin. An anger I try like hell to keep out of my voice.

"Khalil, listen to me, and listen closely, okay?" I wait for him to nod. "The only thing I want you to do is play video games, eat my famous macaroni cheeseburgers, and be the happy little boy you should be. That's it. Me, your grammy and grandad? What'll make us the happiest is if you do that, okay? You understand?"

He stares at me for a long moment, and his wide gaze roams over my face, as if searching. Then, he tilts his head a little to the side, a small frown crinkling his forehead.

"If I keep playing *Minecraft*, will you be happy?"

I swallow a chuckle but nod my head. "Absolutely. As long as me or someone else is there with you. That's our rule, right?" I arch an eyebrow.

"Yep." A grin spreads across his face, and the band squeezing the hell out of my chest slowly eases, and I drag in the first deep, cleansing breath since we started this conversation.

"Good." I kiss him on the cheek before rising and rubbing a hand over his soft curls. "Now, let's go get you dressed so we can go eat that good food your grammy has downstairs."

"Yeah!" Khalil races out the room, and chuckling at all that five-year-old energy, I follow behind him.

◆ ◆ ◆

Skating over to the bench, I swipe up my water bottle and pop the cap. Even though it's cold out here on the rink, I barely feel it. Sweat dots my forehead, and no doubt, when I strip out of this gear, it will be drenched—and smelling like armpit and balls. But for now, I don't smell anything but the bite of cold and the chemical scent from the ice. Inhaling the scents that are as familiar to me as my own, I glance toward the stands behind the boards. Khalil sits on the third row, his head bowed over his tablet, probably playing one of the many games downloaded there. Even from here, though, I can see his lips moving. I don't need to be near him to know that mouth goes a mile a minute, and he's no doubt talking Patrice's ear off.

As if feeling my gaze on them, Patrice lifts her head and smiles at me. When her expression warms and brightens even more, I don't need to glance around to know Ken is behind me. That look of complete adoration belongs only to her husband. A hole the size of a cigarette burn sizzles in the middle of my chest. They remind me of me and Kendra. She used to come sit in these same stands with Khalil during some of my practices, would even join me a few times on the road. Like we used to be, Ken and Patrice are joined at the hip.

"I really appreciate Patrice watching over Khalil. I owe her." I set my water bottle down, and Ken shakes his head as he lifts his own bottle to his mouth.

"No worries. She's more than happy to do it. Said it'll prepare her for when she has ours." A grin slowly spreads over his face, and the love and happiness glow as if a light beams from under his skin, out of his eyes.

"She's pregnant?" I ask, my eyes narrowing on his pretty wife, who's returned her attention back on Khalil.

"Yup. Eight weeks. We're not announcing anything until she's out of the first trimester, though."

A shadow briefly flickers over his face, temporarily dimming some of the light in his eyes. The miscarriage they suffered last year. Though he doesn't say it, I know that's what caused the brightness in his gaze to dampen.

"Well, your secret's safe with me," I assure him. "And congratulations, man. I'm happy for the both of you."

"Thanks, Sol."

"Kennedy, Young, any day now," Coach yells over to us. "You're welcome to join the rest of us."

Smirking, I drop my water bottle back on the bench and return to the center of the rink. As a left defenseman, Ken skates farther down to his position. With a narrow-eyed stare at me, Coach blows the whistle, and practice resumes. For the next hour, we go through team drills, followed by a cooldown period. Coach breaks us up, and we focus on some individual skill work that addresses mistakes from last night's game and today's practice.

Later, when I exit the locker room, Khalil and Patrice are waiting for me right outside. As much joy as hockey brings me, it dulls in comparison to this little boy with his wide grin, my green eyes, and his mother's face. My love for him is damn near painful.

"Look, Daddy!" He holds up a miniature-size hockey stick. "Aunt Patrice gave it to me. It's just like yours!"

"Wow, that's awesome." I mouth *Thank you* to Patrice, who nods at me in return. "What do you say to Aunt Patrice, li'l man?"

"I told her thank you," he tells me, and I should check him over that little attitude that's in his voice—and I would if I wasn't holding back a snort of laughter. "I'm a big boy."

"My bad. And yeah, you're right. Telling someone thank you when they do something nice for you is big-boy behavior." Shaking my head, I hold out a hand toward him, and he doesn't hesitate to slip his into mine. "Thanks again, Patrice. I truly appreciate it."

She waves me off. "Please, it's no problem. At all. I love hanging out with Khalil. He's my little partner." Ruffling his curls with one hand, she holds up her other hand. "See you later."

Khalil smacks her palm with his. "Bye! See you later, Aunt Patrice!"

Chuckling, I lead him down the hallway and out of the building.

"I'm gonna grow up and be you, Daddy! I'ma beat you in hockey!"

He goes on and on, swinging the stick until we reach the parking lot and I load him into his booster seat. Even as I climb into the front seat and drive off, he's still bragging about how he's going to be a hockey player when he's older and be better than me. I would wonder where he gets that cocky-ass attitude from but then I remember. Right. Me.

". . . said you had a girlfriend. I told him uh-uh. Mommy's in heaven. But he said his mommy saw you kiss your girlfriend. You have a girlfriend, Daddy?"

I jerk my attention from the road to the rearview mirror. Khalil plays with the tablet we keep in the car to occupy him, not even looking up at me as he asks the question that sends a fissure racing across my heart.

Clearing my throat, I take a moment to figure out what to say. I've never lied to my son, and I'm not about to start now. But how to explain that, no, the woman whom everyone and their mama—literally—saw me mouth-fuck wasn't my girlfriend? Even though he'd only ever seen me kiss his mother.

"No, li'l man, I don't have a girlfriend, not like how Mommy and Daddy are." *Were.* Shit. "Just a friend who's a girl." I silently cringe at that clichéd, lame-ass excuse.

"Oh. Y'mean like Candice tries to kiss me? I always run from her. I'on like her, though." Who the fuck is Candice? And why she trying to push up on my son? Also, I need to check her parents about their fast-ass daughter next time I go up to that school. "You like your girlfriend?"

"Friend, Khalil. She's a friend," I stress. But another glance in the mirror reveals he's still engrossed in the game he's playing on the tablet. "And sure, I like her." At least my dick does. "She's a firewoman too."

"No way." Now I get his attention. "For real, Daddy? A real fireman?"

"Yeah, for real. And fire*woman*." Or *person*. Shit, what is the correct term?

"Wow," he crows, his excitement obvious in the pitch of his voice. Any higher and we might have dogs start following us. "Cool! Can we go see her? Can we, Daddy?"

"Khalil—"

"Please? Please, Daddy?"

"Khalil, she's busy fighting fires. Maybe another time—"

"Can you call her?"

Shit.

I love that he's smart, but damn, it's inconvenient as hell at times. And right now is one of those times. I could just tell him no. Hell, I'm the parent, and putting my foot down is part of that job description. But denying him would be more about me than him. Especially since every time he sees a fire truck or hears a siren, his face is pressed to the window in excitement, watching it zoom past.

I sigh, glancing in the mirror once more, and this time catching my son's wide eyes and big grin in the reflection. Okay, so what's the harm in just dropping by the firehouse? If Adina isn't there, maybe I can introduce Khalil to her coworkers. Aside from that kiss, there isn't anything between us. I've made that abundantly clear, and she seems to agree. So there's no reason for me to be running scared and avoiding her. Inconvenient lust wasn't a good enough reason . . .

Shit. I've gotten really adept at lying to myself.

"Daddy, can you?" Khalil pleads.

"Yeah, li'l man. I'll call her and ask if we can come by."

Even as I stop at a red light and pull out my phone, I clench my jaw. This isn't going to end well.

Chapter Eight

ADINA

Goddamn, this isn't going to end well.

Pinching the bridge of my nose, I squeeze my eyes shut for a long moment, inhaling a deep breath and holding it for five seconds before releasing it just as slowly, like exhaling through a straw. Grounding exercises, my counselor called them. Followed by isolating the five senses. Focusing on the here and now so I don't dive into an emotional tailspin about the immediate future.

Nope, Solomon wasn't the only person who sought out help. But while he's still seeing his, I stopped after about two months of sessions.

Call it surrendering to toxic thinking, but the fear of someone discovering I couldn't handle Keshaun's death on my own rose above my own concerns of mental health. Women in my field already face enough prejudices and biases, and I couldn't voluntarily pin a target on my back that marked me as weak or not tough enough to handle the loss. Even Dad and my brothers . . . they would never admit aloud or probably even to themselves that they doubt my strength, but the way they're so careful around me speaks volumes.

So yeah, I quit therapy, but some of what I learned manage to stick.

And now, as I stand in the firehouse bay filled with engines, I pray that the slight calming of the chaos whirling inside my head stays that way. Calm. Quiet. Because if I glance down at the text I received just a couple of minutes ago, the disquiet, the doubt . . . the fucking excitement . . . might send me running.

I could've said no when Solomon called and asked if he could swing by with his son. Hell, I *should've* said no. It's not like we've had any communication since that first night Graham followed me home as a bodyguard. But hearing Solomon's deep, crushed-velvet timbre for the first time in nearly two weeks—and throw in the sweet sound of a child's voice—and I caved. With not even a respectable fight.

I fucking suck.

"Oooh, Daddy! A fire truck!" The high-pitched voice I'd heard over the phone jerks my attention to the driveway and the small boy and huge man walking toward me.

Heat fills me like a swollen flood, and though I try to dam it up, my ovaries aren't trying to hear it and throw themselves on the floor of the bay like the thirsty bitches they are.

It's been nearly two weeks since I last saw him, but the way my cheeks prickle even as my pussy clenches around aching emptiness, it might as well as have been two days. Two hours. Mortification mingles with lust as I stare at Solomon, taking in that beautiful face cloaked in a frown that I'm coming to think is his default position, and his tall, big body clothed in a navy cable-knit sweater, dark-blue jeans that hug his powerful, thick thighs, and brown Timbs.

My breath stutters in my lungs, lodging in my throat before softly wheezing out between my lips. Apparently, my mouth, nipples, and all other erogenous zones vividly remember that the last time I saw this man, our lips and tongues were wrestling for domination. And he was winning. And so was I. God, so was I.

Too bad my mind possesses an equally detailed account of his rejection, of the humiliation afterward. Of how I let down my carefully fortified defenses and allowed myself to be vulnerable, only for him to show me why trusting people is overrated.

As Solomon draws closer, I jerk my way-too-infatuated gaze from his hooded green eyes and drop my attention to the mini-me at his side. And no matter how I feel about the larger version of this boy, there's no way in hell I can contain the smile that slowly stretches my lips.

He's as beautiful as his father.

The tight curls that grace his head might be a mixture of his father's sandy brown and a darker shade, and his skin may be a couple of shades darker than Solomon's. But everything else? The bright-green eyes, the strong facial structure, and his sturdy little body . . . they're all his father. But it's that huge carefree smile that has my heart giving an Olympic-gold-worthy flip in my chest. God. In another decade or so, he's going to be hell on the female population.

Sliding my hands into the front pockets of my uniform pants, I smile, and when the little boy's eyes land on me, I fight back a laugh at how round they go. He looks like a life-size anime character, with those big eyes and bigger grin.

"Daddy!" he yells, tugging on Solomon's hand with both of his. "It's a fireman! See?"

Chuckling, I approach them, squatting down to his level when they reach the edge of the bay.

Holding out my hand, I can't ignore or deny the nerves that grip and have a good ol' drunken time in my belly. This is Solomon's son. *Kendra's* son. And though this will most likely be my first and last time meeting him, I want him to . . . like me.

God, I need to chill. Attempting to read too much into his and Solomon's presence here at my firehouse would be a mistake of monumental proportions. Like, Pac-hooking-up-with-Suge-Knight monumental proportions.

"See? That's where you're wrong. I'm no man."

Damn. I mentally wince. There I go again. Impossibly, the boy's grin seems to brighten even more, and I'm thankful he didn't catch that *Lord of the Rings* slip. Flicking a glance up at a silent Solomon, I catch his slight frown, and my stomach goes haywire again, my nerves joining in for shits and giggles.

Yeah, I'll be keeping my attention focused on the son, not the father. The child is safest, between the two of them.

"You're a firelady!" He slides his hand into mine and, tiny grip firm, shakes it back and forth. And he might as well have reached right into my chest, grabbed my heart, and yelled "Mine!" like it's his newest and most favorite toy. Because it's now his. "Hi, firelady!"

Laughing, I slip my hand free of his and squeeze his shoulder. "How 'bout, since we're going to be friends, you call me Adina. And what's your name?"

"Khalil." He turns to his father. "Daddy, Dina's my friend. She said so! I'm friends with a firelady!"

This kid.

Forget a decade, he's hell on the female population now. Me being that population of one.

Standing, I force myself to look at Solomon again.

"Hey. Good to see you again," I lie.

And maybe he knows because, for the first time, the corner of his mouth twitches in an almost smile.

"That's what your mouth saying, ma, but that dry-ass tone is telling something entirely different."

"Ooh, Daddy! You said *ass*," Khalil points out. And if I'm not mistaken, it's utter glee that colors his voice.

"Yeah, my bad, li'l man." He ruffles his son's curls, but that apology seems more automatic than heartfelt. Why do I get the feeling he apologizes a lot for his language? Because from my experience, "agitated adjectives" are always flying outta that mouth. "Thanks for this," he says to me, voice softer yet still somehow rough, like calloused fingers sliding over my senses.

"No problem. It's my pleasure to do this . . . for him," I add pointedly.

Another one of those almost-there smiles, and I redirect my focus to his son. Either that or roll up on my toes and sink my teeth into that corner where his lush bottom lip and slightly thinner top one meet.

Fuck no, my common sense rails.

Fuck yes, sis! my vagina eggs me on.

Since I'm not into self-flagellation, I'm riding with common sense.

"Ready to go, Khalil? I told the other firemen you were stopping by, and they can't wait to meet you. Then we can check out the fire truck. How does that sound?" I ask, using his term for the engine.

"Yay!" He pumps a fist, lifting his knee to meet his elbow. "Can I slide down the pole too?"

I scoff, then grin. "Uh, yeah. Of course. What's a visit to a firehouse without sliding down the pole?"

Khalil cheers again and catches me completely off guard when he grabs my hand and swings it between us. I look over at Solomon, who lifts his gaze from our clasped hands to my face. I wait to see if he's going to object, but when he gives me an almost imperceptible nod, I steer him and Khalil toward the door leading into the firehouse.

Moments later, we enter the common area, where most of the guys are sitting on the couch or at the table, waiting on the lunch that Marco and Paul are in the kitchen preparing for this shift. Almost all gazes swing toward us, and the noise level lowers as we move farther into the rooms.

"Well, who do we have here?" Jared shoves back his chair and approaches us, a wide grin lighting his craggy face. With his arm outstretched toward Solomon, he says, "Solomon Young. Jared Silva." Solomon clasps my godfather's hand in his, pumps it up and down. "Damn, it's good to meet you. Now I can congratulate you in person. Man, that was a fantastic winning shot in the third against the Knights. You and Danver are killing it in the paint."

Solomon nodded. "'Preciate it."

"And who's this?"

Jared bends down to Khalil's level, as I'd done several minutes ago. He extends his hand to Khalil and shakes the little boy's. Khalil's eyes are so round they damn near fill up half his face. The irony. He's awed by the fireman while the fireman is fanboying over his father. It's both cute and hilarious.

"I'm Khalil," he whispers. "And you're a fireman!"

"I sure am. Want to meet the other firemen?" Jared asks, standing, still holding Khalil's hand. He jerks his chin toward Solomon. "Is that okay with you?"

"Can I, Daddy? Can I go with Fireman Jared?" Khalil's practically bouncing up and down, and those big green eyes of his plead with his father.

He's made of stronger stuff than me if he can resist that.

"Yeah, that's cool. Remember our rules, li'l man."

Khalil jerks his head up and down. "Uh-huh. Be nice and don't get in grown folks' business."

A snicker slips free without my permission. If that last one ain't every Black parent's number one rule. That, and don't go over to nobody's house asking for food. Viviane Wright didn't play about either one of 'em.

Jared leads Khalil across the room, and soon he's surrounded by the others, and the boy's smile is so bright it rivals any sun.

"Well, look who finally decided to show his face around here." Malcolm saunters up to me and Solomon, holding a cup of coffee, with a scowl riding his face. "My sister's only been hounded by rabid-ass reporters because of you. Full disclosure? I think she can do better."

Dammit.

I forgot all about Solomon being my fake boyfriend. Shit. I really should've found some time between the outbreak of my sudden celebrity—or infamy—and Solomon's call to tell them we broke up. Or maybe, I don't know, something wacky like the truth. But that ship has sailed and is on its way to the Undying Lands. Not only will I look like the liar I am, but if I ever need to pull the fake-boyfriend ruse again with someone else, no one will fall for it.

Note that I feel not one bit of guilt about being a liar when it will save me from another one of Viviane the Matchmaker's ill-fated hookups.

"Please, Malcolm. Cut the man some slack." I wave him off. "After a few days, all of that drama died down and people moved on to the next story. Besides, the man put an actual bodyguard on my ass. What more did you want him to do?"

"Since he was responsible for them being on your ass in the first place? Be here himself to protect you." He mugs Solomon, who slides his hands into the front pockets of his jeans and arches an eyebrow in reply.

What that man can say with one eyebrow lift is dissertation worthy.

"Listen, Malc—"

A large hand cuffing the back of my neck cuts off the you-doin'-too-much tirade on the tip of my tongue like Jason Voorhees in the middle of a summer-camp session. I know Malcolm's protective, and that's just one of the things I love about him, but damn! Doesn't matter though. That heavy, firm grip on my nape has my thoughts playing a fucked-up game of Telephone. By the time the *Move away!* and *Touching is bad!* messages from my brain reach my nipples and pussy, they've morphed to *Squeeze tighter!* and *What else those fingers do, tho?*

My thirsty-ass body doesn't give a damn that Solomon doesn't want us like that. Just shameless.

"You don't need to defend me, ma," Solomon says. Goddamn. That deep voice should be packaged with batteries and stored in a bedside dresser drawer. "Ay, Malcolm, I get you wanting to protect your sister, and I commend that. And we can disagree on sports and anything else, but don't ever accuse me of not covering one of mine. I couldn't be here because I had away games. But she had one of the best in the business guarding her. She's gonna always be good when it comes to me."

Covering one of mine.

Always be good when it comes to me.

Most of my breath evaporates in my throat, and what's left scorches the lining right off. *Mine.* Why that particular word echoes in my head and ping-pongs off my rib cage, I don't even want to attempt to analyze. I don't even want to touch on what it's doing to my poor vagina.

The charade. It's all for the charade, I remind myself with a ringing bitch slap. Don't read anything else into it. He's not busting me out, and I should just be thankful for that, since there's nothing about Solomon Young that reads *magnanimous.*

Still, Malcolm is Malcolm. And God love him, but it doesn't take much to set off this man's temper. He'd never put his hands on me—or any woman, for that matter—but Solomon is neither of those. And that mouth is reckless as hell.

Knowing this, I shift forward to place myself between Solomon and my brother.

Well, I *try* to shift forward.

That hold on my neck tightens, preventing me from moving, and *holy shit.* I clench my teeth against the moan that trembles up from my stomach to the back of my throat, ready to spill out between my lips. While I trapped the audible sound, I can't do a damn thing about the shiver that shudders through me. With his narrowed gaze fixed on Solomon, my brother doesn't notice my body's involuntary response. But no such luck with the man responsible for it. Next to me, his big frame stiffens. I'm so attuned to him that I pick up the nearly indiscernible reaction. He shifts behind me, coming closer to me so his chest grazes my shoulder blades. And there's *nothing* subtle about the hard, thick length that nudges my lower back.

No. Nope. Uh-uh.

Not possible. Even as flames lick at the soles of my feet, the backs of my knees, and the sensitive lips of my pussy, I stand firm on my denial. Right now it's not only the hill I'm willing to die on but the pyre I'm prepared to throw my carcass on and burn, Viking-style.

He doesn't want me.

Solomon made that abundantly clear.

That *thing* hiding out in his jeans is a biological response. A fluke. Dicks gon' dick, and they get hard for anything and everything.

"You're lucky we're in this firehouse," Malcolm growls, anger flickering in his dark-brown gaze.

"We don't have to be," Solomon returns calmly.

Oh, for fuck's sake.

The arousal toying with me doesn't take a back seat to annoyance; it just moves over.

"Okay, fine. You both have big dicks. Now, would you mind putting them away? Malcolm, stop antagonizing this man. He didn't leave me high and dry, and you know that for yourself since you met Graham. And you." I shoot a glance up and over my shoulder, meeting Solomon's emerald eyes. "You will not invite my brother outside to fight like it's three o'clock in the schoolyard. Your son is right over there, and something tells me he'd be mad as hell at you if you hit the fireman."

Both men snort, and I shake my head.

"Malcolm, can you tell Jared I'm going to grab a couple of things for Khalil?" With one last death glare at Solomon, my brother gives me a nod, then heads off toward Jared. Turning around, I tilt my head. "You want to come with me or stay here?"

He mimics me, cocking his head. "I can play nice when I want to, li'l mama."

Who wants that?

Please God save me from my inner heaux.

"Seeing is believing and, well, call me Ray Charles, 'cause I ain't seen shit."

He arches that damn eyebrow again. "Oh really? So maybe I should go over there and tell your brother the truth about that dinner, since you blind as fuck now."

Why does his rude-as-hell mouth get me twisted up inside? I should cuss him out, tell him to put that cock that was poking the shit out of my back seconds ago in an anatomically impossible hole. And yeah, a part of me still wants to do that.

But a much bigger part of me just wants to ride that mouth and see if it stays mean.

Jesus.

Heat flashes up my throat and pours into my cheeks. I duck my head, afraid Solomon will be able to read every one of my filthy thoughts all in my face.

I blame everything—the dirty images filtering through my mind, my body's unchecked reactions—on that kiss. It awakened a libido that had lain dormant since Keshaun. Though, true, I missed sex, nothing in me ached to have it. Craved it. Was like a bitch in heat for it.

That was then. And this postorgasmic kiss is now.

Yeah, I need to get away from Solomon and get myself together. This ain't what my sanity or my pussy needs.

"I'll be right back. Try to stay out of trouble until I get back." I edge around him and head down the hall at a fast clip.

Not running. I'm not running from anyone or anything.

But I'm for damn sure power walking.

I pass the dormitory-style room with our beds, the lieutenants' offices, and separate sleeping quarters. The chief's office sits at the end, and next to it is the storage room. I enter, then allow the door to close behind me. I flip the switch, bathing the large space in light.

Now, where was that box? The last time I saw it was when one of the third-grade classes in the area came over for a field trip. The chief's admin assistant said it should be on the second shelf from the . . . there it is.

With a satisfied grunt, I reach for the large box and open the flaps. Pulling out a red plastic fireman's hat and a gray badge, a toy walkie-talkie, and a fire extinguisher, I smile, imagining Khalil's reaction to these items. I set the toys on the shelf space next to the box and close it.

"So much for not being a puck bunny. I guess all that shit about not being ready to move on from Keshaun only applied to those of us who aren't rich hockey players, huh?"

Fuck.

Fuckfuckfuckfuck.

So involved in finding the gifts for Khalil, I hadn't even heard the door to the storage room open or close. And now Matt stands between me and the exit. Dammit.

Refusing to betray the clutch of nerves twisting and grinding in my stomach, I gather the toys and turn to face him. Because as sad as it is to say about a fellow firefighter, I'd never give my back to him.

Anger slides under the unease. Anger because this asshole can't take no for an answer. Because his fragile ego can't handle a rejection. Because he has me edgy and mistrustful in my own firehouse.

"You need something in here, Matt?" I ask, not bothering to answer that question that was a statement with a question mark slapped at the end. It was an insult designed to hurt me and get under my skin. And it did. But fuck if I'm gonna let him know that. "If so, close and lock the door behind you."

I don't move forward because I'm not voluntarily bringing myself closer to him.

And he doesn't move.

My pulse throbs in my ears like a drug-fueled drum solo. It's crazy that Malcolm and Jared are on the other side of that door, and yet I feel alone, vulnerable. Scared.

"You not gonna answer my question?" His lips twist into a smirk, but the anger in his dark eyes is clear under the storage room's naked bulb. "You walk around here like you're too good for anyone. And they treat you like some kind of fuckin' saint. When all it took was a few dollars and a big name to get you down in the mud with the rest of us."

"If that's what you think, then move around like I told you to," I say calmly, even though all kinds of *muthafuckas* and *bitches* dance on my tongue with hot coal-lined boots. "I don't see what the problem is."

The smirk deepens into an ugly sneer, and the first drops of fear trickle into the disquiet and anger. I grew up with brothers, a father, *and* a mother who didn't play that turn-the-other-cheek shit. All of them made sure I got hands and could use them on anyone who tries me. But this isn't that easy, that simple. He's a fireman—I refuse to call him a brother. And he can twist the narrative around to make it seem as if I'm the one who made advances and he turned me down. Or that I'm mad because he critiques me hard because of my performance. Or that I'm—my personal favorite—too sensitive when it's just boys being boys.

Any of those could be detrimental to me rising up the ranks in the department. The odds are already stacked against me like a fucking Jenga tower because I'm Black and a woman. But getting the reputation of being *difficult . . . hard to work with . . . a disruptive problem in the house* . . . being Nolan Wright's daughter won't save me. My spotless performance record won't help me.

My race and sex will trump all that.

I'm not naive enough to believe in the fairy tales of equality and diversity the department and this country like to spout. Not when only 12 percent of firefighters are women and even fewer of those women are Black. No, I'm in an overwhelmingly cis-het-white-male field, and as Matt's one of them, his version of the "facts" will likely be granted more weight than mine.

And then . . . then there's the part of me that just doesn't want to complain to my shift CO. And not just because that would be Jared. It's not fair that I *have to* complain. That I can't expect the same freedom of the others in this house—the freedom to not be harassed. To clock in, do a job I love with people I respect, and then head home.

It's not fucking fair, and I *hate* Matt for stealing that from me. For making me feel . . . trapped.

"You and bitches like you are my problem. Acting like you're so much better than you really are. Did you even love Keshaun? That man not even cold in his grave and you on the next man's dick. At least I respected that reason you gave—"

"You didn't respect shit," I hiss, fury rolling through me like a swollen wave.

Pain radiates in my chest as if he slammed a red-hot knife into it. He crossed the line, bringing up Keshaun. Again. The fuck was he questioning my love for him, my loyalty? And no, even though I want to snatch his throat out, it isn't lost on me that slithering underneath the rage is the guilt. Because in those dark, lonely, and unforgiving hours when everyone else sleeps, I've accused myself of the same thing.

That shame shreds my restraint and intentions to rise above this asshole.

Sorry, Michelle. I know I'm supposed to go high when they go low. But today, I'm digging a hole to the fucking basement.

"And I'm not gonna be too many more of your bitches. But speaking of bitches, you'd know a lot about that, since you up here acting like one with your feelings all hurt and your lip poked out. Now, I tried to be nice when I said I'm not ready to date. But since you don't want to live, I'll give it to you straight. I don't want you. I'll never want you. If you were the last man on earth, I'd fuck myself before you. So, you have a choice here. *A*, stop worrying about me and the next man's dick and move on, or *B*, I report your ass for sexual harassment and being a tool. Which one is it going to be?"

Yeah, I should've probably stopped at *speaking of bitches*. Definitely should've put brakes on my tongue at *fuck myself before you*. But he has me hot as hell, and when backed too far into a corner, my default is to come out swinging for blood.

Yet as his features darken, and his brown eyes deepen to an unholy black, I know I've said too much, gone too far. And he has at least fifty pounds and six inches on me. And we're in a small room, with him between me and the door.

"You threatening me? The fuck you think you are? Go 'head and say something. You might be the captain's daughter, but that's not going to save you. At the end of the day, you're still a piece of pussy who got here because the department needed *diversity*"—he spits out the word like it's covered in dog shit—"so the fucking liberals could get off their backs. Your father and a quota push got you through those doors. And everyone knows it. So yeah, go ahead and cry to the brass. When you're out of this house or moved to some dusty desk where they don't have to see you and forget your ass exists, I'll still be right here. Where I belong."

Every one of his words are like bullets piercing my body and leaving seeping wounds behind. Because he's right. I know it; he knows it. He's just reiterating and confirming all my previous thoughts.

Trapped. I'm back to feeling trapped.

"Get out of my way," I grind out.

A mean grin spreads across his face. "Make me."

Oily fear slicks a path to my belly, and my grip on the nearly forgotten toys tightens so the blunt ridges of the fake badge dent my palm.

A knock on the door breaks the taut silence that descended between us. And I both hate and detest the relief that floods through me, nearly dissolving the strength in my legs.

"Dina, you still in there?" Another hard rap. "Hey, we're ready to show li'l man around the house."

Though fifteen minutes ago I wanted to drop-kick my brother for showing his overprotective ass, now I want nothing more than to run to him and bury my face against his chest. And cry.

"I'm coming out now," I call out, thankful my voice doesn't tremble. "You going to move now?"

His lips flatten, anger and what I assume to be frustration glinting in his eyes. I don't give a damn. Just as long as he *moves.*

Matt turns and pulls the door open, coming face to face with my brother. I can't see his expression, but the surprise, then suspicion, on my brother's is crystal clear. He frowns; his dark-brown gaze drags down and then up Matt's frame.

"What're you doing in here, Matt?" He glances over the other man's shoulder and looks at me. "You good?"

Before I can answer, Matt scoffs and steps out of the storage room. Malcolm doesn't move, so he edges past my brother, their chests nearly bumping.

"Yeah, everything's good. I just came in to make sure Adina found the toys for that hockey player's kid. It's been a while since we had to use them."

Malcolm doesn't shift his narrowed gaze away from Matt even as he asks me, "That right, Dina?"

Matt mutters something, as if offended that Malcolm isn't accepting his word on the matter. Not that Malcolm gives a fuck. He still waits on my answer.

And here is where I could admit the truth about the months of Matt pushing up on me, of him getting disrespectful and now verbally abusive. Tell him how I'm being sexually harassed. My lips even part, but . . .

But I already see the suspicion and concern in his eyes. And instead of it making me feel comforted, safe, I'm choking on my own weakness.

He's already dragging out his cape, and more than anything I want him to confidently hand that cape over to me 'cause he's confident I can save myself.

"Yeah, it's all good. And I have what I came looking for." I hold up the toys and walk forward and out of the storage room.

Malcolm steps out of the way for me, but his intense, too-piercing, too-seeing stare remains on me for several long seconds before sliding back to Matt.

"Okay," he finally says. "You can go, Matt. I got her from here if she needs any more help."

Something flashes in Matt's eyes, but he gives my brother a stiff nod and takes off down the hall, back toward the kitchen and common area.

"You sure you're good, Dina?" Malcolm asks, gaze moving over my face.

"Yeah, I'm positive."

"You know you can tell me anything, and I'll always have your back, no matter what it is. You're my family first, a firefighter second. You know that, right?"

"Yes, Mal. I know." Ducking my head, I shift past him. "I should get back, since I invited Solomon and Khalil here. If I leave him with Jared too long, he might sell my virginity for season tickets."

Malcolm mugs me. "Man, go on with that. Don't ever mention that to me again."

"You're a big-ass crybaby."

"I'll be that as long as this conversation is never repeated."

Snickering, I turn toward the hall, following behind my brother's large frame.

Though my mouth is curved into a smile, thick, greasy shame and disappointment coat my throat and chest and puddle in my stomach.

I had no remorse about fibbing to my family about my supposed relationship with Solomon.

But this is different.

It *feels* different.

I just lied to my brother's face and in turn protected a piece of shit that I despise, basically handing over my power to him, now that he knows I won't confess the truth about his behavior toward me.

That shame and disappointment aren't just in the situation, they're in me.

I've just failed *me*.

Some hero I am.

I can charge into burning buildings, fight fires, and save people.

But I can't even save myself.

Chapter Nine

SOLOMON

For the third time, I glance toward the mouth of the hall that Adina disappeared down over ten minutes ago. Does it take this long to grab a couple of things for Khalil?

Shit. I scratch my beard-covered jaw. This is her environment, apparently her home away from home. There's no reason I should be checking for her like she's my kid instead of my . . . hell, I don't know. My nothing.

My nothing.

I exhale a low breath and drag my gaze away from the direction Adina left and back to Khalil. A reluctant smile tugs at my mouth. My son is in his element. Surrounded by all these firemen, and he's the sole focus of attention? Yeah, I'm gonna hear about this for weeks. And I'm good with that. He's laughing, having a good time. He's happy. That's all I want for him.

Yet . . . I look back toward the hall.

An itch tingles just under the base of my neck. It's the same itch that warns me when there's about to be some bullshit on the ice and I need to prepare to fight for myself or my team. It's the same itch that scratched at thirteen-year-old me as I climbed the steps to my apartment only to find my mother on the living room floor with her boyfriend standing over her, his knuckles bloody.

It's that same itch that prickled my skin *that* night I arrived home after a game and Kendra wasn't there.

I've learned to not ignore what I've come to consider my warning system. Yeah, I'm in her firehouse, with her people. And I have no ties to Adina, no relationship other than the one we faked for her family and that the press has concocted with their cameras. But something's up.

Fuck it.

Just as I take a step in that direction, a tall bulky firefighter with close-cut dark hair emerges from the hall. I narrow my gaze on him as he stalks across the room and drops down on one of the couches that has seen better days. He shouldn't catch my interest except for the fact that he just came from where Adina has gone and anger tightens his features. I don't know this man, but anger I'm very familiar with and can easily identify.

Something's . . . off. And that itch hasn't let up.

Again, I move toward the hall, and just as I reach the entrance, Adina and Malcolm appear. Only when I lay eyes on her does the sensation at the base of my neck ease.

Ease, not disappear.

Malcolm meets my gaze, and for once his face doesn't ball up in distaste. He shifts a look down at Adina before returning his attention to me. If this were anyone else but her brother, I'd think he was trying to communicate a message to me.

But yeah, he hates me.

He continues on, heading for the kitchen while Adina stops next to me. Unable to stop myself, I slide a glance back over where ol' boy is sitting. His eyes are on us, face frowned up. Yeah, I'm starting to feel some kind of way about him.

"Everything good?" I switch my regard back to her.

She blows out a breath, rolling her eyes. On another woman, that eye problem would completely put me off. But Adina? My gut pulls tight, an ache like I haven't eaten in days clawing at me. With Adina, I just want to teach her what that will get her. Which is my face buried in her pussy, giving her something to roll them eyes at.

Goddamn, this woman is dangerous. A fucking menace.

"Yes, everything's just fine. You and Malcolm," she mutters. "For two people who don't like each other, you're so much alike."

"Correction, ma. I like your brother just fine. It's him who don't fuck with me because, *A*, he knows I'm right about his team being trash, and *B*, he thinks I'm fucking his sister." She scowls at me, but I catch the soft yet sharp inhale of breath at my mention of fucking her. Her chest, perfectly outlined in her dark-blue long-sleeved shirt, rises and falls, and damn if I'm not jealous of that patch over her breast. Forcing my attention back to her face, I arch an eyebrow and pretend I don't notice the darkening of li'l mama's eyes or the stain of red on her softly rounded cheekbones. "Nah, as long as he believes I know what your pussy looks and tastes like, we never gon' be cool."

I didn't need to add that. But a part of me wanted to see that pretty gaze darken even further. See that flush deepen. And they do.

"This must be fun for you," she says, and I bend my head lower to catch it.

"What?"

She studies me for several seconds then huffs out a dry, short chuckle. "You literally wiped the taste of me from your mouth. I need you to keep that energy."

Adina walks across the room, approaching Khalil, and though she just gave me a tight-lipped, half-assed smile, the one she bestows on my son is open and genuine.

She's right to call me on my shit. I didn't have any business talking to her like that. It could be mistaken as flirting. As toying with her. When that's not my intention.

It isn't . . .

Fuck, I don't know a damn thing anymore.

◆ ◆ ◆

"Daddy, do you see me?" Khalil hoots with laughter, waving his whole arm at me as if I can't peep him in the front seat of the fire engine. "I'm a fireman!"

"Yeah, li'l man. I can't miss you," I call back to him.

He grins, then turns to Adina, who whispers to him, and a moment later the horn blasts, and I'm thankful she drove the truck out of the bay and onto the short driveway. Khalil's giggles fill the air when the noise of the horn fades, and my chest tightens almost to the point of pain.

Other than his grandmother, he hasn't been close to another woman since Kendra . . . yeah, since Kendra. The women who I've fucked in the past were just that—women I've fucked. None of them had ever met my son. None of them had the faintest chance in hell of coming within five feet of him, much less meeting him. But Adina . . .

Khalil not only met her but laughed with her, sat on her lap behind the wheel of the fire truck. And before this, he'd eagerly climbed on her back and slid down the pole with her. I'll hear his giggling and his high-pitched, delighted scream in my dreams, and they'll be good ones.

As the horn blasts in the air again, I absently rub a palm over my chest, directly over my heart. I feel like I should go get Khalil, thank Adina for this favor, and leave. I have to protect my son, not let him become attached to her, because she's not going to be around. I can't *let* her be around. Because the more time I spend with Adina, the more I want to have that pussy collapsing around my dick, creaming on it. The more I need to have those thighs trembling around my face and my waist. Fuck, I want to tear her up, leave my handprints on that perfect ass, on those rounded hips. Hear her voice crack on my name because it's strained and hoarse from all the screaming.

My earlier thought about her being dangerous isn't an exaggeration. Those other women—they weren't threats. But Adina? She wouldn't be faceless, nameless. She wouldn't be forgettable.

And that was a betrayal.

"Daddy!" I blink, so lost in my thoughts I didn't notice Khalil and Adina climbing down from the engine and approaching me. Malcolm and the older fireman, Jared, who I learned is a lieutenant here, join them. Khalil throws his arms around my knees and tips his fire-helmet-covered head back, a grin so wide I can count all thirty-two. "Daddy, Fireman Jared said he's coming to your game! Can he sit with me?"

Adina scoffs, shaking her head. "Did you put him up to that?"

Jared holds up his hands, the smirk quirking his mouth contradicting his wide eyes.

"I'm innocent, I swear. Besides, I have tickets." Lowering his arms, he nods at me. "Thanks again for that, Solomon."

I swallow a snort. "Yeah. No problem."

The man basically extorted game tickets from me in exchange for her parents' address.

"Daddy, can Ms. Dina come with us to the 'seum?" Khalil asks.

I glance at her, and I'm not proud of the sudden bottoming-out of my stomach or the rapid thud of my heart slamming against my ribs.

Or the fierce, deafening *Fuck yes* that roars in my head.

There's little I'm afraid of; other than harm coming to Khalil, I'm numb to that shit. That tends to happen when the worst has already happened. But this sensation crip-walking down my spine?

Fear.

Fear of how loud that voice is and the lust that streams through my veins on the heels of it.

"Li'l man, Ms. Adina is still working. She has to be here just in case there are any fires."

"Oh." He frowns as if he's thinking hard on my excuse. Then his expression clears, and he's smiling up at me again. "Can she come over to our house later? Can we have pizza when she comes? You like pizza, Ms. Dina?"

Holy shit. My head spins from the barrage of questions and switching of topics from my son. I can't even blame anyone else. He inherited that bulldozer of a personality from me. It doesn't feel great being on the receiving end of it. And it feels even worse to have to tell him no. But fuck me, am I finding it difficult to come up with a reason. Well, other than *Sorry, son. But if I have her over to the house, your dad might end up deep in the guts of your new buddy.*

Yeah, not appropriate.

"Khalil—"

"Hey." Adina hunkers down in front of us, and Khalil turns around to face her. "Your dad's right. Me and Jared have to be here all night just in case someone needs our help. But anytime you want to come by and see us, we'll be here, okay? Promise." She holds up her fist, and after a moment, Khalil bumps it. Adina smiles and stands, cupping his shoulder. "I had fun with you today."

"Me too," Khalil says, but his voice has lost some of its enthusiasm, and Adina's expression softens, her gaze flicking to me. The glance is too quick for me to catch what she hides in those brown eyes, but damn if I don't want to grab her chin and force her head back toward me so I can read her, decipher her secrets. "Bye, Ms. Dina."

"Not *bye*, Khalil. See you later."

His voice is slightly lighter when he replies, "See you later, Ms. Dina."

She shouldn't be making promises to my kid. Especially ones neither one of us can keep. Intend to keep.

"Thanks for letting me bring him by. This was cool of you."

"Of course. You have a great boy. Anytime."

Our gazes lock, and for a long beat, there's silence between us that even the honks and dull roar of traffic or Jared's conversation with Khalil can't penetrate.

"I'm going to take Khalil in to say bye to the rest of the guys," Jared says, and I jerk my attention away from her in time to catch the unsubtle smirk riding his mouth.

"Uh-uh! Not *bye*. It's *see you later*, Fireman Jared!" my son loudly corrects him.

Chuckling, Jared dips his chin. "My bad, li'l man. You're right. Let's go tell everyone *see you later*." Hiking an eyebrow at me, he asks, "That okay?"

"Yeah, that's good." I stare after him and Khalil as they head toward the bay with the other fire truck. "He's an all right guy for an extortionist."

"Not extortionist. Opportunist. That man saw an opportunity to score some hockey tickets—I'm still confused about why—and he jumped on it. We firemen are a squirrely bunch. You gotta keep your head on a swivel around us."

I huff out a short laugh, and a ghost of a smile whispers across her mouth.

"If there's any consolation," she says, sliding her hands in her pockets and rocking slightly back on the heels of her black steel-toed boots, "he's a huge fan and is really enjoying the tickets."

I nod, but before I can reply, the sound of a door opening catches my attention. The same guy I'd noticed earlier exits the firehouse and stalks past us, not speaking. But that mug on his face? Yeah, it's a damn soliloquy entitled "Fuck You."

I frown, staring at his retreating back until he climbs his goofy ass in a truck parked halfway down the block.

"You fuck him?"

Surprise and then an emotion that seems too . . . complicated for anger briefly twists her face. There's more in that darkening of her expression, and though I can't accurately pinpoint what that emotion is, it has a flash of heat sweeping up my spine and prickling my skin. On impulse, I turn back in the direction of her coworker just in time to see the vehicle pull away from the curb and fly past us.

"No." Her tone's flat, dry. Not inviting any more discussion.

But shit, when has that ever stopped me? And only to myself will I admit that there's more than curiosity nagging me. And that more, I'm not ready to even touch.

I cock my head. "You sure?"

Her chin tucks into her neck, and her face balls up. "Am I sure that I haven't fucked Matt? What the hell kind of question is that? Not that it's any of your business, but I think I remember who and who hasn't been in my shit."

Matt. I tuck that info away for later.

I shrug. "He's acting like you giving away his pussy. Both back in there"—I tip my head toward the firehouse—"and now. So if he hasn't fucked, then he must want to and you told him no."

She doesn't answer. But the emotion that flashes over her face this time I immediately recognize. Annoyance. Because I'm right.

And I tell her so.

"Yeah, that's what it is." The image of *Matt's* face earlier as he reentered the firehouse's communal space flickers across my mind, and I frown, edging closer into her space until her breasts nearly brush my chest. "He a problem?" I growl.

"No, of course not," she scoffs. But she's also staring at my chest, not meeting my eyes. Suspicion, ugly and dirty, burrows in my chest.

"You wanna look at me when you lie to me?" I shift backward a step and dip my head, forcing her to look at me. When those pretty brown eyes rise to my face, I study her. Seeking out the answers that she's hiding from me. No, I don't have any evidence of that, but something ain't right. "Now, let's try that again. He a problem for you?"

"No," she says, her voice firm, resolute. "And for future reference, I can handle myself and anyone else that comes my way."

"I don't doubt it, ma," I murmur. "Doesn't mean you have to. And for future reference," I say, regaining the scant space I inserted between us, lowering my face until we're almost sharing the same air, the same breath, "I don't believe shit you just said. But I'm gonna trust if *that*"—I jerk my chin in the direction the asshole went—"becomes more of an issue, that you remember who has your back."

"Who? You?" she scoffs, crossing her arms and grazing my chest.

That touch might as well be a stroke down my dick. At least that's how hard I get. How hot lust blows through me like the roughest, wildest storm.

"Yeah, me."

If I wasn't so close to her, I might've missed the darkening of her eyes or that almost imperceptible gasp of air. She looks as stunned as I feel. Yeah, I hadn't meant to say that. Part of me still doesn't know if it's true . . .

Yeah, it's true. If she called, texted, emailed, fucking smoke signaled that she needed me, I would be there. That doesn't mean I don't resent her for that.

Because I fucking do.

"Bullshit." Her lips twist up at the corner in a counterfeit smile, and skepticism saturates that one word. "Why would you come running to the aid of someone you don't like? Someone you consider a mistake? Hell, I'm still trying to figure out how you're here today. I get the why—Khalil. He's the cutest kid, so saying no to him must be an act of Congress. Still, I would've thought you'd bribe, plead, beg—do anything—to get out of being in the same space as me again. Even now, I can practically see your need to get up out of here." She makes a derisive sound, giving her head one hard shake. "So no, I call bullshit. Even if I did have a *problem*, as you call it, you would be the last person I'd admit it to, much less ask for help."

That's fair. I can't fault her for her words or reaction. High-key, I don't know how I'm here either. I love my son, and we all might indulge him a little too much lately, but I don't have a problem saying no to him. One thing I'm not 'bout to do is raise a little badass demon who don't know how to act. My parents didn't play that, and neither do I.

So Khalil asked to come to the firehouse, but I wanted to be here too. Or else I wouldn't be.

I know that about myself too.

I know that.

I also know that I want her. Fuck, I *crave* her. There's no denying it to myself anymore, especially staring down into her dark eyes that reflect glimmers of hurt. Hurt I placed there with my careless handling of her.

If I was on the ice and made a mistake on a play, I wouldn't bench myself like a pussy. I'd get back in there and try to regain whatever I'd cost my team. Shit, I even teach Khalil that—if he does somebody wrong, apologize. But after I hurt Adina when she lowered her guard, allowed herself to be vulnerable with me . . . placed her trust in me . . .

"I'm sorry."

Adina blinks. Blinks again. "Excuse me?"

Her shock should be amusing. Instead, it just makes me feel like shit.

"I said, I'm sorry." When her face balls up, I hold up a hand, and her lips snap shut, but the frown remains. "Not for the kiss. And you were right. I did want to regret it, wanted to pretend it didn't happen. But I couldn't . . . I haven't. Even though I feel like I should be, after having had my mouth on you, my tongue in you, I'm not sorry that I know what you taste like. Like the rawest high-priced whiskey. One hit had me on my ass, and I panicked. You—" I clench my jaw, grinding my teeth together. My survival instincts kick in, warning me not to let the words scrambling onto my tongue free. But that's fear talking. Fear and . . . panic. And for once, I have to put someone else above my own selfish needs. "You are the first woman I've kissed since my wife . . . since my wife. That had me feeling some kinda way, but I should've dealt with my own shit another time and not let you walk away from me believing you were a mistake. That was never my intention, ma."

She stares at me, those pretty brown eyes wide, her features softened in shock.

"I'm the first woman you've ki—that can't be right." She shakes her head. "You told me yourself that you've been with other women in the last two years. That you . . ."

"I have fucked other women. But giving 'em dick and kissing 'em are two different things. One is damn near transactional, a biological need to bust a nut. And the other . . ."

The other is personal. More intimate.

I don't say that aloud, but I don't need to. Adina nods, understanding clouding her gaze.

"Now it's my turn to apologize," she murmurs.

"For what?"

"Because if I'd known that, I wouldn't have asked you to kiss me. I feel like I pressured you into—"

"Put that out your head and mouth, li'l mama. Can't no one make me do shit I don't want to. It's why I kissed you; it's why I'm here now. Khalil wanted to see the 'firelady'"—she gives a soft snort, and I smile—"and so did I. And not just to make my kid's day. But also to make sure you're all right after all that shit went down."

To see if my shit bricking up around you is a fluke.

Nope. No fluke.

Upstairs, when that ass bumped up against my thighs while she talked smack to her brother, my dick sat on swole, ready to drill a hole through her fucking back.

Nah, baby girl gets me hard by just breathing. And something tells me even that's optional.

Damn, that's sick as fuck. Li'l mama got me on some necrophilia shit.

"Thank you." Head tilted, she studies me, those eyes roaming my face. "For coming by and bringing Khalil. Like I said, he's a complete joy to be around. And for the apology. I told myself I didn't need it, but now that I have it, that was a lie." A rueful smile curves her mouth. "Maybe you're not a *complete* asshole. And . . ."

She cuts off the rest of her sentence, a small wrinkle creasing the skin above the bridge of her nose.

"Nah, say it," I urge.

No sense in holding back, especially since we both seem to be in the confessing spirit. Besides, I find myself desperate to know what's on her mind. Hell, desperate for her thoughts, her voice. I hunger to be inside this woman in more ways than the obvious one.

The frown deepens, but she exhales a low breath and shifts her gaze away from me so she's looking at some point over my shoulder. I don't like that shit; I want her eyes on me. But I don't call her on it.

"Okay." It's still several seconds before she speaks again. "Maybe you needed me to be your first kiss, just like I needed you to be mine. With someone who understands you, what you've lost and how feeling a little alive for a few moments is better than the emptiness that convinces you you're dead inside and there's no hope of resurrection. No Easter Sunday rolling of the stone for you. Yeah . . ." She nods, finally lifting her head, and what little breath I still possess she drives away with the darkness in her eyes. A darkness that swirls with sadness, a hint of desperation, and a fuck-ton of lust. "Yeah," she repeats, "when you get a taste of that hope, you'll do anything to hold on to it, try to stretch it from a few minutes into longer. Just as long as you feel something other than that . . . nothing."

Breathe, dammit. Breathe before you pass the fuck out.

But my mentally growled order doesn't penetrate as the rush of air in my head drowns out everything but her softly, carefully spoken words and the ones she once confessed to me on a dark street.

I love sex . . . from the pleasure and the connection to the weight of a man on top of me. I loved the quiet moments afterward, where the sweat is drying and our hearts are calming as we're tangled up in each other.

I'm picturing that shit in my head, and it's not abstract or impressionist art. It's detailed, photographically clear, and anatomically correct.

"I can promise you this, li'l mama." I lift a hand, curl it around the front of her throat, my thumb grazing the bottom of her jawbone. She doesn't make a sound, doesn't move. Nah, that's not right. It's slight, subtle, but she arches into my palm and, narrowing my eyes on her, I act on instinct and tighten my grip. Still no sound—no protest, no gasp.

But she fists my sweater at my waist and those long, thick lashes flutter. God*damn*. Lust roars through me louder than that horn on the fire truck. I bite my bottom lip as my dick throbs, demanding to feel this woman in every which way she'd let it. And shit, I can think of a fuck-ton of ways. "When I'm around you, the last thing I feel is *nothing*."

Taking a further risk, I press my luck and press my body against the curvy length of hers. She tips her head back, and I take a beat, scrutinizing that face. That stunning and absolutely beautiful face.

The sudden need to see it twisted in orgasm slams into me. To see it flushed with pleasure. To see it covered in my nut.

Fuck, the filthy things I want to do to her. The dirty things I want her to acquiesce to letting me do to her.

Instead of backing away—because the smart thing would be to back all the way up—I inch closer, press harder against her. My dick pokes her soft belly this time, not her back. Those full, firm breasts pillow against my chest, and those thick thighs brush mine. She's nearly a foot shorter than my six feet, four inches, and our height difference hasn't been more apparent as I bow my head over hers and sink my teeth into her plump lower lip. That muthafucka is like the damn Bat-Signal, urging me to come and take it, suck on it, slide my dick over it.

It's scary how much I want to tear li'l mama up.

Her rushed pants of breath bathe my lips as I swipe my tongue over the flesh still captured between my teeth. I release her only to treat her top to the same treatment. A groan rips up and out of me. That flavor—that hit of smoky whiskey and heavy sweet cream—hits my tongue, and a hunger pang twists my stomach so tight I damn near flinch from that need, that pain. When you sometimes go to bed with a growling stomach when growing up, you vow to never be hungry again. Now is no different. I'm starving, and she's that second helping I was once denied. No way in hell I'm stepping away from her unsatisfied.

Common sense tries to infiltrate this crimson-tinted haze wrapped around my brain. Tries to warn me that hemming her up by the neck and fucking her mouth in front of the fire station when her brother, who already can't stand me, is just yards away isn't a good look. Tries to remind me that this kiss will be much harder to walk away from than the first.

Yeah, I don't give a fuck about none of that.

Cocking my head, I give her top lip one last lick, then slip into her mouth, reacquainting myself with the taste, texture, essence of her. I wasn't lying about the potency of her flavor. My head is swimming at the first tangle of our tongues. And when I suck on it, each pull echoes in my dick. I grind my pounding, hard-as-steel length against her belly, and though I grunt at the pressure, it's not enough. Only lifting her, shoving her back against that fire truck feet away, ripping away these ugly uniform pants and beating up this pussy will be enough. And I wouldn't bet my autographed Grant Fuhr hockey stick on that.

My hand tightens just a little bit around her throat, and her groan vibrates against my palm. That, too, I feel up and down my dick. Shit, she's a menace. The worst thing she could've done was let me know she's not running from me. Stroking the roof of her mouth, I praise her with a squeeze of her hip.

I lift my head, but rising on her toes, she follows me. This time, she bites me, leaving behind a sting at the corner of my mouth. The tiny flare of pain has me returning to her for another hard, wild kiss of tongue, teeth, and groans.

"Ahem."

Fuck.

What common sense couldn't do, the light clearing of a throat accomplishes. That sound penetrates most of the lust clouding my brain, and I jerk my head up. The afternoon breeze brushes over my face, bringing swift attention to my wet, swollen mouth.

My initial, primal reaction is to drop my hands away from Adina and shove as much distance as possible between us. I even stiffen in preparation of doing just that. But at the last moment, I remember how I fucked up the first time we kissed. How, in my panic, I hurt her. Only that keeps me in place. I drop my hands from her body but only after giving her throat and hip one last squeeze. And when I step away, it's to the side of her, my shoulder grazing hers.

She shivers, and it ripples through me. A fierce, ill-placed gratification courses through me. That shudder wasn't because of the wind; that was pure me.

"Hi, Daddy." Wide-eyed, Khalil looks from me to Adina and back to me like he's watching one of his video games. "Why're you kissing Ms. Dina? I thought you said she wasn't your girlfriend."

"Oh, this oughtta be good," Jared muttered, humor lighting his eyes.

"She's not, li'l man," I say, not looking at Adina. "I was just telling her bye."

His face scrunches. "You don't tell Grandad or Grammy bye like that. You just hug them or do this." He jerks his chin up in a fair imitation of me.

Jared breaks into a coughing fit, but he can't hide his grin behind the fist raised to his mouth. Beside me, Adina softly snickers. I notice she doesn't try to help me out, though.

"You ready to hit the museum?" I ask, not answering his question. Because again, my answer isn't age appropriate.

"Yeah!" He pumps a fist, successfully distracted. Thank fuck. "Bye, Mr. Jared! I'll see you at the game! Daddy"—he swings his attention back to me, grinning big—"Mr. Jared is coming to your next game, an' he's bringing Ms. Dina with him. Isn't that cool?"

"I think that's pretty cool that she's going to a game," I murmur, glancing at her.

"Um," she hedges.

I chuckle, and yeah, it's at her expense. And hell no, I'm not stepping in to bail her out. Payback really is a mufucka. And sometimes it's fast as one too.

"Don't worry about using your extra ticket, Jared," I say to the other man. "I'll leave two more at will call."

"You don't—" she grinds out, but I cut her off, holding up my hand.

"No need to thank me. It's my pleasure." At *pleasure*, I drop my gaze to her mouth and bite my bottom lip. When I raise my eyes to hers, pleasure and a wariness that I can relate to shadow them. "Just say thank you, ma."

I wait, everything in me stilling. Don't ask me why it's important that she comes to one of my games. Why I want her to see me in my element. Prove to her that her lame-ass Patriots don't have anything on me.

Experience the side of me that's important in my life.

Like I said, I don't have an explanation why I want her there. It just is.

"Can she sit in the box with me and Grammy and Grandad?" Khalil asks. Turning to Adina, he raves, "They got popcorn and hot dogs in the box, Ms. Dina!"

If my stomach hollows out, then fills with apprehension at the thought of her sitting in the luxury box with my in-laws, I for damn sure hope my face doesn't betray it. Their reaction to seeing Adina at one of my games, alone, should be enough reason not to press that. Shit, to rescind the offer of tickets.

Should.

But it isn't. And I don't.

It's not like we're dating or even fucking, for that matter. But both me and my dick know that last one is on borrowed time. Especially if she's near me again.

That knowledge doesn't make me back off either.

"Hey," I say, voice low. But she hears me, and her head jerks toward me. "The tickets are yours and will be waiting on you. No pressure if you don't want to come." I pause. Fuck it. "But I want you to."

She briefly closes her eyes, exhales on a long breath.

As if sensing her weakening, like a shark scenting blood in the water, my ruthless son grabs her hand and pulls on it.

"Please, Ms. Dina. Pleeease." He drags out the *please* to about five syllables, and when she sighs, I know he has her.

She shouldn't feel bad. Not many people can withstand that whining with the addition of looking into those big, wide green eyes.

"Sounds good." She smiles at Khalil. "I can't wait."

Yeah, li'l mama is gonna have to work on lying. I don't buy that for one second, and from Jared's low chuckle, he doesn't either.

And when he murmurs "You father and brothers are going to disown you," I know I'm not wrong. The thought of her family—except for her mother, she adores me—up in their feelings because Adina's going to a hockey game sends a trickle of joy raining through me.

"Who's going to tell them?" She narrows her eyes on Jared, and he shrugs, that wide grin saying he most definitely will.

"Khalil, tell Mr. Jared and Ms. Dina *see you later*," I say, remembering Khalil's earlier correction.

"See you later! At the game!" He grabs my offered hand, wrapping his fingers around mine, and waves to them with the other.

I nod at Jared and then look at Adina.

"See you later, Dina," I murmur.

"Yeah, later."

We stare at one another, and fuck if I don't want to lean down and take another of those wet, too-damn-hot kisses with me. Especially when her lips are still puffy from my mouth and tongue. But I don't. Once was temptation enough. And I need to prove to myself that I'm capable of not getting lost in her. If this is headed where I think it is—and it is—I *have* to prove that to myself.

Because there will come a day when I'll walk away from this, from her, without looking back. And there's no better time than the present to start practicing it.

Khalil's hand in mine, I give her a chin jerk and lead my son down the driveway toward the car. But I still catch Jared asking Adina "Am I supposed to pretend I didn't see what I saw?"

"You saw nothing," she hisses back at him.

I smile.

There's no way I'm not coming out of this fucked. But for right now? In this moment?

I smile.

Chapter Ten

ADINA

"I still can't believe I'm at a hockey game." Noni twists in her seat, scanning the rows behind us. "I'm so damn excited. Who thought you bussin' it open for a hockey player would have these kinds of perks?"

"Okay, one, I'm not bussin' it open for anyone," I mutter, and ignore her snort. "And two, what the hell are you looking for?"

"One, if you aren't, you will be. And if you don't, I need a three-page, single-spaced Times New Roman twelve-point-font essay on why the fuck not. With your sources cited." Her crazy ass twists the other way, still scanning the more-than-half-packed arena. "And I'm people watching. Trying to see which ones up in here are most likely to break out in a fight during this game. I bet Minnie there'd be at least two. Ooh." She plops her ass back down and faces me again, dark eyes shining as bright as the lights in the arena. "Do you think we'll be lucky enough to get another person snatching off their artificial leg and beating somebody with it?"

"The hell?" I rear back, staring at her in horror. Because I for damn sure didn't hear her right. "What're you talking about?"

"Oh yeah, bitch. It happened during a Vegas Golden Knights game a couple of years back. They were playing the Edmonton Oilers. She snatched her prosthetic off and got to whooping ass with it."

"Daaaamn."

"Right?" Noni laughs. "That's some crazy shit. Homegirl said what she said with her whole chest. Or leg."

"Stop it. You're going to hell for that." I snicker. She shrugs, and I laugh harder. "Seriously, though. Since when did you become a hockey fan? You have never mentioned liking the sport to me, and you told me ol' boy licked your underarm during sex. Your TMI game is strong."

Noni's mouth screws up in a disgusted twist.

"Eeew. Why go and bring *that* up? I can't wash my armpits without thinking of him." She gives a dramatic shudder. "Now, you know you have no tolerance for anything outside of football. But to answer your question, Minnie was hooking up with this hockey player a few months back. So she started watching all these games on TV so she could show him she was interested in his sport. At first, I thought she was goofy as fuck—well, I still do, if you want to keep it a buck. It's one thing to learn your partner's interests so you can hang out and enjoy quality time together. But that shit's give and take. And that wasn't what she was doing. My twin tried to be something she wasn't to catch and keep the attention of a man. That's some bullshit."

I nod. Listen, me and Minnie, at best, have a cordial relationship. At worst, she's been Narnian seconds from me rocking her shit. Yet hearing Noni's story, I can't help but feel a little sympathy for my best friend's twin. Minnie is beautiful, smart, a gifted hairstylist. But the ain't-shit way she lets men treat her? It's sad because she could pull over a random car on Washington Street and find a better pick than the ones she dated.

But that's her business, not mine.

I just hated it for Noni, who worried about her twin and wanted more for her. Mainly wanted Minnie to love herself more.

"She was hooking up with someone on the Pirates?" I ask, curious if it would be anyone who'd be on the ice tonight.

"Hell if I know." Noni shrugs. "Honestly? I didn't ask any of the details, because I knew what it was, even if Minnie didn't want to see it. He'd fucked and got on. But she wanted to make it into something deeper. When I tried to tell her that so her feelings wouldn't get hurt, she snapped at me. And since I can't miss work because I'm in somebody's jail, I let it go."

"Damn," I murmur again. "Why do I feel bad for her?"

Noni waves a hand. "Babe, you know I love my sister with my whole soul. But save that feel-bad for someone who needs it. Because Minnie's gonna be right back in that same predicament in two weeks. Hell, she might already be falling on that grimy-ass dick as we speak."

It's wrong, but I crack up. This is one of the reasons why Noni's students adore her. She's petite, gorgeous, with reddish-brown natural curls that brush the middle of her back. But that sweet exterior harbors a razor-sharp brain, a sharper wit, and a take-no-shit attitude. And she takes no shit from her students, coworkers, or administration.

My best friend is goals. And while our paths couldn't have taken more different routes—me to the fire academy and her to college and two master's degrees—I still admire her. She's a baddie.

"Well, we can get a jersey for you to take home to her." They live together in a town house over in College Hill. "She'll probably like that."

"So she be mad as fuck that I went to a hockey game without her? Uh, that's a no. I don't feel like hearing that mouth. She'll be fine. Anyway, enough about my sister and her wayward coochie. I'm here to rip a page out of her book. You think your man can introduce me to one of these fine-ass hockey players?" She squirms on her seat, scanning the ice as if the said hockey players are already swarming into the rink.

"He's not my man," I grind out.

She shoots me a look over her shoulder, eyebrow arched.

"Sweetie, you have these bomb-ass seats—what're they called? Right, club seats. We were escorted to said club seats like we're fucking royalty. And you're wearing his jersey. Don't play in my face."

I have a comeback; I promise. But for the life of me, I can't find it at the moment. Because everything Noni's pointed out is true. When we arrived at the arena, I had the option of going to "the box," as Khalil had put it. What he'd been referring to was the luxury box where the owners, family, and other invited guests sat above the stands. I'm sure the description was accurate, and it no doubt offered all kinds of amenities, like the hot dogs Khalil mentioned and alcohol—which, shit, I could use right now. But I chose to sit close to the rink instead. Not only do I have zero desire to be closed in with a bunch of people I don't know, but these club seats are located in the center of the ice, super close to the rink. Since it's my first game, I want to be close to the action, not removed from it. Plus, it's not like we're sitting on bleachers or hard-ass stadium chairs. Nope, these are wide, padded, and super comfortable. And we don't even have to leave for snacks and sodas. We have an actual concierge that brings all that to us. With this kind of catering, who needs a box?

And of course I'm wearing Solomon's jersey. So is she! I mean, Solomon sent them over for us; it would've been rude not to put it on for the game. And it's not like I know any other player. Besides, it's not like we're the only two wearing his number 19.

Why yes, I am making excuses. Again. So?

"I'm teasing you. But y'know, it is okay if you like him," Noni says, her voice gentle. Too gentle.

I glance away from her, pretending to survey the crowds continually streaming into the arena, rapidly filling the seats. A couple of women claim the seats to the left of me, and I politely smile at them. The pretty brunette with golden brown eyes returns my smile, giving me a small wave. I wave back.

"You get to have fun, to live, Dina," Noni continues. "And there shouldn't be any guilt attached to it."

"I know," I murmur. And I *do.* But acknowledging something didn't stop the fear from crawling in. "He scares me," I admit to my best friend on a near whisper.

A frown immediately appears on her face. "Why? Has he done some—?"

"No, no, nothing like that. His mouth is reckless as fuck, and I can't lie, he has hurt my feelings a time or two. But he's not cruel. Not intentionally." I shake my head, hard. "I'm scared because he can fuck my world up. And I'm not talking about sex. Well, not *just* about sex." I huff out a breath, and despite the concern shadowing Noni's gaze, her mouth twitches with a smile. "I mean everything else. I don't know if I can fuck him and turn off my emotions like a faucet. You know me better than anyone—I've never been one for one-night stands or situationships. And Solomon . . ." Without my express permission, my eyes look toward the ice, as if seeking his big, solid form. "Solomon still mourns his wife. Is still very much in love with her. I can't . . ."

I can't play second to anything or anyone again. Not even to a ghost.

I don't need to voice those words, because they ring in my head like a struck bell, loud as hell. As much as I loved Keshaun—and God knows, I did—I understood where his priorities lay. Firefighting. His career. Advancement. And I supported him and his aspirations because they were mine too. Still . . . no one likes to feel like they're . . . forgettable.

"Oh, friend." She reaches out, covering my hand with hers and squeezing. "You're one of the best people I know, and you deserve to be put on a pedestal and worshipped." I roll my eyes and start to sputter a denial, but she squeezes my hand again. Firmer. "I'm serious. Dead ass. Hell, look at your job, Dina. You sacrifice, putting your life on the line every day for others. You're a fucking real-life heroine and deserve someone to go just as hard for you. It's not too much to expect or demand."

She exhales a breath and leans closer to me so I can't avoid looking into her brown eyes even if I wanted to. And a part of me really wants to.

"You lost a good friend, a good man. Someone you loved. Maybe someone you would've ended up spending the rest of your life with."

I frown. *Maybe someone* . . . What did she mean by that? Keshaun was my fiancé. *Of course* I would've spent the rest of my life with him.

"Maybe you're not ready to jump back in to another relationship, and that's fine," she continues. "That's your choice. But Dina, all you've known is Keshaun. It's been him and becoming a firefighter, and the two were so tangled together, I don't know if you can separate on from the other. You need time to sit in and discover who you are apart from him. Apart from being a firefighter. You just need to *be*. To have fun. To relax. To fucking *live*. What do you do when you're not at work? Sit your ass down on that couch and binge the latest season of *Love Is Blind* or whatever the newest trash TV show is on Netflix. Aht." She holds up a hand, forestalling my objection. "Bitch, please. It's trash, I don't even wanna hear it. But my point is"—her voice softens—"enjoy this." She waves a hand, encompassing the stands, the rink. "Enjoy *him*. You already know Solomon's not emotionally available. Repeat that shit, and write it down one hundred times if you need to remind yourself of it. Because this could be a blessing in disguise. That man looks like he can fuck you into astral projection, then tear both you and your soul up in a dirty-ass threesome. And I say, let him. For the first time since Keshaun, you're attracted to someone, and if he reciprocates, do it. Just have fun and get the dick as long as it lasts, and then walk away without looking back, thankful for the experience. And then you move on and find that person who is for you, who will treat you like the queen you are. Or you don't and treat yourself like the queen you are. Shit, do both."

I lower my gaze to my lap and blindly stare at the faded denim hugging my thighs. Noni's words resonate inside me like a word spoken from a Sunday pulpit. They're taking root inside me; doesn't matter that I wish they didn't. That I could reach inside my chest and rip them out. But I can't. No—I won't. Because in a way, my best friend just gave me permission to do what my body has been aching for from the moment I laid eyes on Solomon's mean ass in the Pirates' corporate office.

Can I just take from him what I need, what I crave? Get all the pleasure and none of the pain? Noni seems to believe I'm capable of it, that I'm strong enough to do it.

She has more faith in me than I do.

Sighing, I turn in my seat to fully face the rink. This subject is too heavy for a hockey game. I don't want to think right now. As Noni urged me to, I just want to enjoy.

At that moment, the loud rhythmic cadence of drums fills the arena, and I'm reminded of a college drum line. Next to me, our conversation apparently shelved and put aside, Noni lifts her arms in the air, her body twisting and gyrating to the beat. If she stood from her seat, I have zero doubt she would be bent over, shaking her ass like she was up in the club, not a stadium.

"Ay!" She grins at me, her hips winding in the chair. "They got a whole marching band up in here! Fuck around and have me high-stepping it out on that ice."

I laugh at her silly ass, but she's not wrong. As Lil Nas X's "Industry Baby" echoes throughout the huge space, I glance up and to the left. It seems like an entire university marching band fills the top of the stands. They're setting an electric atmosphere, and excitement pumps through my veins, my body moving to the familiar beat as well.

"They're good, right?" the brunette next to me leans over and asks. Grinning, she nods toward the band. "Every home game this month, we've had a different high school band attend and play for the team and fans."

My eyebrow wings high in surprise. "They're high school? Wow. They're amazing!"

She nods. "They really are. Hi, by the way. I'm Patrice Kennedy. My husband is Arthur Kennedy." That name means nothing to me, but I'm guessing he's on the team. "And you are? Sorry if I'm being nosy. This is the first time I've seen you at a game."

"That's because it is my first time at a game." I smile and shake her hand. "Adina Wright. And this is my friend Monica Crawford. Solomon Young invited us."

Her eyes widen as her head cocks to the side. "Solomon?" Slowly, a grin spreads across her lovely face. "Interesting."

Before I can even begin to analyze the meaning of that *interesting*, the arena erupts in deafening cheers, screams, and shouts. The thick walls of the stadium damn near shake with them. A column of blue, green, and white streams out from one end of the rink. People shoot to their feet, the noise ratcheting to an even louder level. Caught up, I stand, too, and along with Noni and Patrice, yell for the Pirates as they take the ice.

Without intentionally doing so, I search out and find Solomon among his teammates. Even among the group of huge men circling the rink, he stands out. And not just because he's the only Black player. It's his power, his grace, his presence that separate him from the others.

And when he skates past our section and his gaze lifts and connects with mine, that power seems to slide right into me, pulsing inside my chest. Throbbing in my pussy. With one look, he's set me on fire, and it takes every ounce of self-control not to twist and shift in my chair, trying to alleviate the ache he stirred.

"Oh, Dina. You in trouble, girl," Noni says in her best Whoopi Goldberg voice, then snickers.

She tells no lies.

My eyes follow him as he skates toward the bench. God, I want that man. I can admit that to myself.

Doesn't mean I'm still not scared shitless.

◆ ◆ ◆

"Wow, what a game!" Patrice clasps her hands together in front of her, a huge grin lighting her face. "The guys killed it tonight! This extends their winning streak to eight games in a row."

I laugh at her enthusiasm. When I met Patrice earlier in the evening, she seemed like a sweet, demure woman. But once the puck dropped and her husband and his team flew into action, all that sweetness went right out the window. She yelled at the ref, booed the other team, and screamed louder than anyone when the Pirates scored. Between her and the fascinating, fast-paced, and fucking brutal game that played out in front of me, I stayed amused.

"And look at your man, doing the damn thing with a Gordie Howe hat trick." Noni nudges me with her elbow. "He was on fire tonight. Hmm. I wonder why."

"Stop it," I growl at her. "And what's a Gordie Howell hat trick?"

"Gordie Howe," Patrice corrects with a smile, and I don't take offense. Hell, if not for her and Noni, I would've been lost the last two and a half hours. "It's when a player gets a goal, an assist, and into a fight in the same game."

"Ohhh."

Yeah, I wouldn't soon forget the sight of Solomon scrapping like the other player tried to steal his mama's purse. A Detroit player slammed Solomon up against the boards in the third period. Patrice explained it was technically legal but still a dirty hit. Probably because the Red Wings were losing 3–1 by then.

Whatever the reason . . . call me basic, but that shit had got me hot. Even thinking back on it has my belly quivering. The other player had tried to hang with Solomon, but he hadn't been a match for him. Solomon had handed his ass to him with blow after blow before the refs and their teammates broke it up.

"I'm going to head on back and meet my husband. It was amazing meeting you two ladies." Patrice pulls me into a hug, surprising me, but I gladly return the embrace. She stands and treats Noni to a hug too. See? When she isn't yelling at the other team and calling them fucking pussies, she's a delight. "I hope you come to another game. I had fun sitting with you. A lot of the time, it's just me and my sister." She gestures to the other woman beside her, who was a lot quieter throughout the game. "Most of the players' wives sit in the luxury box, so it can get a little lonely down here."

"We had a ball too. Hopefully, we'll see you soon," I say, deliberately not promising to attend another game.

I'd been kind of emotionally blackmailed into coming to this one. I enjoyed myself, but still. Besides, I had no clue what this . . . thing with Solomon was. This game might just be a one-off. My chest tightens at that thought, but I deliberately brighten my smile as Patrice and her sister wave goodbye and one of the stadium's staff appears, escorting them out of our row and up the stairs.

"Let's get out of here. I'm starved. That doughboy was great, but my stomach is gnawing at my back." Another of the Pirates' staff waits at the end of the row, I'm guessing to guide us out to our cars, and I'm ready to go.

"You don't want to wait and see Solomon? Thank him for the tickets? Ask him for some di—"

"I will kill you, stuff you in my trunk, and help people look for the body. Play with me if you want to."

"Fiiine. So savage." She looks me up and down. "If Solomon doesn't fuck you, I might be interested in a little friends-with-benefits situation with you."

"I swear, Noni—"

My threat and her cackle are cut short by the yelling of my name. Even above the shouts and chatter of the people steadily and slowly exiting the arena, I hear that sweet, high-pitched voice screaming my name.

A ball of warmth swirls in my chest, expanding and spreading as Khalil climbs down the stairs, heading straight for me. Apprehension seeps through my delight. Good God, little kids have zero sense of self-preservation or fear. While he leaps from step to step, my heart lodges in my throat, worried he's going to fall and tumble down the long flight.

Moving out of my row, I hurriedly climb the stairs to meet him halfway. When we reach the same landing, he throws his arms around my thighs, hugging me tight. Laughing at his over-the-top exuberance, I kneel and squeeze his small, sturdy body. His arms encircle my neck, and for a moment, I inhale his scent that is pure little boy—a bit of sweat, hot dogs, and that little-boy scent that should be bottled up and distributed with happiness diffusers.

"Ms. Dina! You came!"

"Of course I did." I lean back and grin down at him. "You look amazing in your dad's jersey."

The green, blue, and white jersey with his father's number must've been custom made, because it fit him like a glove.

"Thanks, Ms. Dina! You're wearing Daddy's jersey too!"

"Yep, we match."

Khalil looks over my shoulder and behind me. "Where's Fireman Jared? Is he here too?"

"No, he had to work at the fire station tonight, but he'll be here for the next home game. He told me to tell you hi, though."

"Tell him I said *See you later*!"

I laugh. "Sure will."

"Grammy! Grandad!" He turns around and waves at an older couple standing behind him.

I hadn't noticed them until now, and even if he hadn't called them out as his grandparents, I would've recognized them. Her, especially. I admit, after reading Solomon's journal entries, I looked up him and his wife, the curiosity to see what the woman who owned his heart looked like, a relentless itch that wouldn't let go until I satisfied it.

Tall, slender, with thickly lashed hazel eyes and fine bone structure, her mother is an older replica of her daughter, except she has beautiful dark-brown skin, and gray streaks her dark natural curls, while Kendra had a lighter skin tone and chestnut brown curls, courtesy of her Caucasian father.

Another difference? In every picture I saw of Kendra, she was smiling, the very image of a happy, content wife and mother. Her mother? Her reserved, solemn expression has me slowly standing, a heaviness weighing down my belly.

Yeah, they don't like me.

As soon as the thought pops into my head, I dismiss it. These people don't know me, and I definitely don't know them well enough to determine their feelings toward me. Especially when we haven't spoken one word yet. I'm being ridiculous.

Forcing a smile to curve my lips, I stretch out my arm toward Solomon's mother-in-law.

"Hello, I'm Adina Wright. It's very nice to meet you."

There's a beat of hesitation—so quick I could've imagined it.

But I didn't.

Glancing down at my hand before meeting my gaze once again, she clasps mine for a polite, perfunctory shake.

"I'm Caroline Talley. This is my husband, Nathaniel Talley. It's nice to meet you as well."

Mr. Talley takes my hand as well, giving it the same courteous but abrupt shake as his wife. Several moments of silence follow, and it seems thunderous, drowning out the noise in the arena. Even Khalil is quiet, as if sensing the undercurrents of . . . what? Awkwardness, tension? Anger?

"You look familiar, Ms. Wright," Nathaniel finally says. "Have we met before?"

"She's a firelady!" Khalil says, clasping my hand and swinging it back and forth. He likes to do that. He did the same at the firehouse.

His grandparents' gazes briefly dip to our hands. When they're looking at me again, I force myself to stand in place, to not shrink from the pairs of eyes trained on me. One pair might be hazel and the other blue, but both hold the same emotion.

Disapproval.

No, I'm not imagining it.

And I would lay money from my not-so-abundantly-blessed paycheck that they saw the picture of me and Solomon kissing.

Shit.

"Right, that's why you look familiar. The firefighter who came to the office looking for Solomon," Nathaniel says, the tone polite but cold. "I wasn't aware you and my son-in-law were so . . . friendly. He never mentioned it. But you must be, for him to invite you to one of his games."

"He didn't say anything about you meeting Khalil either." Caroline moves forward and cups Khalil's shoulder. And I get the sense that's she staking claim over her grandson. Over her family. "How well do you two know each other?"

I'm almost speechless at the questions that feel more like an interrogation than a friendly getting-to-know-you conversation. But I scramble to gather my thoughts—and my voice.

Clearing my throat, I say, "Uh, not very well. Solomon and Khalil came by the firehouse a couple of days ago. But a person needs just minutes in this little guy's company to fall for him. He's amazing."

I smile down at Khalil, who happily returns it.

"I met all the firemen, Grammy! And Ms. Dina let me slide down the pole. And I played on the fire truck. It was fun!" He's practically bouncing on his feet, and despite the discomfort of this meeting, I chuckle.

Khalil's joy is infectious. Even the ice coating his grandparents' expressions thaws just a bit. But it freezes right back over, harder than ever, when they return their attention to me.

"Our grandson is very special," Nathaniel says. "We're just a little surprised, because Solomon doesn't just let anyone around his son. He's very protective." He pauses. "We all are."

One of the skills a firefighter has to develop is quickly reading the lay of the land. Yes, we get information about a structure's layout before heading into a fire. But once you're in there, with smoke, flames, and gases, things can get disorienting. So yeah, learning how to read your environment is vital.

And that ability isn't exclusive to a fire. Take now for instance. I've just met the Talleys, but I clearly understand that the Talleys are circling the wagons, protecting their own—and warning me away. Letting me know I'm not welcome in their family.

Why their obvious censure stings, I can't begin to explain. Like I said, I don't know these people. And their opinion of me shouldn't matter. Them letting me know I'm not wanted shouldn't mean a thing to me. Damn sure shouldn't hurt me.

But it does.

God, it does.

"Hey, babe. You ready to go? These guys are waiting to take us to our car." Noni appears at my side, and behind me, she lays a hand on my back, slowly circling it. Comforting me.

I blink back the sudden burn of tears. Mortification razes a path through me. Oh hell no. I won't cry in front of these people. I think the fuck not.

"Yes, all ready." I blink against the still-present sting and force a smile. But I know my best friend can see past it. Her pleasant expression doesn't betray a thing she's thinking. But her eyes? They're spitting fire. "Mr. and Mrs. Talley, this is my friend Monica Crawford. Noni, this is Nathaniel and Caroline Talley, Solomon's in-laws."

Noni nods at them, murmuring a greeting that, to my ears, sounds shoved past grinding teeth. She's fiercely loyal, and knowing my girl like I do, it's in the best interest of all if I cut this short. Noni doesn't play about me, and that helps beat back some of my embarrassment and hurt.

"We're going to head out," I say to them before switching my attention to Khalil. My smile is more genuine with him, and that sweet little face does more to smooth balm over my heart. "It was awesome seeing you again, Khalil."

"See you later, Ms. Dina!" He waves his hand, and I do the same.

"If you'll excuse us. Have a great evening," I murmur to the Talleys and ease around them, climbing the stairs to the exit.

And to a space that isn't filled with the choking, acrid scent of disapproval.

Chapter Eleven

SOLOMON

"Great game." I slap Mont on the shoulder on my way out of the locker room, and the younger man jerks up his chin.

He doesn't say much. Definitely not the gregarious chatterbox Harry Morgan, our former goalie, was. But he doesn't need to say a word when he plays like he does. When he originally joined the team, some of us—yeah, me included—cast judgment. Harry was legendary and one of the best in the NHL. Hell, in the history of the game, period. Plus, he was an integral part of this team, a leader, and a friend. We hated losing him even as we were happy for him voluntarily retiring while he was healthy and to spend time with his family. So this quiet, aloof, younger goalie coming in? Nah, we cast judgment. Until we saw Mont Hannah play. He's a fucking god on the ice. A good part of our successful winning season so far is due to him. His positional saves, phenomenal athleticism, and reflexes, as well as his damn near instinctive balance between aggression and patience, have already made him invaluable to us. Shit, Mont can remain selectively nonverbal as long as he keeps playing like a beast.

Besides, I can identify pain and trauma when I see it. And something in Mont's eyes, his closed-off manner . . . yeah, like knows like, and our goalie has secrets, painful secrets, that he's not ready to share.

I follow him out of the locker room, hooking my duffel bag over my shoulder.

"What're you getting into tonight?" Ares Dent, our right defenseman, asks as we near the door.

A snicker comes from behind me. "We all know what you're getting into. Pussy. Lots of pussy," Erik says.

Completely unoffended, Ares grins. The man's a ho and proud of it. "Don't hate on me. I'm willing to share."

And Ares means that. Literally. The defenseman never met a threesome or orgy he didn't love.

"Yeah, I'm good on that." I pull the locker-room door open. "The only plans I have include reading my son a bedtime story, putting him down for the night, and kicking back with a beer."

"Same," Ken adds. "Except for with my wife."

Ares arches an eyebrow. "You reading her a bedtime story too?"

"Damn right. Whatchu think this is?"

I snort while Ares and Erik crack up.

"Ay, Sol, we saw the chick you got caught tonguing down out there. Is that coincidence or . . ." Ares wiggles his eyebrows, looking manic as hell.

"Yeah, I caught that too. She was sitting beside Patrice," Ken adds.

"Nunya business."

"Damn, it's like that." Erik laughs along with the rest of them.

I don't bother answering them. Not when the electrical current that had crackled through me when our eyes met as I skated out on the ice still throbs in my veins.

"Save it. This is Solomon. He's not going to talk about shit if he don't want to." Ken smirks and walks through the open door.

We step out into the hall. Erik and Ken peel off to head toward the media room, where Coach waits with a few other team members to do postgame interviews. I hate that shit and don't pretend otherwise. Which is why Coach and the organization don't make me or Mont participate before or after every game. Not because I don't like it—shit, it comes with the job. The main reason is they know I don't give a fuck about ingratiating myself to reporters, and anything is likely to fly outta my mouth. Especially if they ask a dumb-ass question. And believe me, they always do. Me with my don't-give-a-fuck answers and Mont with his comically short ones? Yeah, they don't push us.

Instead of heading toward the exit, I take the elevator to the floor with the luxury box. Whenever Khalil attends one of my games, I always meet him and my in-laws up there so he won't be caught up in the crush of the postgame crowd. Also, although I try to protect his privacy and don't post pictures of him, fans still recognize Khalil. And some of them have no fucking home training. So to avoid all that—and to avoid my mug shot ending up on somebody's Instagram account—I separate him from most of this.

I reach the luxury box minutes later and enter. Khalil's engrossed in his tablet, probably playing *Minecraft*, but his head pops up when I step into the room.

"Daddy!" He jumps up, tosses the tablet down, and races toward me. I bend down and scoop him up, then hold him against my chest. Hugging him, I kiss his cheek, and his giggle is better than any hat trick. "You did good!"

"Thanks, li'l man." I laugh, moving him to my hip. "Nate, Caroline. Thanks for bringing him to the game and watching him for me."

"You know you don't ever have to thank us for keeping our grandson." Caroline walks over to us and ruffles his tight curls. "He's our heart."

"Daddy, we saw Ms. Dina! I said hi."

"Did you?" I wondered if she would come through. Satisfaction pulses within me. So does a gnawing curiosity to see what she thought about the game.

"Yes, we met her as well," Caroline says, and something in her tone has me tensing and switching my attention to her. "Nice young lady."

"She is," I carefully agree, setting Khalil down on the floor.

"Khalil," Nate says, moving toward us. "Go play on your tablet for a minute, Grandson. Let your grammy and me talk to your daddy for a moment."

"Okay." Khalil races back to his seat, and I wait until he picks his tablet up and is lost in his game before turning back to my in-laws.

"What's up?" I ask, although the stillness crouching right behind my rib cage clues me in that I'm not going to like where this is heading. "Something wrong?"

"Not wrong but . . . concerning," Nate says. He looks at Caroline, and they share some kind of silent communication. "Like Caroline said, we met Ms. Wright. Khalil saw her sitting in the section for the players' family and wanted to go down and speak to her. It caught us off guard, since we didn't know, one, that you were still in contact with her, as you'd told us there was nothing between you two. And two, that you'd invited her to the game."

"Of course, your friends aren't our business. But when it involves Khalil . . ." Caroline trails off.

Anger flares inside me, and it takes everything in me not to tell her that she's right—it isn't their business. But I clench my jaw, trapping the words behind my teeth. Respect and love for them curb my tongue.

"Khalil asked to go to the fire station, and he had a good time. There's no problem or need for concern."

"I disagree, Solomon." Nate crosses his arms, his eyebrows arrowing down in a small frown. "When it has to do with him, we will always be concerned. He's our grandson—"

"And I'm his father." I cut him off before he says something that will make me say fuck the respect and love I have for them. "And I would never do anything to place him in harm's way, physically or emotionally."

"Not intentionally, honey. We know that. Of course we do." Caroline sets a hand on my arm. "And of course we understand that you'll have"—she briefly pauses—"friends. It's unreasonable for us to expect that you won't. But not all of them need to be introduced to your son. He could get confused. And with that picture floating around the internet . . . then for you to bring that same woman around him? He could very easily mistake this Ms. Wright for someone else in your life. In his life."

Part of me agrees with her; I do. No one will ever take Kendra's place in my heart, and I'm for damn sure not trying to bring anyone in my son's orbit for him to think I'm replacing his mother. And that *Not all of them need to be introduced to your son*? What the fuck was that about? They act like I'm out here hoing and then sitting every woman I fuck across from my son at the breakfast table. They know me better than that. Yeah, I get they're hurting, they're protective. Even scared. But that shit gets me hot.

Grabbing on to my temper by my fingernails, I crook my fingers at him and dip my chin in the direction of the box's bar. They follow me over to that corner of the room, placing even more distance between us and Khalil. He's a boy; he doesn't need to be in adult business, even if it's just overhearing us.

Once they stand in front of me, I slide my hands in my pockets. I love the two people standing in front of me. And not just because they're Kendra's parents. Nate welcomed me onto the Pirates, initiating the trade that brought me here. He's been fair, kind, even coaching and guiding me about other business ventures outside of hockey. And Caroline has been the mother figure I didn't know I needed when mine is so far away from me. So yeah, I hide my hands, not wanting them to see my fisted fingers. Not wanting them to guess the anger simmering inside me on a low, steady burn.

"Adina Wright is a friend. And that's all she is." Hell, I can't even call her that, seeing as how every time we're together, we tear into each other. Would that *tearing into each other* remain only verbal? With the way my dick bricks up when I'm within breathing distance of her, I highly doubt that. "But even if that changed, it would be my decision. Just as anything having to do with Khalil and his well-being is my decision. And as his father, you have to trust that he, his happiness and safety, will always come first with me."

"You wouldn't be the first man to have his head turned by a woman. To be caught up and preoccupied by something pretty and new. Like you're his father, we're his grandparents. His mother is—" Nate pauses, swallows, and his jaw flexes. "Was our daughter. That gives us the right to question what's going on in his life, how your *entanglements* will affect him."

Entanglements? Fuck I look like? Jada Pinkett Smith?

"The fact is you're bringing someone into Khalil's life, introducing her, letting him be familiar with her, and Caroline and I have never met her. We don't know anything about her other than she's a firefighter who sought you out and doesn't mind public displays of affection." His mouth twists, and he shakes his head. "The fact that you allowed yourself to forget who you are, *what* you are, and got caught out there on the street like some college kid on spring break speaks volumes to where your head is. So no, forgive us if we're questioning your judgment on this one. We're family. That's what we're here for. To offer you advice and point out when your actions aren't lining up with who you are."

His criticism stings. No, it burns.

"Your argument would mean something if my relationship or non-relationship with Adina would affect Khalil. And while I appreciate everything you've done for me and Khalil, that doesn't give you the right to dictate who I choose to bring into his life. You're right. You don't know Adina. If you did, you wouldn't accuse her of trying to ride my shit for a come-up. She has her own career, and I guarantee you, that picture didn't make anything easier for her. She didn't court the press or give them interviews or try to get paid. And she could've easily done it."

"You're willing to take that chance? I don't know her, but you do? She came to the offices a handful of weeks ago. So that makes you an expert on her? And now she's met your son. Maybe that was the intention all along. A bigger payday."

Why is Nate being so insistent on this? It's pissing me off that neither one of them seems to trust me. Even right after Kendra died, when I was at my worst, I never did anything to endanger Khalil.

"Nate, I—" I growl.

"Solomon, honey." Caroline's soft voice drags my narrowed gaze from Nate, who's about to make me forget that he's my father-in-law and employer. If he keeps questioning my parenthood, he's gonna see another side of me. "All we're asking is that you be a little more conscientious and circumspect. There's never anything wrong with that."

"With all due respect, Caroline, when you're insinuating that I haven't been careful with my son's welfare, then there's something wrong with that." I try to keep the bite out of my voice, but when she blinks, her shoulders dipping, then I figure I wasn't successful.

"The truth is you weren't careful. Or clearheaded. And you're doing it again," Nate snaps. Red flushes his sharp cheekbones, and his blue eyes glitter with anger. "When you invited that woman to the game, did you even stop and consider how that placed you and her back into the public's eye? If any of that gossip had died down, seeing her there at your game would've certainly have stirred it back up. And there were still plenty of people in the arena when Khalil went down to see her. They could've had their phones out, recording that little interaction. And it wouldn't have just been you out on these gossip sites, but him. And he's entirely too young and innocent for the bullshit that comes along with all of this."

So why did you let him go down into the stands, then? The question hovers on my tongue, but I let it die there. But damn, I should be the one pissed—well, more pissed. Instead of telling Khalil no, they let him get his way. So really, whose fault would it have been if he and Adina ended up trending?

I inhale a deep breath. Before I can end this conversation, before any of us say something that can't be taken back, Nate's frown deepens.

"Also, we talked about this too: you're an athlete, Solomon. A celebrity. You don't belong to just yourself. Whatever you do—good, bad, or indifferent—reflects on this organization. On your team and teammates. With the addition of Mont Hannah, the exit of several longtime players and addition of new ones, and talk of conflict in the locker room, we can't afford any distractions that will sidetrack us from the goal of playoffs and the championship. And that includes unnecessary drama that has nothing to do with Pirates hockey."

"Nate, you're the owner of this team, my employer, and my father-in-law. You're the closest thing to a father figure I've had since my own dad passed years ago. And I love and respect you. But what's not going to happen is you telling me how to conduct myself on or off the ice. Or how to live my life. Because at the end of all this shit, I'm a grown-ass man and a father myself. I will fuck all this shit up before I let you talk to me like I'm not either one of them. And I mean that."

I cock my head, silently daring him to speak one more disrespectful word to me. Because we both know he wouldn't pull this with any other player. I'll call him out on that shit if he tries to deny it. And this is the second time he's brought up the team, and that's not sitting right with me. A more suspicious and paranoid mind would think he was low-key threatening my job.

"Now, we gon' end this right here before we say some shit we can't walk back. And I don't want that. I hope you don't either."

I don't wait for them to add anything else. At this point, we're just going around in circles, repeating the same thing, and I get hotter every time they put it out there, just with different adjectives and verbs. Moving around them, I stalk back toward Khalil, who's still engrossed in his game and, thankfully, doesn't seem to have overheard any of our exchange.

"Ay, Khalil, let's head out."

His head pops up, and he grins at me. He grabs his little backpack, stuffs the tablet inside, zips it, then runs toward me. He hands me his bag, then cuts a path to his grandparents. Caroline bends down, scooping him up in a tight hug. Nate stares me down, and I steadily meet it until he looks away to pull Khalil close. He whispers something in li'l man's ear, and Khalil nods so hard he looks like a damn bobblehead. On Black Jesus, he better not be telling him no bullshit.

There was a time that wouldn't even occur to me. Now? I don't put anything past a muthafucka.

Caroline walks Khalil back over to me, concern wrinkling her brow and darkening her eyes. When they reach me, she bends down and places one last kiss on Khalil's cheek.

"We'll see you later, sweetheart," she murmurs to Khalil. As she rises, her gaze connects with mine again, and she whispers low enough for my ears only, "Please don't let this come between us, Solomon."

"Nothing will ever come between us." I brush my mouth over her cheek, then switch my attention to Khalil. "Let's hit it, li'l man."

As we leave and walk down the hall toward the elevator, Khalil's nonstop chatter fills the air, but I'm only half listening. Because my mind is on the woman who showed up tonight and is the center of my first major disagreement with my in-laws.

If anything, what just happened should be a red flag. Should give me an added reason to stop . . . whatever this is between me and Adina. Nate's warnings creep through my mind, and I can't evict them.

But even as those warnings bounce off my skull and fill my ears, I know I'm not going to heed them.

It's much too late for that.

Chapter Twelve

ADINA

With a long, relieved sigh, I dump the last of my grocery bags on the kitchen counter, then retrace my steps down the hall back to the foyer. I close and lock the front door and spend the next fifteen minutes putting away food.

It's only eleven thirty in the morning, but I need another shower. Sometimes I hate my internal alarm clock. After dropping Noni off at home last night, I didn't get home and asleep until a little after one in the morning. Too much whirled in my head, and calming the chaotic tornado of thoughts had taken reruns of *Frasier*, deep breathing, and a couple of Benadryl. But did my body care that I'd just lain down a few hours earlier? Nope. I was up again at 5:30 a.m. and couldn't go back to sleep. So I went to the gym, stopped by my parents', and went shopping. And now I'm ready to chill out on my couch, turn on the extended versions of the *Lord of the Rings* trilogy, and enjoy the rest of my day off.

As I stuff the empty plastic bags into a bigger plastic bag under the sink, I'm planning the food that will accompany my weekly *LOTR* binge when my cell rings. I frown. The ring is generic, so it's no one from my family. And if it's not one of them or Jared, I have no desire to talk to anyone. Especially if it's going to be a request to take my ass out of the house.

I walk past the counter, eyeing the phone like it's about to swing on me. When it stops ringing, I take that as a sign that it couldn't have been that important—but then it starts up again.

Damn.

Telemarketers aren't usually this tenacious. They just leave a useless voicemail to call them back—uh, that's a hell no—and move on to the next sucker that'll answer. Peering down at the screen, I jerk to a halt, and my heart thumps in my chest like a heavyweight champion intent on taking one of my ribs out.

That Asshole.

There's only one person with that name in my phone.

Solomon.

Why is he on my phone? I'm not going to lie. Part of the reason I couldn't sleep was wondering if he would call. I mean, I went to the game, we had that "moment" before his game, and then I saw his son afterward, along with his in-laws, who I'm pretty sure view me as an untrustworthy home-wrecker. Which should sound silly as hell. But nope, I refuse to ignore my intuition. I don't need the Mirror of Galadriel to know Nathaniel and Caroline Talley saw me as an interloper and didn't like that I was familiar with their grandson or son-in-law. Or that they most likely aired their feelings to Solomon.

So am I surprised he didn't call last night to even see if I liked the game? Nope.

But am I just a little hurt? Yep.

Hurt and petty enough to hit End Call so his ass knows I see the call and don't want to talk to him? Oh, most definitely.

At least that's my plan. On the fourth ring, I growl "Dammit" and hit the answer button. Because the need to hear the low sex-at-midnight voice just edges out my need to be trifling.

Shit. If Solomon ever discovers the effect he has on me, I'm fucked.

And not in the wet-ass, quivering-pussy kind of way either.

"Hello."

"Adina."

A beat of silence passes between us. I don't know what he's thinking—I can't tell when I'm in front of him, since those pretty green eyes and prettier face give nothing away, and I for damn sure can't tell over the phone.

On my end, though, I'm absorbing the impact of his voice wrapped around my name. I close my eyes, thankful that he's not in front of me. Because I can't hide the shiver that ripples through me.

"You called me, remember?" I point out. And if my voice is a little snappy, well . . . sexual frustration is a bitch.

"Ay, ma. That mouth gon' write a check your ass can't cash."

Who can't?

Stop being so fucking thirsty, I order my nipples and sex. No damn shame at all.

"I'm sorry. If you called just to issue threats, I got a toilet to wash. A drain to unclog of hair. Paint to watch dry. So if that's all . . ."

A raspy, *menacing* chuckle echoes in my ear, the dark sound shooting fire through my veins. I close my eyes, clench my teeth, fighting to trap the moan that's determined to make a jailbreak.

"Hang up on me if you want to," he says. "I'ma just take that as an invitation to pull up. And Dina, I don't hand out threats. Just IOUs and promises."

Well. Damn.

This man's mouth is so reckless and *rude.* I can't stand it.

Then why are my legs in danger of parting like the Red Sea?

Huge-ass sigh.

"What do you want, Solomon?"

"What're you doing right now?"

"About to go shower, then not move from the couch for the rest of the day unless it's to get food from the DoorDasher."

"Come hang with me."

I jerk the phone away from my ear, stare down at the phone. Blink. Because surely I couldn't have heard what I think I did.

"I'm sorry, what?"

"Come hang with me, ma," he repeats, tone gruffer, but it still sounds way too much like an order than a request.

"Why would I do that?" I ask, and I'm not even being facetious. Hell, I really want to know.

There's a part of me that wants to jump in the car and go to—wherever he lives. But the other, smarter half that values the preservation of my sanity, feelings, and vagina is beaming images of not just that incendiary kiss at the firehouse but the faces of the Talleys.

I have enough drama in my life with this Matt situation. I don't need any from Solomon and his in-laws.

"Because I'm asking," Solomon says. "I can provide more privacy for you here than if I came to you. And because you want to, Adina. You want to come to me."

God.

In this moment, I hate him for being right.

My belly gives a vicious twist, and heat pours into the hollowed-out bottom. How? How does he have me trembling and my pussy clenching around an emptiness that never bothered me until I met him? This need that I've try to deny and then convince myself I couldn't—shouldn't—have is not just physical, though. It's mental. Because this man is a total mindfuck.

The grief he wears like a custom-made Tom Ford suit. The I-don't-give-a-fuck-ness that drips off him along with his confidence that borders on arrogance. The sexual magnetism that has to be etched into his DNA. All of it screws with my head.

"Don't think about it, ma. Don't think about why you shouldn't or why it's a bad idea. Just go with what you want."

I huff out a short dry laugh. "Are you talking to me or to yourself?"

A beat of silence. "Both."

Damn. I wish he'd lied.

If he'd lied, it would've been much easier to say *Sorry, not sorry. Aragorn calleth* and go 'bout my business.

But he'd been honest. Even a little vulnerable. And that glimpse of softness on Solomon Young is my catnip. And my downfall.

I sigh. "Give me an hour."

"See you then, ma."

He ends the call, and I'm still standing in my kitchen, phone pressed to my ear. Shaking my head, I slowly lower the cell, pinching the bridge of my nose.

What did I just agree to?

◆ ◆ ◆

"Holy shit."

Like an awed child, I practically press my nose to the rear window of the black Mercedes-Benz Maybach S600. Ten minutes after he ended the call, Solomon texted and let me know he was sending a car to pick me up. I damn near drooled over the gorgeous luxury car idling at the curb when I stepped out of my house exactly an hour later. The Maybach wasn't the vehicle he'd been driving the evening he popped up at my parents' house.

With Solomon's almost rough mannerisms and blunt speech, I sometimes forget that he's a multimillionaire. But as the driver guides the car up the curved brick driveway and slows to a stop in front of the beautiful and utterly charming white-and-gray-blue Cape-style home, I'm reminded just who I've been dealing with. A wealthy man who can afford a sprawling home in Barrington that sits right on Smith Cove with a perfect view of Narragansett Bay. A three-car garage, a cupola on top of the pitched roof, columns on either side of the arched doorway, glistening bay windows lining the front of the home . . . I don't know what I was expecting, but this wasn't it.

Nerves attack my stomach, twisting, churning. What the hell am I doing here? With him? I don't belong here.

I almost order Demarcus to turn the car around and take me back home. This isn't me. This isn't my world—

Whoa. I straighten away from the window. *Stop that. Right now.*

Between last night and the way his in-laws looked and treated me as if I were beneath them and my first glimpse of this house, I let my insecurities get the best of me. No, I don't earn millions of dollars and can't afford a house that wouldn't be amiss on the pages of a magazine. All my clothes don't bear designer brands either. But I'm educated, I have a job I love most of the time, and I own my own home.

And besides, *he* invited *me* here.

Setting a hand over my stomach, I swallow past a very dry throat. As Demarcus parks the car and exits, coming around to my door, I inhale a deep breath and get my shit together. One thing I've learned about Solomon in the past few weeks—he's very observant. And if I walk up in his house with my shit not together, he'll latch onto that. I can't afford to be vulnerable around him.

Demarcus pulls my door open, holds out his hand to me. With one hand wrapped around my coffee cup, I slip my other one in his, accepting his help to step out of the Maybach. The front door of the house opens. Solomon strolls out, and *dammit.* I should've kept my happy ass at home. With this man looking like a whole endless dinner buffet *and* snack, in a plain white T-shirt that hugs his broad, muscled chest, gray sweatpants that do nothing to hide his dick print, white socks and slides, I'm walking into my doom.

Death by dick. That'll be a new one.

Because I'm not in the habit of lying to myself. As sure as that man is working with *at least* eight inches, if I enter that house, there's an 82 percent chance I'm going to end up stuffed full of him. That knowledge alone should've been enough to keep me out of his car and most definitely out of his home.

Yet here I am. Walking toward him like a mouse heading for that muthafucking cheese. Ready to be taken down.

"Thanks, D," Solomon says to Demarcus, his gaze fully trained on me.

I try my hardest not to fidget under those eerily beautiful eyes. But when his head cocks to the side, eyes scanning over my topknot, bubble coat, gray leggings, and Converse before returning to my face, my cheeks flame hot. Through my clothes, that slow, long perusal strokes over my skin, my breasts, in between my thighs. I shiver. And his eyes narrow a little more, becoming hooded.

Like I said, nothing escapes him.

Oh bitch. It's over for you.

"You coming in, or do you like standing out in the cold?"

I ball up my face. And that quick, he reminds me of why I still have an 18 percent fighting chance.

That loose-ass mouth.

"If you welcome all visitors to your house like that, no wonder you live so far out here in the country."

He slides his hands in the pockets of his sweatpants, and I dare my eyes to follow the motion and get another look at the outline of his dick. Of course, they flip me off and do what they please. And god*damn* . . . that monster is at ease and it's still reaching down his thigh. My poor li'l pussy clutches her pearls.

"No," Solomon says, and I snatch my attention away from his dick and back to his face. "Barrington isn't the country. It's not my fault that anything more than fifteen minutes away is like driving to a different state for anyone born in Providence. And you got it backward, ma. I live out here so I don't have unwelcome visitors. Your ass is gonna sit down and think about it before you decide to pop up on me."

I swallow down my snicker. He's right. Most Providence natives are going to whine if we have to travel fifteen minutes away from anywhere. And even though Barrington is a suburb of Providence, it might as well be Boston.

"Whatever," I mutter. Brilliant comeback, but hey, the man is still standing there hot as fuck and delicious. It's the best I can do.

Striding pass him, I head for the door. He left it open, so I'm accepting that as my *C'mon in.*

I hear murmured words behind me, and then before I can grab the handle of the storm door, Solomon's there, arm reaching around me. He grasps the handle, his other wide, too-warm palm settling low on my back. I briefly close my eyes, absorbing the impact of that touch, the punch of it ricocheting through me. Only when he applies the slightest amount of pressure, silently urging me forward, do I move, embarrassment surging inside me.

As I step inside the huge foyer, my discomfiture evaporates like mist under a morning sun.

"One doesn't simply walk into . . . wow."

"There you go, quoting that movie again." He scoffs, closing the front door. "Your brother mentioned that you only do that when you're nervous. What's got you nervous, ma?"

I squint up at him. "You remember that?"

"There's not much about you I don't remember," he mutters, coming up beside me. My lips part on a soft gasp, but before I can question what that exactly means, he says, "You said an hour, li'l mama. That was closer to two."

I arch an eyebrow at his complaint. "Well, that was before I knew you lived out in the boonies. And I didn't have coffee this morning, so . . ." I hold up my white to-go cup with the blue lettering and green tree symbol.

If you're from the Northeast, it's always Dunkin' Donuts over Starbucks. And for most Rhode Islanders, it's Cumberland Farms—or Cumby's, as we call it—over all of them. Their coffee is the shit.

"Where's Khalil?" I glance toward the stairs, as if his son will come running down them any minute.

"At kindergarten."

"Oh, okay." Wisps of smoke curl and dance inside me. Ignoring them for now, I say, "Damn, Solomon. This is gorgeous."I stop short of twirling in a complete circle like Maria on top of an Austrian mountain in *The Sound of Music* as I peel off my coat and hand it to him. "Almost worth making the trek all the way out here."

He stares at my Annual Mordor Fun Run sweatshirt, with its picture of Frodo and Sam on their trek to Mount Doom.

"Cute shirt."

Since I can't tell if he's being facetious or not, I'm taking it as a compliment.

"I think so."

He snorts and hangs my coat on the end of the stair banister as I continue ogling the beauty of his home. From my vantage point, I can see all the way to the rear of the house and the water sparkling under the early-afternoon sun through floor-to-ceiling windows. A huge living room sits to my left, and unlike what I would've expected for a house this size, the space looks warm and cozy instead of austere and stuffy. The same goes for the second living room to my right. That's some shit, when you need two living rooms. Why anyone would, I have no clue. But the room is as gorgeous as its twin. Fireplaces and obviously expensive but comfortable-looking furniture fill them. My favorite part of the second room? The child's play area right under the bank of bay windows. Toys, books, a small TV, and a video game console claim the space, and my chest gives another of those uncomfortable pinches.

Pressing a hand to the small of my back again, Solomon guides me forward, his socked and my sneakered feet falling soundlessly on the gleaming hardwood floors. We reach the end of the hallway and step into an immaculate kitchen that would be any cooking enthusiast's wet dream. I am not among that number, but still—wow. Top-of-the-line appliances, gray-and-white marble counters and island, what have to be custom light-gray cabinets, a farmhouse-style sink . . . Everything is absolutely perfect.

The floor-to-ceiling windows I glimpsed from the foyer adorn the kitchen and the breakfast nook nestled behind a half wall, and the view beyond is breathtaking. A wide, long expanse of green is broken by a stunning deck with a firepit, low couches and chairs, a huge pool, and a dining area. A latticed covered walkway reaches the deck from another path that curves around the side of the house.

So this is what wealth looks like up close and personal.

"I knew you were paid, but you're *paid* paid." I circle the island, where sits a spread of salad, steaks, baked potatoes, condiments, and a couple of bottles of wine and beer chilling in a bowl of ice. I look up from all that food and gape at him. "Who else did you invite?"

He frowns. "What the hell you talking 'bout, ma? You lucky you in my shit. For damn sure no one else is coming over here."

"I'm lucky I'm in your shit?" I glare at him. But when he stares back at me, completely unperturbed, I shake my head. There's no use in explaining to him that *his rude ass* invited *me* over to his house, not the other way around. "I'm surprised no one has beat your ass yet," I mutter.

"Who?" His chin jerks toward his neck, and *now* he looks offended. "Who's going to beat me, li'l mama?"

Sighing, I pick up a salad and a dinner plate from the set stationed at one end of the island.

"You lucky this food look good as hell and I didn't have a chance to eat lunch. Fortunately, my stomach chewing on my back is louder than the voice telling me to go home. So I'm going to eat this buffet that's enough for five people and just say thank you. And please don't say shit else until I've eaten at least half this steak and all of my potato."

He smirks and picks up plates of his own. I get to piling food on mine, but he's not fooling me. No way he stays silent and lets me eat uninterrupted. It's not in him.

Minutes later, we're sitting across from one another at the square table in the breakfast nook, digging in to our food. The only sounds are our forks and knives scraping against the plates. And the occasional moan. That's from me. Because damn! Everything is perfection.

Another moan slips free, and Solomon picks up a beer bottle and tips it to his mouth. The way a man swallows has never fascinated me before—before Solomon, that is. The purse of his lips over the mouth of the bottle. The smooth up-and-down motion of his Adam's apple in that strong throat. I lightly bite the inside of my bottom lip, wishing it was that tendon running alongside his neck that's under my teeth.

"Make another of those sounds, and that steak ain't the only thing that's going to be spread out across my plate," he almost casually warns.

I blink.

Did he just . . . ? No, he didn't . . .

But the sharp clenching in my lower belly and the scorching heat racing through my veins and pooling into a hot puddle between my thighs assure me that, oh yes, he did.

"Close your mouth, ma." He chuckles, and it's low, a little ominous, a hell of a lot sexy. "Unless you're trying to—"

I pop up a hand, palm out.

"Don't say it. Don't you fucking say it," I growl.

But he doesn't need to finish it. My imagination effortlessly supplies the ending of that sentence, and it includes my tongue and his dick. My mind jumps on the bandwagon, and in slow, vivid motion, a carousel of images parades past my mind's eye.

Me, on my knees, head tipped back, lips parted around the thick, long dick he slowly feeds to me. My scalp tingles as if I can feel his big hands tangled in my hair, tugging.

Lust tumbles through me, and I fight the urge to fidget in my seat. Fight and win.

Thank God.

What did my grandma say? God may not show up when you want him, but he's right on time. I've always been skeptical about that bit of wisdom, but now? Call me a believer.

He lifts his beer for another sip, and I set my fork and knife down on my plate next to my half-eaten steak and decimated baked potato.

Leaning back in my chair, I tilt my head, studying him just as closely as he appears to be looking at me.

"What am I doing here?" I bluntly ask.

He watches me over the bottle, several beats of silence pulsing between us. It's so loud; this room seems like an echo chamber, bouncing it back to us over and over again.

"Because I want to spend some time with you."

"You mean you want to fuck."

"Yeah." My whole body damn near flinches at his bald honesty. He leans back against his chair, hooking an arm over the back while he continues to toy with the beer in his other hand. "You've seen yourself, ma. I don't need to tell you you're fine as fuck. Your sick body—those perfect tits, the ass that made even those ugly-ass uniform pants sexy, thick thighs . . . then there's that face. Your body gets my dick hard, but that face?"

He shifts in his chair, and for a second, the flex and bunch of muscle in his arms, along his chest, snatch my laser focus from his mesmerizing words. But as sensual as that display of power wrapped in flesh is, nothing can distract me for too long from his words. His raw, dirty, and utterly lovely words.

"That face could make a man pray again. Because only something that fucking beautiful could be God created." He licks his full lips, and I almost whimper. Order him not to do that, not one more time. Order him to lick *my* lips. "So yeah, you being you, it's impossible not to wanna fuck. Doesn't mean I was happy about it. Doesn't mean I *wanted* to want to fuck."

"So what changed? When?" I murmur.

Because I'm here, in his house. A house, he admitted himself, that he allows only a select number of people to visit. And I'm not naive enough to believe he asked me to "come to him," as he put it, just to talk.

The question is, Am I willing to take it there? Take it there, knowing he's going to hurt me. That one day I'll be relegated to one of those nameless, faceless women he's fucked in the last couple of years. That his heart, his soul, is owned by a dead woman, and all I'll get from him is a nut.

No, I won't walk away from him unscathed.

And yet I don't get up and run from this house back to the safety of my own. Loneliness hurts, but not in the same way of the kind I'm courting.

"I love my wife." *And there it is.* I battle against the urge, the desperate need to glance away from him. But my pride trumps my fear of him seeing how that statement of fact disturbs me. Jabs a wound in my carefully guarded heart. "Never say never, but other than Khalil, I don't know if I'll ever love anyone as much as I do her. No cap, I don't think I want to love anyone like that again. But that's not what this is."

"Right." I try to hold in the serrated chuckle, but it escapes. And the food I'd just scarfed down sits at the bottom of my stomach like my body's weight in lead. "I'm a fuck. We've established that, thanks."

He doesn't blink at my sarcasm. As a matter of fact, for a long, long moment, he doesn't move at all. Then, in one sinuous motion, he lowers his arm from the back of the chair and straightens. Leaning forward, he props his arms on the table, bracketing his nearly empty plate.

Though he doesn't touch me, I'm still pinned by that green gaze, the force of it heaving on my chest, my neck.

"I said I want to fuck you. But if that's all you were, ma, trust and believe, you wouldn't be in my chair, at my table, with food I cooked, in front of you. I wouldn't go to all this trouble for pussy when it's so easily available for free."

How pathetic am I that his words loosen the suffocating weight on my chest? That I'm soaking up his almost vulgar assurance that I'm more than forgettable ass to him? I can't lie; shame slinks on its belly through me. Shame that I won't, again, get up and walk away. I'm settling for crumbs, and I know it. I know it, and there's a part of me who's willing to gather those measly remnants and hoard them. Because they're all I have of him.

"Cool. Great." Yeah, I'm done. Shoving my chair back, I shoot to my feet, the napkin I'd spread across my lap soundlessly tumbling to the floor. "Thanks for . . . this. It's been real."

Too muthafucking real. God, I wish he'd try to lie to me sometimes. At least it wouldn't make me feel like a walking vagina.

I round the end of the table, but before I can make it to the kitchen door, the sound of his chair scraping across the hardwood precedes his big hand cuffing my upper arm, halting me midstep.

"Wait." I jerk my arm, and he lets me go. But he doesn't move back. No, he shifts closer, and the wide wall of his chest grazes my shoulder. "I didn't finish. Yeah, I want you. We've already established that. But that's not all there is. Shit would be a lot easier, a lot simpler if it were. I can't get you out of my head, ma. Not from the moment I walked into that conference room. And I've tried. God knows I've tried. But I like . . ." He pauses, and his frustration and . . . and *need* seem to bleed out of his pores, cascading over me like the sweetest fragrance. Or pheromone. "I like how I feel when I'm with you. I like how shit quiets in my head. It could be that you have my head so gone and my dick hard that everything else fades into the background. I don't know. I don't give a fuck. All I care about is the pressure cooker inside me that's been on ten since . . . for years . . . eases. I've missed feeling fucking normal, Adina. You've given that to me, and on some real shit? I don't want to give it up. Not right now."

My breath heaves out of me on loud exhalations. Or maybe they're deafening only to me in this too-quiet room.

His lips brush the top of my head, and I can't suppress the shudder ripping through me. Almost hesitantly, he lifts his hand, and it circles around my neck. Just like the first time he did it at the firehouse, my heart stutters in my chest, then races as if there's a gold medal at the end of a track. The air that had been leaving my lungs in loud puffs snags in my throat, trapped by the not tight but firm grip on my throat. That heavy, big palm and the long, thick fingers brand me. Moisture slips out of me, and I know my panties are in a sorry state.

Even as I mentally yell a warning to my body to *stand still*, I unconsciously lean into that hold, pressing his hand harder against my windpipe. Urging him to . . . yeah, no point in denying it. Urging him to tighten his grip, threaten my ability to drag in air.

Like he has the handbook to my body, he does just what I'm silently begging for. And the groan rolling up from my stomach all the way to my throat sounds like a ragged, wrecked thing in the room.

Just as I'm ready to throw all caution—and my drawers—to the wind and ask him to lay me out on this table next to my half-eaten steak, he releases me, and this time, my whimper is in disappointment. His fingers pinch my chin, tipping my head back. I lift my lashes and meet his gaze that seems to glow green fire.

"You feel that?" His hips roll against me, and I swallow back a gasp at the steely, huge length pressed to my hip. My pussy contracts so hard I'm wondering if a vagina can have freaking labor pains. "That's what you do to me. That's what I can't wait to pry that pretty little cunt open with."

My body jerks at the see-you-next-Tuesday. No one's ever used that word with me, and until this moment, I could've sworn I didn't even like it. Turns out, from the way my clit pulses like a separate heartbeat, I'm not too opposed. My lashes flutter, and I'm on the verge of closing them when he pinches my chin harder, demanding my attention. Helplessly, I give it to him.

Hell, right now, he could have my attention, firstborn, and soul.

"Listen to me, li'l mama," he murmurs, and the heat in his gaze dims just a bit. The sight has another feeling trickling through me. Not fear. Dread. Apprehension. "I don't want to hurt you, but I refuse to lie to you either. This"—he grinds his dick against me again—"is all I got to offer you. I'm not promising a relationship; I was being honest when I told you about not wanting another one. Shit, I doubt I have it in me to give that to anyone else again. But I can give you friendship, a willing body to push back the loneliness, just like you do for me."

He frees my chin just enough to rub his thumb over my bottom lip, the caress this side of rough. He's making me feel that touch, leaving an imprint on me. The tip of his thumb breaches my lips, and he scrapes the pad over the edge of my teeth.

A lust that's almost too brutal, too fierce to look at, darkens his face, and it's several seconds before he returns his gaze to mine.

"Call me a selfish muthafucka, Adina, but I want to be the first person whose hands you put your body and trust into since your fiancé. I *need* to be that person. You gave me the first kiss, and I want the rest. I want *you*."

I study the golden brown skin pulled taut over his cheekbones, the bright emerald eyes, the thick sandy-brown curls and beard of the same color that surrounds his lush, full mouth.

I have to give him credit; he *is* honest. A lot of men wouldn't have bothered with that disclaimer. They would've fucked, then played a woman off like she was getting too clingy. But Solomon has always been honest. Sometimes brutally so.

That doesn't mean a fist isn't squeezing the hell out of my heart. Or that a tight curl of foreboding isn't twisting my stomach into knots.

"Say something, ma."

I part my lips, but nothing emerges. Licking my suddenly dry lips, I say, "Thank you for being straightforward with me."

Silently, he looks at me, his eyes roaming over my face.

"That's it?" he asks.

I shake my head. "Can I finish my steak?"

After a protracted moment, he lowers his hand from my face and takes a step back. And I suck in a low, deep breath. How I wish it wasn't saturated with his distinctive scent. The brisk, sharp freshness of the ice he so loves. The undertones of sandalwood and a sensual musk that could be from his soap. But instinct tells me, it's him. His skin. His essence.

"You the one who was about ready to roll up out of here without finishing eating," he reminds me, moving farther away from me.

Gratitude and disappointment skate through me at his easy acceptance of my avoidance. I'm not one who's ever been a pushover, but damn if I don't love that aggressive side of him.

"Yeah, well, I didn't think you'd pack me up a to-go box, so . . ."

He snorts, sinking back down into his chair, and I do the same. For the next half hour, we eat, drink, and don't mention the intense conversation or the proposition he basically placed in my lap.

I have no clue how I keep up my end of the conversation, because my head is all over the place, constantly replaying his words, his admission. Before I realize it, I'm helping him take the dishes over to the sink, ignoring his protest. The whole time we rinse everything and load the dishwasher, I sneak peeks at him like I'm sixteen instead of twenty-six.

Everything in me longs to hop up on that big, powerful body, lock my arms and legs around him, and grind my heavy, swollen pussy over his ridged abdomen. Another slick glance at his sweatpants and dick print, and the emptiness in my sex becomes more pronounced. It spasms around air, and it's almost a physical ache, crying to be filled, stretched, possessed.

My head and body continue their battle, even as we exit the kitchen, walking side by side down the hall toward the front door. I'm quiet, lost in this tug-of-war.

Solomon grabs my coat from the end of the banister and holds it up. Even as I slide my arms through the sleeves, a feeling akin to panic spreads in my chest, reaching to my throat and lower to my belly. A hollow . . . sadness filters through like dark, sticky strings.

Oh God.

I stare at his broad back as he turns toward the front door, reaching for the knob and holding his cell up to his ear. Dimly, as if through a long windy tunnel, I hear him talk to Demarcus. I should be right behind him, ready to walk out that door and into the car his driver is probably about to pull up in, here in the next few minutes.

I'm doing the smart thing. The *right* thing.

I've always prided myself on being reasonably intelligent. In this moment, though? I'm questioning that.

I can walk away, resume the existence I had before Solomon Young came into my life, and probably save myself a world of pain.

Or I can risk popping the bubble that has surrounded me the last year and grab this chance at having this man break me with the pleasure his kisses have already promised. At being touched again, at physically connecting with someone again. At feeling needed, desired.

The choice is clear. The sane one, that is. Protect my peace, my sanity.

But that's just it, isn't it? I've been just *existing*. Going to work, spending time with family and Noni, then returning to an empty home. Alone. I'm so tired of *alone*. When I consider that, the choice isn't so cut and dried.

I want to be the first person whose hands you put your body and trust into since your fiancé. I need *to be that person. You gave me the first kiss, and I want the rest. I want* you.

I want him too. With a hunger that's unwise and probably unhealthy.

"D should be pull—"

"I don't want to go," I blurt out. Did I consciously intend to say that? No. Am I taking it back?

No.

He doesn't immediately reply, and that beat of silence is just long enough for fingers of doubt to drum down my spine.

"If you've changed your—" I stutter, but his narrowed glare and words cut me off.

"Shut up." He stalks forward, eating up the few feet separating us, not stopping until he's all up in my space. His breath that smells and tastes of the beer he just drank brushes my face, and his dick once more nudges me. A whole-body shiver runs through me, and lust is right on its heels, flooding me, setting my whole *being* on fire. "Don't even finish that bullshit you're about to say." He mugs me, and moisture drips out of me at the sight of it. "What I am is mad as fuck right now."

"Why?" I frown.

"Because you're leaving me with only an hour and a half before I have to leave and pick my son up. That's not nearly enough time to fuck your life up like I want to."

He's not bragging or lying. I haven't even had the dick yet, and I know with complete certainty that sex with him will be life changing.

I hike a shoulder in a half shrug as disappointment pinches behind my rib cage. "We can wait until later. That's not—"

Solomon interrupts me again, this time physically shutting me up with a long finger pressed to my lips.

"I've fucked you a hundred different ways in my heads since you stepped out of my car. Twisted this badass body up in as many positions. No way in hell I'm letting you walk out that door without me tasting and beating up this pussy."

He punctuates *this pussy* by cupping me between my legs.

"Holy shit."

My knees buckle, and a shocked cry escapes me. Oh my God, the pleasure—knife sharp, bright, and almost painful—spears me, and I'm no match for it. The heel of his palm presses against my clit, and the tips of his fingers unerringly locate the entrance to my sex, slightly pushing into it. My leggings are no protection against his touch or the pleasure threatening to choke me out. I can't brace myself against it—don't want to. Incredibly, the electric tingling behind my clit heralds the oncoming of an orgasm.

It's been a long time, but *damn*.

"So if that's not what you want, say it now."

Say? As in talk? My brain isn't capable of forming complete sentences with his uncompromising grip on my pussy. Actually speaking? Yeah, not possible.

"Adina?"

He starts to pull his arm back and, panicked, I reach down between us and grab his wrist with both hands, holding him. Right. There.

"Yes."

He cocks his head, his hooded gaze sensual, determined.

"Yes, what?"

Okay, so he's really serious. Consent is sexy, no doubt, but the ironclad grip I have on his wrist should be answer enough. But since he doesn't move, doesn't speak, I guess not.

My impatient huff emerges sounding more like a desperate whimper, but I can't find it in me to care.

"Yes. Taste me. Slide up in me. Fuck. Me." I pause, briefly closing my eyes. "Please."

"Goddamn you, girl," he mutters harshly, but the crush of his mouth on mine not a second later eliminates the harshness from those words.

His tongue thrusts between my lips, tangling with mine, pulling, sucking, demanding. It's a prelude to what he intends to do to my body, and I open wider for him . . . just like I intend on doing with my body.

Sliding free the hand between my thighs and gently but firmly dislodging my hold on him, he bends, cups the backs of my thighs, and hoists me in the air. On a startled cry, I tightly wrap my arms around his neck and legs around his waist. Did he really just throw my ass up here in his arms like I'm a backpack instead of a full-grown woman?

Why yes. Yes, he did.

And it was hot as fuck.

I don't wait for him to kiss me again. This time, I rake my teeth over his beard-covered jaw, then absorb the shudder that ripples through his big body, moan as it vibrates in my pussy that's pressed against his abdomen. Lifting my head, I take his mouth, giving him my tongue and insisting on him returning the favor. And he does. Immediately. Even as he adroitly climbs the stairs, he tries to turn the tables on me, snatch control away from me. I almost let him. He starts to pull his arm back and, panicked, I reach down too. Because damn, if there's one thing

I've learned in the times he's introduced his mouth, tongue, and teeth to me, it's that surrendering feels so fucking good.

But trusting him not to drop me, I slide both hands up over his neck and the back of his head, scraping my nails over his scalp. Another shiver coursing through him is my reward, and as I double fist his short curls, the kiss turns nastier, greedier, rougher.

Hunger rises in me, and it's relentless, coming at me, threatening to swallow me down in great big, ravenous gulps. I'm no match for it. So I stop fighting it and roll my hips, stroking my pussy over his hard stomach. Oh God. I'ma have to twist these leggings to wring them dry by the time I peel them off. They're *soaked.* This man has me running like a damn faucet. And while I should feel a little embarrassed at how needy and hot I am for him, what's the point? As soon as he puts his hand back on my pussy, he's going to discover the truth for himself.

He has me in this state.

He has me on the verge of begging for his fingers, his mouth, his dick.

He has me feeling so alive it's almost painful.

Tightening my grip on his hair, I tilt his head back and to the side, diving deeper between that mean mouth. I claim it, knowing it's a temporal stake. But while it's mine for the next hour or so, I'm branding myself on it, stamping my ownership so he feels it long after I'm gone.

Solomon shifts his hands from my thighs to my ass, squeezing. And it's not tender; it's hard, demanding, possessive. And it drags a whimper out of me, closely followed by another roll of my hips, another drag of my sex, another molten pulse of pleasure.

"Fuck this," he growls against my lips. Seconds later, we reach the second floor, and he has my Converse, leggings, and panties off and tossed aside and my back propped against the wall.

I choke off a surprised cry as he drops to his knees, hauls my legs over his shoulders, spreading me wide. I squirm, afraid of falling. Only his strength holds me up, and I flatten one palm against the wall beside my waist and grab at his shoulder with the other one.

"What you scared for?" He nuzzles the place where my thigh and torso connect, making my breath catch in my throat. And when he places an open-mouthed kiss to the top of my mound, that same breath propels past my lips. "C'mon, ma. You were just throwing that pussy at me; keep that same energy. Ride this mouth."

He slides his tongue over my clit, circling it, then closing his lips and pulling on it. I couldn't hold in my scream even if I wanted to, not with pleasure slamming into me from all sides, from inside me and out. Both of my hands fly to his head, holding him in place, holding him *right there* as I writhe against him, body rolling and bucking, doing just as he demanded.

Riding that mouth.

He hums, and the vibration against my sex is fucking *divine*.

I press my head hard against the wall, closing my eyes. But then I pop them open and bend my head, peering down my chest, stomach, and to the place between my legs that now has a new owner. An owner who's exploring every part of his new territory and claiming it. I can't *not* look as he kisses my pussy like he just took my mouth. Open. Wild. Nasty. So dirty that staring down at his tongue sliding through my folds, then flattening over my clit has my thighs shaking around his ears.

"Fuck, you taste good," he mutters. I've never been one who gets off on praise, but hearing the words on his lips? I've discovered a new kink. Delight blooms inside me, right under the ecstasy, warming my skin. "I could fucking hate you right now for holding out on me, when you walking around here with pussy like this."

That's a first.

And later I might take the time to think about how a man telling me he could hate me while eating me out makes me feel. But at this moment, with his mouth opening wide over my sex and trying to damn near suck it all in at once, I'm a fucking fan.

"Please," I beg, modesty and pride on the floor along with my leggings and panties. "Solomon, I need it. Please."

"Need what, ma? Tell me and use your words."

I grunt, my hips jerking as he shifts me on his shoulders, his long arms reaching up so his hands can cover my breasts. A long, raggedy moan escapes me as his talented and foul-ass fingers pinch my nipples through my sweatshirt, twisting them to the point where pleasure edges up against pain like long-lost friends.

"Adina, talk to me."

Talk? Use words? What the hell are those?

He lifts his head, and my hands fist his short rough-silk curls tighter, trying to force him back to where he belongs.

Where he belongs.

Even *thinking* shit like that will have me messed up. I can't risk that. Not even in the heat of the moment, with his mouth turning me silly.

"I'm not gon' tell you again, ma." His warning deepens the craving for him, excitement shooting through me.

Part of me wants to find out what he'd do if I pushed him to do just that—tell me again. But the thumping heat and moisture leaking out of my pussy hiss at me to shut the fuck up and give him what we want.

"Make me cum, Solomon," I whisper. "Make me cum hard. I need it."

It's been so long since I've had an orgasm that wasn't self-delivered. I'm trembling with the anticipation, the hunger.

"Say less."

His hands abandon my breasts and fall to my thighs, tilting my hips, spreading me wider. And he thrusts his tongue inside me, shattering my mind in the process.

"*Fuck.*" I fold over, trusting him to keep me lifted . . . keep me safe.

One of my hands remains gripping his hair, and the other claws at his shirt-covered back. That's what he's transformed me into—a scratching, clawing, sexual creature chasing an orgasm. Currents race from the back of my neck, down my spine to my ass and even to the soles of my feet. God, I could light up a whole damn street grid with the electricity running through me.

He moans, and I swear my pussy swallows it along with his tongue. There's something about Solomon . . . I don't know. Maybe the sincere, unshakable knowledge that my body, my pleasure are safe with him, even if my heart isn't. It releases this lock that has trapped me frozen behind grief, guilt, and fear. He frees me to share this part of myself—a part that has been gone for so long I'd forgotten she existed—without worry or shame.

And as he licks a path back to my clit, wagging his tongue back and forth, kissing it, sucking it, I release everything.

Every inhibition.

Every concern.

Every piece of me.

"Give it to me, Dina. Gimme my nut."

I give it to him.

Pleasure combusts, sending me scattering in every direction, flying so high, so far, I hear my scream from a distance. I should be afraid of something this powerful, this huge. But I'm not. I'm grateful. I'm so fucking grateful.

I'm still floating, waiting for the many pieces of myself to find their way back, when he hikes me in his arms again, this time bridal-style, and carries me down a hall. I turn my face into his neck, opening my mouth over the taut skin there and lazily draw circles over his skin, humming at the delicious musk that greets my tongue and nose.

His arms squeeze me close, and I take that as encouragement to suck lightly, graze my teeth over him. Am I trying to mark him? I don't know. Don't want to think about how any brand would be as temporary as what we're doing here. Not permanent. He's already been permanently claimed, and not by me.

I shut my eyes, dropping my forehead to his wide shoulder. *Stay in the moment. Stay in the moment.* This was about sex. About beating back the loneliness for a little while. About—how had he put it?—feeling normal again.

It isn't until he sets me down on my feet that I open my eyes and, lifting my head, survey the bedroom we entered. The big sleigh bed piled high with soft gray and cream pillows and a comforter to match. A wardrobe that wouldn't surprise me if it contained a portal to another land sat in one corner. A small dove gray couch and smoked-glass coffee table form a sitting area on the other side of the room. Matching bedside tables and a vanity.

It's luxurious.

It's pretty.

It's impersonal and obviously a guest room.

There aren't any pictures, no personal knickknacks, no random items like change or receipts thrown on the bedside table to mark this room as a room where someone regularly lays their head.

He took me to a guest room in his home. And there can only be one reason why.

His bedroom is his sacred space where he shared a place and bed with his wife. I don't belong there. That's not a domain meant for me.

A hurt I have no business feeling wells up in me, knotting so hard and tight in my belly I barely stifle a groan. Pain throbs in my chest like someone slammed their fist there. Instead of ignoring it, I embrace it.

I needed this reminder that this is just sex. No matter how greedily he ate me, how gently he held me, how tenderly he touches me, this is. Just. Sex.

He can't put me in second behind his wife because I'm not vying to place.

So I should be thankful he brought me here. At least in this room, this bed, the ghost that haunts him and the rest of the house will be shut out. There aren't any memories in this space, and I need to be grateful for that.

I repeat that to myself as he skims his hands up my hips, over my stomach, slipping beneath my sweatshirt to raise it and tug it over my head. My bra quickly follows, and I'm standing naked and vulnerable in front of him while he remains fully clothed.

Oh God. There's so much meaning in that, I'm scared to mentally touch it.

"Hey." His hard, big hand pinches my chin, tilting it up, while his other hand slides into my hair, gripping the curls so tight my scalp tingles. I draw in a breath, my lashes fluttering down at the pinpricks of pleasure dusted in pain that echo in my pussy. "Where're you in your head?"

I shake my head. Well, as much as his hold will allow it. But he's not accepting that nonverbal answer, if his tugging my head farther back is any indication.

He mugs me, his narrowed gaze scouring my face before returning to me.

"One thing you not gon' do is lie to me. Just tell me you don't feel like talking about it, and then we can talk about it."

Despite the doubts and hurt still clinging to me like damp fog at dawn, I snort.

"You know that doesn't make any damn sense, right?"

He shrugs, but he also doesn't release his grip on my hair or chin.

"Where'd you go, Dina?"

It's on the tip of my tongue to say *nothing* or make up a lie on the fly. But staring into his beautiful green eyes, I can't. I may not be able to give him the entire truth, but I can give him some of it.

Sighing, I dampen my bottom lip with my tongue and watch his stare follow the motion like a cat studying a skittish mouse.

"I'm a little scared of what this will mean for me, how I'll change," I whisper.

His gaze immediately softens, and on Solomon, the expression is fucking *mystifying*. My heart throws a haymaker against my ribs, and I almost stumble backward from the power of it. Only his grip steadies me, supports me.

"Yeah, baby, I get it. You think this shit don't scare me either?" My eyes balloon, and he gives a low laugh, his thumb rubbing over my bottom lip, swiping through the moisture there. "This might not be my first time fucking since . . ." He doesn't complete that sentence and he doesn't need to. I know very well what that *since* means. "But it's the first time I give a fuck about it. The first time I'll look in a woman's eyes while I'm deep in her pussy and know who she is. The first time it'll mean something past getting off."

My throat closes tight, and I stare up at him, robbed of words and thoughts at his rumbled confession. It doesn't take away all the hurt from being banished to this impersonal room, but damn if it doesn't ease most of it.

God, I'm in so much trouble. So much.

He releases my chin and lowers his hand to my throat, to the necklace with the pendant resting just below my collarbone.

"What's this?" He brushes his fingertips over the image of Saint Florian.

"Saint Florian medal." My throat tightens further, but for a different reason this time. His touching Keshaun's necklace. I clench my jaw, battling back the guilt and shame trying to shove their way to the forefront of my mind, my heart. I gently nudge his hand away from it, closing my fingers around it. "The patron saint of firefighters. It was . . . Keshaun's."

His body stiffens, and for a moment, I think he's going to jump back and away from me. His eyes blaze green fire as it remains fixed on the necklace. When he lifts his eyes to me, long moments later, it's me who has the urge to shift back and away. The objection lurches to my tongue. I'm in the house where he lived with his wife; this place is a whole tribute to her. He better not ask me to remove my one connection to my dead fiancé . . .

As quick as that heat flared, it banks, and he strides around me, heading for the do—bed.

I frown.

I didn't imagine that anger in his eyes, and I would've bet my beloved Argonath bookends that he was leaving the room. But no.

He sinks down on the bed, legs sprawled and spread wide, one palm planted on the mattress beside his hip and the other beckoning me over.

I wait for the instinctive bust of irritation at that impervious curl of his fingers, like he's a king summoning his subject. But apparently my pride is now bowed down to the power of the pussy, because she is doing all the thinking. My walls spasm, clenching as if I didn't just experience the most cataclysmic orgasm of my life. And since he is named after a king, it shouldn't be a wonder that my vagina has prostrated herself in front of him.

My feet move forward, carrying me the short distance until I'm standing between his powerful thighs. He traces two fingers down my throat, over my collarbone—evading my necklace, I notice—around each of my breasts, pausing to swirl a caress around my nipples, before trailing a path down my stomach and over to my hip. I glance down, halfway expecting to see the road map that feels branded into my skin.

"I'm clean, Adina. Had a physical at the beginning of the season, and I haven't been with anyone else in weeks. Even then, I used a condom. Always have. I can't lie; I don't want anything between my dick and this pretty-ass pussy. But if that's not where you at, what you want, then I can go get a condom. Your choice."

"I'm on the pill," I breathe, my belly constricting and sex pulsing at the thought of him pushing inside me, bare, nothing separating us. "And I haven't been with—"

"Yeah, I know," he softly and yet sharply cuts me off. "Need you to say it. You good with me going up in you raw?"

"Yes." Craving that more than I want to dwell on.

He lifts his arms, reaches behind him, and drags his T-shirt off and over his head. I sink my teeth into my bottom lip, not wanting to be shook by that. But *ohhh bitch*, I am.

"Climb up then and get your dick."

Your dick.

I shiver, knowing how he meant it, but my foolish heart and pussy take it another way.

Sex. This is about sex.

Hot, dirty, mind-warping sex, but still . . .

I repeat the mantra in my head as I obey him, straddling his thighs, feeling the pull in my own as they spread over his.

And as he dips a hand in his sweatpants and pulls his dick free, I notch up the volume and speed until it's echoing in my head on ten.

Goddamn.

He's beautiful. Long, thick, deliciously veined, and a couple of shades darker than his light-brown skin. The sight of it sends swirls of heat and flickers of fear skating through me.

He's going to rearrange my fucking insides with that thing.

With him fisting and pumping that too-big column, it only seems to grow before my eyes. Not even the glistening beads of precum that have my mouth watering for a taste can stifle the heap of *hell naw* piling on top of itself in my belly.

"What the hell you shaking your head for?" He snorts, and when he mentions it, I realize that, yep, I was really shaking my head. "All that bark you got, and no bite behind it? Ma, you gon' take this dick." He cups my ass, pressing until I lift on my knees. Angling my hips forward and his length forward, he slides that monster through my folds, wetting himself up. I tip my head backward, loosing a lush, low moan and then a whimper as that bulbous, wide head bumps my clit. Shuddering, I grab at his shoulders, holding myself steady. "Look at you, playing. Over here shaking an' shit. Get on this dick, baby. And you better fuck it like you own it."

He emphasizes that command with a slap to my ass cheek, and I jolt at the flare of pain and flash of heat that almost immediately follow.

With his urging, I rise higher on my knees, and he tucks the head at my soaking-wet entrance. Between his gravelly, sexy voice, and dirty, uncompromising words, and that pop to my flesh, I'm damn near dripping.

He fists the lower half of his dick, and then he lifts his gaze to mine, refusing to let go. And with me staring into those gorgeous green depths, I *get on this dick*.

I sink down, and my pussy parts, giving way. Flickers of pain lick at me, overwhelming the pleasure that's been swarming my veins, my blood. I frown and can't contain my whimper. Fuck. And it's just the tip inside me.

There's no way . . . I can't . . .

"Yeah, you can," Solomon growls. And, like the one on mine, a frown darkens his face. But his eyes belie the fierceness of it. They're heated, nearly blazing bright, but there's a . . . tenderness there too. A tenderness that seems out of place for *just sex*. "You're going to do it too. This was made for you. It's yours. Now be a bad bitch and take it."

There goes my praise kink again, making itself known.

On a moan, I press down, and he surges up. He doesn't stop, and neither do I. Though my entire body shakes with the pressure and dense mingling of pain and pleasure, we don't pause until he's fully buried inside me.

Oh God. *OhGodOhGodOhGod.*

I'm too full. Too overwhelmed. Too . . . *everything*.

In this moment, I'm no longer only Adina but Adina *and* Solomon. We're melded so tight I can't tell where I end and he begins.

And that scares the shit out of me.

"On you," he grinds out, the strain from holding still evident in his voice and in the taut lines of his face and body.

Deep inside me, he throbs, that beautiful big dick letting me know he's ready to do some damage. But only when I am too.

Tentatively, I circle my hips and gasp at the wisps of pain but the wave of sweet, terrible pleasure. *Damn.* I don't think I've ever . . .

I shut that thought down. This is us in here, joined. No room for the past or future. Just the present, and that's what I'm focusing on.

Well, that and this dick.

Digging my nails into his solid shoulders, I slowly lift my hips, sliding up his thick length until only the head remains notched inside me. Then both of our moans saturate the room as I slide all the way back down.

"Oh fuck," I breathe, dropping my head back on my shoulders. I repeat the ride. Again. Then once more. Every glide has me moving more sure, more confidently. And has ecstasy lapping at me in greedy licks. "Oh fuck," I whisper again.

His low, positively wicked chuckle reverberates against my nipples, inside my sex. I feel him every—damn—where.

I find my rhythm, and soon I'm lost in him, in me, in this filthy, beautiful fucking. He leans forward, capturing a nipple between his lips and teeth, worrying it, while his other hand cradles, plumps, and plucks at the breast waiting for the attention from his mouth. It all just adds to the sensory overload threatening to take me under. So far under I won't find my way back.

"Goddamn, ma." He lifts his head after placing an oddly gentle kiss on the beaded tip. Sliding a hand up the middle of my chest, he circles it around my neck, and I almost cry from that possessive, primal touch. Lightly squeezing and ripping a soft cry from me, he stares down between us, where he's driving inside me at a speed and pace that I fight to keep up with. "Why you got this good-ass pussy?" he snarls. "This good-ass, wet pussy."

With each word of praise, he pounds into me, showing neither one of us any mercy.

He promised to beat up my pussy, and if Solomon Young isn't anything else, he's a man of his word. The sound of our raw, hard, and fierce fucking fills the room. His low grunts, my staccato whimpers, the thick, sticky sound of his dick in my sex, the wet slap of skin against skin.

My fingers curl around his wrist, and I dig my nails in there, urging him to tighten his own grip. With a low, dark rumble, he does. He squeezes until my breath is trapped beneath his hand.

And that's all it takes to tip me over.

On a strangled scream, I come, splintering, spinning. I'm in a free fall, and I don't care how far I plummet or how hard I land. Nothing matters except the pleasure breaking me, reshaping me. Renewing me.

Beneath me, Solomon slams up into me, his dick sending electric shots through my pussy, my body. After a moment, he goes rigid beneath me, and he throbs high and deep inside me. And the pulses of cum coating my pussy trigger aftershocks to shiver through and over me.

My name is a furious growl in my ear, and then . . . nothing.

Perfect nothing.

Chapter Thirteen

SOLOMON

If anyone had told me even weeks ago that after I fucked the hell out of the firewoman who showed up at the arena, we would end up sitting in McDonald's while my son went wild in the play area, I would've told them to hold on to that good Kush they were obviously smoking so I could get a hit once the season's over.

Khalil's excited yells reach us as he slides down one of the colorful tubes, and I avoid analyzing the unexpected turn of events—and the shadowy, elusive emotion playing hide-and-seek with my heart.

This is so not how I imagined my day would end up.

Yeah, when I issued the invitation for her to join me at the house, I hadn't anticipated sex would be the outcome. But I'd hoped. Hell, Adina's bad as fuck, and having her in my private space that very few people could claim they'd entered? Hell yeah, I'd hoped.

Yet if it ended up going that way, I saw me sending her back to Providence with Demarcus. Definitely not inviting her to ride with me to pick up Khalil from school and take him to McDonald's. At the time, I rationalized it as running late after sex and a shower.

Low-key, I could've had Demarcus in my driveway in minutes. Charge it to the loose, much-needed peace after a good fuck. But the truth is I didn't want to send her home; I wanted to keep her just a little while longer. Bask in this place a little longer.

Not gonna lie, though. When I returned to the car after collecting Khalil, and he climbed in and saw Adina, his delight and excitement had a tangled mess of emotions colliding and winding around my rib cage.

Satisfaction and amusement that he obviously likes Adina and enjoys being in her company.

Guilt, sadness, and maybe a little disgruntlement that he obviously likes Adina and enjoys being in her company.

A selfish part of me wanted that special, happy response to be only for his mother.

Selfish because his mother's not here and he deserves the affection from someone other than me and his grandparents or my teammates. I shouldn't begrudge my son that.

But I also can't allow him to become attached to Adina. Both of us understand what this is. And even if I wanted it to be more, it couldn't be her, no matter how hard she makes my dick or how she brings me some semblance of quiet.

The very nature of her job puts her in the direct path of danger. Most people try their damnedest to avoid it, but she literally runs to and into it. She puts her life on the line every day she goes into work. I lost Kendra to a random accident. Contemplating a future with a woman who willingly runs into burning buildings for a living? No, I can't do it. I *won't* do it. That would be setting me or my son up to experience a pain I've barely survived once. I won't do it again.

So yeah, this is sex and companionship until it isn't.

Even as the thought runs through my head, I remember that moment in the guest room when my gaze first settled on the pendant hanging around her neck. In that second of anger, of—fuck me—possessiveness and jealousy, it hadn't felt like just sex and companionship. I'd wanted to snatch it from her neck, burying it along with any thoughts of her former fiancé.

But seeing as how I had her in my fucking guest room because I couldn't sleep with her in my own bed, I had no cause or right to do that.

I drop my gaze to her throat, where the necklace is hidden beneath her sweatshirt.

And damn if that need doesn't flicker, scratch at me.

Fuck.

"He's such a happy little boy," Adina says, and I look across the table at her, faintly surprised and thankful that she echoes some of my thoughts. It drags me out of my fucked-up head. "That's a testament to you as a father."

"He's been through a lot," I murmur. "Sometimes I wonder how much he really understands. He was just three when he lost his mother. I think he'll really grasp it when he's a little older and begins to see the difference in how our family looks compared to other kids'. Still, between me and his grandparents, we try to compensate and hope he doesn't lack any love."

She nods. "He seems so friendly and open. I don't know that much about kids, but I was one. To me, that's a sign that he's secure in who he is, and that comes from being so well loved and protected that he's confident in himself."

She falls silent, and her words stroke something in me, soothing a worry that's never far from my mind. Even with the support of Nate and Caroline, being a single father is hard. Being unexpectedly and cruelly thrust into single fatherhood is even harder. And I'm always anxious that my inexperience and fumbling will negatively affect him.

"Thank you," I say quietly.

Again, she nods and tilts her head. "Speaking of his grandparents, I met them last night after the game. They brought Khalil down to the stands to see me."

"Yeah, they mentioned it."

An emotion passes over her face, there and gone too fast for me to catch and decrypt.

After a moment, she inhales a deep breath, and her gaze flickers to the remnants of the fish sandwich and fries she ate, before lifting to me again.

"I don't think they cared for me," she says carefully.

"Don't take it personally." For a moment, I considered evading the truth or dismissing her observation. But she's a smart woman; she would peep that lie for what it was, and besides, there's no reason to hide the truth from her. It's not like she and my in-laws will be running in the same circles. This thing between us is just that—between us. Not anyone else's business but ours. "They're very . . . protective of Khalil." And possessive. "He's their only grandchild, and they have a tough time accepting anyone new around him. Especially if they don't know them."

"Especially if that person is a woman." A small smile lifts the corner of her mouth, but it bothers me. There's nothing humorous in it.

"That's probably true. But I wouldn't know for certain, since I've never brought another woman around him, other than my teammates' wives."

Adina glances away from me again, and her throat works on a swallow. I almost tell her not to read too much into that, but I'm not that much of an asshole. Well . . . actually, I am. But I don't want to be that toward her. Besides, I made my position clear on what this is between us. There's no need to repeat it.

"I can understand their hesitation and reserve. I can only imagine if I was in their position, I would feel the same." She goes quiet again, and after a few seconds, shakes her head and returns her pretty brown gaze to me. A more genuine smile ghosts across her mouth. "When I first saw Khalil, I thought he was your mini-me. But after meeting his grandmother, I can definitely see he shares her features too."

"Yeah, he does. Which pisses my mother off to no end, since I'm a replica of my father. She says everyone edged her out of her own grandson." Her soft laughter joins mine. "It's tough on her because she still lives in Halifax and doesn't get to see him but two or three times a year, when I take him for a visit after the season ends or she and my sister fly here."

"Canada?"

I smirk. "You trying to tell me you didn't google me, ma?"

"No." She balls up her face. "Okay, yeah, I did. But," she adds over my snort, "I only read about your career, not your personal background."

"Okay."

"I'm serious." She laughs, holding up her hands. "I didn't. Going farther than that would've meant . . ."

I hike an eyebrow. "That you were interested?"

She smacks her lips, scowling at me. "Well, yeah. It meant exactly that."

Chuckling, I return my attention to the play area, checking on Khalil. It doesn't take long to scope him out. He's found himself a friend—a couple of them. A little girl and boy scramble after him in one of the tubes, and their laughter and loud chatter can be heard all the way inside the restaurant. My son has never met a stranger. I'm both proud of and nervous about that.

"If your mom is back in Canada, I'm assuming you were born there. How long have you lived in the States?" she asks.

"Seven years. I was twenty-three when I left the Edmonton Oilers and joined the Pirates. Another thing my mother's still pissed at." I snort. "Hockey is serious for us Canadians. Hell, I have friends who stopped talking to other family members because they switched up on teams. We don't play that shit. And for me to leave the Oilers for the Pirates? Yeah, I'm lucky I'm her only son, otherwise she wouldn't even acknowledge me on the street if I passed her."

Adina blinks. Then a smile slowly spreads across her face, blooming into a wide grin. The laughter that rolls out of her is pure and joyful. I'm caught up in that sound, in her beautiful face, even more beautiful in true amusement than she is midorgasm.

And she is fucking gorgeous midorgasm.

"I wish my father and brothers could hear that. They would be all over your ass, finding out you abandoned the family ship."

I grimace. "Then this stays here between us, right? Cone of silence?"

"Sure."

"I don't trust that shit for a minute." I scoff, shaking my head. "But yeah, regardless of her complaining, my mom is glad to come here—to the States—to visit. She's lived in Halifax for thirty years, but she's originally from Chesapeake, Virginia. My father, who's from Canada, had been going to college there when they met. They married right after he graduated. When they found out she was pregnant with me, they left and returned to Canada. Mom said the racism here scared him and he wanted to raise his family back home." I huff out a short laugh. "Granted, the racism there isn't the same as it is in the US. But make no mistake, it exists. It's more polite but still manages to maintain the viciousness required to be racist. Canada is a big-ass gaslighter. Always pointing the finger at the US instead of looking within itself." I shrug. "But as a French Canadian, my father hadn't experienced it. Not until he brought his Black wife home and raised his Black son, that is."

"I didn't want to ask," she murmurs. "It seems rude, but I wondered . . ."

I nod, the corner of my mouth lifting, already guessing what she means.

"Yeah, I get that all the time. Ever since I was a kid. People trying to figure out *what* I am before giving a damn about *who* I am."

Adina flinches. "I'm sorry. I didn't mean—"

I cut off her apology with a wave of my hand. "Nah, I didn't mean that as a dig toward you. Shit, you didn't dislike me based on whose blood runs through my veins. In your case, it was the *who* that formed your opinion of me. About that . . ."

I check for Khalil again, and after spotting him running past the large window, I turn back to Adina.

"It's me who has to apologize, and it's long overdue." A sick churning starts up in my gut, and I reach for my soda, taking a long sip. Wishing it was something much stronger. "Our first meeting, you called me out on my abusive language. That fucked with me. I've been called a lot of shit in my life—asshole, bastard, muthafucka. And I'm not gonna lie, I've probably earned every one of 'em, both on and off the ice. But never have I been called abusive, and it terrifies me that I was so cruel, my mouth so loose, that you felt that way. No, that it affected you that way. I'm sorry, ma. I promised myself a long time ago that I would ne—" I break off, but it's too late.

Understanding dawns in her eyes, and her face softens. Falling against the back of the seat, she doesn't say anything, granting me room to continue or change the subject. I appreciate that. Most people would rush in with questions, and I've only spoken about the ugly details of my past with Kendra.

And now Adina.

"I watched my mother survive an abusive relationship. That changes a person, one way or another. For me, I vowed never to put my hands on a woman in anger or verbally tear her down, stripping her of confidence, power, and spirit. It's also why I've never, and will never, spank Khalil."

Her eyes slightly widen in surprise. "Your father . . . ?"

I vehemently shake my head. "Never. Fuck no. He died when I was eight and my sister, Mia, four. But I still remember him. Remember the man he was. Remember how much he worshipped my mother and us. Nah. He'd cut off his own hands before hitting any of us, but especially Mom." I exhale, dragging a hand down my face and beard, the edge of my hand hitting the brim of the baseball cap I wear. "Like I said, he died when I was eight." Funny how I can say *that word* in relation to my dad but not to Kendra. "Afterward, my mom fell apart. In that year directly after, it was me getting Mia up for school, dressing her, fixing our breakfast and lunches. Same thing for after school. Mom rarely came out of the bedroom she shared with our father. And when she did, it was like something in her . . . shifted. The first boyfriend came around two years after Dad died. He was a piece of shit who had a hand problem. When they broke up came boyfriend number two. His mouth was a chain saw, and he had no problem directing the shit that came out at my mother. When she eventually broke up with him, a month later, Brian showed up."

At just the thought of him, my jaw clenches. I don't realize my fists have followed suit until Adina covers them with her hands. I stare down at her smaller, delicate fingers, spread out over my larger hands, and without intending to, I flip mine over, encompassing hers. It almost feels like I cling to her, holding on while taking this fucked-up trip into my past.

"Brian." I loose a dry chuckle that sounds and feels like sandpaper scratching my throat. "He had an issue with his hands and mouth. He also lasted longer than the two before him. Hearing your mother cry as a grown man slaps and kicks her, and being helpless, powerless to stop him or help her? It's fucking torture. Then, I couldn't understand why she put up with it. Why my sister and I weren't enough that she had to keep bringing these muthafuckas into our home, our lives. It wasn't until I was older that I realized that, after losing my father, she'd been so lonely, in so much pain, that she'd been searching for anything, anyone to fill the void he left behind. To replace the love they shared."

That understanding extinguished the anger burning inside me for a good part of my teenage years. Sympathy replaced it. But witnessing how she fell apart, how she was never the same without Dad—and how losing him made her accept some unthinkable shit—put me off love for years. I wanted no part of something that held that much power over me.

But then I met Kendra.

And then I lost her.

And then I really understood.

"I know what I felt after Keshaun died. Yet I still can't imagine the pain and grief she experienced, having loved and lived with your father for so long. Having a family with him." Her fingers tighten on mine. "Is she still with Brian?"

"No." Pride streams through me. Pride and love for the strongest woman I know. "He lasted a year before he put his hands on me. One day after the bus dropped me off, I came home to the sound of him beating her. Mia had stayed home from school that day, sick. And I could hear her crying even before I opened the door. Seeing Brian crouched over my mother wasn't something new. But this day . . . maybe it was seeing Mom curled up so he couldn't hit her face and hearing Mia's screams. Whatever it was, I threw myself at that bastard. I was big for an eleven-year-old, but he was a grown man, and he easily threw me off of him. Backhanded me. And that was it. Mom picked up this glass vase from the coffee table and smashed it over his head. When he came to, the police had arrived, and we never saw him again. Come for her kids, and he saw another side of her. That was also the end of the boyfriends. At least until I was older, bigger. My mom isn't just a survivor; she's a warrior. And I couldn't love her more. She raised us on her own, never complaining, always showing up. That's my rock, right there."

A fierce frown darkens Adina's face. "Good," she growls. "I hope she left a scar, so whenever he looks in the mirror, he's reminded that she beat his ass for touching her and her son."

Despite the heavy topic, I chuckle.

"Ay, you bloodthirsty as fuck."

She hikes her chin up, loosing her hold on me and folding her arms on the table.

"I get it, honestly." She smirks. "I wish someone would put their hands on me or my mother. My father and brothers would flip all this shit over. They don't play about us." Her smile softens, then disappears, and her face sobers. "She had you, but I can't help but wish she had brothers, a father. Hell, cousins. But it doesn't sound like she had that support system."

I shake my head. "No, she didn't. Most of her family still lives in Virginia, and even then it's just her, my grandmother, a couple of uncles, and some cousins. Her side isn't that huge. And my father's side . . ." I comb my fingers through my beard, heat starting to prickle at my skin. Thoughts of those assholes never fail to elicit that response. "His family, especially his parents, didn't want anything to do with their son's Black wife or children. Nah, we were on our own. Not that we didn't have a tight-knit community in Halifax. Where we lived—North Preston—is Canada's largest Black community. And it's just that, a community. We take care of each other, and after my father died, the people in our neighborhood gathered around Mom and us. So in a sense, I had a big-ass family of aunts, uncles, and cousins. I believe if my neighbors had known what was going on in our house, they would've shown the fuck out. But Mom didn't say anything. Didn't ask for help. And Dad's side for damn sure wasn't coming to North Preston to find out about their son's wife and kids."

"I'm surprised they didn't come out the woodwork when you went pro," she mutters, and a glance at that lovely face and the fire in those eyes gives me a smile that would usually never grace my mouth when talking about the Youngs.

Turning back to look at the play area, I find Khalil and am completely unsurprised to find more children gathered around him. He's like a magnet and, even at five, a leader. The confidence in him, the intelligence, the loving spirit—I'm in awe of him, and the fact that Kendra and I created him. How anyone could look at that beautiful, amazing boy and dislike him on sight because of his skin? I've been on this earth thirty years and it still astounds me.

"My father's brother and a few cousins did," I quietly say. "But I didn't have shit for them. How're you gonna show up for me, your Black nephew and cousin, but ignore my mother, my sister? They got me fucked up. And make no mistake. I'm a Black man. How did Obama put it? I've been seen *and* treated like a Black man all my life by society. And I'm fucking proud of it. And here, in this climate, that's how I'm raising my son. I'ma teach him to move and operate as a Black man in this world we live in. Damn if I'm going to have him out here unprepared for how people come for him simply because of who he is."

Mia, on the other hand, identifies as biracial. And hell, I'm cool with that, respect it and don't give her any shit about it. I remember reading a study a few years back that more biracial women identify as such, while more biracial men identify as Black. I can't begin to unpack why; I only have my experiences in Canada, in the NHL, and here in America to explain why I do. But mine are different from Mia's, our experiences and our views. And neither are wrong. They just are. And so are we.

"God, I could crawl under this table right now and suck your dick. That was sexy as hell."

I stare at Adina, shock rippling through me in waves. At her grimace and "Fuck. Did I say that out loud?" shock gives way to my loud bark of laughter.

I draw more than a few glances my way, and even when recognition crosses several of those faces, I still can't stop laughing.

Can't stop my shit from bricking up either.

She smiles, shaking her head even as red stains her cheeks. "And if I didn't say it before . . ." She pauses, then after a brief hesitation, reaches back across the table and grasps my hand. That touch arrows up my arm and burrows into my chest. "I accept your apology. Gladly. For the record, I've never been afraid of you. Wanted to punch you in the throat to shut that big-ass mouth up? Yes. But afraid? No. Never."

I chuckle again, and damn. It hits me that this is the most I've laughed in . . . well, a long time. Two years, to be exact.

Should that have me running scared? Yeah. More than anything that has happened with us today, that should have me terrified. And tomorrow—long after she's gone and it's just me, Khalil, and my thoughts as I lie in the bed I shared with Kendra—I will be.

But now?

Now, I'm just going to be.

Chapter Fourteen

ADINA

I'm going to kill him. Forget solidarity and all that other brotherhood bullshit. Matt isn't my brother—and never will be. He's a pain in my ass who's acting like a baby denied breast milk. Oh. He's also a bitter bitch.

"You good?" Michael, a member of my crew, asks, voice low as I strip out of my turnout gear next to our engine.

I nod, head bent as I shrug out of the flame-resistant coat and pants. Looking into his face and spying his concern is beyond my ability at the moment. I'm doing everything I can to hold it together and not cry out of sheer fury and frustration. Out of powerlessness. My eyes sting, watering.

Fuck.

Not here. Not in front of everyone. Definitely not in front of *him*. I refuse to give that asshole the satisfaction of seeing my tears.

"She's a big girl, Mike. No need to baby her." The Asshole walks by us, and the condescension practically drips from his words. "If she can't accept constructive criticism without crying about it, then she's in the wrong profession."

"That's enough," Cam orders quietly. All activity in the bay stops, and a glance up reveals the lieutenant staring Matt down.

A sneer curls Matt's lips. "No disrespect meant, but, Lieutenant, we all know we're only as strong as our weakest link."

"I said. That's. Enough," Cam reiterates, his expression hard and brooking no more of Matt's lip.

Matt balls his face up, but he wisely deads whatever more he wants to say and stalks out of the bay. An uncomfortable, tension-filled silence fills the area. I'm too pissed to try to ease that tension. Sorry, but I'm busy trying to convince myself that yes, homicide is bad.

I'm not there yet.

Eventually, the bay empties out, everyone heading to the showers. Everyone except for me and Malcolm.

"Dina, I want you to be honest with me," Malcolm says, cupping my elbow and halting me gathering up my turnout gear. He waits until I meet his solemn gaze. "Is there something going on between you and Matt?"

I bark out a jagged laugh. "Hell no."

He frowns, and though pain sparks inside my chest, I can't blame him for doubting me. Especially after today's fucktastic display.

This morning, we were running drills. Training is an ongoing process; it doesn't stop when we leave the fire academy. Every day we're doing something if we're not out on a call. Today, Matt, as the driver engineer, ran a hose-lead-out drill. The purpose of the training is to reinforce the skills necessary to place an initial attack line into operation. And to do it quickly and efficiently. It doesn't matter if it's a full engulfed-structure fire or a small car fire; how fast and smoothly we're able to lead out the attack line—or deploy the first hose stream while additional lines are laid out—determines the difference between success and failure. It's a timed drill, since quickness is key.

Apparently, I'm not only as slow as a constipated snail, but my technique sucks shit too. From the way Matt stayed on my ass, I couldn't do anything right today. No one in the company except me received the harsh treatment he doled out. But because he's a driver engineer and I'm still at firefighter rank, snapping back on him would've been viewed as insubordination. So I had to eat each sharp "critique," stay silent with each jab.

It was humiliating and demeaning. And I couldn't do shit.

"You sure, Dina? I hope you know you can tell me anything, and there's no judgment." Malcolm persists, his dark gaze closely studying me. "That out there"—he waves behind me toward the open bay doors—"seemed personal. If you two've had an argument or even something . . . intimate that went left—"

"No, there is nothing between me and Matt. Never has been, never will be." Truth. I can't stand him.

Malcolm continues to look at me, not saying anything, and guilt worms its way under my skin. I battle not to fidget under his scrutiny. Again, I have the strongest urge to tell him the truth. That I rejected Matt and now he's taking it out on me through the job. But the same thing that's kept me silent still wraps around my throat. Anxiety. Worry.

Even now, though he doesn't know it, Malcolm's placing the burden on me to police Matt's actions, to explain them away. He, Cam, and everyone else who witnessed his behavior today should be on his ass, calling him to task. But no. They're asking me if a relationship went bad.

This is just a glimpse into how it would be if I reported him. They would scrutinize me, *my* actions, *my* behavior. What did *I* do to cause his reactions? Though he's the one harassing me, it would be my responsibility. My fault. Did I lead him on? Did I try to make nice? Even questions about why I'm just now reporting him.

No. It's tough enough being a woman—a Black woman—in the fire department. In a lot of ways, we've made progress. But in many more, it's still a good ol' boy institution built and intended for white men. And it operates in that manner.

And even being very aware of that . . . I don't want to lose my job. I love being a firefighter, and I refuse to allow anyone, especially Matt Husband, to steal that away from me.

"All right." Malcolm dips his chin. "I'm going to take you at your word. But driver engineer or not, promotion or not, Matt comes at you like that again, and we're gonna have problems. Well, more than we already do, because I got something for his ass."

"Malc—"

"Nope." He holds up a hand, cutting me off. "You can dead that, Dina. He was out of line today. And before all this shit, you're my sister first. And if he can't respect the firefighter, he's gonna respect that."

"Malcolm, please. I don't want you to get reprimanded over some dumb shit."

"Nothing about protecting you is dumb. Nothing about one firefighter respecting another is dumb. And don't worry about being reprimanded. I got this."

He pecks a kiss on my cheek and walks away, leaving me to groan and pinch the bridge of my nose.

I stare after him, damn near choking on a scream. The same way I felt like I wasn't being seen or heard during those drills, I'm battling the same anger, the same need. I love Malcolm for wanting to have my back; hell, I'm his sister, I get it. But he's ignoring—or refusing to see—how him rushing in to deal with my problem steals my power. I'm not weak. I'm *not*, dammit. Losing Keshaun didn't steal my strength. No, dealing with the loss, the soul-agonizing pain, forged a strength in me like flame hardening steel. And they need to recognize it.

Or I need to show it to them.

Fuck, I don't even know anymore. Is it my fault that I don't yell *Look at me! I'm not a baby. I'm not powerless, voiceless! Let me handle my own shit!* Or is it their fault that they won't open their eyes, look past their own needs to protect and shield me, and *see* it? *See me?*

Dammit.

I don't know. The only thing I'm crystal clear about is Malcolm "having something" for Matt?

That is just what I *didn't* want to happen.

◆ ◆ ◆

"Thanks for coming with me tonight, ma. This isn't exactly what I do."

I tip my head back, smiling up at Solomon's chagrined expression. Everyone around us in the VIP section of the club is chilling, dancing, drinking, and smoking. In other words, they're having a good-ass time as Drake blasts through the speakers.

The glassed-in VIP section is roped off, with security standing at the entrance, preventing anyone who hasn't been invited to celebrate Ciaran Mahone's birthday from entering. God, how I want to yell, "You cannot pass, bitches!"

But I refrain.

It's packed in here, full of Solomon's teammates, their friends, and a whole herd of nearly naked, gorgeous women. The bottle girls maintain a steady flow in and out, bringing more and more alcohol. The right-winger is going big for his twenty-eighth birthday. And from what Solomon mentioned when he texted earlier and asked if I would join him tonight, his friendship with Ciaran is the only reason he agreed to come out.

I chuckle.

Mostly everyone is shouting and laughing, and Solomon's frowning, sitting in the same spot he claimed on one of the leather couches since the time we arrived over an hour ago. I met the man a few weeks ago, have been his lover for a couple of weeks, and still it's like I *know him* know him. And yeah, this is so not his scene.

"From the reaction you got when you stepped up in here, I'd say your teammates are glad you came out."

When he and I arrived, a loud roar and spontaneous applause broke out, growing more deafening when Solomon flipped them off.

"Yeah, well, they need to thank you. Because if you'd turned me down, I would've kept my ass home. All this fucking peopling makes me itch," he says, lifting his beer bottle up to his mouth for a deep drink.

I laugh, taking a sip from my own vodka and cranberry. Does my ridiculous heart trip over itself at his casual words? Yes. Yes, it does.

"It's not a problem. At all. I'm off tomorrow, and after the last shift I had, I needed this."

He frowns, his gaze sharpening on me, and mentally, I groan. Damn. I hadn't meant to let that slip. I want to forget the last twenty-four hours happened and enjoy this night, hanging out with Solomon.

It scares me that when I spend time with him, all my problems and worries evaporate under the heat of his body, his beautiful eyes, and just . . . him. What happens when he takes that away? Because contrary to my most recent decisions, I'm no fool. This . . . situationship with him has an expiration date. I may not be able to pinpoint that exact day, but it's going to happen. Either he'll pull the trigger or I will.

Either this lust between us will burn out and he'll move on.

Or I will get tired of pretending I'm not second best to a ghost.

One of them is bound to give, sooner or later.

In the meantime, though, I'm going to enjoy the time. And the sex. Good God, the sex.

I flick my gaze over him. From the tousled sandy-brown curls to the thick beard framing that sit-on-me mouth, down his wide black-T-shirt-covered chest, over the long, thick thighs wrapped in jeans of the same color. One of his powerful arms stretches across the back of the sofa behind me, and the hand not toying with my curls rests on his leg.

He's such a beautiful, beautiful man, and I've gone past the point of wanting him to *craving* him. These last couple of weeks have been . . . I sigh silently. Wonderful. Too wonderful. When he hasn't been on the road and when I'm not on shift, I've been spending days and evenings with him and Khalil. The only thing that comes close to being sexier than watching this man twist in orgasm is seeing him with his son.

Single dads.

I get why they're so popular in movies and books.

Fatherhood is hot as fuck.

"I suggest you start thinking about something other than what's running through your mind right now. I have no problem finding the nearest bathroom and bending your ass over in one of those stalls." He drops an abrupt wet kiss on my lips, then lifts his head, arching his eyebrow. My mouth tingles, and so does my pussy. This man has me so gone. "Don't think you're distracting me, though. What happened on your shift?"

I sigh, wishing he would just follow through on his threat. Not only would I enjoy the hell out of it, but I'd rather be riding his dick than talking about my day. Also, I can't deny that I'm surprised he even asked about my job. If there's one topic we don't discuss often, it's firefighting. As a matter of fact, it seems as if he actively avoids anything having to do with my job.

"Just butting heads with someone at the firehouse," I say, downplaying the run-in with Matt. "We don't exactly see eye to eye on some things."

His frown returns. "Is it that guy from a couple weeks back, when we were there? The one with the eye problem?"

Damn. He forgets nothing.

"Yes, him."

"You don't see eye to eye on what?"

I shrug, glancing away and looking over the partying guests as if I've never seen them in the time I've been here.

"Just work stuff. Nothing major."

"Adina." Solomon raises a hand to my chin, pinching it and tilting my head back so I'm staring directly into his eyes. "Is everything good? He's not giving you problems, is he? I didn't like the way he looked at you then, and he seems off to me."

"It's nothing." I shake my head, dislodging his hold on me. "Nothing I can't handle. I'm a big girl," I say, mimicking Matt's words.

His eyes narrow on me. "That don't mean shit to me, ma. Just because you can handle something doesn't mean you should or even have to. I can just imagine some of the bull you have to deal with."

"The same you have to deal with, being one of how many Black hockey players in the league?"

"Yeah, but my teammate doesn't have my back, we lose a game. You? You could lose your life."

Silence falls between us, and it's louder than the music blaring in the club. Unease curls inside my chest, curdles in my stomach. That, I attribute to this conversation and the undercurrent of fear running through it. The ripple of trepidation rappelling down my spine? I don't know its origin. And I don't desire to analyze it.

"Just like you train to be the best at what you do, so do I," I murmur just loud enough to be heard over the chatter, laughter, and music. "My dad once told me that in our field, we have to recognize when we're mentally and physically ready to go. The first five and last five years are the most dangerous to firefighters. It's when people are most prone to get hurt. In the first five, we're still learning and training; we're still new. And in the last five, we might believe we know everything and there's nothing else to learn. That's equally dangerous. Yes, I'm in my first five, and I continue to train on the calls as well as when I'm not on them. I acknowledge that I'm still green in some ways, and accepting this keeps me aware, careful. But in all that, I'm not ready to go. I'm mentally and physically capable of doing this job that I love, just like your body and heart will let you know when you're ready to retire from a sport you're passionate about."

He doesn't reply, but the hard set of his sensual mouth telegraphs that he's not happy about what I've said. And here's another issue with us other than the obvious. Another reason he'll never trust me with his heart, if it was even an option. My job.

And a part of me resents him for that. Athletes are injured all the time when they go out on the ice or field or pitch. But I would never ask him to reconsider his profession or hold it against him because he loves it too much.

I drop my gaze to my drink, then raise it to my mouth for another sip. Hopelessness digs out a hole inside me, and for the second time in two days, angry tears burn my eyes.

"Hey." Once more, he cups my chin and lifts my head, granting me no option but to look at him. He frowns as he studies my face, but then his expression softens. "I didn't ask you here to argue or bring you down. I'm sorry."

He leans down, brushing his lips against mine. Once. Twice. Then firmer, tracing his tongue across the seam of my lips, then thrusting in between them. On a groan, I open wider for him, letting him sweep me up and away in this crazy high only he creates within me.

Belatedly remembering where we are—and that people have cell phones with cameras—I reluctantly pull away from him. "Solomon," I whisper, settling a hand on his thigh.

But the muscles under my palm flex, pushing another blast of lust through me. On reflex, I curl my fingers into the tight, rock-hard flesh beneath me, and he covers my hand, pressing it hard. I shift my gaze up, and it crashes into his. The heat there touches me like a physical caress, and I sink my teeth into my bottom lip.

"Don't tempt me, ma," he growls. "I ain't been inside you in six days. And from the way you're shifting and shit on this couch, I know that pussy's dripping wet for me. Isn't it?"

I nod. Why lie? Especially when I'm dying for him to find out for himself.

"Let's get out of here," he mutters.

Don't have to tell me twice.

Just as he removes his arm from behind me and grabs my hand, Noni and Minnie walk into the section. My friend grins, waving at me. Her eyes go comically wide as they land on Solomon, and her grin grows wider, showing all thirty-two teeth.

"Oops, I forgot Noni was coming. You said I could invite her. That's still cool, right?"

"Of course. Like Ciaran knows everyone in this section. His motto is, for damn sure, the more the merrier."

I laugh, rising from the couch, tugging down the hem of my beige off-the-shoulder bandage dress.

"Fuck, ma," Solomon grunts.

I glance behind me, and he's staring at my ass, his bottom lip caught between his teeth. Snorting, I snap my fingers in his face. But secretly? I'm flattered and thrilled. Sue me. I love that this gorgeous man finds me sexy.

"Hey, eyes up here," I order.

Slowly, he drags his gaze up my body, over my hips, belly, and breasts until he meets my eyes.

"My bad. Firefighting does a body good." He smirks, standing next to me.

Smiling, I turn back to my best friend and her twin. As I round the table, I reach Noni and pull her in for a hug. She returns the embrace, squeezing me tightly and squealing in my ear like we haven't seen each other in years instead of a couple of days.

"Hey, Minnie. Nice to see you again." I release Noni and greet her twin.

As usual, she wears a stale expression, giving me the barest of smiles. I swear, this girl. She's so lucky I love Noni or she would definitely see another side of me.

It's a shame she's always wearing that sour-ass face too. At least with me she does. Because she's a beautiful woman. Noni and Minnie are fraternal twins, but both share petite curvaceous figures that a lot of women pay out money for. Noni has stunning, smooth dark skin and upturned brown eyes, with a mouth I've heard more than one rude-ass man describe as a dick teaser. Her twin's complexion is several shades lighter, and though they share the same eye color, Minnie's are more oval shaped, and her features are delicate, while Noni's are as bold as her personality.

My girl and her twin are bad as fuck. Unfortunately, so is Minnie's personality. I reiterate, at least with me.

But I'ma let Minnie live tonight. This is Solomon's friend's birthday, and I'll control my mouth. As long as she does the same.

"Solomon." I turn to him, smiling wide. Yeah, I'm pretty delighted that my girl is meeting my . . . well, whatever the hell he is to me. The intrusion of that thought threatens to dampen my mood, so I shove it along. "This is my best friend, Monica, and her twin sister, Minerva. Or Noni and Minnie. Noni, Minnie, this is Solomon Young."

"Of course I know who you are," Noni raves, grinning hugely. "It's amazing to finally meet you."

She shakes the hand Solomon extends toward her. A strange expression crosses Minnie's face as Solomon turns to her, offering his hand. I frown, but maybe I imagined it, because she politely smiles and accepts his greeting.

"Good to meet both of you." He jerks his chin up at Noni. "You're the one li'l mama's always texting. And she told me you came to our game with her."

"That's me, and a belated thank-you for the ticket. I thoroughly enjoyed myself." She hikes up an eyebrow. "And I regret nothing about the texting. How else am I supposed to get time with my best friend when she always holed up under you?"

I groan, and the corner of Solomon's lips quirks.

"Excuse her. Whatever is in her head comes straight out of her mouth. No checkpoint," I say to him.

"Nah, I like that. But now I'm wondering why you complain about my mouth when you have her?"

Noni laughs, and I grin. He's not wrong.

I glance at Minnie, who's been quiet, and she's staring off toward one of the glass walls separating our section from the rest of the club.

Determined not to worry about her and her moods—hell, she's lucky I extended the invitation—I wave toward the bottles littering the table.

"Do you guys want a drink? They have some of everything up in here."

"Uh, is Nick Cannon out there making baby number fifty-two as we speak?" She scoffs and bends down, nabbing a bottle of D'Ussé and a glass. "You want some, Minnie?"

"I'm good."

"Okay, sis." A frown briefly wrinkles Noni's forehead, but she shrugs and busies herself with pouring the cognac.

"What's up with your girl's sister?" Solomon murmurs in my ear.

I tilt my head back, and he bends from his towering height so I can say in his ear, "Who knows? I was being nice, inviting her because I didn't think Noni would want to come here alone. Ignore her. I do."

He huffs out a laugh, straightening. Just as he slides an arm around my waist, the birthday boy, Ciaran, ambles up to us. From the flush on his high cheekbones and the glaze in his eyes, he is having a really good time.

"Solomon, damn. I'm surprised you're still here." He cackles and slaps Solomon on the shoulder. I wince. If not for both of them being behemoths, I'm sure one if not both of them would've fallen over from that pound. "Who do we have here?"

He stares at Noni and Minnie, his mouth nearly split from ear to ear. Not that I can blame him. Noni looks sexy as hell in her white sleeveless bodysuit and tight black leather pants. And from her wide smile and subtle hip pop, she doesn't seem to mind his ogling.

"This is Adina's friends, Noni and Minnie." Solomon nods toward them. "Noni and Minnie, this is my teammate, Ciaran Mahone."

"We know who he is," Minnie pipes up for the first time, other than her hello to Solomon. "We're huge fans of the Pirates."

"Aw, see? That's what the hell I'm talking 'bout. Well, welcome, ladies. Any friends of Adina's are friends of mine." He says the cheesy line as if we've known each other longer than the almost two hours I've been here. "C'mon, Noni and Minnie." He moves forward and steps between them, offering his bent elbows to each of them. Glancing from one to the other, he asks, "Are you two related?"

"Twins," Noni says.

"Twins?" Ciaran's blue eyes gleam. "Shit. I've always wanted to be between—I mean, meet twins."

I roll my eyes. He couldn't be more cliché-ish if he tried.

"Seriously?" Solomon balls up his face. "I hope that shit's because you're drinking."

"Ignore him, ladies." Ciaran sniffs, and I chuckle. He's a little obnoxious, but he's charming in a douchey kind of way. "Let me introduce you to some of my teammates, since you're fans. Hang around that one"—he jerks his chin in Solomon's direction—"and your heart might shrink three sizes too small."

I crack up at the reference to the Grinch. So does Noni, and even Minnie gives a small smile.

"He's hilarious," I say.

"Yeah? I hope he remembers that slick shit tomorrow when I accidentally send him into the boards at practice."

I blink. "Sorry? You have practice tomorrow? And all of you are partying like this?" I wave a hand, encompassing the hockey players in various states of fucked up.

"Hungover or not, we'll all be there."

"Wow." I whistle. "That's discipline."

"Nah, that's wanting to be the next Grant Fuhr and Jarome Iginla."

I stare blankly at him.

Chuckling, he shakes his head. "The first Black hockey player to win the Stanley Cup and the first Black captain of an NHL team. C'mon, ma. If you're fucking a hockey player, you're gonna have to learn something about the sport."

I suck my teeth, lightly slapping his chest with the back of my hand. "Whatever." I roll my eyes. "Anyway, are those your idols?"

"Yeah, Grant Fuhr was one of the reasons I wanted to play for the Edmonton Oilers, and Iginla is a legend. They both are."

I study him for several moments, and he cocks his head to the side. "What?"

"You keep surprising me." I shrug, ignoring the melting sensation in my chest. "You're so different from the jerk I first met. I mean, your mouth is still as wild, but you're . . ." I twirl a hand. "More. So much more."

He stares down at me, those green eyes vibrant, intense. Part of me longs to glance away, afraid of what I'm projecting back to him with my own gaze. But I can't. He's too . . . everything.

A big hand curls around my hip, and the other settles low on my back, right above my ass. He tugs me closer until my breasts press against his chest, my thighs align with his, and his dick digs into my abdomen.

Bending his head over mine, he growls, "I got more for you, ma. You gon' let me give it to you? You gon' take it?"

Holy shit.

My eyes briefly close. This man is slowly turning me into someone I don't recognize. Hot in the ass. Needy.

Compromising.

Pushing aside that last one, I lift my lashes and nod.

His face tightens, and I recognize that look. He's getting ready to fuck my world up. Again. And again.

Turning, he grabs my hand. I look up and catch Minnie watching us, wearing that same expression from earlier. I still can't read it. Is it anger? Irritation? Hurt?

No, it can't be any of those. I don't have anything to do with Minnie other than the occasional *hi* and *bye* when I'm talking to or with Noni. So what could I have done to elicit any of those feelings?

Solomon tugs on my hand, and I promptly forget about Minnie and her weirdness tonight. I only focus on him leading me out of the VIP section, down the steps, and toward another door guarded by more security. Spotting Solomon, they both give him head nods and step aside, opening the door.

We enter a quiet, shadowed hallway, and when we reach the second door on the left, he pauses in front of it, twisting the knob. I follow after him into a private bathroom with a gleaming double sink, a privacy stall, and a couple of chairs with a round table.

He doesn't give me too long to survey the room, because in seconds, he closes the door behind me and then turns back, lifting me up and setting my ass on the sink.

"Six days, ma." His fingers go to the zipper under my right arm, pinching the tab and slowly drawing it down. "Six days without your mouth on me." When the zipper stops just under my hip, he releases my arms from the sleeves one at a time and pushes the top down to my hips, leaving me clad in a nude strapless bra from the waist up. He trails a fingertip over the top of my flesh. "Without tasting these pretty-ass titties. Six days without getting in this perfect pussy."

Getting in this perfect pussy.

The five words reverberate in my head and my sex. An ache sets up deep inside me, and it's an itch I can't scratch. *I* can't. But damn, *he* can.

Lowering his head, he trails his lips over my collarbones, from one shoulder to the other. Still avoiding my necklace. I shiver, eyes closing at the soft, damp caress with a hint of tongue. Gasp as he reaches behind me and unhooks my bra, slipping it off me.

"Why won't you leave me alone, Dina? You're in my head." He buries his face in my neck as his hand comes up and forms a necklace around it. My breath catches. But not because of the grip around my throat. His words choke off the air in my lungs. That note of pain, of quiet desperation, leaves me breathless. "I've fucking begged you to over and over, but you won't."

Anger filters into his voice, as if he's blaming me for his preoccupation with me. Am I supposed to feel guilty about that? Shit, I think it's only fair, since he refuses to be evicted from my head too. "I'm tired of fighting it," he whispers, and my stomach clenches in excitement, fear . . . hope. "Tired of fighting myself. Especially when there's no way in hell I'll win."

His head lifts, and when he stares down at me, I try not to allow the shadows of defeat in his eyes to steal the light trickle of joy in my chest, and instead focus on the arousal in them. Center on the need deepening his already deep, sensual voice. Focus on the possessive hold on me.

"I'm lying to myself," he continues. "That's become a bad habit of mine since meeting you. Because no way in hell will this"—he squeezes his hand around my neck, brushes a kiss up the column—"be enough. It won't be enough time. Not to do every nasty thing I want to do to you. I look in those pretty, soulful eyes, and the innocence there is like waving a fucking red flag in front of my face."

God, I can turn a blind eye with the best of them.

I can pretend that his plan to fuck me out of his head and his system has transformed into something more. Something more emotional and affectionate.

Something that has a chance of maybe, just maybe, lasting longer than our expiration date.

"Kiss me," I whisper. Demand.

And he does.

But not my lips.

The breath explodes from my chest as he cups my breasts, molding his hands to them, plumping them. My hands fly up to clutch his thick forearms, and his low, dark chuckle has a spear of lust arrowing straight to my pussy. My already slick walls clench as if begging for the same treatment my titties are receiving.

"Perfect," he mutters a second before he closes his lips around my nipple, sucking it hard, raking the edge of his teeth across it.

Pleasure capsizes me, and I arch into his touch, feeling as utterly and completely *perfect* as he called me. Is it wrong of me to seek that kind of affirmation? To hold it close? I know I'm pretty and have a tight, thick body honed by years of hard work and training. But hearing that word in his rough voice, feeling that praise ghost across my skin?

I don't think it's wrong. Nothing that feels this *good* can be.

My head tips back on my shoulders, my belly tugging tight with each pull of his mouth on my breast. He switches up—tweaking, pinching, licking. And when he switches to the other, neglected breast, I whine in relief, in pleasure.

"Gimme that, ma," he orders, his mouth a little rougher, more demanding. His touch on the wet tip a little harder. "Goddamn, I've missed that."

He returns to my flesh, alternating between the mounds. Cupping them and bringing them together so the tips nearly touch. I stare down at him, trapped in the erotic torture he's wielding on my body like a sadist. I'm willingly helpless as he sucks on both nipples at the same time, lashing them in a wicked rhythm that has moisture leaking from me, wetting my panties and probably my dress.

I squirm on the sink, grasping his head, holding him close, refusing to let him go. Frustration careens through me as the tight skirt of my dress prevents me from spreading my legs so I can wrap them around his waist. Get that thick, hard dick pressed against my pussy.

"Fuck, Solomon." I whimper as a telltale tingle starts low in my back and stomach. "Solomon, I—"

"Do it."

I can't. Not just from him sucking on my nipples. Right?

But as he curls his tongue over and around the tips, then pulling and sucking so hard, so deep . . .

Fuuuuck.

I release a cry as shock and pleasure burst in my pussy. The orgasm is tight, damn near painful, without his fingers, tongue, or cock enabling it to fully bloom. But shit. It steals my breath, my body trembling, aching. Seriously, aching. Like I've been both satisfied and left starving.

"That's the fuck I'm talking 'bout," he snarls, then rears up, capturing my mouth in a searing kiss. I claw at his shirt-covered shoulders, desperate for more of what only he can give me. I'm ready to shamelessly beg for it.

He grips my waist, lifting me from the counter and setting me on my feet. My impatience doesn't seem one-sided as he reaches for the hem of my dress and jerks it up until it forms a band just above my hips. Slipping his hand between my thighs, he unerringly finds my clit and rubs his finger over it, tracing the nub over the insubstantial material of my thong.

I clutch his arms, depending on him to keep me standing.

"Fuck you so wet for?" He dips between my folds, stirring, and the sound of my soaked flesh should embarrass me. But it doesn't. It only enflames the lust marching through me like a marauding army set on seizing and conquering. "This for me, ma. All for me."

I can't answer. And my response isn't necessary, since it literally coats his skin, glistening under the soft lighting of the bathroom. He slips his fingers between his sensual lips, sucking them clean. My pussy throbs, yelling "Gimme some of that!"

He thrusts his hand back between my legs, cupping my flesh, grinding the heel of his palm against my clit, and my thighs shake, my knees tremble as I impossibly hover on the crumbling edge of another orgasm.

"Oh shit," I whine, plead. "Oh shit, please."

"This, li'l mama? You want this?" He shoves his fingers inside me, and there's no way in hell anyone standing on the other side of the bathroom door can't hear my scream. One of his big hands moves to the nape of my neck, cupping it while he drives deeper, higher in my sex. "Wet me up one more time before I dig in this pussy, lose myself in it." He crushes a hard, hot kiss to my cheek. "Die in it."

His words—words I'm not 100 percent sure he meant to utter—and the steady, merciless thrusts of his fingers propel me faster and harder to a release that has tiny wings of anxiety fluttering against my stomach. But when he strokes inside one more time, his palm grinding against my clit and his fingertips rubbing over a place sometimes even my vibrator has a time reaching, I shatter. I come so hard and long, I sag against his chest, clutching at him, my breath hot, serrated puffs over my throat.

"Goddamn, that was hot as fuck. *You're* hot as fuck and so damn beautiful, I'll never get tired of seeing you come for me." As he praises me, he rips at his pants, jerking them open and freeing his dick. Then hikes me in the air, urging my still-shaking legs around his waist, and walks across the bathroom, not stopping until my back hits the wall. "Now my turn. Open up for me and take your man, Dina."

Take your man.

My already labored breath snags in my throat at that guttural command. Even as he works his dick inside me, I'm still reeling.

Does he mean it? Did he mean to say that?

My heart does this traitorous and hopeful leap, and only when he buries his dick fully inside me, sparking off that too-full, too-much-pressure sensation do I drag myself out of my head . . . and into my pussy.

"I've missed this. Fuck, I've missed this. This pussy. This heat. This good, wet shit," he mutters against the base of my throat where his lips are pressed.

I don't need to ask what *this* is, as his hands and weight prop me up and he withdraws, then surges forward, circling and grinding his hips so the base of his cock caresses my clit. My arms wind around his head, fingernails scraping his scalp, tunneling through his hair, grabbing onto any part of him I can as he turns me out.

My pussy is stretched, branded, and my mouth opens against his temple. But not to complain. No, I whisper nonsensical shit in his ear. Telling him how good he feels. How he owns this pussy. How this pussy curves to just his dick. And by the pounding my flesh takes as he slams up into me over and over, I know he hears me. And it affects him.

Long, hard thrusts rock though me, and I open myself as wide as I can in this position, taking each drive, each stroke. The symphony of sex echoes off the walls of the bathroom, and I never want this to end. But as his wide, bulbous tip continually hits a spot high up inside me, I hold on tighter. I'm not going to last much longer.

"Solomon." I gasp, feeling a pressure low in my belly, low in my sex. "I . . . I . . ."

Can't finish a sentence or take a breath, that's what. And I don't ever have to in life, just as long as he keeps fucking me. God, I don't want him to stop.

"Get there, Dina," he snarls, his hips snapping against me, his dick filling me over and over. "Get there, goddammit."

On a keening wail, I throw my head back, and I erupt. All over him. Over us. He grips my shuddering body tighter, his fingers digging into the flesh of my ass as he holds me still and pounds away, chasing his own nut, throwing me higher into my own.

The next scream clawing from me is soundless, my lips parting, but the sound is trapped in my tight throat. His grunts and low growl fill the space along with slapping skin as he jerks inside me, once, twice, then bathes my walls with his cum.

For long, long moments we cling to one another, like shipwreck victims. Maybe we are. Tossed and broken by lust and . . .

I burrow my face in the nook between his shoulder and neck, unwilling to even mentally finish that thought. I can't. Though, God, I want to. Am terrified to.

"Let's go home," he rasps, and I nod.

Home.

I won't ask where that is. If he means my place or his.

All that matters is I'm going to follow.

Chapter Fifteen

SOLOMON

I open the door to Nate's office and step in, my gaze going to his administrative assistant. The elegant older woman has been with Nate as long as I've been a member of the team. She smiles, her dark eyes welcoming behind her glasses.

"Hey, Solomon. How're you doing today?"

"Good, Maev. Is Nate busy? He sent a message for me to come by and see him."

"No, you can go right in."

"Thanks."

Nodding at her, I stride past her desk and up to the large double doors bearing Nate's name in gold lettering. After rapping on the gleaming wood, I wait until his voice rings out. I turn the brass knob, open the door, and enter his spacious office.

It's been a minute since I've been up here; I see my father-in-law all the time when I'm dropping Khalil off at his home or picking him up. Or when they invite me over for family dinners. Which is why when the same woman who came to find me weeks ago with a message about Adina approached me again with a summons to Nate's office, I was curious and a little confused. Still am. Whatever he has to tell me must be important if he can't wait until later, when he's home.

"Nate." I close the door behind me and cross the floor, walking toward his desk. "I received your message."

Nate looks up from his computer monitor, and instead of his customary smile, he's stone faced. Curiosity gives way to irritation. I don't know what put that expression on his face, but it can't have anything to do with me. Still, I feel like he about to be on some bullshit. He's been a little distant since that conversation in the luxury box after the game Adina came to. While I love my father-in-law, him running me or how I parent will never be a thing. So I've been giving him room to get up out his feelings.

Looks like he needs some more.

"Solomon." He gestures toward the two armchairs in front of his large oak desk. Part of me wants to say *Nah, I'll stand.* But I'ma behave. Once I sink into one of the chairs, he props his elbows on the desktop and temples his fingers. I hope he isn't expecting me to fidget or speak first. Hell, he called me here. And those kinds of games don't and never have worked on me. After several silent minutes where we wage visual combat, he finally says, "I'm going to take it you haven't watched television or been on social media anytime today."

I shrug. "I don't really have the time or patience for that. Why? What's happened now?"

Pictures from Ciaran's birthday party at the club started leaking the day after. More and more popped up in the four days since. And some of them featured players, well . . . partying. They included them with drinks in hand and women hanging off them. But so what? Even Coach didn't say anything to us about them. We're grown-ass men, and we all have lives. And none of us are saints.

Yeah, Nate can be a bit old fashioned and reserved, but c'mon, damn. He works around hockey players for God's sake, not *golfers*.

His eyes narrow, and his lips flatten in so much disapproval that shit could be tattooed on his face. Instead of answering me, he turns his computer monitor around and clicks his mouse. I immediately recognize Twitter—oh, excuse me, X—and there's a still of a video. Above it, someone named @kaykaylive posted "Solomon Young gets it in! Yooo! Where do I sign up to get me summa dat?"

Nate clicks his mouse again, and the video starts to play. For a second, I'm not recognizing what I'm watching. Like my brain refuses to accept the signal my eyes are sending. But a few more seconds in, and I can't deny what's on that screen.

Me.

And Adina.

In the private VIP bathroom at the club.

I have her pinned against the wall, so my back is to the camera. And thank God, but I remember that night with crystal clear clarity. Just like I do every moment, second, I've been inside her, had my hands on and in her. She's topless, and her dress is a ring around her waist. But her nakedness isn't really visible. Just the tops of her shoulders. Never in my life have I been grateful for how big and wide I am. From the very top of my ass being visible and how I'm working my hips, it's obvious we're fucking. That's bad enough. But if anyone saw her bare breasts or her pussy . . .

Fury razes a path through me, incinerating every rational thought. And when I bury my face in her neck, and her face, saturated in pleasure, becomes visible in the video, the fury transitions to pure rage. I need to hit someone. Destroy them for recording a private, intimate moment and posting it on social media for people to perv over, comment on, and jack their fucking views up.

The video lasts for maybe ten seconds at the most, but it feels like ten minutes. The longest and most humiliating ten minutes of my life. This is worse than when someone captured a picture of us kissing. This feels . . . dirty. Ugly.

A silence coated in ice covers the room. I can feel Nate's glare burning a hole in the side of my face, but I continue staring at that fucking screen even though the video stopped.

Adina.

Has she seen this? Does she know about it? *Jesus.* I need to call her, warn her. She's going to . . . *fuck.*

"You don't have anything to say?" Nate snaps.

I tear my gaze from the monitor and meet his glacial eyes.

"What do you want me to say? To apologize? For what? I didn't do anything wrong. The muthafucka who snuck into that bathroom and recorded us without our permission and decided to post that shit should apologize. In the very least. They deserve to pay. And let me find out who it is . . ."

I scowl. I bet I can get in touch with the owners of the club and see if they have any security footage from that night. As soon as I leave here, I'm calling my attorney and getting her right on that.

"Are you kidding me, Solomon?" Nate looses a harsh bark of laughter and falls back against his chair. "What the hell? Has that woman pussy whipped you so hard that you can't see what's happening right in front of you?"

My chin jerks back, and I slowly straighten in my chair. Heat streams up my spine, up from my gut and into my neck, my face. I fist my fingers on my thighs, then move them to the arms of the chair, curling them around the wood. I need something to hold on to so I don't go across that fucking desk.

He's Kendra's father.

He's your employer.

You love him.

That last one saves him more than the other two. Because I don't give a damn. No one disrespects me.

"Nate, I get I'm your employee and your son-in-law, but don't ever speak to me like that. Give me the same respect I've always given you. That's my only warning."

The anger doesn't leave his face. Red floods into his cheeks, staining them. With a muted curse, he shoves back his chair and shoots to his feet. He marches over to the floor-to-ceiling window and stares out at the view of downtown Providence. Although I doubt he's really seeing or appreciating it. Like me, he's probably trying to get a grip on his temper.

If he knows me like I do, he better.

"Solomon." He spins around, scrubbing a hand over his carefully styled gray-and-blond hair so several of the short strands stand on end. "I'm frustrated and, yes, angry as hell, because you're not appreciating the magnitude of this video. Both professionally and personally."

"The fuck?" I scoff, rising to my feet too. "Yeah, I do. Someone violated my privacy and now my ass—literally—is everywhere. And even if I'm able to get them taken down, which I'm damn well going to try, the damage is already done. Then there's Adina—"

"Wake up, Solomon!" he barks. When I arch an eyebrow, he growls under his breath and drags a hand over his hair again, trailing it down his face. "Forget that woman. She's brought nothing but trouble and problems since you met her. If you'd only stayed away from her like you promised—"

"I didn't promise that," I interrupt him, slicing my hand through the air as if I'm cutting through that lie. "I never promised that. You heard what you wanted to hear. I said there was nothing between us, but that was then, and this is now. I have a right to change my mind and make decisions about my private life. Why do I have to stand here and justify that to you?"

"Because you do," he bites out, stepping toward me but drawing up short. "Because this is not just about you. You're an employee here who represents this organization. You're a father whose son will be affected by this. You're a hus—"

"Don't you say it," I rasp. "Don't you fucking say it." Guilt slams into me like a hockey puck to the chest. My hand flies to cover my heart that slams against my rib cage like a wild, feral animal desperate to get free of its cage. "Don't bring Kendra into this."

Maybe he realized he went too far, because Nate falls silent and turns back to the window. After several seconds he faces me again, and regret lines his face. For a moment, he appears older, tired. I almost feel sorry for him, because I know he's thinking about his daughter.

Almost.

I'm too busy trying to suck in air that doesn't carry the metallic taste of pain and shame.

"I'm sorry," Nate says, voice low. "That was out of line and below the belt." Blowing out a breath, he rubs the back of his neck. "Listen, Caroline and I don't expect you to live like a monk or even never get into a relationship again. It's just . . ." He swallows. "It's too soon; it's only been two years, and the pain for all of us is still fresh. It's too soon for Khalil and for you. Hell, you just got out of counseling, and we had to force you to go through with that."

"You mean it's too soon for you."

"That too. I won't lie. I'm not ready to see another woman around Khalil. Not when Kendra isn't here, where she's supposed to be." He looks away, his jaw clenching. "And even if we were all ready for this step, this . . . Adina isn't the right woman. Not for Khalil, and with this shit"—he flings a hand toward his desk and the monitor—"obviously not for you. I stand on her bringing nothing but issues with her."

I don't address what he said about none of us being ready for me to be in a relationship. Hell, I believe that. But how does he get to decide that for me? Who made him God—a God I'm still on the outs with, so I'm not even listening to Him—where he determines when I'm good enough to move on?

It's the truth, sometimes the two years Kendra has been gone feel like two weeks. But the days when I can't move out of bed are much fewer and farther between. The grief, the loss . . . it's getting better. Slow as fuck, but it is getting better. Khalil helps. Hockey helps.

Adina . . . helps.

Shit.

I backpedal away from that last thought, erasing it from my mind like it never appeared. But the knowledge of what I won't accept echoes in my head, my chest. Because it's true.

And fuck if that doesn't feel like a betrayal.

I shake my head, refocusing on Nate.

"So that other people have intruded in her life and caught us in certain compromising moments is her fault? Like the bullshit from the picture and that this video is sure to bring makes her life easier?"

"And what if it does?" he shoots back, that fierce gleam in his eyes again. "Just take a moment, step back, and think about it, Solomon. Both times you're with a woman, someone's around to capture it? A little too coincidental, don't you think? Yes, there were images of you and Kendra, but never ones like this. This stinks, son. It stinks to high heaven, and there's only one common denominator."

"Nate, you're reaching. What the fuck could Adina possibly gain from that?" This time, I jab a finger toward the monitor. "She's exposed. Put under a microscope. She's a fucking firefighter, for godsakes. This doesn't help her in any way. Nah. I refuse to believe she's behind that shit. There's no way. I know her."

"You've had your dick in her, Solomon. That's a big difference from knowing someone. You knew Kendra. Regardless of spending four months with her before you got married, you knew my daughter down to her soul, and vice versa. The years, the time, the family you built enabled that. You just met this woman, what? Weeks ago?"

The way he keeps saying *that woman* and *this woman* gets under my skin and on my nerves.

"And you ask what could she gain from this?" he continues before I tell him to check that. "Notoriety, which for some of these people out here is better than fame. What about attention? Money. Firefighting doesn't pay much; we're both aware of that. What if she decided to supplement her income by selling compromising pictures and video of Solomon Young? What if she's decided being a firefighter is no longer for her and this is a stepping stone to something else? Social media influence? Hell, I don't know. Because, let's be honest, Solomon. You have much more to lose, to protect. Your image. Your brand. Endorsements. Your privacy, and that of your son. Are you willing to take that risk? I'm telling you now: I'm not."

Just take a moment, step back, and think about it, Solomon. Both times you're with a woman, someone's around to capture it? A little too coincidental, don't you think?

What if she decided to supplement her income by selling compromising pictures and video of Solomon Young? What if she's decided being a firefighter is no longer for her and this is a stepping stone to something else?

My immediate reaction is to dismiss his accusations as bullshit. The woman I've let in my space, my house, my son's life . . . the woman whose body I've been balls deep in, have had wrapped around my own . . . the woman whose smile can banish away the shadows in my mind, my chest, whose voice and laughter bring a calm to my chaos . . .

No, she wouldn't sell me out like that. She wouldn't use my son for a buck or fifteen minutes of fame.

And I stand on that. But . . .

What am I doing? Yeah, I've only known Adina for weeks. But in that time, I've lost focus. Got caught up maybe—just maybe—believing this could be what I stressed to her from the beginning that it wasn't . . . permanent. Nate has his own motives and agenda, but he's not wrong.

Shit has changed. It's spun out of control.

Since Adina came into my life, I am on the blogs more. But it isn't her fault. *It's mine.* She's been exposed *because of me.* It's affected her because of her association *with me.* I've convinced myself it doesn't bother me, but shouldn't it? And not just for her but for Khalil? I'm his father first; it's my job to shield him whenever and wherever I can. And by involving him in this . . . thing with Adina, I'm giving him unfounded hope and thoughts that she's not temporary, when that was our agreement. That's what we both said we wanted.

I briefly close my eyes, and a vision of my boy's fear and uncertainty when he lost his mother wavers across my mind. I couldn't prevent a car accident. But Adina courts danger every damn time that alarm rings, and the risk of losing her, of putting Khalil right back in the position of losing another person he loves . . .

I can't do it.

Not for the bullshit reasons Nate and Caroline are throwing at me, but because I'm a father first. I must protect him.

And Adina too.

She didn't ask for this shit. And not just the unexpected and unwanted exposure. Bringing her further into a relationship with people who won't accept her, who actively resent her . . . how in the hell is that fair?

It's not. Not to any of us.

Nate walks back behind his desk and plants his fist on the top, leaning forward.

"I've said it before, and I'll repeat myself one last time. This is a distraction you and the team don't need. When people should be talking about our thirteen-game winning streak, they're focused on this . . . sex tape. You're my son-in-law, the father of my grandson. But this is business. And I can't allow you to mess with business. Fix this or there will be consequences."

"Are you threatening to bench me?" I growl.

"If that's what you heard. I don't want to take any action, but if you force my hand . . ."

I stare at Nate, and his eyes meet mine.

The fuck? He's threatening my career?

This is a power move, plain and simple, to try to force my hand. Let's be honest. If this had happened to Ciaran or Ares, Nate would've let Coach handle it, and they for damn sure wouldn't be benched behind this bullshit.

Anger eats at me, and yeah, I need to get the hell up out of here before I say something I can't take back.

Giving him a short nod—and he can thank my mother for that, because she would beat my ass if I disrespected an elder by simply walking out—I pivot on my heel and stalk out of the office.

My day is fucked.

And so am I.

Chapter Sixteen

ADINA

The Range Rover I'm currently sitting in the rear of pulls to a stop in the parking lot behind the firehouse. I close my eyes, and mental images of the throng of reporters and cameramen swarming the sidewalk across from the station assault me. The only reason they aren't crowding the front of the house is because of the barriers set in place. And if some brave soul decided to crawl over or under it, they'd have to face the four firemen standing out there to make sure they keep their distance. My brother front and center among them.

I've brought this chaos to my station. That goddamn video.

I bow my head, tears stinging my eyes.

"Fuck."

"Dina, this isn't your fault," Noni says, voice soft with concern.

Ever since that video of me and Solomon surfaced, she's been over at my house or on my phone, talking me down off a ledge. Noni's the only one I've allowed in my house, to see me. There's one other person I wanted to be there, to comfort me. But in the last two days, I've discovered I'm on my own.

Except for Graham. Again.

Good ol' Graham.

"Yeah, that's not how people are seeing it." I made the mistake of going on social media, and all the keyboard warriors are out in full force. I've been accused of everything from arranging the filming and releasing of it myself to being a ho to clout chasing. It seems only a handful of people get that I'm a victim of whoever did this foul shit. Everyone else seems too busy delighting in watching me get fucked against a wall and then fucking me over on all the social platforms. Sighing, I press my forehead against the back of Demarcus's seat. "Logically, I get that, Noni. But I *feel* dirty. I *feel* responsible. I *feel* so goddamn violated. And now I have to walk into this building knowing everyone has seen that shit. Seen my fucking . . . sex face."

Including my father and brother. Jared.

Jesus, I've never been this humiliated.

"Babe, if anyone's going to have your back, it's your people at the fire station. Other than your house, you should be the safest there. No one is going to let people fuck with you."

I haven't told Noni about the situation with Matt. I don't know why; she would 100 percent be on my side. But like this thing with the video, I'm embarrassed, feel guilty. Like somehow it's my fault. Which, yeah, it's ridiculous. I did nothing to court Matt's attention, just like I didn't ask someone to sneak into a club bathroom and film me getting fucked.

But there's no rationalizing feelings. It is what it is.

"Noni, I've never felt so damn alone in my life. How do I feel like everyone's eyes are on me and invisible at the same time?"

"Solomon hasn't called or answered the phone yet?"

"No."

Admitting that is like acid poured across an open wound. Two days ago, a knock on my front door had woken me up. At the same time the house phone I never used started ringing. Getting the door first and seeing Graham standing on the other side clued me in to who was calling. It was like déjà vu. Suddenly, I was taken back to when that picture of Solomon and me kissing had made the rounds. Only this time, it's worse. Much, much worse.

At least then, Solomon called me because he'd been out of town. He doesn't have that excuse here. The Pirates' next two games are here in Providence. But he hasn't reached out, hasn't answered his phone when I called, hasn't replied to texts.

Just sent Graham. If the bodyguard hadn't shown up at my door, I wouldn't even have known Solomon knew about the video.

It hurts.

It hurts like hell not hearing from him. Not seeing him.

It reminds me that I'm expendable. Replaceable.

Forgettable.

"Dina, he probably has a lot on his plate, too, with—nope. You know what? Fuck that. I made excuses for him the first day, but yesterday? Today? Nope. So what, he got the video taken down? That's what the fuck he's supposed to do, since you don't have that kind of pull. But I don't care. I don't care. There ain't that much muthafucking busy in the world where he can't drop a fucking text, send a message by fucking pony express. He used to be my boy, but now he can kick rocks with open-toed shoes."

Despite the weight pressing down on my shoulders and chest, I snicker.

"Pony express, Noni?"

"I said what I said."

God, I love her.

"This is what I want you to do. Get out that car, lift your damn head up, and walk into that fire station like the bad bitch you are. You have nothing to be ashamed about. The person who did this owns all of that, not you. So go to work, and fuck anyone who got something slick to say. Tell them—nah, fuck that. Call me and I'll tell 'em."

I laugh, and it's the first time in days. Sighing, I nod, though she can't see me.

"You're right. I know you're right." Inhaling, I hold the breath, then slowly blow it out. "Let me go clock in and get to work."

"That's what I'm talking 'bout. And remember. Bad bitch."

"Got it."

Shaking my head, I end the call.

"Ready, Ms. Wright?" Graham twists halfway around in the front passenger-side seat to look at me.

"Ready as I'll ever be."

I reach for the handle, but he's already out of the car and rounding the rear. Seconds later, he opens my door, scanning the lot. Only when he's satisfied does he step back and let me exit. His big hand settles on the middle of my back as he walks me to the rear entrance of the firehouse.

"Thanks, Graham. I really appreciate it," I say, grabbing the door handle.

He nods. "I'll see you in the morning. If you need to leave before then, don't forget to call me. Please don't go on your own unless it's work related."

"Got it." Waving at him, I pull the door open and enter.

The familiar scent of Pine-Sol greets me, but unlike most mornings, it doesn't bring familiarity or solace. There is nothing familiar about my world as of two days ago. If not for my job, I would've stayed curled up in my bed, under the covers, hiding from everyone.

But no one's trying to hear I have to call in because of a sex tape. Hell, I don't even know if that would be a valid excuse. For damn sure would be a new one.

"Huh. So you're actually here. I'm surprised you showed your face here today. I just knew you were going to call in."

I tell my feet to keep moving, but the shame barrels into me in waves, crashing down over me. Freezing me midstep.

He must've been waiting on me. Like a spider hiding, waiting for its prey to enter its web.

Slowly turning around, I face Matt.

He smirks. "Not so mouthy now, are you? Not when everyone—and I do mean everyone—has seen you getting fucked. Must be a very proud moment for your father and brothers."

His low laugh creeps over my skin, leaving a filthy film behind.

"Good to know. Thanks for that." I start to walk off, but his next words jerk me up short.

"I'm not even gonna lie. I'm glad this happened. It's what I've known all along. You're a whore, and now everyone knows it."

His words are blows to my chest, abdomen, and soul. I'm bleeding internally from each strike, and I can barely breathe. The pain is physical and nauseating.

But quick on its heels is rage. Pure rage. Maybe because I've been called a ho so many times over the last two days by people who don't know me, hearing it from this piece of shit, who does know exactly *who* I am and *what* I stand for, sends my fury through the roof.

Maybe because I've been adamant about handling it on my own, about standing in my own strength, but *I haven't.* I haven't done anything but let him get away with denigrating me, tearing me down, and stealing my power.

I'm tired.

I'm *done.*

I whirl around on him.

And snap.

"A whore." I take a step toward him, and the sneer riding his lips starts to slip. "You're pathetic. A joke. A bitch-ass muthafucka who probably got up extra early this morning so you could be right here to unload all of your bitter, petty, insecure bullshit on me. Did you stand in the shower and plan what you were going to say? Make sure you delivered it with the correct affect? Well, good for you." I slow clap. "Are you feeling better, Matt? Did you get that one off your chest? I want to make sure you're good." I cock my head, baring my teeth at him in what couldn't possibly be considered a smile. "Because, *bitch*, you will never talk to me like that again. I've let you slide, and now you feel a little too comfortable disrespecting me. You shouldn't have come for me today, Matt, because I damn sure didn't send for you. But now that you're here, get this, okay, *bitch*? If you ever fix your mouth to speak to me in any capacity outside of our job, then I will report your ass. And that's after I knock your fucking teeth in. You better find something safe to do, Matt. Because this ain't what you want, *bitch*."

Spinning around, I don't give him time to reply but continue up the stairs leading to the locker room. My heart pounds in my chest, the throbbing echoing in my ears. His expression spurs me faster up the steps.

I'd seen Matt angry.

But what I saw before I left? The ice-cold, almost blank look flattening his features sent a chill tripping down my spine. I have to watch him. I don't trust him for shit.

Just as I reach the second floor, the alarm starts blaring throughout the station. Relief sweeps through me, and I hurry to my locker to dump my bag and get to my gear.

I would never wish a disaster or harmful circumstance on anyone.

But I would rather face a fire than stay here.

It's a shame that I feel safer with the fire than I do here in my own firehouse.

◆ ◆ ◆

"Other than smoke inhalation, you check out fine. Your vitals are good as well. I'm going to keep you on oxygen for another couple of hours, and then you can be discharged. But"—the doctor checks her chart, then returns her attention to me—"you'll need to rest for the next twenty-four to thirty-six hours. When you get home, take cough drops and the full course of antibiotics I'll bring to you before you leave. Even after you feel one hundred percent, continue to take them as prescribed. After the first two days, if you have abnormal throat irritation or you don't feel any better, go see your general practitioner or come back here. Okay?"

I nod, pulling the oxygen face mask away to rasp, "Thank you."

Even saying those two words scratches my throat painfully.

"Of course." She closes my chart and places it back in the sleeve at the foot of my hospital bed. "I'll come back to check on you before you're discharged."

She—her white coat reads **Dr. Evans**—gives me a smile before exiting my room in the emergency department. As soon as she leaves, my parents and brothers file in. I'm sure there must be some rule against so many people back here in the ED, crowding into one room. But with my father and brothers in uniform and Ma being . . . Ma, I assume they're making an exception.

They all wear the same worried expressions and gather around my bed. Dad and Ma on one side, Malcolm and Malik on the other.

"Hey," I croak.

"Sweetheart." Mom grasps my hand in hers and brushes the other one over my hair. Tears pool in her eyes. "Oh my God. I'm so glad you're okay."

"You scared the shit out of us, sis," Malik says, his gaze running over me as if assuring himself that I really am good.

"Yeah, don't ever do that to us again," Malcolm orders.

The corners of my mouth lift in a feeble smile under the face mask.

"I'll try. Can't make any promises." Even saying that has my throat on fire.

I hoped my flippant answer would ease some of their tension, but it fails.

"We're going to need to discuss what happened," Dad says, his anger practically vibrating in his voice. "Both officially and unofficially."

I nod.

Yes, there's no getting around that.

I close my eyes, and immediately images of that hot smoke-filled room I'd been trapped in just hours ago appear in my mind's eye. I can feel the flames that ate at the walls, the window. Popping my eyes back open, I meet Dad and Malcolm's furious gazes.

They know.

Maybe not the why, but they definitely know the what.

The first call of my shift had been to a structure fire in a two-and-a-half-story family home. When we pulled up, black smoke billowed in the air, red-and-gold flames licked at the first-floor side windows and the back of the house. Dad, Jared, and Cam did a quick assessment.

Jared quickly asked the owners if anyone was still inside the home, and receiving a negative answer, he and Cam started issuing orders. Attack lines ready, we prepared to enter.

It'd shocked me that Cam had assigned Matt to be my partner. But on the scene at an active fire, I couldn't argue. So I went into the fire with a man who despised me.

At first, everything went fine. We hosed down the walls and floor in what appeared to be the dining room. After that, things start to get a little hazy. I remember the smoke thickening, the flames encroaching closer. A crash.

Then . . . nothing.

No, not completely true.

I remember Matt not being there.

He'd left me.

Terror and anger rise up inside me like an inferno, threatening to choke me.

Two in, two out. Never go into a structure by yourself. That's a cardinal rule in firefighting, and our unbreakable one. Even if one of our tanks goes off, we tap our partner, letting them know, and we both leave.

Matt broke that rule and left me in there by myself.

And I spy the knowledge, along with the fury, in my father's and brothers' eyes. So, yes, they're aware of the what—Matt abandoning me—but not the why.

Retaliation.

There's no doubt in my mind that's the reason behind his actions. I don't give a fuck what explanation he gives. He purposefully left me.

Lifting the mask, I ask, "Why?"

Understanding my question, my father grinds out, "He claims he tapped you on the shoulder to let you know he was leaving because something was wrong with his mask. He thought you were behind him and didn't realize it until too late. At least that's what he says," Dad reiterates. "Don't worry, baby. He will be reprimanded and written up. And I will make sure he goes before a disciplinary panel. And no, not just because you're my daughter. We don't leave our partner. Under any circumstances."

"If he makes it to the disciplinary panel," Malcolm mutters, and Malik growls an agreement.

Usually, Dad would've stopped that kind of vigilante talk. But from his narrowed eyes and tight jaw, I think the fire captain is stepping back and the father is in full control.

"Don't think about any of this right now," Ma murmurs, squeezing my hand and clinging to it as if she's afraid I'll disappear if she lets me go. "Concentrate on healing and getting well. And after you're discharged, you're coming home with us. No argument." She holds up her other hand as my lips part to protest. "You'll have to forgive me for being overprotective when my daughter is injured on the job. Let me get over the fear that almost took me out of here when I got that phone call. In the meantime, you're coming home with us."

"Well, if you're going to mom-guilt me . . . ," I rasp.

Truthfully, I don't want to be alone.

"Stop talking," she orders gently and leans down, kissing me on the forehead.

A commotion of raised voices reaches through the room's closed door, and seconds later, it opens, and Solomon charges in. His breathing is labored, and his eyes are wild as they quickly scan the room before settling on me. When our gazes connect, his body deflates like a balloon pricked with a needle. His shoulder hits the wall as he sags against it, head bowed until his chin nearly rests on his collarbone. A visible shudder ripples through his big body, and though it's the first time I'm seeing him in days, I want to rise up out of this bed and go to him. Comfort him.

Me and my stupid, foolish, foolish heart.

Mom releases my hand and walks over to Solomon. She rubs soothing circles over his back, murmuring something in his ear. Solomon nods and, after several moments, slowly straightens, pushing off the wall. He looks at me, and though he's composed, his face revealing nothing, pain and anxiety darken his emerald eyes.

"We'll give you two a couple of minutes." Mom shoots pointed stares at Dad and my brothers, and, grumbling, they back away from my bed and file out of the room.

Malcolm even pauses, lifts a hand, and after a brief hesitation, squeezes Solomon's shoulder. If I wasn't suffering just from smoke inhalation, I would believe Dr. Evans had given me the good drugs. Because surely I'm hallucinating that Malcolm was *nice* to Solomon.

Soon, the door closes behind my family, and I'm alone with him.

We silently watch each other, then Solomon approaches my bed.

"Hey," he murmurs.

"Hey."

He winces at the sound of my voice, and briefly closes his eyes. A spasm of emotions crosses his face. Pain. Fear. Sadness.

All three.

"Are you going to be okay?" he asks, voice just above a rasp.

I nod. "Smoke inhalation." I swallow, wincing at my sore throat. "Discharge in a few hours."

This time, he nods and fists the sheet covering me.

Silence permeates the room again.

"How did you . . . ?"

Damn. My throat is on fire, and the more I talk, the more it hurts. I glance around, peeping the carafe of water and the plastic cups on the small silver tray next to my bed. I reach for it, but Solomon beats me to it.

He quickly removes the plastic from the cup, pours water into it, and then hands it to me. Grateful, I accept the cup and force myself to slowly sip the cool liquid, even though I want to gulp it down like a person just crawling out of a desert. The water feels like heaven over my throat, and I sigh, leaning my head back against the thin hospital-issue pillow.

"Your brother must've found my number in your phone, because he called me," he says, answering my previous question.

That makes sense. Especially because if Malcolm had called Solomon from my phone, he most likely wouldn't have answered. As he hadn't been for the last couple of days.

"Jesus, Adina." He sinks into the seat next to the bed and grasps my hand in his. Lowering his head, he presses his forehead to my knuckles. "I was so scared. All I could think of—"

He breaks off but he doesn't need to finish that sentence.

Kendra. All he could think of was losing Kendra.

I close my eyes, a maelstrom of emotions whipping inside me. Sadness and hurt for him that, even momentarily, he relived that trauma of when his wife died. A little bit of joy, because he obviously cares. A caustic laugh echoes inside my head. What have I devolved to that I'm actually delighting in the fact that he cared if I lived or died. The bar is super low.

And then there's pain because, in the scariest moment of my life, I couldn't call him, couldn't lean on him because he disappeared on me. Abandoned me. It's difficult to swallow that even when I reached out to him, he ignored me.

Piling that on top of the humiliation I've suffered, it's too much. It's too fucking much.

So many times I've waited for others to put me first.

My father with firefighting.

Keshaun with his career.

Solomon with his wife.

When do *I* decide to put *myself* first? Why am I allowing anyone else to determine how I feel about myself? What I *do* for myself?

Now. That's when.

He rolls his head from side to side, rubbing his forehead against me. "*Fuck* this job," he whispers harshly. "I knew—"

The ringing of Solomon's cell is overly loud in the room and breaks off whatever else he would've said. He reaches in the pocket of his coat and removes it. Glancing down at the screen, he frowns, his sensual mouth flattening.

"I need to take this," he says, looking up at me.

I wave toward the phone and lift the cup of water for another sip. Sighing, I recline against the pillow again.

"Hello." Pause. "Nate, yeah." Pause. "What the hell?" he snaps. "Is that Khalil? What's wrong with him?"

My eyes pop open at his son's name and the worry lacing Solomon's voice. On the other end of the call, his father-in-law is so animated I can catch snatches of his conversation.

"Heard you say her name and *hospital* . . . crying and screaming . . . here," Nate yells.

"You're here at the hospital? Dammit, Nate, why?" Solomon growls, shooting up from the chair. "I told you I would call when I left here. You can't just give in to him when—"

". . . traumatized . . . told you about this . . . trouble. Get your priorities straight! Your son . . ."

Solomon's eyes and the skin across his striking cheekbones both flare.

"Yeah, Nate. I got you. I'll be out in a few minutes. Tell Khalil that Adina's fine. She's going to be okay. Will you do that, please?" There's nothing polite about his tone as he grinds out the request through gritted teeth. "Thanks. See you in a few."

He ends the call with a jab at the screen and, eyes closed, taps the cell against his forehead.

"Shit," he mutters under his breath. When he looks at me again, the regret etched into his face also lines his voice. "My in-laws brought Khalil here to the hospital. We were with them when I got the call from Malcolm, and Khalil overheard my conversation. I immediately left the house, but apparently, Khalil started crying, upset over you being hurt. They think hearing you were hurt probably triggered something about his mother. He wanted to see you and wouldn't stop crying so they brought him down to the hospital. But they can't bring him back here, so . . ."

He trails off, and I shake my head, not needing him to continue. I get it. And my heart breaks for Khalil. If I'm not mistaken, I heard him screaming in the background, so I don't doubt he most likely thought of losing his mother. I don't begrudge him having to leave and go to his son.

But . . .

I point at his phone and curl my fingers in a *gimme* motion. Solomon cocks his head but, after a moment, hands the cell to me. The home screen hasn't locked, since he just used it, so I quickly locate his texting app and bring up a new message.

Thumbs moving over the keyboard, I type out a note and hold up the phone so he can read it.

"I understand. Go to him. Please let him know I'm fine," Solomon reads aloud. Relief washes over his face. "Thank you for that, ma." He exhales, dragging a hand down his face. "Look, I'm sorry I haven't been—"

I violently shake my head, bringing the phone back to me.

No need for an apology.

When I hold the phone out to him again, and he reads my message, his frown returns. My heart tightens, and pain flares in my chest. God, I'm going to miss that frown, which is Solomon's default expression. Somewhere along the line, instead of annoying me, it became endearing.

"Nah, I do need to apologize. I got in my head after that fucking video and let . . . *shit*," he hisses when his phone vibrates in my hand. It's another incoming call. From Caroline this time. "Decline that," he orders. "Listen, I have to go, but I'll come by to see you later this afternoon or tomorrow. We need to talk."

My thumbs move over the keyboard again.

You can leave.

He nods, thrusting his fingers through his hair and fisting the short curls while reading my note.

"Yeah, I need to get to Khalil, but I promise I'll—"

I hold up a hand, stopping him. And type again.

Go. Don't come back.

Solomon stares at the screen, confusion shadowing his eyes, turning the corners of his mouth down.

"What're you talking about?"

This is the out you were looking for. I'm good.

Then I hand the phone back to him, done texting. His face doesn't clear. If anything, his scowl deepens. I thrust the phone at him, and slowly he accepts it.

"Adina," he whispers.

I lift the face mask and croak, "I'm done."

He mugs me. "Because I have to leave and go to my son?" he snaps.

"Because you're not free. You never have been."

For a moment, he stares at me, hard. Then understanding softens the harshness around his eyes, his mouth.

"Dina," he breathes.

But I close my eyes and turn my head away from him.

I'm done.

I can't get past him not showing up for me. I deserve someone who would feel some type of way about leaving me to handle all the reporters. Yes, he sent Graham to protect me, but I haven't been sharing my body, my . . . heart with Graham. Solomon abandoned me when I needed him most. He pretty much warned me that I wouldn't be a priority for him. I should've listened. It would've saved me this pain radiating and throbbing in my chest.

He loves his wife, and I get that. I *admire* that about him. And I never wanted to take her place for him or Khalil.

I just want to share in that place. Wish he would make room for me. But he won't.

I deserve more. I *need* more.

And he can't give that to me. No, he's *unwilling* to give that to me. I'm worthy of that.

So, I'm done.

Even falling in love with this broken, rude, beautiful man.

I'm done.

Moments later, I hear the door to the hospital room open and close.

Only then do I let the tears stinging my eyes fall.

Chapter Seventeen

SOLOMON

With a sigh, I sink down into the airplane seat next to the window. I shift, buckling my seat belt, then stretch. My ribs protest from the hit I took earlier in the game against Dallas. I barely feel it. I've had worse, and this won't even be a twinge in a few days.

What hurts more is my shitty playing.

Overshooting passes. Missing goals. Fighting.

It's been two weeks of this, and, fed up, Coach tore into my ass tonight. I'm not saying it's all my fault, but I definitely contributed to our winning streak ending in our last game. And again tonight. I haven't stepped up for my team, for Coach, for me. And it's killing me.

When I lost Kendra, I found temporary solace in hockey. Being on the ice, immersed in the game I love? It offered me a haven, a place where I could forget my grief, my anger, my pain. I channeled it all into the game.

I haven't been able to do that this time around.

Which doesn't make sense. It's not like Adina passed. It's not like she doesn't live and work a half hour from me and Khalil. But for all intents and purposes, she might as well be gone. That's how distant she is, how far away.

Not from Khalil, though. Just me.

She's mailed cards, games, and other gifts to my son, staying in contact with him. Even as anger and this heaviness that feels a little too close to grief weigh down my chest, I'm thankful to her for not cutting off my son. She might not want anything to do with me, but she hasn't disappeared from his life. But that hasn't stopped Khalil from asking about her. Demanding to know when she's coming back over to the house to see him, spend time with him.

It chips at another piece of my soul when I have to tell him I don't know.

I turn in my seat, staring down at the tarmac of Dallas Fort Worth International Airport. But I'm not really seeing the wing of the plane, the lights in the air traffic control tower, or the staff loading the last of the team's luggage.

Images of Adina as she lay in that hospital bed, the resolution and sadness in her pretty brown eyes drowning out the pain from her injury as she held up my phone with the message to leave and not come back.

I can't lie; I felt like shit. I still do.

Because the truth is when I got Malcolm's call about her being injured and taken to the hospital, I lost my shit. Terror, agony, and a horror so profound, so deep, I lost the ability to breathe for several seconds. Thought I was having a damn heart attack.

Not again. Not fucking again.

Those words ricocheted off my skull. When I got myself together and left Nate and Caroline's house at a dead run and jumped into the car, another thought took its place.

I can't do this again. I can't.

After making sure Adina was okay, I planned to break off our . . . relationship. Because against my best intentions it became that. When you get excited about seeing someone. When a person trusts you with their body, their pleasure. When you share private thoughts you've only confided in very few people. When you allow someone around your child.

It's a relationship.

And that scared me.

No, I didn't understand true fear until I got that call from her brother. And I intended to run, like a fucking coward.

But Adina beat me to it, sending me away.

And it's nothing but what I deserve.

My smart ass called myself setting boundaries before becoming involved with her. As if those boundaries would protect me from getting in too deep. From feeling more for her than a hard dick.

I've heard people call me a cocky bastard, and they couldn't be more right. The hubris of me believing I could police her emotions.

Or mine.

"Hey, bro." Ken drops down in the seat across from me and buckles his seat belt. Sighing, the sound happy, relaxed, he looks down at his phone, smiles. His thumbs fly over the screen; then, after a few seconds, he lowers the cell and focuses his gaze on me. "Tough game tonight." He drums his fingers on his thigh. "Tough couple of weeks. Anything you want to talk about?"

My immediate, reflexive answer is no. Me, talk? What, are we gonna braid each other's hair too?

I open my mouth to tell him just that when "Adina broke up with me" jumps out.

Shiiiit.

Ken arches an eyebrow, leaning back in his seat and silently studying me. I'm already regretting my verbal diarrhea.

"I wasn't aware you and her were together like that, for her to break up with you. And let me be clear from the jump. You probably did some bonehead move that justified that move."

I scoff. And again, my instinctive response is a *Fuck you*, but hell, he's right. This is my fault. Adina just beat me to the punch.

"We weren't together—well, not like that. We were hanging out." And I sound like I'm thirteen instead of a grown-ass man.

“Well, I’m here, listening.” He spreads his long arms wide. “Let me have it.”

And miracles of all miracles, I do. I let him have it. And I hold nothing back. Not our first meeting. Not the kiss. Not her meeting Khalil. Not about Nate and Caroline. Not about the video or Nate’s threats.

Not about how it ended in the hospital.

Ken sits quiet, tugging on his bottom lip.

“So let me get this straight. When that video came out, instead of going to your woman—because make no mistake, from what you described, she’s your woman—and comforting her and protecting her, you let Nate get into your head and sent your bodyguard in your place? And *then* you avoided her calls for two days? *And then*, you went up to that hospital, where she’s lying injured and probably scared from the incident on her job, to break up with her? Do I have that right?”

Yeah, when he puts it like that, I sound like a li’l bitch making bitch moves. I knew I’d been a coward, but hearing it out loud? The shit sounds worse, and I burn with embarrassment. Adina deserved better. Much better.

“You got it right,” I murmur. “I’m an asshole. I admit that.”

“At least there’s that. Then I don’t have to spend too much time explaining to you exactly how fucked up that was. You left her uncovered, my guy. Graham wasn’t in that video with her; you were. Graham wasn’t the one she probably wanted to hear everything was going to be okay from. That was you. Nate had his own reasons and agenda for suspecting her of recording and leaking the picture and the video, but Nate doesn’t know her. Hasn’t spent time with her. Didn’t read her secrets. You did. So there’s no damn way he should’ve been able to get in your head and make you doubt her integrity and the character of the person you came to know over these past few weeks.”

"I know, Ken. I know all of this. And the truly fucked-up part? I didn't believe she was behind it. Not for real. But I jumped onto that as an excuse to back away from her."

"What was the truth, then?"

"I was running scared. I got so caught up in her that I let her get closer than I intended. Than I should have. Two times I was so into her that I forgot I was on a public street, a club bathroom. The truth is I put us both in those positions because I forgot who I was. Whose father I am. Who I be—"

I clamp my lips shut around the rest of that sentence, dropping my head and staring down at my clasped hands resting between my thighs.

"Just go ahead and say it. Who you belong to?" Ken quietly asks. I don't respond, but then I doubt he expects me to. On a long sigh, he leans forward, dropping his voice low. "On some real shit, Solomon? A part of you will always belong to Kendra. I saw how you guys were together. The love was real and pure. Nothing that strong can die simply because one of you did. But the fact is one of you did die. She did. And you're still here, alive. Even though you've tried your best these past two years to be the walking dead, it's not true. As clichéd as it is, Kendra wouldn't want you to be this . . . angry, lost shell that you've been. The woman I knew would've actually been pissed as hell. Because love doesn't suffocate. It doesn't wish harm. It's generous and open. And she wasn't just *in* love with you; she *loved* you. Wanted the best for you. So being alone doesn't honor her. It dishonors everything she stood for and what your marriage stood for."

He rubs the back of his neck, his lips rolling in, and he stares out the airplane window. But like me, it's doubtful he's actually seeing what's beyond the glass.

"When Patrice miscarried last year, I didn't want to try again. After witnessing her grief, her pain, and hearing her sob like her heart was literally breaking, I refused to suffer through that again. So about four months later, when my wife told me she was ready to get pregnant again, I flat-out said no. For me, I had her. I didn't need anyone else. And that pain had never left. Shit, I'd wake up some nights, seeing her thighs and our bed coated in blood. Hear her crying in my head. But then one day, months later, I opened up my eyes and really saw what my refusal was doing to her. It was denying her not just my love but the love of a child she desperately wanted. And I had closed a part of myself down. Shut it off so I wouldn't feel that same desire. I didn't want to remember how fucking happy I'd been when she told me she was having our baby. All I could remember was the pain, the sadness. The hollow caving-in of my chest."

Jesus. I'd had no idea any of this was going on. I'd been so swallowed up in my own heartache, I hadn't been aware my teammate, my friend, had been grieving as well.

"What did you do?" I briefly close my eyes. "I mean, what made you decide to try again?"

"One, having my wife tell me I was being a selfish asshole." He chuckles, rubbing his knuckles over his clean-shaven jaw. "And two, realizing that by holding on to the baby I'd lost, I was holding up my blessing and not making room for the child I could have. The family I could have. The laughing, wonderful, caring wife I had. Because while I closed myself off to the possibility of that child, I also closed myself off from Patrice. Solomon, bro." He picks up his phone again, fiddles with it for a few seconds, then turns the cell to me. It's a picture of him and Patrice, grinning widely as she holds up a sonogram. "This could be yours. It *should be* yours. If you're alone, that's your choice. But you're not just punishing yourself, but Khalil too. You can tell yourself you're protecting him, but in truth, bro, you're only isolating him. He needs more than you and his grandparents. He deserves more, just like you do. Happiness. Peace. Security. Love. That's what you both should have. But if you have a death grip on the past, you'll never open your hand to the future and all that's waiting for you there."

A huge suffocating weight bears down hard on my chest, and I suck in a wheezing breath. My eyes burn with tears I hide behind closed lids.

I want what he's talking about. The picture he just showed me and the one he's drawn for me with his words.

I want all of it. And when I think of it, there's only one woman who's there in that picture.

Adina.

But . . .

"I feel so guilty." I inhale a shuddering gulp of air. "Kendra should be here. Raising our son. Seeing him grow. And the guilt that she's not and I am tears me apart. The guilt that I'm betraying her by bringing another woman into Khalil's life. That I'm . . ."

"Go on and say it, bro." Ken unbuckles his seat belt and reaches across the space separating our seats to grasp my hands. As if he's giving me physical and emotional support to say the words that are lodged in my throat but expanding in my chest until my ribs threaten to crack under the pressure. "That you're falling for another woman," he supplies when I can't.

I open my eyes, meeting the steady strength in his.

"Yeah," I rasp. "That I'm falling for another woman."

Fear speeds through me, whistling and screaming like a runaway train. But it's a bright, painful blast. And afterward . . . afterward, that weight starts to shift, crack, and slowly fall apart. Am I still afraid? Yeah. Hell yeah. And not just because I've decided to walk out of the anger, guilt, and sorrow of my past.

But because I'm also choosing to walk into an uncertain future that looks nothing like what I'm leaving behind.

I'm through running, though. Thinking back on the last two weeks without Adina in my life—talking to her, touching her, seeing her smile, fucking her—I've been miserable. And so has Khalil. Nate and Caroline have been preaching about putting his best interest first. What if Adina is his best interest? He's blossomed under her attention. He adores her. How can that not be the best for him?

And me.

I'm not going to lie; her job still terrifies me. And getting that call and walking into that hospital room to see her lying in the bed? It reminded me of all that I'd lost—all that I still had to lose. But Ken's right. I can no longer live my life like that, because it's not living. It's white-knuckling life. It's existing, and I'm tired of that.

In no time since Kendra's passing have I ever regretted a second spent with her, regretting the family and amazing years we shared. Even if it meant losing her all over again just to have those years with her, I'd do it again in a heartbeat.

So how can I not embrace this possible future I could have with Adina? I'm not God. I can't predict what will happen, but I can enjoy and cherish the fuck out of the time I have. Loving Adina is worth the risk of possibly facing one day without her.

"Thank fuck for that." Ken smiles, falling back against his seat. "My next move was getting your ass out on that ice and slapping you a few times with the puck. You know I'm a pacifist, but I would've made an exception for you."

I snort. Pacifist. This is the same person who was just in the penalty box twice tonight for fighting.

Shaking my head, I stare down at my ring finger. And for the first time in two years, there's a peace mingling among the sadness. There's hope.

"Thanks, Ken. I mean that. I appreciate you."

"Nah, Solomon." He waves off my words. "You're my brother. If I can't snatch you up, who can?" He stretches, then pulls down the shade on the window as we receive instructions from the pilot that we're about to take off. "But now I feel like I need to crush a few beer cans against my head to balance all this sensitive shit."

I laugh, tugging down my shade, too, and it feels . . . light. Real. "Now, if that's not some toxic-masculinity bullshit."

He smirks. "Spell it."

Flipping him off, I smile and settle back in my seat. We'll arrive home in Providence in about four hours. Plenty of time to figure out how to begin reversing the damage I've inflicted.

And how to convince Adina that we belong together.

◆ ◆ ◆

"I don't need you to get my door, Graham. But if you'll wait here, I'll be back out."

Graham nods from the front seat of the Range Rover, and I push out of the car, climbing the steps to my in-laws' house. I knock, my stomach twisting and nerves spilling through me as I wait for the door to open.

Moments later, Caroline answers, and she smiles at me, stepping back so I can enter.

"Hey, Solomon," she greets. "C'mon in."

"Thanks." I move inside the foyer and glance up at the staircase leading to the second level of their palatial home. "Khalil's asleep?"

"Oh yes. He's been down for a couple of hours," she says, closing the door behind me. "I had the guest room prepared for you since it's so late and—"

"I appreciate that, but I'll go get him. We're headed home tonight."

She was headed in the direction of the kitchen, but she draws up short, glancing at me over her shoulder with a small confused frown.

"Oh, but he's been in bed for so long, it'd be a shame to disturb him when you both can just sleep over and leave in the morning, like you always do."

That's the problem. I always did it because they subtly insisted and I would feel like an asshole if I declined. But there were many nights after getting off that plane that I wanted to spend my first night home from an away game in my own bed. But I put their needs above my own.

That stops here. Tonight.

"I know. And like I said, I appreciate your thoughtfulness, but after spending the past six days in hotel rooms, I'd like to go to sleep in my own bed tonight."

"Oh. Okay." Concern darkens the eyes Kendra inherited from her. "Well, I can go get him up . . ."

"No need. I'll do it. But I do want to speak with you and Nate first."

She hesitates, tilting her head, still frowning.

"Okay," she says again. "We were just in the kitchen. I was preparing a plate for you when you arrived."

"Thanks."

Another flash of irritation, even though the gesture is kind and considerate. But still, they just assumed instead of asking me. Not that I can place all the blame on them. This is my fault, too, because I've given in for so long.

What's the saying? Putting the cow back in the barn after the doors are open? Hell, I don't know, but this situation with Nate and Caroline is going to be like that. Placing boundaries when I haven't established any up until now is going to be tough for all of us. But they're needed.

"Nate," I greet my father-in-law, entering the kitchen.

"Hello, Solomon." He looks up from the slice of apple pie and coffee set in front of him at the table. "Tough game."

His perceptive gaze holds a note of concern and of censure.

"Yeah, it was."

Caroline rounds the large island in the middle of the room and walks over to a cabinet, opens the door, and pulls down a container. She crosses back to the oven and moves the food there into the clear bowl.

"What're you doing, honey?" Nate asks her, frowning. "Solomon can eat down here." He switches his attention to me. "You plan on taking your dinner up to the guest room?"

"No," Caroline says before I can. "He's taking it home. He's decided to head home tonight instead of staying over."

There's hurt in her even tone, and the me that climbed on that airplane prior to my talk with Ken would've caved and said *Never mind.* Nah, that old me would've just carried my bag up those stairs and not protested at all.

This ain't him, though. And the sooner they realize that—the sooner they accept that there will be changes—the better we all will be. And if not? Well, that'll be their choice.

I've made mine.

"You're taking that baby out this late?" Nate demands. "Why? What's going on?"

Instead of answering his questions, I pull out a chair across from him and wait until Caroline sets the to-go container on the table and sits next to her husband.

"I need to speak with both of you." I inhale, silently ask Kendra to guide me in the words needed to speak to her parents and not hurt them. "I love and appreciate both of you. Since Kendra's . . ." I inhale, hold that breath, then slowly, so slowly release it. "Since Kendra's died," I say, my voice trembling on the word that I haven't uttered since she's been gone, "I've leaned on you two heavily, and you've never complained, have always been there for both me and Khalil."

"Of course we are. That's our grandson, and you are family too. Kendra wouldn't have it any other way," Nate gruffly says.

"Yeah, I know she wouldn't." I smile. "That said, I've been unfair to you and to myself. And to Khalil. I've allowed you to coparent when you are not his parents, and crossing those lines has made boundaries nonexistent. I can't allow that anymore. If the last few weeks have proven anything to me, it's that I have to be Khalil's parent—his only parent left. And you have to fall back and be his grandparents."

"What're you saying?" Caroline whispers, her fingers floating to the base of her neck.

"Are you trying to cut us out of his life?" Nate snaps. "Because I won't allow that to happen."

"See? That right there." I lean forward, settling my arms on the table. "You *won't allow*. I'm your employee at the arena, not here in your house or mine. Not when it comes to my family. You can't allow anything, because he's *my son*. We're your family, but I make all the decisions regarding Khalil and hope you support me. When it comes to decisions about him, about me and my life, you have no control."

"Is this about that woman?" Nate sneers.

"Adina. Her name's Adina, not *that woman*," I say quietly, but fuck yeah, there's bass in my voice. He's going to respect her, or he won't be around her. That's if I can convince her to be around my ass. "But no, it's not about her. Yeah, she might've shown up in my life and been the catalyst for this change, but it really has nothing to do with her. This is about us."

"Are you punishing us, Solomon?" Caroline softly asks. "All we've done has only ever been out of love for both you and Khalil."

"I know that, Caroline. If I didn't, I wouldn't be sitting down here having this conversation with you. It's because I understand your actions are motivated by not just love for us but Kendra. We all lost her, and nobody hands out handbooks on how to move on when you lose a child or a wife or a mother. We did the best we could, but when it's no longer working for everyone, you change. And it's no longer working. Not the intrusion and questioning of my parenting. Not the policing of who I date. You've known me for seven years—the man I am, the parent I am. You should be able to trust that Khalil's best interest will always come first and that I would never do anything to harm him or bring someone around him who would hurt him."

"We do trust you. That's never been an issue," Nate asserts. "But if we can see what you can't because you're too close to a situation, you're saying we can't question you? Offer our opinion? Even when it's going to affect our grandson?"

"That's what I'm saying." Nate's lips snap close, but he glares at me. He's not pleased with my answer at all. Possibly offended. That's also his problem, not mine. "Can you offer an opinion? Sure. We're also friends. But you give it, trust me to take it into consideration, and then drop it. You don't keep hammering your opinion or try to force it on me. Let me repeat—I'm his father. I love my son and know what's best for him. If you can't trust that, then I don't know what to tell you. And Nate." I pin him with an unwavering, steady stare. "If you can't learn to separate personal from professional, then we're gonna have a problem. I respect you for the businessman you are, but if you threaten my job again over private issues between us, then I'll leave the Pirates and we can just be in-laws. I won't be emotionally or professionally pressured."

Nate glances away from me, but not before I catch the remorse in his gaze. At least he has the grace to regret his decisions and actions. That's a starting point, because I want to stay with my team. But I won't allow him to use it to control me either.

"Understood," Nate finally says. He looks at Caroline, and she slips her hand into his, wrapping her fingers around his. "I apologize for that. I just . . ." He huffs out a breath, shifting his gaze to his half-eaten pie for a moment. "We miss her," he finishes, voice thick, husky.

"I do too." I swallow past my suddenly tight throat. "More than I can ever express. Would I have wanted our lives to turn out this way? No. But I can't live in what-ifs. None of us can. I just want to be . . . happy. My son to be both happy and healthy."

"I'm sorry." Caroline wipes at her eyes, then trails a trembling hand through her curls. "From your perspective, I can see how we overstepped. And I promise to try and do better. You'll probably need to remind me a few times, but . . ." She looses a shaky laugh. "But please, I just don't want to lose my place in Khalil's life. I don't want him to forget Kendra."

"That'll never happen. Anyone I bring into our lives would never replace her. She was one of a kind. That doesn't mean they won't be just as special as her, just as loving. And I need you two to try and accept that."

"We'll try, son." Nate nods. "We'll definitely try."

"That's all I'm asking. We'll begin from there."

Chapter Eighteen

ADINA

Shutting my car off, I stare at the building that has been home to me for the past several years. The building I'd been so excited to be assigned to along with Dad and Malcolm. The building where I became part of a family. A building where I saw my future.

Then Keshaun dying happened.

Then Matt happened.

Then Solomon happened.

Funny that three of the most impactful events in my life so far revolve around three very different men for different reasons.

One loved and left me.

One tried to break me.

And one damn near did but instead put me on the path to recovering my power and voice.

Heaving a sigh, I push my driver's door open and step out, then close it behind me. The sound of it shutting shouldn't echo so loud in the morning air. But maybe it's because, for the first time in two weeks—the weeks since I ended up in the hospital and I ended things with Solomon—my head is quiet. Calm. And resolved.

I inhale a deep breath and don't move toward the building. Not just yet. I need a few more moments before I go into the station and either fuck up my career or set a wrong right, with the support of my officers.

Whichever way it goes, I'm going to be all right.

Whichever way it goes, I'm going to be free.

It's taken me almost those two weeks to get here. To heal not just from my injury but from Solomon.

Just because I finally put myself first doesn't mean I don't still hurt or think about him or . . . want him. But it does mean I decided my heart, my feelings, my autonomy over my life are a priority. And though it took me a while to get here—this emotional and mental place as well as this physical place—I'm here. I'm ready to walk into my station house and take back my power.

And I'm going to finish this and let the proverbial chips fall where they will. Here's the thing. They're *my* chips. It's *my* decision to toss them. It's *my* decision to accept where they land, no matter how this all turns out.

That thought is enough to propel me forward, and I stride toward the building. Reaching the door, I pull it open, step inside, and draw up short. Malcolm and Dad stand there in the back hall.

Shit.

I'd managed to hold in my tears, but seeing them here, even though this isn't even Dad's shift, has my eyes stinging. Yeah, I can't walk into that office with Jared and Cam with red eyes. But as they smile at me and Dad stretches out his arms, I don't really give a damn if my lieutenants see I've been crying.

This support, this unconditional love—it's everything. I'm standing on my own, but it's so fucking nice to know they're also standing. At my back. Letting me take the lead on this but giving me a solid front to depend on.

Only a little less difficult than making this decision was telling my family the truth.

At our Sunday dinner, I revealed everything to them.

Saying they were pissed would be an understatement. Hurt and pissed. Dad, Malcolm, and Malik, because I didn't feel like I could come to them. Especially Malcolm, because he flat-out asked me if something was wrong. And Mom, because of the same reason, but also because we're women. She would've understood, being a Black female professor in academia, but I couldn't trust that she wouldn't tell Dad.

Now, I know the error of my ways. I isolated myself from those who would've gone to war for me. It's commendable to be self-reliant and walk in my own strength. But that doesn't mean I have to do it alone.

Once they got over their immediate anger, they wholeheartedly supported my decision to report Matt. With that encouragement, I didn't waste another moment in calling Jared and asking if I could see him and Cam before my shift started on Tuesday. Procedure dictates that I report the incidents to my shift commanding officer, which is Jared. But I requested Cam be there as well so no one could accuse Jared of not being impartial.

Like I said, that was Sunday, and now I'm minutes from walking into that office.

"You got this, baby girl," Dad murmurs, closing his arms around me and pressing a kiss to the top of my head.

For the first time I don't say anything about him calling me that while we're in the station. Probably because I need that *baby girl* now, reminding me who I am and who I come from.

"We're going to be waiting for you when you're done. Right there," Malcolm assures me, settling a hand on my back. "I'm proud of you, sis."

I embrace that pride in his voice and in Dad's face.

More importantly, I embrace the pride in myself.

Nodding, I say, "Let's do this."

They follow behind me as I climb the steps and make my way to Jared's office. I stop at the closed door, lifting my fist to knock on it. But at the last moment, I pause, reach behind my neck, and remove Keshaun's necklace.

I'm not forgetting my past; I'm just stepping into my future without any crutches. And though my love for him is something I'll always treasure and he'll always live in my heart, the time has come to let go. And as I tuck the necklace into the pocket of my uniform pants, that's just what I do.

I knock on the door, and at Jared's deep "Come on in," I grasp the doorknob and inhale a deep breath that would have my old therapist giving me a thumbs-up. Deliberately relaxing each muscle in my body, I briefly close my eyes, offer up a short prayer, and enter the office.

◆ ◆ ◆

I step out of the office, leaving Jared and Cam behind inside. Shutting the door behind me, I blow out a breath, dropping my head and closing my eyes.

I did it.

"You did it," Malcolm says.

I open my eyes, and Malcolm and Dad smile down at me. Reaching out, Malcolm, then Dad draw me into a hug. I return each of their hugs, squeezing them tight.

"I knew you could," Dad adds.

"I did too." I smile.

"You're happy you did it, though?" Malcolm asks.

I nod, squeezing his hand, which hasn't released mine. "Yeah. I'm happy and proud of myself."

I am going to let everything with Matt go. It's taken me a minute to get here, but I refuse to let him pollute my spirit any longer. Not one more second.

I'd already made the decision to report him, but it'd been solidified when Dad informed me that Matt would most likely be put on paid leave and the write-up would go in his file, which could affect his promotions, but that was it. He would be right back in this house after his suspension was up, and while he might not make lieutenant in the near future, it could—and probably would—still happen.

In other words, he could return here and continue to be the same POS he's always been.

And that's *if* he faces those consequences. What's to say what will happen when he gets in front of the panel, lie to wiggle his way out of this, frame the incident as an accident? Because he's for damn sure not going to tell the truth, that he intentionally left his partner in a burning building because she wouldn't give him no play or pussy.

If that happened, no one would ever know the truth. If I hadn't spoken up, it would leave him free to subject another woman who rejects him to the same behavior. He's not safe to work with. For anyone. And when I thought about another person suffering through the harassment and fear that Matt's inflicted on me these past months, there was no way I could sit on this. And though it hurts me to even think his name, Solomon had a very valid point. Our house? We're a team. Our lives literally depend on us being cohesive and having one another's backs. He's shown he can't compartmentalize, that he'll bring his petty, bitter shit onto the job, possibly endangering other firefighters. If he harmed another person—another woman—because I chose to stay silent, though, then that would be on me. That would be my fault.

Now, standing with Dad and Malcolm, I feel stronger than I have in months. I reclaimed my power and my voice, and I will never allow another person to strip me of it.

"You should be proud, sis." He drops a kiss on the top of my head and releases me, but still grasps my shoulders. "All of us are. But I want you to know, whatever decision you'd gone with, we still would've been proud. Full disclosure, though? If you hadn't reported him, he would've seen me. And I would've made that fist to his mouth that he got after that drill shit look like a love tap."

I crack up. My brother needs someone to calm his ass down. But that person would have to possess the patience of Job, because if I believed Solomon's mouth was reckless . . .

The joy warming my chest dims a bit.

Nope. I shake my head as if I can shake thoughts of Solomon loose in my head. I let that go.

Let *him* go.

I give myself permission to be okay with that and not beat myself up over compromising who I am.

I am enough. I did enough. I can let go.

I force a brighter smile to my lips, grasping at the peace and happiness I felt leaving Jared's office. Focusing on myself—that's my goal. My future. And when I'm ready, finding someone who will accept me for me and put me first. Until then? I'll enjoy the blessings God has given me. If getting injured in the fire taught me anything, it's that every day isn't promised, and I must treat each moment as a gift. Keshaun taught me that too.

Moving on isn't forgetting. It's living.

"I'll see you two later. I have to make a meeting downtown. We're celebrating later, Wright," Dad says, smiling and using my last name. I grin up at him. "So don't make any plans for tomorrow after shift."

"Got it, Captain."

Then he ruins it by pressing a kiss to my forehead. I snort. But I don't mind. Not this time.

"C'mon." Malcolm hooks an arm around my neck after Dad leaves. "I gotta surprise for you."

I squint my eyes at him. "What is it?"

He sighs. "Why do people always ask that question when you tell them you have a surprise? *Surprise*, man. Where did I stutter?"

I snicker. "Fine. But you know damn well I don't like—oh, wait." I pull my vibrating phone out of my pocket and glance down at the screen. "That's Noni. I promised I'd call right after my meeting."

"Cool. Meet me downstairs in the bay."

"Be right there." After hitting answer, I hold the phone up to my ear. "Hey, girl. No worries." I walk away from Jared's office and head toward the locker room for a little privacy. "It went great. They took my report, and I swear, Jared tried to keep it professional, but if he'd had Matt in front of him at that moment, we'd probably be investigating a work-related homicide." I cackle. "Seriously, though, they both seemed like they believed me and told me it would be handled."

"That's amazing, babe. I'm so happy for you."

I push open the door to the locker room, stopping just inside.

"You don't sound too happy, friend." I frown. "What's wrong?" A beat of silence, and then Noni's sigh echoes in my ear. "Okay, now I'm worried. Did something happen at the school? You good?"

In general, Noni's an upbeat, positive person. To hear her not cheering and cussing has my stomach bottoming out and anxiety flooding in.

"Dina, I found out who recorded you and Solomon that night at the club."

I fall back against the wall, not expecting her to say *that*. What the hell?

"Hey, you still there?"

"Yeah," I whisper. Clear my throat. "Yeah, I'm still here. What do you mean you found out who did it? How? From what Graham told me, even Solomon couldn't track down—"

"Minnie did it."

Noise crashes inside my head, and my knees tremble, wobbling under me. I bend over at the waist, sucking in air. Funny how I haven't eaten a thing today but my stomach churns with nausea.

"Dina. Dina, are you still there?"

"Yeah." I close my eyes. "Did you say . . . Minnie recorded us in that bathroom?"

"Yes. I'm so sorry, Dina! I swear, I didn't know until last night when I mistakenly picked up her phone, mistaking it for mine. I saw the video in her photos. She didn't even have the decency to delete it after causing all this shit and so much fucking harm." Disgust drips from her words.

Noni loves her twin; even though we haven't gotten along in the past, she's stayed Switzerland, somehow remaining understanding and patient with Minnie. So to hear her . . . revulsion shocks me almost as much as this startling news.

Almost.

Because, *what the fuck*?

Gathering myself together, I slowly straighten, focusing on my best friend. She's hurting, and I need more answers.

"Why are you apologizing?" I ask. "You didn't do anything wrong. You're not responsible for what your sister did. But God, Noni, I'm still having a hard time understanding this."

"Same. If I hadn't seen it with my own eyes, hell, I wouldn't believe it. How could she . . . ?"

Noni goes silent, and I ask, "Why? Why would she do that to me? I mean, sure, we don't care for each other, but I've never done anything to her. Called her a bitch or two in my head, but never anything that called for *that*."

"Once I busted her ass out and she stopped trying to lie her way out of it, she admitted something I didn't know. Trust me, if I had, I would've handled a lot of things differently. Remember when I told you she fucked a hockey player and deluded herself into thinking that they could have a relationship?"

"Yes." Oh shit. I think I have an idea where this is going.

"That hockey player was Solomon." I knew it. Damn. "She never said anything when she knew you had your little situation with him. Didn't say a word when I invited her to the club, knowing he'd be there. She said her feelings were hurt when he didn't recognize her. Like, bitch, is that a reason to disseminate porn?" Noni sucks her teeth. "Minnie didn't admit it, but she was on some get-back. For both of you. She's always been jealous of you. No matter how many times I tell her I love both of you, she's felt like I favor you. And then you ending up with the man she wanted? I guess it was all just a little too much for her."

Her sarcasm reaches through the phone, and I cup my forehead.

"She humiliated me and him over a quick fuck, an imagined connection, and some petty bullshit?" I question, because I'm hearing everything Noni said but I'm still not fully grasping that Minnie would try to ruin my career and destroy my reputation over nothing.

Literally nothing.

"Yeah, Dina. God, I'm so sorry. And yes, yes, I know you said I don't need to apologize, but she's my sister, my twin, so I have to. What do you want to do?"

"What do you mean?"

"What do you want to do? I can go to the police and report her. If you or Solomon have an attorney, I can speak with them. Just let me know what you want."

"Seriously, Noni? You would turn in your sister? For me?" I quietly ask.

"Hell yeah. You're my sister too. Not by blood, but most definitely by choice. And right now, you are my choice. What she did was foul as fuck, and she should face consequences. She's not some toddler having a tantrum. And doing that to another woman? Oh no, I'm down with whatever you want to do."

Love for this woman fills me so fast and so hard I spread my fingers over my heart. For so many years I focused on people who didn't prioritize me, when I had a friend who'd been doing it all along. Like now.

"I love you, Noni."

"Girl, don't—"

"No, I mean it. I love you, and thank you. Let me think on it? Solomon had the video taken down, but you're right. The harm was done. So let me think on what I want to do, because I don't want to decide on emotion. And right now, my emotion is all about strangling the shit out of your sister. But at the end of the day, she's still your sister. I don't want to be like her and cause further harm."

"You better than me," she grumbles. "But it's on you. And as far as my sister, I'm good on her for a long while. I've been thinking about getting my own place for a while, and now seems as good a time as any."

"I ain't wanna say it, buuut . . ." I chuckle. "Let me go, though. Malcolm said he had some kind of surprise for me."

"Now, he knows good and damn well you don't like surprises."

"Tell me about it. As a matter of fact, I should let *you* tell him."

I can practically see her balling up her face. "Girl, three-point-seven seconds around your brother and I want to choke his ass out. No thanks." I cackle at her silly behind. "Ay, I may not have sounded like it, but I am happy for you. Proud too. Congratulations, babe. And I love you too."

Before I can reply, she hangs up, and I lower the phone, smiling. She's going to be all right. But I'm going to plan a girls' night so she isn't sitting up in her house brooding over her sister.

Fucking Minnie.

Making my way downstairs, I turn over what to do with this information. Unlike the whole thing with Matt, I'm not going to try to make this decision on my own. I'll talk to my mom about it. Not Dad, Malcolm, or Malik. I already know their answers.

I wish I could discuss it with the other person who was affected, but that's out of the question . . .

"Khalil?"

I jerk to a stop in the middle of the bay, for a second doubting my own eyes when I see Solomon's little boy jumping and pumping his fists in front of Malcolm as he quickly dons his turnout gear. It's one of the things we do for kids when they visit the firehouse, putting the gear on and stripping it off. Children always enjoy it. Khalil isn't any different, if his yells to "Go, go, go!" are any indication.

But at the sound of my voice, he turns and spots me, a huge grin nearly splitting his face, then races toward me, arms and legs pumping.

Joy and love I have no business feeling, since I'm technically not a part of his life anymore, fill my chest and throat. I bend down, scooping him up when he reaches me. Spinning him around, I laugh at his slightly manic giggles. I've missed him. Spending time with him firmly entrenched him in my heart, and digging him out has proved to be impossible.

"What're you doing here?" I ask, setting him down on his feet.

"My daddy brought me here!"

He turns and points toward the open door of the bay, and I don't know how I missed him. Huge, wide, and gorgeous as ever. Even my broken heart can admit that.

Yes, my broken heart.

Because at some point in the last two weeks, I stopped denying how I felt about him. Hell, I probably fell for Solomon the first time he called me a liar in that conference room. And I never stopped, only sinking deeper and deeper, like in quicksand. An appropriate comparison, since I am in over my head.

But I can love someone and recognize they're bad for my mental and emotional health. People like to throw *falling in love* around like it's an infectious disease they had no choice in succumbing to. Which is bull. My heart might want who it wants, but it's my choice on whether I'm with him. It's my choice to stay.

And I made that choice.

"We miss you, Ms. Dina." Khalil throws his arms around my knees, and, tearing my gaze from his father, I glance down to catch him tipping his head back.

I chuckle at his adorable pout and ruffle his curls.

"I miss you, too, sweetheart. Did you enjoy the puzzles and games I sent you?"

"Yeah! Can you come play them with me?" Oh, he was breaking what remained of my heart. "Daddy said you can!"

"Did he?" I murmur.

"Yeah, he did. Actually, he'd like it if you came back over and hung out."

I slowly shift my gaze from Khalil and raise it to meet Solomon's. My heart races for the back of my throat and lodges there. It's nearly a physical pain, being this close to him.

"Is that right?" I manage to say, thankful it emerges even, calm.

"Yeah, it's right." He stares at me, his green eyes so intense, so bright, it's difficult maintaining eye contact. "Son," he says, not releasing me from that visual hold, "give me and Dina a second, all right? Hang out with Mr. Malcolm."

"Okay!" He looses his arms from around me and takes a step back, but then stops. "You're not going anywhere, Ms. Dina? You're staying?"

I'm going to murder Solomon. Because his kid is killing me.

"No, I'm staying right here."

His smile returns and he runs off.

"Real low, bringing the kid," I say, returning my attention to Solomon. "You figure I could tell you to leave, but not him?"

"Yeah."

I mug him. Still blunt to a fault and rude. That shouldn't make my pulse trip over itself or have my pussy clenching like she's performing Kegels.

Crossing my arms, I glance around him, and sure enough, Malcolm and now Jared are hanging out here.

"You're a brave man. Both my brother and Jared are here. You must like playing with your life."

He shrugs. "Nah. I called them a couple of days ago to apologize, and they told me about your plans to come in today and report that muthafucka who's been harassing you." His eyes narrow, and a flash of anger brightens them. "We're gonna have a discussion about that, ma. You shouldn't have had to deal with that shit alone. Especially when you had so many people willing to have your back."

I cock my head. "Are you really here to go off on me—hold up. What do you mean, you called to apologize to them?"

"Just what I said." He mimics my pose, crossing his big arms over his bigger chest. "I didn't show up and protect their daughter and sister when that video came out. I failed you, and, man to man, I needed to own up to that to the men who have been covering you since you were born."

"If that ain't some patriarchal shit." I suck my teeth. "And my mother? Or me, for that matter? We don't deserve an apology?"

"I went by your mother's office at the university and personally apologized earlier that same day. You're her daughter, and as a woman she gets, more than your father and brothers, how that video hurt you. As for you, that's why I'm here now. I couldn't call you, because you have me blocked." Sure do. "And besides, when I did, it needed to be to your face, looking in your pretty brown eyes so you could see how sorry I am for failing you. For abandoning you. I should've never put my fears above your safety and mental well-being. I'm sorry, Adina," he softly repeats.

Well, that stole some of my mad. Damn him.

"You hurt me," I tell him. "You need to know how much you hurt me."

"I know, sweetheart."

I close my eyes at the endearment. *Ma. Li'l mama.* Those two set my panties on fire each and every time he uttered them. But this *sweetheart*? It touches my heart. Like a butterfly's wing brushing across it. Why now?

Good question.

"Why now?" I ask him. "Why are you giving this to me now and not more than two weeks ago?"

"Because I'm a coward. Or was. I'm trying to do better, be better. But, then, I was too afraid to admit that you meant more to me than sex. That we could be more than sex."

"What you mean is I wasn't—am not—your wife," I murmur.

"No, you're not." I drop my arms, take a step back from that verbal smack. He's gonna stop hurting my feelings— "Stop, ma." He cuffs my upper arm, letting his hand slide down to grab my hand. "Let me finish. No, you're not Kendra. You're Adina. Brave, beautiful, sweet, smart-ass-mouth, take-no-shit, sexy-as-fuck Adina. And there's not another person like you. I don't need you to be anyone but you."

He scrubs a hand over his head, leaving me speechless. Shivering. Disbelieving.

"You terrified me from the first moment we met. Because I came alive in that conference room. Against my will, you dragged me back into the world of the living. And part of me worshipped you for that. And the other half was just fucking scared. Scared that if I allowed myself to become attached to a person again, it would mean eventually losing them. And with your job . . . I jumped on that as an excuse to hold you at a distance. You asked why now? Because now I realize that having you, loving you, is worth the risk. And because asking you to give up who you are to appease my fears is a bitch move. So I decided to give up my fears instead of you."

Loving you is worth the risk.

I stare at him, studying every feature of his face. Searching his eyes for the truth, afraid I'm projecting what I need to see. What I long to see.

But no. It's there. Right there.

And it's all for me.

Love.

Mine, if I'm brave like he called me. Brave enough to claim it, him and his son.

I don't know if I'm brave. But I am in love with him. So fucking in love with him and Khalil.

I move forward.

He meets me halfway.

We lean toward each other at the same time, and one of his hands circles my neck, the other cups my cheek. Then his mouth is on mine, and I'm falling into him, trusting him to catch me.

His tongue thrusts between my lips, and I open wide for him, moaning at the taste of him, the feel of him after going so long without him.

"This mean you forgive your man?" he growls against my lips.

"Who that?" When his hand tightens around my neck, I chuckle, rising on my toes so I can press my mouth harder against his. "You already had it. I'm just glad you came and claimed it."

"I didn't have a choice. Khalil was about to run his little ass away from home if I didn't come get his Ms. Dina."

I laugh, tipping my head back and throwing my arms around his neck.

Happiness, bright and huge, surges inside me, and I can't believe I'm here. I close my eyes and press my forehead to his shoulder, inhaling his heady scent.

He releases my neck and pinches my chin, tilting my head back.

"Just in case I didn't make myself clear. I'm in love with you. I love you. I want you. I need you."

"I love you too. Mean ass and all."

He grins, and it's the first carefree, easy one I've seen. It's gorgeous on him. More so because that smile is all for me.

"Ay, bruh. This declaration of love come with season tickets?" Malcolm calls out, and I laugh, shaking my head.

"You don't even like hockey," Solomon reminds him, turning around but with me still in his arms. He's not letting me go, and I'm more than okay with that. "Football's your sport, remember?"

"And is. But if you're going to be hanging around, I guess we'll have to stop hating on you. And we need to get to know my li'l man here." He picks up a squealing Khalil. "So I might as well go to one of these ice-skating games."

I snicker as Solomon mugs him.

"I take it back, ma. Maybe this whole we-together thing might be moving too fast."

"Nope." I kiss his chin, jaw, and when he lowers his head, his lips. "No take-backs. We're all a package."

"Damn. Ayight." He tunnels his hand through my hair, tugging my head back and staring into my eyes. All traces of humor disappear from his gaze, though a small smile tips the corners of his mouth. "As long as I have you, I try not to body your brother."

Chuckling, I cup his cheek.

"Bet."

Acknowledgments

To my heavenly Father, who constantly and faithfully blesses me. You have seen me through some of the most difficult years of my life without ever leaving or forsaking me. “Thank You” isn’t enough, but I’ll say it anyway. I love You.

To Gary, for never giving up on me and always supporting me. Without you, your love, laughter, and silent and not-so-silent strength, this world would be colder and lonelier. Thank you for being my real-life hero.

To Stephen Wyatt, for coming through with your help and connections. Research would’ve been a lot more painful of a process without your assistance!

To Marc Williams. Thank you for sharing and being so generous with your wealth of knowledge as a member of the Montclair, New Jersey, fire department. You didn’t have to give me your time and answer so many of my questions—even the ones that seemed weird! LOL!—but I’m so grateful you did, and I appreciate you! You’re definitely one of Montclair’s finest!

To Crystal Perkins. I’ve known for years that you’re amazing, and you just proved it over and over again, sharing your knowledge of all things hockey with me! Whenever I hit you up, you never hesitated to answer my questions, and I adore you for your generosity of spirit as well as your knowledge. You’re everything that’s true and lovely about the romance world!

To Viviane Alston. Thank you for answering my desperate call when I needed to know about all things Providence. Also, thank you so much for giving me a crash course about the African diaspora in Canada and Black Canadians. I'm in awe of you; I really am. Also, lastly, thank you for letting me know how passionate Canadians are about their hockey teams. I got it! LOL! I'm proud to call you my aunt!

To Lauren Plude and Lindsey Faber. Thank you for your patience and never-failing upbeat and positive attitudes. And I can't express how grateful I am for your enthusiasm toward this book, its story and characters. You got me even more excited! LOL! Your thoughtful—and spot on—insight and criticisms helped make this book so strong and made me fall even more in love with it. I have loved working with you!

To Rachel Brooks. I may run out of ways to thank you, but I'll never run out of gratitude and love for you. You've been my adviser, my advocate and cheerleader, and I am so thankful to have you in my corner. The way you support my dreams and do your damnedest to make them come true is a blessing. And as the Rev said, "We're with God and we're with Rachel!" I need that T-shirt too!

About the Author

Photo © 2023 Sean Evans Photography

First published in 2009, *USA Today* bestselling author Naima Simone loves writing sizzling romances with heart, a touch of humor, and snark. Her books have been featured in the *Washington Post* and *Entertainment Weekly*, and her style has been described as balancing "crackling, electric love scenes with exquisitely rendered characters caught in emotional turmoil."

Naima is wife to Superman—or his non-Kryptonian, less bulletproof equivalent—and mother to the most awesome kids ever. They all live in perfect, sometimes domestically challenged bliss in the southern United States.